Y0-CAR-830

Dear Reader,

Welcome to the third and final book starring the Creed cowboys. First Steven and now his cousin, Conner, have settled down to married life, against all odds. But Conner's twin, Brody, has never been one to put down roots; residents of Lonesome Bend, Colorado, know it will take a special woman to tame this restless spirit for good. Carolyn Simmons might be perfect for the job . . . too bad Brody is the opposite of everything she thought she'd been waiting for!

I also wanted to write today to tell you about a special group of people with whom I've become involved in the past couple of years. It is The Humane Society of the United States (HSUS), specifically their Pets for Life program.

The Pets for Life program is one of the best ways to help your local shelter—that is, to help keep animals out of shelters in the first place. Something as basic as keeping a collar and tag on your pet all the time, so if he gets out and gets lost, he can be returned home. Being a responsible pet owner. Spaying or neutering your pet. And not giving up when things don't go perfectly. If your dog digs in the yard, or your cat scratches the furniture, know that these are problems that can be addressed. You can find all the information about these—and many other—common problems at www.petsforlife.org. This campaign is focused on keeping pets and their people together for a lifetime.

As many of you know, my own household includes two dogs, two cats and six horses, so this is a cause that is near and dear to my heart. I hope you'll get involved along with me.

With love,

Praise for the novels of
Linda Lael Miller

"Miller tugs at the heartstrings as few authors can."
—*Publishers Weekly*

"[Miller] is one of the finest American writers in the genre."
—*RT Book Reviews*

"Strong characterization and a vivid western setting make for a fine historical romance."
—*Publishers Weekly* on
McKettrick's Choice

"Completely wonderful. Austin's interactions with Paige are fun and lively and the mystery . . . adds quite a suspenseful punch."
—*RT Book Reviews* on
McKettricks of Texas: Austin

"Miller is the queen when it comes to creating sympathetic, endearing and lifelike characters. She paints each scene so perfectly readers hover on the edge of delicious voyeurism."
—*RT Book Reviews* on
McKettricks of Texas: Garrett

"A passionate love too long denied drives the action in this multifaceted, emotionally rich reunion story that overflows with breathtaking sexual chemistry."
—*Library Journal* on
McKettricks of Texas: Tate

"All three titles should appeal to readers who like their contemporary romances Western, slightly dangerous and graced with enlightened (more or less) bad-boy heroes."
—*Library Journal* on
the Montana Creeds series

"Miller's prose is smart, and her tough Eastwoodian cowboy cuts a sharp, unexpectedly funny figure in a classroom full of rambunctious frontier kids."
—*Publishers Weekly* on
The Man from Stone Creek

LINDA LAEL MILLER

THE CREED LEGACY

DOUBLEDAY LARGE PRINT HOME LIBRARY EDITION

This Large Print Edition, prepared especially for Doubleday Large Print Home Library, contains the complete, unabridged text of the original Publisher's Edition.

ISBN: 978-1-61129-679-2

Copyright © 2011 by Linda Lael Miller

All rights reserved. Except for use in any review, the reproduction or utilization of this work in whole or in part in any form by any electronic, mechanical or other means, now known or hereafter invented, including xerography, photocopying and recording, or in any information storage or retrieval system, is forbidden without the written permission of the publisher, Harlequin Enterprises Limited, 225 Duncan Mill Road, Don Mills, Ontario M3B 3K9, Canada.

This is a work of fiction. Names, characters, places and incidents are either the product of the author's imagination or are used fictitiously, and any resemblance to actual persons, living or dead, business establishments, events or locales is entirely coincidental.

This edition published by arrangement with Harlequin Books S.A.

® and TM are trademarks of the publisher. Trademarks indicated with ® are registered in the United States Patent and Trademark Office, the Canadian Trade Marks Office and in other countries.

Printed in U.S.A.

This Large Print Book carries the
Seal of Approval of N.A.V.H.

Also available from

LINDA LAEL MILLER

and HQN Books

The McKettricks of Texas

McKettricks of Texas: Tate
McKettricks of Texas: Garrett
McKettricks of Texas: Austin

The McKettricks series

McKettrick's Choice
McKettrick's Luck
McKettrick's Pride
McKettrick's Heart
A McKettrick Christmas

The Montana Creeds series

Logan
Dylan
Tyler
A Creed Country Christmas

The Mojo Sheepshanks series

Deadly Gamble
Deadly Deceptions

The Stone Creek series

The Man from Stone Creek
A Wanted Man
The Rustler
The Bridegroom

The Creed Cowboys

A Creed in Stone Creek
Creed's Honor

Coming soon

A Lawman's Christmas
Holiday in Stone Creek

For Nicole Blint, with love.

THE CREED LEGACY

CHAPTER ONE

Lonesome Bend, Colorado

Ranching, Brody Creed thought, shifting in the saddle as he surveyed the sprawling range land from a high ridge. *It can mend a broken heart, this life, and then shatter it all over again, in a million and one different ways and twice that many pieces.*

There were plenty of perils. Cattle starved or froze to death when a hard winter came around, which averaged once a year up there in the high country. Spring calves and colts fell prey to wolves and coyotes and sometimes bears, hungry after hibernating through the coldest months.

It was now May, and all was well, but come summertime, wells might dry up for lack of rain, and turn the grass to tinder, ready to blaze up at the smallest spark. He'd seen wildfires consume hundreds of acres in a matter of hours, herds and houses and barns wiped out.

Year round, good horses went lame and pickup trucks gave up the ghost, and every so often, somebody drowned in the river or one of the lakes.

On the other hand, Brody reflected, the beauty of that land could heal, take a man by surprise, even though he'd called the place home all his life. That day, for instance, the sky was so blue it made Brody's heart ache, and the aspens, cottonwoods and pines lining the landscape were shimmering splashes of green, a thousand hues of it, ranging from silvery to near-indigo. The river wound like a ribbon through the valley, clear as azure glass.

After a few moments, Brody adjusted his hat and sighed before giving the gelding a light nudge with the heels of his boots. The buckskin, long-legged with a black mane and tail, picked his way cautiously down the steep slope that led to the water's edge.

Behind them and a hundred yards farther along the riverbank, in a westerly direction, hammers clacked and power saws screeched, and Brody glanced back, pleased, as always, to see the steel-and-lumber skeletons of his house and barn rising.

Not so long ago, there had been a campground and RV park on the site, owned by Tricia McCall, now his sister-in-law and therefore a Creed. The picnic tables and the concrete fire pits were gone, along with the public showers and electrical hookups for trailers. Only the log building that had once served as the office remained; Brody had been bach-ing in it since last Thanksgiving, when he'd moved out of the main ranch house.

The peace between him and twin brother, Conner, could be a fragile one at times, and they both benefited by a little distance.

Now, ready to get moving, Brody

clucked his tongue and gave the gelding, Moonshine, another tap with his
heels.

"Come on, now," he told the buckskin, his tone reasonable. "The water's
shallow here, and it's real calm. If we're
going to be working livestock on both
sides of this river, then you've got to
learn how to cross it."

Moonshine, recently acquired at an
auction in Denver, was young, and Brody
hadn't had a chance to train him in the
ways of a cow pony.

No time like the present, he figured.

Brody was about to get down out of
the saddle and lead the horse into the
water, which lapped gently at the stony
shore that used to be a swimming beach,
back when the River's Bend Campground was a going concern, when
Moonshine suddenly decided he was
willing to get wet after all.

He plunged into the water, up to his
chest, making a mighty splash in the
process. Brody, gripping the barrel of
that horse hard between his knees, just
to stay in the saddle, laughed out loud
before giving a whoop of pure delight.

His boots filled, and within moments his jeans were soaked to the tops of his thighs, but he didn't care. Moonshine swam that river like he had Olympic aspirations, his powerful legs pumping, his head high and his ears pricked up.

"Good boy," Brody told the horse, with gruff appreciation. "You're doing just fine."

Reaching the other side, Moonshine bunched his haunches for the effort and bunny-hopped up the steepest part of the bank, water pouring off him in sheets. Once he'd gained level ground, the animal shook himself like a dog and Brody laughed again, for no other reason than that life was good.

He was home.

And, for the most part, he was happy to be there.

Drenched, he got down from the saddle to pull off his boots, empty them and yank them back on over his sodden socks. When he got to the main house, he'd swap his wet duds for dry ones from Conner's closet.

Having an identical twin brother had

its advantages, and one of them was access to a whole other wardrobe.

There'd been a time when Conner would have groused about Brody's tendency to borrow his stuff, but last New Year's Eve, Brody's "little brother," born a couple of minutes after he was, had taken a wife. Conner was happy with Tricia, and these days it took more than a missing shirt or pair of jeans to get under his hide.

They were on a perpetual honeymoon, Conner and Tricia, and now, with a baby due in three months, they glowed, the both of them, as if they were lit from within.

Brody mounted up again and reined Moonshine toward the home-place, feeling a mixture of things as he considered his twin's good fortune.

Sure, he was glad things were working out so well for Conner, but he was a little envious, too.

Not that he'd have admitted it to anybody.

Tricia was beautiful, smart and funny, and she'd taken to ranch life with surprising ease, for a city girl. Essentially a greenhorn, she'd gone horseback riding almost every day since the wedding, when the weather allowed, anyway— until her pregnancy was confirmed. Then Conner had put a stop to the pursuit.

No more trail rides until after the baby's arrival.

Period, end of discussion.

Brody grinned, recalling how adamant his brother had been. For the most part, the marriage appeared to be an equal partnership, but this time, Conner had laid down the law. And Tricia, normally the independent type, had capitulated.

That was just common sense, to Brody's mind, though a lot of country women continued to ride when they were expecting a baby, herding cattle, rounding up strays, checking fence lines. Conner's strong opposition was a no-brainer—Rachel Creed, Conner and Brody's mother, had continued to enter barrel-racing events long after she learned she was carrying twins. There hadn't been a specific incident, but soon after giving birth to Brody and Conner, Rachel's health had begun to go downhill.

She'd died when her infant sons were less than a month old.

Blue Creed, their father, hadn't lasted much longer. Overwhelmed by the responsibility, he'd brought the babies home to the ranch, right around their first birthday, and handed them over to his brother, Davis, and Davis's wife, Kim. Soon afterward, Blue himself had been thrown from a horse and broken his neck. He'd been in a coma for six weeks, and then died.

Now, crossing the range between the river and the two-story house Conner and Tricia had been sharing since they got hitched, the grass rippling around him like a green sea, Brody did his best to ignore the clammy chill of wet denim clinging to his legs—and the old, deep-seated sorrow rooted in his soul. He did take some consolation from seeing the cattle grazing all around, most of them Herefords, with a few Black Anguses to break the red-brown monotony. Two dozen broncos, specially bred for the rodeo, and six Brahma bulls completed the menagerie.

Clint and Juan and a couple of the

other ranch hands wove in and out among the different critters on horse-back, mainly keeping the peace. Brody touched his hat-brim to the other men as he passed, and those who were look-ing his way returned the favor.

By then, Moonshine was restless, try-ing to work the bit between his teeth, so Brody gave him his head. That cayuse might be skittish when it came to cross-ing rivers, but he sure did like to run.

Brody bent low over the buckskin's neck, holding his hat in place with one hand and keeping a loose grip on the reins with the other.

And that horse ate up ground like a jet taxiing along a runway before take-off.

Brody was enjoying the ride so much that the corral fence sprang up in front of them as suddenly as a line of magic beanstalks.

Moonshine soared over that top rail as if he'd sprouted wings, practically stretched out flat, and came in for a magnificent landing about one foot short of the place where Conner stood, looking like he'd had rusty nails for breakfast instead of bacon and eggs.

Brody gazed down into a face so like his own that the sight of it even took *him* aback sometimes, and he was used to being pretty much an exact duplicate of his brother.

Conner was scowling up at him, through swirls of settling dust, and he looked as though he'd like to grab hold of Brody, haul him off that horse and beat the holy bejesus out of him. So much for personality improvements resulting from wedded bliss!

"Oops," Brody said cheerfully, because he knew that would piss off Conner and he still enjoyed doing that now and again, even though they'd been getting along well for a respectable length of time. "Sorry."

He swung down and faced Conner, who was taut with annoyance, his shoulders squared, his fists clenched and his attitude contentious.

"Damn it, Brody," he growled, "am I having one of my invisible days, or are you going blind? You darn near ran me down, and it'll take me the better part of the morning to get this mare calm enough to work with again!"

Prior to the leap, Brody hadn't noticed his brother *or* the pinto mare, now nickering and tossing her head over on the far side of the corral, but he didn't think it would be smart to say as much. Instead, he decided to come from a place of helpfulness.

"You starting horses yourself these days, instead of letting one of the wranglers do it?" he asked, bending to pick up the lightweight saddle the mare must have tossed when he and Moonshine came over the fence.

Conner grabbed the saddle and jerked it out of Brody's hands. "Yes," he snapped in response. "You dropped out for a decade, Davis broke both legs the last time he rode a bronc and Clint and Juan are downright creaky at the hinges. Who the hell did you *think* was starting the horses?"

"Whoa," Brody said, recoiling slightly and still grinning. "What's chewing on you? Did you have a fight with the little woman or something?"

"No!" Conner yelled.

Brody chuckled, adjusted his hat and then turned to get Moonshine by the reins. After the river crossing and the hard run over the range, not to mention that spectacular jump, he figured the horse deserved some stall time, free of the saddle and bridle. "Well, what's the matter, then?" he asked reasonably, starting toward the side door of the barn.

"Nothing," Conner bit out, setting the dusty saddle on the top rail of the fence and turning to the mare.

"Something is," Brody insisted calmly, pausing.

Conner looked at Brody then, through the haze of slowly settling corral dirt, and sighed. "Tricia and I might have had words," he said grudgingly.

"Trouble in the vine-covered cottage?" Brody teased, knowing it couldn't be anything serious. He'd never seen a man and a woman more deeply in love than his brother and Tricia were.

"She says I'm overprotective," Conner said, taking off his hat and swatting his thigh with it before putting it back on.

Brody flashed a grin. Rubbed his beard-stubbled chin with one hand.

"You?" he joked. "Overprotective? Just because you'd wrap the lady in foam-rubber padding, if she'd let you, so she wouldn't stub her toe?"

Conner glared, but there was a grin to match Brody's brewing in his blue eyes. He held it off as long as he could, but then it broke through, like sunlight penetrating a cloud-bank.

"Put your horse away," Conner said. "I might as well turn the mare out to graze for the rest of the day, now that you and that gelding scared her out of three years' growth."

Brody led Moonshine into the barn, put him in a stall and gave him a couple of flakes of hay. When he left by the main door, Conner was waiting for him in the yard, throwing a stick for the Lab-retriever mix, Valentino.

In Brody's opinion, that was a prissy-assed name for a ranch dog, but the poor critter had already been saddled with it when Conner and Tricia took up with each other. Conner had tried calling him "Bill" for a while, but the former stray wouldn't answer to that, so Valentino it was.

Brody looked around. There was no sign of Tricia, or the Pathfinder she drove.

"She's gone to town to help Carolyn at the shop," Conner said. He usually had a pretty fair idea what Brody was thinking, and the reverse was also true. "The woman is pregnant out to here." He shaped his hands around an invisible basketball, approximately at belly level. "What would be so wrong with staying home for one day? Taking it easy, putting her feet up for a while?"

Brody chuckled and slapped his brother on the shoulder. "She's running a small-town art gallery, Conner," he said, "not bungee-jumping or riding bulls in a rodeo."

Conner's face tightened momentarily and, once again, Brody knew what was on his twin's mind because they so often thought in tandem.

"There's no connection between our mom's pregnancy and Tricia's," Brody added quietly. "Stop looking for one."

Conner sighed, managed a raw kind of grin. Nodded.

It struck Brody then, though not for

the first time, of course, just how vulnerable loving a woman made a man. And after the baby came? It would be way worse.

Brody shivered, momentarily swamped with recollections.

"What happened to your clothes, anyhow?" Conner asked, looking him over. He tended to get around to things in his own good time.

"Moonshine got a little overenthusiastic crossing the river," Brody replied.

They headed into the house, the dog trotting behind them, and Brody ducked into the laundry room to swipe a pair of jeans, a T-shirt and some socks from the folded stacks on top of the dryer. After a quick shower to thaw out his bone marrow, he dressed in the room he and Conner had shared as kids, with their cousin Steven joining them in the summertime, and emerged to find his brother still in the kitchen, brewing a cup of coffee with one of those fancy single-shot machines designed for the chronically caffeine-deprived.

"How's the new place coming along?"

Conner asked, holding out a steaming mug, which Brody took gratefully.

"It's a slow process," he replied, after a sip of java. "The builder swears up and down that it'll be move-in ready by the middle of August, though."

Conner gave a snort at that, retrieved a second cup from under the spout of the shining gizmo and raised it slightly, in a little salute. "Nice clothes," he observed wryly. "I once owned some just like them."

Carolyn Simmons held her breath as she watched her very pregnant friend and business partner, Tricia Creed, making her wobbly way down from the top of a ladder. Tricia had just hung a new batik depicting a Native American woman weaving at a loom. The work of a local artist, the piece wouldn't be in the shop long, which was possibly why Tricia had placed it so high on the wall. No doubt she reasoned that if the picture wasn't within easy reach, she and Carolyn could enjoy it for a while before some eager buyer snatched it up.

With her long, dark braid, loose-fitting

cotton maternity clothes and attitude of serene faith in the all-around goodness of life, Carolyn thought Tricia resembled the weaver a little.

Taller than Tricia, with artfully streaked blond hair, Carolyn wore her usual garb of jeans, boots and a fitted T-shirt. Tricia liked to joke that if an opportunity to ride a horse came up, Carolyn was determined to be ready.

"What were you doing on that ladder?" she asked now, propping her hands on her hips as she regarded Tricia. "I promised Conner I'd keep an eye on you, and the minute I turn my back, you're teetering on the top rung."

Tricia dusted her hands together and smiled, stepping back a little way to look up at the batik. "I was nowhere near the top rung," she argued cheerfully, her face glowing in the sunlight pouring in through the big front window. She sighed. "Isn't she beautiful?"

Carolyn, following Tricia's gaze, nodded. Primrose Sullivan, the artist, had outdone herself this time. The weaver was indeed beautiful. "I think some of our online customers would be interested," she mused. "I'm not sure it would photograph all that well from this angle, though—"

The hydraulic squeal of brakes interrupted.

Tricia moved to the window and peered through the antique lace curtains. "It's another tour bus," she said. "Brace yourself."

The business, a combination boutique and art gallery, filled the first floor of Natty McCall's venerable Victorian house—Carolyn lived upstairs in Tricia's former apartment, along with her foster cat, Winston. The items the two women sold ranged from goats' milk soap and handmade pincushions to one-of-a-kind dresses and near museum-quality oil paintings.

"I'm braced," Carolyn confirmed, smiling and taking her customary place behind the counter, next to the cash register.

Tricia straightened an already straight display of handmade stationery.

The shop wasn't going to make anyone rich, but for Carolyn, it was a dream come true. In Lonesome Bend, she had a comfortable place to live—not a small thing to a person raised in no fewer than fourteen foster homes—and an outlet for the various garments, decorative pillows and retro-style aprons she was constantly running up on her sewing machine. Formerly a professional house sitter, Carolyn had been selling her designs online for years. Her online business brought in enough extra money to build a small savings account and buy thread and fabric for the next project she had in mind, but that was the extent of it.

The little bell over the front door jingled merrily, and the busload of customers crowded in, white-haired women with good manicures and colorful summer clothes, chatting good-naturedly among themselves as they thronged around every table and in front of every shelf.

The store, loftily titled Creed and Simmons—Tricia's great-grandmother, Natty, said the name sounded more like a law firm or an English jewelry shop than what it was—barely broke even most of the time. Tour buses heading to and from Denver and Aspen and Telluride stopped at least twice a week, though, and that kept the doors open and the lights on.

For Tricia, having sold property inherited from her father for a tidy sum and then having married a wealthy rancher to boot, the place was a hobby, albeit one she was passionate about.

For Carolyn, it was much more—an extension of her personality, an identity. A way of belonging, of fitting into a community made up mostly of people who had known each other from birth.

It *had* to work.

Without the business, Carolyn would be adrift again, following the old pattern of living in someone else's house for a few days or a few weeks, then moving on to yet another place that wasn't hers. House-sitting was a grown-up version of that old game musical chairs, only the stakes were a lot higher. Once or twice, when the figurative music stopped unexpectedly, Carolyn had been caught *between* houses, like a player left with no chair to sit in, forced to hole up in some cheap motel or sleep in her car until another job turned up.

Thankfully, there were plenty of opportunities around Lonesome Bend—movie stars and CEOs and high-powered political types kept multimillion-dollar "vacation homes" hidden away in private canyons, on top of hills and at the ends of long, winding roads edged with whispering aspen trees.

Carolyn still did some house-sitting now and then, for long-time clients, but she much preferred the cozy apartment above the shop to those enormous and profoundly empty houses, with their indoor swimming pools and their media rooms and their well-stocked wine cellars.

In the apartment, she was surrounded by her own things—the ceramic souvenir mugs she'd collected from cities all over the country, a few grainy photographs in cheap frames, her trusty laptop and the no-frills workhorse of an electric sewing machine that had been a parting gift from her favorite foster mom.

In the apartment, Carolyn felt substantial, *real,* rooted in one particular place, instead of some ethereal, ghost-like being, haunting lonely castles.

For the next forty-five minutes, Carolyn and Tricia were both so busy that they barely had a chance to look at each other, let alone speak, and when the tour bus pulled away at last, it was almost time to close up for lunch.

The cash drawer was bulging with fives, tens and twenties, and there was a nice pile of credit card receipts, too.

The shelves, racks and tables looked as though they'd been pillaged by barbarians, and the air still smelled of expensive perfume.

"Wow," Tricia said, sagging into the rocking chair near the fireplace. "*That* bunch just about cleaned us out."

Carolyn laughed. "That they did," she agreed. "Bless their hearts."

Tricia tilted her head back, sighed slightly and closed her eyes. Her hands rested protectively over her bulging stomach.

Carolyn was immediately alarmed. "Tricia? You're all right, aren't you?"

Tricia opened her eyes, turned her

head and smiled. "Of *course* I am," she said. "I'm just a little tired from all that hurrying around."

"You're sure about that?"

Tricia made a face, mocking but friendly. "You sound just like Conner. *I'm fine,* Carolyn."

Frowning slightly, Carolyn went to the door, turned the Open sign around, so it read Closed, and turned the lock. She and Tricia usually had lunch in the downstairs kitchen at the back of the house, and sometimes Tricia's husband joined them.

Tricia was still in the rocking chair when Carolyn got back.

And she'd fallen asleep.

Carolyn smiled, covered her friend lightly with a crocheted afghan and slipped away to the kitchen.

Winston, the cat, wound himself around her ankles when she entered, purring like an outboard motor. Like the house, Winston technically belonged to Natty McCall, Tricia's great-grandmother, now a resident of Denver, but because he stayed with Carolyn whenever his mistress was off on one of her frequent and quite lengthy cruises, she loved him like her own.

Apparently, the feeling was mutual.

Or he just wanted his daily ration of sardines.

"Hungry?" Carolyn asked, bending to stroke the cat's gleaming black ears.

Winston replied with a sturdy meow that presumably meant *yes* and leaped up onto a sideboard, where he liked to keep watch.

Smiling, mentally tallying up the take from the power-shopper invasion, Carolyn went to the fridge, got out the small bowl of sardines left over from the day before and stripped away the covering of plastic wrap.

She set the bowl on the floor for Winston, then went to the sink to wash her hands.

Winston came in for a landing squarely in front of his food dish and, at the same time, a knock sounded lightly at the back door.

Conner Creed pushed it open, stuck his head inside and grinned at Carolyn, flashing those way-white teeth of his.

Her heart skipped over a beat or two

and then stopped entirely—or at least, that's the way it felt—as he stepped into the house.

Because this *wasn't* Conner, as she'd first thought.

No, siree. This was *Brody.*

Carolyn's cheeks burned, and she barely held back the panicked "What are *you* doing here?" that sprang to the tip of her tongue.

The grin, as boyish and wicked as ever, didn't falter. Clearly, their history didn't bother Brody at all. It shouldn't have bothered Carolyn, either, she supposed, since almost eight years had passed since they were *together*-together. And what they'd shared amounted to a tryst, not an affair of the heart.

Be that as it may, every time she encountered this man—a recurring problem now that his brother was married to one of her closest friends—she wanted to flee.

"Is my sister-in-law around?" Brody asked, well aware, Carolyn would have bet, that he'd rattled her.

Carolyn swallowed hard. Once, when she'd been on a trail ride with Conner and Tricia and a number of their friends and neighbors, Brody and his now-and-then girlfriend, Joleen Williams, had raced past on horseback, their laughter carried by the wind. Carolyn, taken by surprise, had played the fool by bolting for the barn, without so much as a good-bye to the other members of the party, and she'd been kicking herself for it ever since.

"Tricia is in the front," she replied, in a remarkably normal tone of voice. "We had a busy morning, and she fell asleep."

Brody closed the door behind him, crossed to the cat and crouched, extending a hand.

Winston hissed and batted at him with one paw.

"Whoa," Brody said, drawing back.

Carolyn chuckled, relaxing a little. Clearly, Winston was a good judge of character, as well as an expert mouser and a connoisseur of fine sardines.

Having made his position clear, the cat went back to snarfing up his lunch.

Meanwhile, Brody rose off his haunches, still holding his hat in one hand, and looked disgruntled. Being drop-dead gorgeous, he probably wasn't used to rejection—even when it came from an ordinary house cat.

"Animals usually *like* me," he said, sounding baffled and even a little hurt.

Carolyn, realizing she'd been gawking, turned away, suddenly very busy getting a can of soup, a box of crackers and a loaf of bread from the pantry.

Glancing back, she saw Brody approach the inside door, push it open carefully and peer into the next room.

He turned, with a kind of brotherly softening in his eyes, and put his index finger to his lips.

"Shh," he said.

"I didn't make a sound," Carolyn protested, in a whisper.

Why didn't the man just *leave* now, if he didn't want to disturb Tricia?

Instead, he lingered, one-hundred-percent cowboy, with his hat in his hands and his mouth tilted sideways in a grin.

"We don't have to be enemies, you know," he said quietly.

Carolyn, in the middle of slapping a slice of bologna onto a piece of bread, opened her mouth and then closed it again.

"Do we?" Brody persisted.

Carolyn recovered enough to reply, though the words came out in a terse little rush of breath. "Tricia is my friend and business partner. You're her brother-in-law. Therefore, we have to be civil to each other."

"Is it that hard?" Brody asked. "Being 'civil,' I mean?"

Suddenly, all the old feelings rose up inside Carolyn, nearly overwhelming her. Tears stung her eyes and she turned her head quickly, bit down hard on her lower lip.

"Carolyn?" he said.

He was standing right behind her by then; she felt the heat and hard masculinity of him in every nerve in her body.

Just go, she thought desperately, unable to risk turning around to face him.

Brody Creed had never been one to leave well enough alone. He took a light hold on her shoulders, and Carolyn found herself looking up into the treacherous blue of those trademark eyes.

"I'm sorry for what I did, way back

when," he told her, his voice a gruff rumble. "I was wrong. But don't you think it's time we put all that behind us and stopped walking on eggshells every time we happen to be in the same room?"

He was *sorry.*

As far as Carolyn was concerned, *sorry* was the emptiest, most thread-bare word in the English language. People hurt other people, said they were *so sorry* and then, in her experience at least, turned right around and did the same thing all over again.

Or something worse.

Carolyn glanced nervously in the direction of the inside door, afraid of up-setting Tricia. When she spoke, her voice was a ragged whisper. "What do you want me to say, Brody? That I forgive you? Okay, for what it's worth, I forgive you."

Brody's expression was bleak, but his eyes flashed with frustration. He was famous for his temper, among other things.

"You'll forgive, but you won't forget, is that it?"

"I might conceivably forgive a rattle-snake for biting me," Carolyn responded. "After all, it's a snake's nature to strike. But I'd be worse than stupid if I forgot and cozied up to the same sidewinder a second time, wouldn't I?"

A muscle bunched in Brody's cheek. He was already sporting a five o'clock shadow, a part of Carolyn observed with a strange detachment. Or maybe he hadn't shaved at all that morning.

Oh, hell, what did it matter?

"You think I'm asking you to 'cozy up' to me?" Brody almost growled. His nose was an inch from Carolyn's, at most. "*Damn* it, woman, I can't avoid being around you, and you can't avoid being around *me,* and all I'm suggesting here is that you let go of that grudge you've been carrying for seven-plus years so we can all move on!"

Carolyn would have loved to slap Brody Creed just then, or even throttle him, but suddenly the door to the next room opened and Tricia peeked through the opening, stifling a yawn with a patting motion of one hand.

"Have you two been arguing?" Tricia

asked, her gaze shifting from one of them to the other.

They stepped back simultaneously.

"No," Carolyn lied.

"Everything's just *great,*" Brody added, through his teeth.

CHAPTER TWO

Mischief lit Tricia's blue eyes as she studied Brody and Carolyn, the pair of them standing as still as cigar-store Indians in the middle of Natty McCall's kitchen.

Just looking at her took the edge off Brody's irritation. He'd always wanted a sister, after all, and now he had one. He felt a similar affection for Melissa, his cousin Steven's wife, but he didn't see her practically every day, the way he did Tricia, since Steven, Melissa and their three children lived in Stone Creek, Arizona.

"Did Conner send you to check up on me, Brody Creed?" Tricia asked in a tone of good-natured suspicion, tilting her head to one side and folding her arms before resting them atop her impressive belly.

Out of the corner of his eye, Brody saw Carolyn turn away. Her streaky blond hair swung with the motion, brushing against her shoulders, and just that fast, she was busy thumping things around on the counter again.

"Brody?" Tricia persisted, while Brody was untangling his tongue.

"It was my own idea to look in on you while I was in town," Brody finally answered, grubbing up a crooked grin and turning the brim of his hat in both hands, like some shy hero in an old-time Western movie. "I don't figure Conner would object much, though."

Tricia smiled broadly, flicked a glance in Carolyn's direction.

The can opener whirred and a pan clattered against a burner.

Brody sighed.

"Join us for lunch?" Tricia asked him.

Carolyn's backbone went ramrod-straight as soon as Tricia uttered those words, and Brody watched, at once amused and confounded, while she jammed slices of bread down onto the beginnings of two bologna sandwiches. She used so much force to do it that the things looked like they'd been made with a drill press.

Deciding he'd stirred up enough ill will for one day, Brody shook his head. "I'd better get back to the ranch," he said. "We're replacing some of the wire along one of the fence lines."

"Oh," Tricia said, as if disappointed.

She moved slowly to the table, pulled back a chair just as Brody went to pull it back *for* her and sank onto the seat.

"Hey," Brody said, concerned. "Are you feeling all right?"

Tricia sighed. "Maybe I'm a little tired," she confessed. "It's no big deal."

At that, Carolyn stopped flinging food hither and yon and turned to look at Tricia. "I think you should go home and rest," she said. "This morning was crazy, and we've been taking inventory for a couple of days now."

"And leave you to straighten up the

shop and restock the shelves all by yourself?" Tricia asked. "That wouldn't be fair."

"I can handle it," Carolyn said. She spoke in a normal tone, but Brody could feel her bristling, all over, like a porcupine fixing to shoot quills in every direction. She didn't deign to glance his way, of course. "And, anyhow, I'd like to close the shop early today. That way, I could catch up on the bookkeeping, then put the finishing touches on that gypsy skirt I've been working on and get it posted on the website."

Brody neither knew nor cared what a gypsy skirt was. He was feeling indignant now, standing there on the fringes of the conversation as if he'd either turned transparent or just disappeared entirely.

He cleared his throat.

Tricia didn't look at him, and Carolyn didn't, either.

The cat fixed an amber gaze on him, though, and Brody was affronted all over again. He'd never met a critter that didn't take to him right away—until this one.

"Tell you what," Tricia finally said to

Carolyn, after a few moments spent looking happily pensive. "I'll take the afternoon off. *If* you promise not to stay up half the night stitching beads and ribbons onto that skirt."

"I promise," Carolyn said quickly.

Most likely, by her reckoning, persuading Tricia to go home was the best and fastest way to get rid of *him,* too.

Brody felt his back teeth mesh together.

"All right, then," Tricia conceded. "I guess I *could* use a nap." With that, she headed off into the other room, probably on the hunt for her purse, and thus Brody and Carolyn were left alone again, however briefly.

On the stove, soup began to boil over the sides of the saucepan, sizzling on the burner and raising a stink.

Brody automatically moved to push the pan off the heat, and Carolyn did the same thing.

They collided, sideways, and hard enough that Carolyn stumbled slightly. And Brody grabbed her arm, an instinctive response, to steady her.

He actually felt the charge go through

her, arc like a bolt of electricity from someplace inside Carolyn to someplace inside *him.*

Instantly, both of them went still.

Brody willed his fingers to release their hold on Carolyn's arm.

She jerked free.

And Tricia was back in the kitchen by then, taking it all in.

Although he and Carolyn were no longer physically touching each other, it seemed to Brody that he'd been fused to her in some inexplicable way.

The very air of the room seemed to quiver.

"I'll drive you home," Brody managed to tell Tricia, his voice a throaty rasp.

"I'll drive *myself* home," Tricia countered, friendly but firm. There'd be no more use in arguing with her than with any *other* Creed. "I don't want to leave the Pathfinder behind, and, anyway, I *told* you—I feel just fine."

Carolyn favored her friend with a wobbly smile. "Take it easy, okay?" she said.

Tricia nodded on her way to the back door. She noted the spilled-over soup on the stove and, with the smallest grin, shook her head.

Brody happened to see her expression because he'd just leaned past her, to take hold of the knob. Where he came from—right there in Lonesome Bend, as it happened—a man still opened a door for a lady.

And this particular lady was trying hard not to laugh.

Brody's neck heated as he stood there, holding the door open for his brother's wife, all too aware that she'd drawn some kind of crazy female conclusion about him and Carolyn.

He clamped his jaw down tight again and waited.

Once Brody and Tricia were gone, and far enough along the flagstone walk to be out of earshot, Carolyn let out a loud, growl-like groan of sheer frustration.

The sandwiches were smashed.

Most of the soup—tomato with little star-shaped noodles, her favorite—coated the stove top. The rest was bonded to the bottom of the pan.

All of which was neither here nor

there, because she wasn't the least bit hungry now anyway, thanks to Brody Creed.

Winston, having finished his sardine repast, sat looking up at her, twitching his tail from side to side. His delicate nose gleamed with fish oil, and out came his tiny, pink tongue to dispense with it.

Comically dignified, his coat sleek and black, the cat reminded Carolyn suddenly of a very proper English butler, overseeing the doings in some grand ancestral pile. The fanciful thought made her laugh, and that released most of the lingering, after-Brody tension.

Carolyn frowned at the catch phrase: *After Brody.* In many ways, that simple term defined her life, as she'd lived it for the past seven years. If only she could go back to *Before Brody,* and make a different choice.

A silly idea if she'd ever heard one, Carolyn decided.

Resolutely, she cleaned up the soup mess, filled the saucepan with water and left it to soak in the sink. She wrapped the flattened sandwiches care-fully and tucked them away in the refrigerator. When and if her appetite returned, she'd be ready.

Winston continued to watch her with that air of sedate curiosity as she finished KP duty and returned to the main part of the shop.

Winston followed; whenever Carolyn was in the house, the cat was somewhere nearby.

She tidied the display tables and put out more goats' milk soap and handmade paper and the last of the frilly, retro-style aprons that were so popular she could barely keep up with the demand.

That task finished, she stuffed the day's receipts into a zippered bag generously provided by the Cattleman's First Bank, double-checked that the front door was locked and there were no approaching customers in sight and went upstairs to her apartment.

Every time she entered that cheery little kitchen, whether from the interior stairway, like now, or from the one outside, Carolyn felt a stirring of quiet joy, a sort of lifting sensation in the area of her heart.

She rented the apartment from Natty McCall for a ridiculously nominal amount of money—nominal was what she could afford—so it wasn't *really* hers. Still, everything about the place, modest though it was, said *home* to Carolyn.

Sure, she was lonely sometimes, especially when the shop was closed.

But it wasn't the same *kind* of loneliness she'd felt when she was constantly moving from one house to another and her address was simply General Delivery, Lonesome Bend, Colorado.

The irony of the town's name wasn't lost on Carolyn.

She'd ended up there quite by accident, a little over eight years ago, when her car broke down along a dark country road, leaving her stranded.

Her unlikely rescuers, Gifford Welsh and Ardith Sperry, both of them A-list movie stars, had been passing by and stopped to offer their help. In the end, they'd offered her the use of the guest house behind their mansion-hideaway three miles outside of town. After a series of very careful background checks, the couple had hired Carolyn as nanny to their spirited three-year-old daughter, Storm.

Carolyn had loved the job *and* the child. Most of the time, she and Storm had stayed behind in the Lonesome Bend house, while Gifford and Ardith crisscrossed the globe, sometimes together and sometimes separately, appearing in movies that invariably garnered Oscar nominations and Golden Globes.

Although Carolyn had never given in to the temptation to pretend that Storm was her own child, strong as it was some of the time, she and the little girl had bonded, and on a deep level.

For Carolyn, life had been better than ever before, at least for that single, golden year—right up to the night Gifford Welsh had too much to drink at dinner and decided he and the nanny ought to have themselves a little fling.

Carolyn had refused out of hand. Oh, there was no denying that Welsh was attractive. He'd graced the cover of *People* as the World's Sexiest Man, not just once, but twice. He was intelligent, charming and witty, not to mention rich and famous. She'd seen all his movies, loved every one of them.

But he was married.

He was a father.

Those things mattered to Carolyn, even if he'd temporarily lost sight of them himself.

After fending off his advances—Ardith had been away on a movie set somewhere in Canada at the time—Carolyn had resigned, packed her belongings and, once a friend had arrived to pinch-hit as Storm's nanny, left that house for good.

Within a few months, the property was quietly sold to the founder of a software company, and Gifford, Ardith and Storm, reportedly having purchased a sprawling ranch in Montana, never set foot in Lonesome Bend again.

Even now, years later, standing in the kitchen of her apartment, Carolyn remembered how hard, and how painful, it was to leave Storm behind. The ache returned, like a blow to her solar plexus, every time she recalled how the little girl had run behind her car, sobbing and calling out, "Come back, Carolyn! Carolyn, *come back!*"

Before that—long, long before that—another little girl had frantically chased after another car, stumbling, falling and skinning her knees, getting up to run again.

And that child's cries hadn't been so very different from Storm's.

Mommy, come back! Please, come back!

"Breathe," Carolyn told herself sternly. "You're a grown woman now, so act like one."

Indeed, she *was* a grown woman. But the child she'd once been still lived inside her, still wondered, even after twenty-five years, where her mother had gone after dropping her daughter off at that first foster home.

"Reow," Winston remarked, now perched on the kitchen table, where he was most definitely not supposed to be. "Reow?"

Carolyn gave a moist chuckle, sniffled and patted the animal's head before gently shooing him off the table. He immediately took up residence on the wide windowsill, his favorite lookout spot.

Being something of a neat freak, Carolyn moved her portable sewing machine aside, replaced the tablecloth beneath it with an untrammeled one and washed her hands at the sink.

The gypsy skirt, the creative project of the moment, hung on the hook inside her bedroom door, neatly covered with a plastic bag saved from the dry cleaner's.

Carolyn retrieved the garment, draped it carefully over the side of the table opposite her sewing machine and silently reveled in the beauty of the thing.

The floor-length underskirt was black crepe, but it barely showed, for all the multicolored, bead-enhanced ribbons she'd stitched to the cloth in soft layers. She'd spent days designing the piece, *weeks* stitching it together, ripping out and stitching again.

It was exquisite, all motion and shimmer, a wearable fantasy, the kind of original women like Ardith Sperry wore to award ceremonies and premieres.

Carolyn hadn't sized the piece for a

movie star's figure, though. It was somewhere between a ten and a twelve, with plenty of give in the seams, allowing for a custom fit.

Carolyn, a curvy eight since the age of seventeen, had deliberately cut the skirt to fit a larger figure than her own, for the simple reason that, if she could have worn it, parting with it would have been out of the question.

She'd been making purposeful sacrifices like that since she'd first learned to sew, in her sophomore year of high school. Once she understood the basics, she hadn't even needed patterns. She'd sketched designs almost from day one, measured and remeasured the fabric, cut and stitched.

And she'd quickly made a name for herself. While other kids babysat or flipped burgers for extra money, Carolyn whipped up one-of-a-kind outfits and sold them as fast as she could turn them out.

That made *two* things she did well, she'd realized way back when, with a thrill she could still feel. Carolyn had an affinity for horses; it seemed as though she'd always known how to ride.

Over the years, most of her foster homes being in rural or semirural areas, where there always seemed to be someone willing to trade riding time for mucking out stalls, she'd ridden all kinds of horses, though she'd never actually had one to call her own.

Now, determined not to waste another second daydreaming, she shook off the reflective mood and picked up the skirt again, carefully removing the plastic wrap and holding it up high so she could admire the shift and shiver of all those ribbons, the wink of crystal beads.

It was silly, she supposed, but she *coveted* that skirt.

Aside from the money the sale would bring in, which, as always, she needed, where would she even *wear* a garment like that? She lived in blue jeans, cotton tops and western boots, and for good reason—she was a cowgirl at heart, not a famous actress or the wife of a CEO or a cover model for *Glamour.*

With a sigh, Carolyn put the skirt back

on its hook on the bedroom door—out of sight, out of mind.

She crossed to the small desk Tricia had left behind when she moved to the ranch, and booted up her laptop. While the magic machine was going through its various electronic thumps, bumps and whistles, Carolyn heated a cup of water in the microwave to brew tea.

Winston, still keeping his vigil over the side yard from the windowsill, made a soft yowling sound, his tail swaying like a pendulum in overdrive. His hackles were up, but his ears were pitched forward instead of laid back in anger. While Carolyn was still trying to read his body language, she heard someone coming up the outside stairs.

A Brodylike shape appeared in the frosted oval window at the door, one hand raised to knock.

Before he could do that much, however, Carolyn had yanked the door open.

"I don't believe this," she said.

Over on the windowsill, Winston expressed his displeasure with another odd little yowl.

"What is that cat's problem, anyway?"

Brody asked, frowning as he slipped past Carolyn, graceful as a billow of smoke.

Carolyn shut the door. Hard.

"Winston," she said stiffly, "is a very discerning cat."

Brody sighed, and when Carolyn forced herself to turn around and look at him, he was gazing at Winston with an expression of wounded disbelief on his handsome face.

"Does he like Conner?" Brody inquired.

Carolyn hesitated. Brody threw an emotional wrench in the works every time she encountered him, but she didn't hate him. Not all the time, that is. And she didn't enjoy making him feel bad.

"Yes," she replied, eventually. "But you shouldn't take it personally."

"Easy for you to say," Brody answered.

"Tricia's okay, isn't she?" That was it, she decided. He was there because he had bad news. Why else would he have come all the way back in from the ranch, where he was supposed to be stringing new fence lines with Conner and the crew?

Brody must have seen the alarm in Carolyn's eyes, because he shook his head. Holding his range-battered hat in one hand, he ran the other through his shaggy, tarnished-gold hair.

Sighed again.

In a searing flash, it came back to her, the feel of that mouth on her skin.

"As far as I know, she's taking a nap." Another grin flickered in Brody's eyes and twitched at one corner of his amazing mouth. "As soon as Tricia turned in, Conner decided he was a little tired, too. That was my cue to make myself scarce."

Carolyn's cheeks were stinging a little, but she had to smile. "Probably a good call," she agreed. And then she waited. It was up to Brody to explain why he'd come back.

His remarkable blue eyes seemed to darken a few shades as he looked at her, and the gray rim around the irises widened. "I know the word doesn't mean much," he said, at long last, "but I meant it before, when I told you I was sorry about the way things ended with us."

Suddenly, Carolyn wanted very much to cry. And this was a sign of weakness, an indulgence she rarely allowed herself. All her life, she'd had to be strong— as a matter of survival.

She swallowed painfully and raised her chin a notch. "Okay," she said. "You're right. We'll just . . . let it go. Act as though it never happened." She put out her hand, the way she might have done to seal a business agreement. "Deal?"

Brody looked down at her hand, back up at her face. "Deal," he said hoarsely. And in the next moment, he was kissing her.

Carolyn felt things giving way inside her and, as good as that kiss was, she wasn't about to surrender so much as an inch of the emotional ground she'd gained after the cataclysm that was Brody Creed.

She wrenched herself back out of his arms, put a few steps between them and then a few more.

Brody merely looked at her, with his mouth upturned at one corner, a bemused *I thought so* gleaming in his eyes.

Stunned, not only by his audacity, but also by what he made her feel, Carolyn touched her lips, as if relearning their contours after a long absence from her own body.

"Don't you dare say you're sorry," she muttered.

Brody chuckled as he opened the door to leave. "Oh, believe me," he intoned. "I'm not the least bit sorry—not for that kiss, anyhow." His gaze shifted to Winston, who watched him from the windowsill, ears laid back, fur ruffled. "So long, cat," he added. "For now."

In the next moment, Brody was gone—so thoroughly gone that Carolyn felt as if she might have *imagined* the visit, at the same time certain that she hadn't.

After that, her concentration was shot.

She waited until Brody had had plenty of time to drive away. Then she logged off her computer, pulled on a lightweight blue corduroy jacket and retrieved her purse and car keys.

Sewing was out of the question, and so was doing the bookwork. She was too jumpy to sit still, or even stay inside.

So she drove to the Creed ranch, taking the long way around, following the back roads and bumpy logging trails to avoid running into Brody.

After some forty minutes, she reached Kim and Davis's place, parked beside the barn and then stood next to her car for a few moments, debating with herself. She and Kim were good friends; she really ought to knock on the door and say hello, at least.

The sprawling, rustic house had an empty look about it, though, and besides, Carolyn didn't feel like chatting. Kim was perceptive, and she'd know something was bothering her friend just by looking at her.

Because she had permission to ride any of the Creeds' horses anytime she wanted—with the exception of the rescued Thoroughbred stallion, Firefly— she could go ahead and saddle up one of the cow ponies without asking first.

Firefly, a magnificent chestnut, was "too much horse" for anybody but an experienced jockey, according to Davis. When they'd learned that the animal was about to be euthanized because his racing days were over and, being a gelding, he couldn't be put to stud, Kim and

Davis had hitched a trailer behind their truck and driven all the way to Kentucky to bring him home.

Passing the corral, an enclosure as large as many pastures, Carolyn stopped to admire Firefly, who had the area to himself that cool but sunny afternoon. He towered against the blue of the sky, and his beauty all but took her breath away.

She stood still as he tossed his great head and then slowly approached her.

Carolyn reached up to pat his velvety nose. Normally, if she planned to ride, she stuffed a few carrots into her jacket pockets before leaving home. Today, though, she'd made the decision impulsively as, let's face it, a knee-jerk reaction to Brody's kiss.

"Sorry, buddy," she told the former racehorse. "No carrots today, but I'll be sure to remember them next time."

Firefly nodded, as if to convey understanding, and Carolyn's spirits rose a little. For her, there was something therapeutic about horses—even as a kid, cleaning stalls and stacking bales of hay to earn riding privileges, she'd felt better just for being around them.

"Wish I could ride you," she told the former champion, "but you're off-limits."

He stretched his long neck over the top rail of the fence, and Carolyn patted him affectionately before moving on.

Besides coming there to ride when the mood struck and time allowed, she'd spent a lot of time in that place, house-sitting and looking after the horses while Davis and Kim were off on one of their frequent road trips, and everything about the barn was blessedly familiar. In fact, Carolyn figured if she ever went blind, she'd still be able to go straight to the tack room, collect the saddle and bridle Kim had given her and get the pinto mare, Blossom, ready to ride.

The horse knew every trail on that ranch by heart. Blossom would cross the creeks without balking, too, and she was as surefooted as a Grand Canyon mule in the bargain. Snakes and rabbits didn't spook her, and Carolyn had never known her to buck or run away with a rider.

Blossom, standing in her stall, greeted Carolyn with a companionable whinny.

Five minutes later, the two of them were out there under that achingly blue sky. Carolyn tugged at one stirrup, to make sure the cinch was tight enough, and then mounted up.

Once she was in the saddle, her jangled nerves began to settle down. Her heart rate slowed and so did her breathing, and her mouth curved into a smile.

She reined Blossom toward the green-festooned foothills, headed in the opposite direction from the main ranch house and away from the range as well, still wanting to avoid Brody if at all possible, but beyond that, she allowed the mare to chart her own course.

Blossom strolled along at a leisurely pace, stopping to drink from the icy, winding creek before splashing across it to the high meadow, one of Carolyn's favorite places to be.

Here, wildflowers rioted, yellow and pink, blue and white, and the grass was tall and lush. From the ridge, Carolyn could not only see the river, but also Lonesome Bend beyond it.

Brody's new house and barn, both sizable buildings, looked like toys from that distance. The workmen were no bigger than ants, moving over the framework, and the sounds of construction didn't reach her ears, though the horse might have heard them.

Blossom grazed contentedly, her reward for making the climb to high ground, and Carolyn stood in the stirrups, in order to see even farther.

There was the highway that led to Denver and points beyond.

Immediately after Brody's return to Lonesome Bend the year before, Carolyn had considered loading up her things and following that road wherever it might lead—like in the old days, she'd had no particular destination in mind.

Just somewhere *away.*

But her stubborn pride had saved her.

She'd loved Lonesome Bend and its people.

She'd had friends, a library card, a charge account at the local hardware store. Not a lot by most folks' standards, Carolyn supposed, but to her, they were important. Leaving would have meant starting over somewhere else, from scratch, and the idea of that had galled her.

She'd decided to stand her ground. After all, Brody was bound to take off again, sooner or later, because that was what Brody did.

He took off.

Looking out over the landscape, Carolyn sighed. Trust that man to break his own pattern by staying on this time, buying the land that had belonged to Tricia's father, Joe McCall, making it part of the family ranch.

Still, staying out of Brody's way hadn't been very difficult at first, as small as the town was. No doubt, he'd been doing his best to steer clear of *her,* too.

Then Tricia and Conner fell in love, and everything changed.

As Tricia's friend and eventually her business partner, Carolyn was included in every gathering at the Creed ranch and, since they were a sociable bunch, tending to go all out for holidays or anything that could possibly be construed as a special occasion, it happened often. Even in the rare month without a red-letter day on its calendar page, it seemed there was always a picnic, a barbecue, a trail ride, a potluck or some kind of party.

Most of the time, Carolyn attended the shindigs and did her best to have fun, but Brody was inevitably some-where around, seldom speaking to her, or even making eye contact, but *there,* nonetheless, a quiet but dynamic pres-ence she had to work hard to ignore.

And just doing *that* much required a level of concentration tantamount to walking barefoot over hot coals, like a participant in some high-powered semi-nar.

Frankly, Carolyn resented having to make the effort but, besides pulling up stakes and leaving town herself, she didn't seem to have any options.

She kept waiting to get over Brody.

Get over the hurt.

Get over caring about him.

So far, it hadn't happened.

Carolyn drew the scenery into her mind and spirit the way she drew breath into her lungs.

A hawk soared overhead, riding an invisible current of air.

Small animals rustled through the grass.

And beneath it all, Carolyn heard the steady *tick-tick-tick* of her biological clock.

At thirty-two and counting, she wasn't getting any younger.

How long could she afford to wait around for fate to make her dreams of a home and a family come true?

She leaned forward to pat Blossom's long, sweaty neck. Shook her head in silent answer to her own question.

She'd wasted enough time waiting around for the proverbial prince to ride up on a snow-white steed and whisk her away to Happily-Ever-After Land.

Okay, sure, she'd hoped a grand passion would be part of the package. But she'd *had* that with Brody Creed, hadn't she—for a whole week and a half?

And where had it gotten her? *Heartbreak Hotel, that was where.*

Obviously, love wasn't going to just *happen* to her, like in all those fairy tales she'd lost herself in as a child. It happened to some people—Tricia and Conner and a few others—but those were probably flukes.

Bottom line, she could wish all she wanted, but the fulfillment of said wishes was her own responsibility. Nobody was going to wave a magic wand and make things happen *for* her.

It was time to do something, time to *take action.*

Gently, she drew back on the reins so Blossom would stop grazing and continued the solitary trail ride, thinking as she went.

She'd been resistant to the idea of signing up for one of those online dating services, afraid of attracting, oh, say, a serial killer, or a bigamist, or some sort of con man set to make an appearance on *America's Most Wanted*. In light of a statistic she'd recently come across—that twenty percent of all romantic relationships begin via a matchmaking website of some sort—she was willing to reconsider.

Or, more properly, she was *willing to be willing* to reconsider.

Denver was probably full of nice men

looking for a partner. Maybe there were even a few eligible guys right there in Lonesome Bend.

It wasn't as if she needed a doctor, a lawyer, or an Indian chief. She'd settle for a mature man, a grown-up with a sense of humor and a steady job.

The word *settle* immediately snagged like a hook in the center of her chest.

She drew a few deep breaths as she and Blossom started back toward Kim and Davis's barn, traveling slowly. She wasn't signing up to be a mail-order bride, she reminded herself. Posting her picture and a brief bio online wasn't a lifelong commitment, but just a way of testing the water.

"You can do this," she told herself firmly.

Now, all she had to do was start believing her own slogan.

CHAPTER THREE

Brody gazed wistfully toward his half-finished house—the barn had stalls and a roof roughed in, so Moonshine had shelter, at least—and swung down out of the saddle.

It was twilight—the loneliest time of all.

In town and out there in the country-side, where there were a dozen or more farms and ranches, folks were stopping by the mailbox, down at the road, or riding in from the range after a day's work, to be greeted by smiling wives and noisy kids and barking dogs. Dishes and pots and pans clattered cheerfully in kitchens, and the scents of home cooking filled the air.

At least, that was the way Brody remembered it, from when he was a boy.

Back then, Kim baked bread and fried chicken in honest-to-goodness grease. She boiled up green beans with bacon and bits of onion, and the mashed potatoes had real butter and whole milk in them. Usually, there would be an end-of-the-day load of laundry chugging away in the washer, in the little room just off the kitchen, since "her men"—Davis, Conner and Brody and, in the summer, Steven—went through clean clothes like there was no tomorrow.

With a sigh, Brody led Moonshine into the partially completed shelter, placed him in one of the twelve stalls and removed the saddle and bridle and blanket. He filled the feeder, and made sure the waterer was working right, and took his time brushing the animal down, checking his hooves for stones or twigs. The overhead lights weren't hooked up yet, but he didn't need them to do this chore. Brody had been tending to horses

and other critters all his life—he probably could have performed the task in a
catatonic state.

He patted Moonshine on one flank
before leaving the stall, making his way
back to the doorway, which was nothing
more than a big square of dusk framed
in lumber that still smelled of rawness
and pitch, and took off his hat so he
could tip his head back and look up at
the sky.

It was deep purple, that sky, shot
through with shades of gray and black
and navy blue, the last fading line of
apricot light edging the treetops. A
three-quarter moon, the ghost of which
had been visible all afternoon, glowed
tentatively among the first sparks of
stars.

Something bittersweet moved in Brody's chest, both gentle and rough, a
contrary emotion made up of sorrow
and joy, and a whole tangle of other
feelings he couldn't name.

He wondered how he'd ever managed
to stay away from Lonesome Bend, from
this land and its people, for so many
years. His soul was rooted in this land,

like some invisible tree, tethered to the bedrock and pulling at him, pulling at him, no matter where he wandered.

This was the only place he wanted to be.

But that didn't mean *being here* didn't hurt sometimes.

Figuring he was getting a little flaky in his old age, he grinned and put his hat back on, raised the collar of his denim jacket against the chill of a spring night in the high country and surveyed the house he'd been building in his head for as long as he could remember—he'd drawn the shape of this room or that one a thousand times, on a paper napkin in some roadside café, on the back of a flyer advertising some small-town rodeo or a stock-car race, sometimes even on paper bought for the purpose.

And now, here it was, a sketch coming to life, becoming a real house.

The question was, would it ever be a *home,* too?

Brody looked around, taking a mental tally of what was finished and what was yet to be done. The under-floor had been laid throughout, the walls were framed in and the roof was in place. The kitchen—the heart of any country house—was big, with cathedral ceilings and skylights. There was space for one of those huge, multiburner chef's stoves. The massive double-sided fireplace, composed of stones from the fields and pastures around Lonesome Bend, and from the bans of the river, was ready for crackling fires, except for the hardware.

He moved on, into what would become the combination dining-and-living room. He paused briefly to examine that side of the fireplace. In this part of the house, the skylights were still covered in plastic, turning the shimmer of the moon murky, but the bowed windows overlooking the river would brighten things up plenty during the daylight hours.

There were five bedrooms in that house, besides the master suite, and almost as many bathrooms. Brody planned on filling those bedrooms with rambunctious little Creeds, ASAP, but there *was* the small matter of finding a wife first. He was old-fashioned enough to want things done in their proper order, though, of course, when it came to babies, that first one could come along anytime, as Davis liked to say, whenever there was a wedding. Invariably, he'd add that the others would take the customary nine months, and Kim would punch him playfully in the arm.

Kim and Davis had a solid marriage, the kind that lasted. The kind Brody wanted for himself, only with kids.

He smiled to himself, there in the gathering darkness of his new house. If she could have heard that thought, Kim probably would have said they'd *had* kids—him and Conner and Steven.

They'd been a handful, Brody reflected. Most likely, keeping up with two boys year-round, and a third when the school term ended, had been plenty of mothering for Kim. Either way, she'd never complained, never withheld love or approval from any of them, no matter how badly they behaved, but she'd been strict, too.

Chores and homework and church on Sunday were all nonnegotiable, and so was bedtime, until they all reached their teens. Scuffles were permissible, even considered a part of growing up country, but they had to be conducted *out-side.*

Of course, Davis usually refereed, though he was always subtle about it.

Bullying, either among themselves or out there in the bigger scheme of things, was the biggest taboo. It was the one infraction that would guarantee a trip to the woodshed, Davis told them.

None of them had ever wound up there, but they'd sure gotten their share of skinned knuckles and bloody noses interceding when kids at school picked on somebody.

Brody roped in his thoughts. Quieted his mind. Carolyn Simmons popped into his brain. She had a way of doing that.

Which was a waste of thinking power, since that woman had about as much use for him as a stud bull had for tits.

And who could blame her, after the way he'd done her?

He leaned against what would be a wall, someday, and took off his hat. Lowered his head a little.

He'd never set out to hurt Carolyn, and he'd meant it when he apologized. He'd been young back then, and foolish, and when the call from his most recent girlfriend, Lisa, came late one night, her voice full of tears and urgency, he'd panicked.

It was as simple as that.

"I'm pregnant," Lisa had told him. "The baby's yours, Brody."

After she'd calmed down a little, she'd gone on to say that she wasn't cut out to raise a baby by herself, and she wasn't about to hand an innocent child over to a rodeo bum like him, either. No, sir, she wanted her child to have a mom and a dad and grow up in one house, not a series of them. If he didn't marry her, pronto, she knew an attorney who handled private adoptions.

Brody hadn't discussed the matter with Conner, or with Davis and Kim, because he'd been estranged from all of them during those years. In fact, he'd made damn sure they weren't around before he showed up on the ranch, badly in need of a hideout, a place to lick his wounds.

And he sure as hell hadn't brought the subject up with Carolyn. He hadn't known what to say to her. So he'd simply packed up his gear, within an hour after hanging up with Lisa, and loaded it into his truck.

Carolyn, still flushed from their love-making earlier in the evening, had been smiling in her sleep when he leaned over and placed a kiss as light as a whisper on her forehead. Except for a note, hastily scrawled and left next to the coffee-maker on the counter beside the back door, that kiss was all the goodbye he could manage.

There was no way to sugar-coat it, then or now. He'd skipped out on her.

End of story.

All during the long drive to San Antonio, where Lisa was living at the time, though, it had been Carolyn haunting Brody's heart and mind, not the woman he was heading for in that beat-up old truck, not the life they would make together, him and Lisa and the baby.

Before Lisa's call, he'd been this close to telling Carolyn he loved her, that he wanted to marry her. Start a family as soon as they were settled.

He'd planned to make up with his kin,

too, and, if they'd have him, make a home right there on the ranch.

Fortunately, Brody reflected, remembering his long-ago honorable intentions, he'd had enough sense to override that particular impulse, on the grounds that he and Carolyn had only known each other for about ten days, and that flat-out wasn't long enough for anything real to get started.

Reaching San Antonio, he'd driven to Lisa's tiny rental house, hoisted her few belongings into the back of his truck and the two of them had headed straight for Las Vegas. Within a couple of days, they were man and wife, setting out to follow the rodeo.

They'd been happy enough together, Brody supposed. Especially after the baby came.

Marriage hadn't cured Brody's penchant for Carolyn, though. He'd been with Lisa for about a month, when, one night in a seedy bar, after guzzling too much beer with some of his bull-riding buddies, he'd tracked down the pay phone and punched in Davis and Kim's number, without a hope in hell that Carolyn would answer.

By then, she'd surely have finished her house-sitting stint and moved on, but he had to try. If Kim answered, he'd ask her how to reach Carolyn. Beyond that, he had no clue how to get in touch with the woman he still loved.

Miraculously, though, Carolyn *did* answer the phone. His aunt and uncle were on the road again, she'd said, and then she'd fallen silent, waited for him to explain himself.

He'd meant to, but it didn't happen. Brody was thrown and then hog-tied by his own tongue and, in the end, all he said was that ever-inadequate phrase, *I'm sorry.*

Carolyn had hung up on him then, and justifiably so. Brody had stood in the corridor of that dive of a bar, with his hand still on the receiver and his forehead against the graffiti-covered wall, feeling as though he'd been gut-punched.

After that night, Brody had kept his alcohol consumption to a minimum. He knew Lisa loved him, and he'd made up his mind, then and there, to love her back. Even if it killed him.

It had taken some doing, but he *had* come to care for his pretty young wife, especially after their son, Justin, was born. One look at that kid, and Brody would have done anything—*given up* anything—for him.

And he *had* given up things he'd once believed he couldn't do without.

Carolyn.

The old and tired dream of going home, setting things right with his family, settling down to a rancher's life. He wanted to show Justin off to the folks, but he was scared shitless of running into Carolyn, so he stayed away.

He'd regret that particular choice forever, probably, because three weeks before he would have turned two, Justin was killed in a car wreck, along with Lisa.

The pain of remembering that time was as fresh as ever, and it nearly doubled Brody over, even now. He'd quit the rodeo after the accident, and stayed drunk for a solid year.

Eventually, he sobered up, but he

stayed mad at the world, and he stayed ashamed. More in need of his home and family than ever, he'd denied himself both—as a sort of self-punishment, he supposed.

If he hadn't been off riding bulls, after all, he'd have been driving that snowy night, not Lisa. He might have been able to avoid the drunk driver doing ninety on the wrong side of the freeway.

And if he'd brought his wife and son home, where they belonged, the greatest tragedy of his life might never have happened.

It was all about choices, Brody reflected, forcibly hauling himself back into the present moment again. The past was over. A man made choices, and then he had to live with the consequences, whether they were good, bad or indifferent.

Brody squared his shoulders, walked on toward the small log structure where he'd been bunking for too damn long.

He switched on the lights as he stepped over the threshold, but two of the three long fluorescent bulbs in the ceiling fixture were burned out, the third flickering ominously, and the ambience was just plain gloomy.

The original furnishings were gone, except for the long counter that had served as a sign-in place for campers, when Joe McCall was still running River's Bend, and the ancient woodstove. Brody slept on a roll-away bed he'd borrowed from Kim and Davis, never made up now that he and Joleen were in an "off" stage of the on-again-off-again thing they had going. He'd had a shower installed in the small rest room, and he did his laundry either at the Wash-and-Go on Main Street or out at the ranch. He owned a double-burner hot plate and a minifridge with a microwave the size of a matchbox sitting on top, and his desktop computer served as TV, DVD player and general, all-around communication device. He used a cell phone when he had something to say to somebody, or he went to see them in person, face-to-face.

What a concept.

Tricia's dad had always referred to the shack as a lodge.

Brody called it a log cabin—or a shit-hole, depending on his frame of mind.

That night, despite his best efforts to alter his attitude, it was a shit-hole.

He'd *kissed* her.

Try though she might, even after the ride on Blossom and the meandering drive back to town, Carolyn could not get past the fact that Brody Creed had had the nerve, the unmitigated *gall,* after all he'd done to her, to haul right off and *kiss her.*

"Unbelievable," she told Winston in the apartment kitchen as she set his nightly kibble ration down in front of him. "The man is *unbelievable.*"

"Reow," Winston agreed, though he went straight to his food dish.

Carolyn shoved up one T-shirt sleeve, then the other, still agitated. She was hungry, but not hungry enough to cook. Remembering the flat bologna sandwiches from lunch, she went downstairs, retrieved them from the refrigerator in Natty's former kitchen and pounded back up the inside steps.

She tossed one wrapped sandwich

into her own fridge—maybe she'd have it for breakfast—and slowly removed the plastic from the other one.

Winston was still noshing away on his kibble.

Carolyn washed her hands and then plunked down in a chair at the table, along with her sewing machine, the day's mail and a rapidly cooling cup of herbal tea.

"I'm talking to a *cat*," she told the cat.

Winston didn't look up from his bowl. "It's pathetic," Carolyn went on. She took a bite out of her sandwich, and it was soggy, tasteless. The crusts of the bread were curling a little, too, and none of that even slowed her down. The meal wasn't about fine dining, after all. It was about making her stomach stop grumbling. "*I'm* pathetic. And do you know what, Winston? I'm no closer to achieving my goals than I was last year, or the year before that, or the year before *that*—"

Winston paused at last, gave her a disapproving glance for talking with her mouth full and finished off the last of his supper.

Carolyn offered him part of her sandwich, but he wasn't into people-food, except for sardines, and he'd already had his daily ration of those.

"You tried to warn me, didn't you?" she prattled on, dropping the remains of her supper into the trash and then washing her hands again. She squirted a dab of lotion into one palm and then rubbed the stuff in with vigor. "You made your opinion of Brody Creed absolutely clear, but did I pay attention? Did I keep my defenses up?"

"Reoooooow," Winston said wearily.

"This is ridiculous," Carolyn said, addressing herself now, instead of the cat. Was talking to herself better than talking to a pet? Seemed like six of one thing and half a dozen of another. "I've got to get a grip. Do something constructive."

Winston, curled up in his cushy bed now, yawned, wrapped his tail around himself with typical feline grace and dozed.

"Am I boring you?" Carolyn asked sweetly. Then, getting no answer, naturally, she laughed, flung her hands out from her sides and let them slap against her blue-jeaned thighs. "I'm certainly boring *myself.*" She approached the laptop, drew back the chair and sat down. Pressed the on button and waited.

Maybe she could find a helpful website. Say, getalife.com, or something along those lines.

She checked her email first—nothing much there.

Then she went to the online banking site and posted the day's sales receipts.

"Look at that," she said, squinting at the screen, though she knew Winston wasn't listening. "If we have many more days like today, Tricia and I are in serious danger of *making a profit.*"

There was more bookkeeping to do—there was *always* more bookkeeping to do—but, being in a low-grade funk, even after a horseback ride, Carolyn decided not to do today what she could put off until tomorrow. Things were usually slow in the shop on weekday mornings and, besides, she'd be fresh then. Capable of left-brain pursuits like balancing debits and credits in a virtual ledger.

She'd brew another cup of herbal tea and sew, she decided. Let her ever-energetic right brain run the show for the rest of the evening.

It couldn't hurt to just *look* at the on-line dating services, though, she mused, still sitting at the desk and sinking her teeth into her lower lip as she entered a request into her favorite search engine.

The number of choices, as it turned out, was mind-boggling.

There were sites for people who wanted a same-religion partner.

There were sites for dog-lovers, cat-lovers, horse-lovers and just about every *other* kind of lover. A person could sign up to meet people who enjoyed the same hobbies, political beliefs, movies, foods and wines, books, etc.

Hooking up by preferred profession was an option, too. Just about every legal vocation—and a few that were distinctly iffy—was represented by not just one website, but *dozens* of them. If she wanted to meet men with a certain first name, or a particular sign of the zodiac, no problem.

It was overwhelming.

It was also intriguing, especially for a woman who'd eaten a squashed bologna sandwich for supper and carried on an impassioned and fairly lengthy discourse with a cat for her only audience.

Reminding herself that fortune favors the bold, not the lily-livered, Carolyn settled on one of several sites based in Denver, and serving the surrounding area. The main page was tastefully designed, and the questionnaire for trial members was short and relatively nonintrusive—some of the sites required enough personal data to trace a person's ancestors back to the Ice Age.

Well, *practically* that far.

The first two weeks of the proposed trial period were free, giving her plenty of time to pull out, and all she had to do was post one photo of herself and give her first name, age and a few minor details.

Carolyn decided to call herself Carol for now. She uploaded a recent picture, taken at the town's Independence Day picnic, admitted that she'd hit the big 3-O, and then—well—*lied.* Just a little.

She loved to bowl, she wrote, in the

little panel labeled Little Tidbits About Me, and she worked in a bank. She had two rescued dogs, Marvin and Harry, and she'd been married once, when she was very young.

Reading over what she'd entered, Carolyn sighed, propped an elbow on the desk and sunk her chin into her palm. None of this was true, of course, but she couldn't help being creative—it was in her nature. Besides, she was starting to like the fictional Carol.

She sounded like a good person.

Reassured by the certainty that prospective dates could contact her only through an assigned email address connected with the site, Carolyn moved the cursor to the little box in the lower right-hand corner of the screen, marked Go For It!, and clicked.

Dater's remorse struck her in the next second, but it was too late now. She was *out there* in cyberspace, albeit under an assumed identity, and it was kind of exciting, as well as scary.

She'd taken a step, after all. Made a move, however tentative, toward her heart's desire: a home and family of her own.

Carolyn slumped back in her chair, glumly scanning the Friendly Faces web page for a button that would allow her to back out of her trial membership— what had she been thinking?—but the best she could come up with was the Contact Us link.

That would have to do. She'd send a brief message, say she'd changed her mind about online dating and that would be that.

But then a message popped up.

Someone likes your friendly face! it crowed, in letters that appeared to be dancing across the screen. Click on the heart to get acquainted!

Carolyn hesitated, amazed and curious and wishing she'd worked on the gypsy skirt as planned, instead of surfing the Net.

She thought about Tricia, happily married and expecting a baby.

She thought about Brody Creed, who apparently believed he could just go around kissing women he'd dumped.

Dumped? He hadn't even had the decency to do that. He'd just boogied, abandoned her in the middle of the night, while she was sleeping.

She clicked on the pulsing heart icon.

A photo of a nice-looking—as in, he looked as though he was probably nice—man popped up immediately. Hi, the message bar read. My name is Darren.

Darren wore a mild expression on his roundish face, and his hairline was receding, just a little. He was a dentist, divorced with no kids and he loved dogs and bowling and computer games.

At least appearance-wise, he was *nothing* like Brody.

A point in his favor, for sure.

Carolyn drew a deep, shaky breath, let it out slowly, and clicked on the chat button. Hello, she told him. I'm Carol.

Darren, in addition to his other talents, was a speedy typist. He flashed back with an immediate, Wow. That was fast. Hi, there, Carol.

Carolyn felt a pang of guilt. She'd been acquainted with the man for two seconds, and she was already lying to him. *Lying* to a divorced dentist, with no kids, who loved dogs.

What kind of person was she, any-way?

A careful one, she thought.

Hi, there, Darrell, she wrote back.

Darren, he corrected.

Carolyn stifled a groan. Sorry. Darren. I haven't had much experience at this, as you've probably guessed. *And my name isn't Carol, it's Carolyn. I don't work in a bank and I'm looking for a husband to father my children. Anybody who isn't a Creed and doesn't have a criminal record will do.*

Darren replied with an LOL and an animated smiley face that was winking. Everybody was new here once, he added, in his rapid-fire, e.e. cummings style. On the Friendly Faces site, I mean. It's a great way to meet new people. Very low-key.

It's a virtual singles bar, Carolyn thought but did not type. *And the secret password is probably* loser.

Really? Carolyn wrote in response. Have you met a lot of people through the site? *And if so, why are you still trolling the web for prospective dates?*

Sure, Darren answered. I'm making friends right and left. So far, it's just been dinner and a movie, but, hey, at least I'm doing something besides filling cavities and begging patients to floss. Ha ha.

Darren had a sense of humor, then.

Sort of.

Carolyn sat with her fingers poised over the keyboard, and no earthly idea what to say next.

Carol? Darren asked. Are you still there?

I'm here, Carolyn replied.

You're shy, Darren said.

Carolyn blew out a long breath, making her bangs tickle her forehead. Not really, she answered. There, she'd said something honest. She *wasn't* shy. She was merely cautious. Sensible.

It finally occurred to her that if *she* was stretching the truth, Darren might be, too. Maybe his name was Dave, and he was married and not a dentist at all. Maybe he owned the Friendly Faces website, and this was his way of making people think they were in for some action.

Nice "talking" to you, Darren, she wrote. But I should be going. Lots to do.

Wait! Maybe we could meet for coffee? he replied.

Maybe, Carolyn said.

Your picture is great, Darren hastened to add. Promise we can chat again, at least?

Carolyn sighed. We'll see, she wrote.

She logged off the computer, pushed back her chair and stood. Stretched, enjoying the pull in her muscles, and turned around. There was the sewing machine, the plastic box full of ribbon scraps saved from various projects, her quilted-top basket, where she kept scissors, thimbles, needles and other notions.

Sewing, like horseback-riding, had long been a refuge for her. She could lose herself in either pursuit . . . usually.

But tonight was different.

All because Brody Creed had kissed her.

The bastard.

The good-looking, sexy *bastard.*

Carolyn squared her shoulders, spun around on one heel and marched herself back to the desk, and her computer.

She switched on the laptop and waited impatiently for the system to reboot.

Then she went online and clicked her

way straight to the Friendly Faces website.

Who knew? Maybe Darren—Darrell?—the dentist was still hanging around.

Carolyn's eyes widened when she spotted the message-box counter. "Carol" had over a dozen emails waiting.

After pushing her sleeves up again, Carolyn plunged in.

Brody tipped what was left of his microwave-box dinner into the trash and looked up at the last of the functioning lightbulbs. Might as well change them out, he figured. It wasn't as if he had anything better to do.

He rustled up the extras he'd bought days before, but never gotten around to installing, and vaulted up onto the counter to take out the dead bulbs first. The job was tricky—he'd seen these thingamajiggies shatter into a jillion tiny, razor-sharp shards for no sensible reason—so Brody took his time.

He'd just finished, his eyes still a little dazzled by the glare of three fluorescent tubes, when he heard what sounded like a thump, or maybe a scratch, at the door.

He got down off the counter. Listened.

That was when he heard the whimper. It was faint, and almost human.

A chill trickled down his spine. He sprang to the door and wrenched it open, half expecting to find a person on the other side, injured and bleeding, looking for help.

Instead, his gaze fell onto the skinniest, dirtiest, most pitiful dog he'd ever seen. It was just sitting there, looking up at him with a sort of bleak tenderness in its eyes.

Brody, a sucker for anything with four legs and fur, crouched down, so he wouldn't be looming over the poor critter like a grizzly or something.

"Hey, buddy," he said huskily. "You selling something? Spreading the Good News?"

The dog whimpered again.

Brody examined the animal. No collar, no tags.

Fleas were a sure thing, though, and maybe something worse, like ringworm.

Brody stood up, slow and easy, and

stepped back. "Come on in," he said to the dog. "Nothing to be afraid of—you're among friends."

The stray just sat there for a few moments, as though he might have heard wrong. He was obviously used to fending for himself.

"Come on," Brody repeated, speaking gently and giving the dog room.

Slowly, painfully, the wayfarer limped over the threshold and right into Brody Creed's heart.

CHAPTER FOUR

The dream was disturbingly vivid.

Carolyn was in a supermarket, surrounded by dozens, if not hundreds, of eager suitors. There were men of every size and shape, color and type, a regular convention for fans of the Village People.

They nudged at her cart with theirs.

Some of them carried signs with her modified name printed on them in ransom-note letters, and one wore a sandwich board that read Marry Me, Carol! and Have Free Dentistry for Life!

"Carol," all the others chanted, in creepy unison, "Carol, Carol, Carol!"

Carolyn's feet seemed to be glued to the floor, but she looked wildly around for an escape route anyway. The freezer aisle was completely blocked, in both directions. She was trapped. Cornered.

Heart-pounding panic set in, washing over her in sweeping, electrified waves. A man with an elaborate wedding cake teetering in his shopping cart pushed his way past the others, to the forefront.

Carolyn recognized Gifford Welsh. He smiled his big movie-star smile, and his piano-key teeth sparkled cartoonishly, like something out of an animated mouthwash commercial.

"You're already married!" she said, turning her head when Gifford tried to stuff a handful of cake into her mouth. Then, pressing back against the cold door of the ice-cream freezer, she shouted, "I don't want to marry *any* of you! You're not—you're not—

"Brody." She started awake at the name. Could still feel its singular weight on her lips.

Winston, curled up at her feet, made a halfhearted hissing sound. There was no telling whether the noise was a com-

ment about Brody or annoyance because she'd awakened him from a sound
sleep.

Carolyn's heart thumped against the
back of her rib cage, and her breathing
was fast and shallow. She lay there, in
her dark bedroom, looking up at the
ceiling and fighting tears.

Don't be a crybaby, she heard one of
her long string of foster mothers say.
Nobody likes a crybaby.

Carolyn had subscribed to that belief
ever since, and she blinked until the
sting in her eyes abated a little.

Going back to sleep was out of the
question, lest the dream go into rewind,
so she got out of bed and padded into
the kitchen, barefoot. She was wearing
flannel pajamas she'd sewn herself, covered in a puppy-dog pattern, and the
fabric was damp against her chest and
between her shoulder blades. Perspira-
tion.

The nightmare had been a doozy,
then. Normally, dreams didn't cause her
to sweat.

But, then, this hadn't *been* a normal
dream, now, had it?

You're not Brody. The words still reverberated through her mind.

She took a mug from the cupboard, this one a souvenir of Cheyenne, Wyoming, filled it with water, added an herbal tea bag and stuck the works into the microwave to heat.

A dog, she thought peevishly, would have gotten up when she did, to keep her company, lend silent reassurance. Winston, by contrast, did not put in an appearance, sympathetic or otherwise.

That was a cat for you.

Not that Winston was *her* cat—he was a frequent boarder and no more. Just passing through.

Somebody else's cat.

Somebody else's house.

Everything in her life, it seemed, belonged to somebody else.

Including Brody Creed. Whenever Joleen Williams blew into town, she and Brody were joined at the hip. It was probably only a matter of time before Joleen roped him in for good.

He was building a house, wasn't he? A *big* house, obviously not meant for man to live in alone.

The bell on the microwave dinged, and Carolyn carefully removed the cup. Took a sip.

The tea had the usual placebo effect, and she calmed down a little.

In need of something to occupy her mind, but scared to log on to the computer again, lest more men should pop up, in search of her alter ego, Carol, she flipped on the light at the top of the inside stairway and made her way down the steps.

The shop looked magical in the moonlight. Like some enchanted workshop, where elves ran up ruffly cotton-print aprons on miniature sewing machines and made more goats' milk soap whenever the supply was low.

Carolyn gave a little snicker at the thought.

She made the aprons, and they bought the soap from a woman who ran a small goat farm a few miles out of town. A few elves would certainly come in handy, though, even if it *wasn't* Christmas.

She loved the shop; it grounded her, like sewing and riding horseback usually did, and she loved the twinkling quiet surrounding her.

A shaft of silvery light struck the batik of the Native weaver, high on the wall, illuminating the image as though to convey some message.

There was no message, Carolyn thought. Not in the picture, at least.

The dream, now? That had clearly been a manifesto from her subconscious mind.

As usual, she wanted what she couldn't have.

Right or wrong, for better or worse, she wanted Brody Creed.

She gave a loud sigh of frustration, set her mug of tea down on the glass top of the handmade-jewelry display and shoved all ten fingers into her hair, pulling just a little.

Why couldn't she just *let go?* It had been over seven years, after all, since that awful morning when she'd awakened in a guest-room bed at Kim and Davis's place to find Brody gone.

At the time, she'd figured he was merely out in the kitchen making coffee, or even whipping up some breakfast.

He was a fair cook, and he seemed to enjoy it.

She'd gotten out of bed, pulled on a robe and headed for the kitchen, in search of the man she loved.

Instead, she'd found the note.

Have to go, Brody had written. *Something came up.*

That was it.

Have to go, something came up.

The tears that had threatened before, after the dream, sprang up again. Carolyn hugged herself, chilled, and gazed at her own woebegone face, reflected in the big mirror behind the counter.

"Nobody likes a crybaby," she told her image.

And then she cried anyway.

"Where'd you get the dog?" Conner asked the next morning, with affable interest, as Brody carefully lifted the bathed, brushed and still-skinny critter down from the passenger side of his truck, onto the grassy stretch of ground between the main ranch house and the barn.

"His name's Barney," Brody replied.

He'd hung that handle on the stray after taking him by the vet's office that morning for a checkup. And he'd been so glad over the dog's clean bill of health that he'd named him after the doctor. "He showed up at my door last night, in pretty sorry condition, so I took him in."

Conner grinned and crouched to look the dog in the eyes, much as Brody had done the night before, when Barney turned up on his doorstep.

"Well, hello there, Barney," Conner said, putting out his hand.

To Brody's mingled amazement and irritation, the dog laid a paw in Conner's outstretched palm.

Man and dog shook hands.

"I'll be damned," Brody muttered, impressed, then worried. Maybe whoever had taught Barney to shake hands was out combing the countryside for him, right now. Maybe somebody loved him, wanted him back.

Conner, meanwhile, stood up straight again. "I guess Doc must have checked for a microchip and all that," he said.

"First thing he did," Brody replied. "No chip, no identification of any kind."

"You gonna keep him?" Conner ventured, as Valentino trotted out of the back door, joined the group and sniffed Barney from head to tail.

"Yeah," Brody said. "I'll keep him. Unless his original owner tracks him down, anyway. Doc's assistant took his picture, and she'll upload it onto several lost-pet websites, just in case . . ."

"But?" Conner prompted.

"But my gut says he's in need of a home."

"Mine, too," Conner agreed. He had been frowning until then, but suddenly, the grin was back. "It'll be good for you," he preached. "The responsibility of looking after the poor critter, I mean."

The words, though he knew they were well-meant, raised Brody's hackles a little just the same. Was he going to be the Irresponsible One for the rest of his life, while Conner got to play the Good Brother?

Before he could figure out a way to answer, Davis came barreling down the hill in his truck from his and Kim's place. Kim rode beside him, her smile visible even through the dusty grunge covering the windshield.

"Kim's pinch-hitting for Tricia today at the shop," Conner said.

Brody felt a pang of alarm, remembering how tuckered out his sister-in-law had seemed the day before. "Tricia isn't having trouble, is she?"

"No," Conner replied, raising a hand to greet the new arrivals. "She just enjoyed yesterday so much that she wanted today to be just like it."

Brody chuckled, partly amused and partly relieved.

An instant later, though, the worry was back. Women were fragile creatures, it seemed to him. Lisa, for instance, couldn't have weighed more than a hundred and ten pounds sopping wet; she hadn't stood a chance against two tons of speeding steel, not driving that little car of hers.

He'd always had access to his inheritance and his share of the ranch profits, even when he was staying as far away from Lonesome Bend as he could. Why hadn't he gotten her a sturdier rig to drive?

"Brody," Conner said suspiciously. "Where's your head right now?"

"You know where," Brody replied, as Davis parked the truck and he and Kim got out of the vehicle and started toward them. Kim was wearing a lightweight sweater with big pockets, where her impossibly small dogs, Smidgeon and Little Bit, were riding.

Barney whimpered and moved behind Brody, leaning against the backs of his legs. He could feel the animal trembling.

Seeing that, Kim smiled, crouched down and set the two Yorkies on the ground. Ignoring Valentino, who was probably considered old news by now, they wagged their stumpy little tails and one of them growled comically.

"Now, come on out here," Kim cajoled, addressing Barney. "Smidgeon and Little Bit aren't going to hurt you."

Kim definitely had a way with animals, and Barney's reaction was proof of that. Probably drawn by her gentleness, as well as his own curiosity, he came out of hiding to stand at Brody's side. His plume of a tail wagged once, tentatively.

The Yorkies nosed him over and then lost interest and tried to start a game of tag with Valentino. They were absolutely fearless, those two. Or maybe their brains were just so small that they couldn't grasp the difference between their size and Valentino's.

"Come have supper with us tonight," Kim told Brody, when she was standing upright again. "You look a little ribby to me, like this dog."

Brody's mouth watered at the mere suggestion of Kim's cooking, not to mention a chance to avoid another lonely evening.

"Is this a setup?" he asked good-naturedly. It didn't take a rocket scientist to figure out that everybody was hoping he and Carolyn would get together.

"Of course it is," Kim replied with a laugh, looking at Brody but slipping an arm around Davis's waist and giving him a brief squeeze. "Why fight it?"

Brody laughed, too, despite the little thrill that quickened in the pit of his stomach at the thought of being in the same house with Carolyn. He folded his arms and countered, "Why not?"

Kim punched him. "You're just like your uncle," she said.

Whatever that meant.

That he was a stubborn cuss, probably.

The quality came free with the Creed name, one to a customer but guaranteed for life.

Conner and Davis, meanwhile, moved off toward the house, where Tricia surely had a pot of coffee brewing.

Smidgeon, Little Bit and Valentino ambled along after them, leaving Brody and Kim in the yard, with Barney.

"Carolyn's probably wise to your tricks, Kim," Brody ventured, serious now, his voice a little husky. "She'll know you've invited me to supper, and she'll think of some excuse to get out of it."

Kim, still a striking woman in her mid-fifties, shook her head and mimicked his stance by folding her own arms. "Could you *be* any more negative, Brody Creed?" she asked. "You and Carolyn are perfect for each other. Everybody seems to know that but the two of you."

Brody recalled kissing Carolyn the day before, and an aftershock went through him. When it was over, she'd looked as if he'd slapped her, and he'd made some smart-ass remark about not being sorry for doing it.

Oh, yeah. He was zero-for-zero in Carolyn's books, no doubt about it.

Kissing her had only made things worse.

He just hadn't been able to resist, that was all.

"Brody?" Kim prompted, evidently reading his face.

He smiled, laid a hand on Kim's shoulder. "I'm all right," he told her. "Stop worrying about me, okay?"

"Okay," she said, in a tone of bright irony. "Are you coming to our place for supper tonight or not?" Not waiting for an answer, Kim added, "Six-thirty, on the dot and don't be late." She looked around, parodied a frown. "If Davis Creed thinks he gets to keep Smidgeon and Little Bit with him while I'm in town, covering for Tricia at the shop, he's got another think coming."

With that, she turned and headed resolutely for the house.

Brody watched her go, one side of

his mouth quirked up in a grin. It was anybody's guess whether Carolyn would accept Kim's supper invitation or make up some excuse to get out of it, but he sure hoped it would be the former.

He wanted to see Carolyn again, even though the idea pretty well scared the crap out of him.

"Women," he told Barney ruefully.

Barney gave a little yip of agreement.

Brody chuckled, bent to ruffle the dog's ears and the two of them started for the house, where the others were gathered and the coffee was on.

"You have dark circles under your eyes," Kim announced, the moment she stepped over the threshold at the shop. "Aren't you sleeping well?"

Carolyn smiled as her friend took the pair of tiny dogs from her sweater pockets and set them down carefully on the floor, where they proceeded to romp like a couple of kittens.

Winston, long since resigned to the occasional presence of the canine contingent, ignored them.

"I slept just fine, thank you very much,"

Carolyn lied, in belated reply to Kim's question. She'd eventually managed to get to sleep again the night before, but she'd promptly tumbled right back into a variation of her dream. This time, with the added fillip of Brody riding through a conglomeration of suitors and shopping carts on horseback, reaching her side and then leaning down to hook an arm around her and haul her up into the saddle in front of him.

The dream hadn't stopped there, either. With no noticeable transition, Brody and Carolyn were alone in a forest, both lying naked in a stand of deep, summer-fragrant grass, making love.

She'd awakened in the throes of a very real orgasm, which was downright embarrassing, even if she *was* alone at the time.

"I don't believe you," Kim said, moving behind the sales counter to put away her purse.

Smidgeon and Little Bit were rolling across the center of the floor now, in a merry little blur of shiny fur and pink top-knot ribbon.

Carolyn, thinking of the spontaneous

climax, was blushing. "Would I lie to you?" she retorted, with an attempt at a light tone.

There weren't any customers in the shop yet, and she'd been keeping her mind off the nightmare/dream by catching up on the bookkeeping on the store's computer.

"Depends," Kim replied mischievously. "How about joining Davis and me for supper tonight? I'm thawing out a batch of my world-famous chicken-and-pork tamales."

A bar of that old song "Suspicion" played in Carolyn's head. "Hard to resist," she admitted. Kim's tamales were fantastic. "Are Conner and Tricia coming, too?"

Kim nodded, but she averted her eyes and was busying her hands rearranging costume jewelry in the glass case.

"And Brody?" Carolyn asked, rather enjoying herself, despite all her nerves being on red alert.

"Maybe," Kim said, her manner still evasive. "Did you know he adopted a dog? Brody, I mean? It's a very good sign. He really *is* serious about settling down in Lonesome Bend—"

"Dogs travel pretty well," Carolyn said, amused and, at the same time, wickedly excited over the perfectly ordinary prospect of sitting across a supper table from Brody Creed.

The bastard.

Kim straightened, looked at her directly. Her smile was a little weak. "You think he's planning to leave again? Even though he's building that big house and a fancy barn to go with it?"

Carolyn's casual shrug was, in reality, anything *but* casual. "He could always sell the house and barn, if he wanted to move on," she reasoned. In truth, though, she didn't like the idea of Brody going back to his other life any more than Kim did, and that surprised her. The prospect *should* have been a relief, shouldn't it?

Kim's gentle blue eyes filled with tears. "Brody's had a tough time of it," she said.

Carolyn needed a few moments to recover from that tidbit—she'd always imagined Brody whooping it up, as the cowboys liked to say, riding bulls and winning gleaming buckles and bedding a different woman every night.

"How so?" she asked, finally, in an oddly strangled voice.

Kim sniffled, squared her shoulders and straightened her spine. "I can't say," she told Carolyn, in a forthright tone. "I'm not supposed to know what Brody went through, and neither is Davis. He'd be furious if he knew Conner had told us."

"Oh, boy," Carolyn said.

"He'll tell you himself, one of these days," Kim said, with new certainty. "And that's the way it should be."

Just then, the bell over the front door jingled and Smidgeon and Little Bit ran, yapping, to greet whomever was there.

Kim rolled her eyes and chased after them. "Little devils," she muttered, with abiding affection.

Carolyn smiled, but on the inside, she was shaken.

She knew better than to go to supper at her friends' place, since it was a given that Brody would be there. Just being around him was playing with fire, especially in light of that stolen kiss—and last night's dream.

She'd be there, just the same.

Maybe she'd take in the gypsy skirt—just baste it to fit temporarily—and wear that.

Brody watched with a combination of affection and envy, that evening, in Kim and Davis's kitchen, while Conner and Tricia flirted like a pair of teenagers.

It was enough to make Brody roll his eyes.

Get a room, he wanted to say.

Davis, sitting beside him at the unset table, nudged him with one elbow. "You remember how it was with those two?" Brody's uncle asked, keeping his voice low. "When they first noticed each other, I mean?"

"I remember," Brody said, grinning a little. A stranger would have given odds that Conner and Tricia would never get together, but everybody who knew them wondered when the wedding would be.

Was Carolyn going to show up for supper or not?

He hoped so.

He hoped not.

"You and Carolyn remind me of them," Davis said, with a twinkle in his eyes.

That got Brody's attention, all right. He swiveled in his chair to look at his uncle with narrowed eyes. "What's that supposed to mean?"

"Just what I said," Davis replied, undaunted. "You know me, son. If I say it, I mean it."

Tricia snapped a dish towel at Conner, who laughed, and the dogs all started barking, while an apron-wearing Kim tried to shush the lot.

It was happy chaos.

It was a *family.*

Again, Brody felt that bittersweet sense of mingled gratitude and loneliness.

"Give things a chance, boy," Davis told him, pushing back his chair and heading for the back door. His uncle had always been able to read him and, clearly, that hadn't changed.

Brody hadn't heard the car drive up, what with all the barking and shushing, dish-towel snapping and laughing, but Davis must have.

He opened the door just as Carolyn was raising one hand to knock.

She looked shy and sweet standing there, wearing black jeans and a gossamer white shirt. Her sun-streaked hair was pulled back in a French braid and, unless Brody missed his guess, she had on just a touch of makeup, too.

"Hi," she said to Davis, with a little wobble in her voice, shoving a large plastic food container into his hands and not sparing so much as a glance for Brody. "I brought pasta salad. It's from the deli at the supermarket, but I'm sure it's good."

"That's fine," Davis said, in that Sam Elliott voice of his, sounding amused. "Come on in and make yourself at home."

Conner and Tricia knocked off the prelude to foreplay to greet Carolyn— Conner with a smile, Tricia with a hug. When Kim joined in, it was like something out of a reality-show reunion.

All Brody could do was wait, though he did remember enough of his manners to stand in the presence of a lady.

Carolyn finally forced herself, visibly,

to look at him. Pink color pulsed in her cheeks and hot damn, she looked good.

"Hello, Brody," she said.

"Carolyn," he replied, with a nod of acknowledgment.

Brody immediately grew two left feet and felt his tongue wind itself into a knot.

It was junior high school all over again.

Only worse.

In junior high, it had been all about speculation. As a man, he knew, only too well, what it was like to kiss this woman, to make love to her.

Stand in a puddle and grab hold of a live wire, he thought.

That's what it's like.

"Kim says everything's fine at the shop," Tricia told Carolyn, with a sparkling little laugh. "I was hoping I'd be missed a *little bit,* though."

Carolyn smiled, no longer looking quite so much like a doe poised to run after catching the scent of a predator on the wind. "Oh, you were definitely missed," she said.

"Absolutely," Kim agreed cheerfully,

opening one of the big double ovens to check on the tamales.

They smelled so good that Brody's stomach rumbled.

Things settled down to a dull roar over the next few minutes—Carolyn and Tricia washed up at the sink and began setting the table, while Davis pulled the corks on a couple of bottles of vintage wine.

It came as no surprise to Brody—and probably not to Carolyn, either—that they wound up sitting side by side at the huge table in the next room. The others made sure of it, the way they always did.

Brody and Carolyn were so close that they bumped elbows a couple of times. The scent of her—some combination of baby powder and flowers and a faint, citrusy spice—made him feel buzzed, if not drunk, which was weird because he let the wine bottle go by without pouring any for himself.

Tricia passed on it, too, of course, being pregnant.

Carolyn, by contrast, seemed uncommonly thirsty. She nibbled at the salad, and then the tamales and Kim's incomparable Mexican rice and refried beans, but she seemed to be hitting the wine pretty hard.

"So, anyway," Kim said, her voice rising above the others. "Carolyn signed up for Friendly Faces—that dating website—and she's practically *under siege,* there are so many men wanting to meet her."

Out of the corner of his eye, Brody saw Carolyn go pink and then mauve. Obviously, she hadn't expected Kim to spill the frijoles in front of God and everybody.

Brody wanted to chuckle. He also wanted to stand on Carolyn's front porch with a shotgun and make sure no other man got past him.

"Oops," Kim said, widening her eyes. She'd let the news slip on purpose, and everybody knew it, but since the horse was already out of the barn, so to speak, that was that. "Sorry."

Davis gave his wife a look.

Carolyn looked down at her lap, still red and making no pretense of eating.

Casually, Brody leaned over, took hold

of the nearest wine bottle and refilled her glass. She glanced at him with an expression of mingled desperation and gratitude and practically drained the thing in a few gulps.

Brody bit back a grin. Well, there was *one* bright spot to the situation, he reflected. Now he had the perfect excuse to drive Carolyn home, because she was obviously in no condition to get behind the wheel.

An awkward silence fell, broken only by the clinking of silverware against colorful pottery plates.

"I think it's wonderful," Tricia piped up, breaking the verbal stalemate. "The dating service thing, I mean. More and more people are meeting their soul mates online these days. Why, the statistics—"

Carolyn looked so utterly miserable by then that Brody felt downright sorry for her. She swallowed hard, raised her chin and bravely interrupted, "It's only a trial membership. I was curious, that's all."

"She's *swamped* with guys wanting

to get to know her," Kim said, warming to the topic all over again.

Another wine bottle was opened and passed around.

Carolyn sloshed some into her glass, avoiding Brody's eyes when she shoved the bottle at him to keep it moving.

"Are you sure you ought to . . . ?"

At last, Carolyn looked at him. She flashed like a highway flare on a dark night, because she was so angry.

Because she was so *beautiful.*

"I'm of legal age, Brody Creed," she said, slurring her words only slightly.

The others were talking among themselves, a sort of distant hum, a thing apart, like a radio playing in the next house or the next street, the words indistinct.

"Besides," Carolyn went on briskly, before he could reply, "I've only had two glasses."

"Four," Brody said quietly, "but who's counting?"

"It's not as if I normally drink a lot," she informed him, apropos of he wasn't sure what.

"Have another tamale," Brody counseled, keeping his voice down even though they still seemed to be alone in a private conversational bubble, him and Carolyn, with the rest of the outfit someplace on the dim periphery of things.

"I don't *want* another tamale," Carolyn told him.

"You're going to be sick if you don't eat something," Brody reasoned. He didn't think he'd used that particular cajoling tone since Steven and Melissa's last visit, when he'd been appointed to feed his cousin's twin sons. He'd had to do some smooth talking to get them to open up for the pureed green beans.

"That's my problem, not yours," Carolyn said stiffly.

"Around here," Brody said, "we look out for each other."

She made a snorting sound and tried to snag another passing wine bottle, but Brody got hold of it first and sent it along its way.

That made her furious. She colored up again and her eyes flashed, looking as if they might short out from the overload.

Brody merely held her gaze. "Eat," he said.

She huffed out a sigh. Stabbed at a tiny bite of tamale with her fork. "There," she said, after chewing. "Are you satisfied?"

He let the grin come, the charming one that sometimes got him what he wanted and sometimes got him slapped across the face. "No," he drawled. "Are you?"

It looked like it was going to be the slap, for a second there.

In the end, though, Carolyn was at once too flustered and too tipsy to respond right away. She blinked once, twice, looking surprised to find herself where she was, and swayed ever so slightly in her chair.

"I want to go home," she said.

Brody pushed his own chair back and stood, holding out a hand to her. "I think that's a good idea," he replied easily. "Let's go."

Kim and Davis, Conner and Tricia—he was aware of them as a group, rimming the table with amused faces but making no comment.

"I guess I have to let you drive me, don't I?" Carolyn said.

"I reckon you do," Brody said. "We'll take my truck. Somebody can bring your car to town later."

Carolyn, feisty before, seemed bemused now, at a loss. "But what about washing the dishes and . . . ?"

"Davis and Conner can do the cleaning up." Brody slid a hand under her elbow and raised her to her feet, steered her away from the table and into the kitchen, Barney sticking to their heels like chewing gum off a hot sidewalk.

He squired her to the truck and helped her into the passenger seat, careful to let her think she was doing it all herself.

Barney took his place in the backseat of the extended cab.

Once he was behind the wheel, Brody buzzed his window and Carolyn's about halfway down. She was going to need all the fresh air she could handle.

"You're going to hate yourself in the morning," he said easily, as they drove toward the gate and the road to town.

He'd only been teasing, but Carolyn's sigh was so deep that it gave him a pang, made him wish he'd kept his mouth shut.

"It might not even take that long," she said sadly. "I'm—I'm not used to drinking and I—well, I'm just not used to it, that's all."

Brody reached over, gave her hand a brief, light squeeze. "That's pretty obvious," he said gently.

"I feel like such a fool," Carolyn lamented, refusing to look at him.

"Don't," Brody said.

She looked down at her hand, where his had been rested for a second, and frowned, seemingly surprised to discover that he'd let go.

"You probably think I'm pathetic," she went on, staring straight through the windshield again.

"Nothing of the sort," Brody assured her gruffly.

"Getting drunk. Signing up for a dating service—"

Before he needed to come up with a response, she turned to look at him, straight on. And she was pea-green.

"Stop!" she gasped. "I'm going to be—"

Brody stopped, and she shoved open the door and stuck her head out.

"Sick," she finished.

And then she was.

CHAPTER FIVE

If she'd deliberately *set out* to make a lasting impression on Brody Creed, Carolyn thought wretchedly, as she stared at her wan image in the mirror above her bathroom sink later that evening, she couldn't have done a better job.

First, being the proverbial bundle of nerves, she'd had too much wine at supper. Then, with ultimate glamour and grace, she'd *thrown up,* right in front of the man. Just stuck her head out of his truck door and hurled on the side of the road, like somebody being carted off to rehab after an intervention.

"Very impressive," she whispered to her sorry-looking one-dimensional self.

With the spectacle playing out in her mind's eye, Carolyn squeezed her eyes shut, mortified all over again. Brody had reacted with calm kindness, presenting her with a partial package of wet wipes and following up with two time-hardened sticks of cinnamon-flavored chewing gum.

She'd been too embarrassed to look at him afterward, had hoped he would simply drop her off at home and be on his way again, with his dog, leaving her to wallow privately in her regrets.

She couldn't be that lucky.

Instead of leaving her to her misery, he'd told Barney to stay put, insisted on helping Carolyn down from the truck and escorting her not only through the front gate and across the yard, but also up the outside staircase to her door.

"I'll be all right now," she'd said, when they reached the landing, still unable to meet his eyes. "Really, I—"

Brody had taken her chin in his hand; sick as she was, the combination of gentleness and strength in his touch

had sent a charge through her. "I believe I'll stay a while and make sure
you're all right," Brody had replied matter-of-factly.

Though she was painfully sober by
then, Carolyn didn't have the energy to
fight any losing battles, so she merely
unlocked the door and allowed him to
follow her inside.

Winston, perched on the windowsill,
greeted him with raised hackles and a
hiss.

"Whatever, cat," Brody had said, with
desultory resignation. "I'm here, like it or
not, so deal with it."

Carolyn had hurried into the bathroom
to wash her face and brush her teeth,
following up with a mouthwash swish
and two aspirin from the bottle in the
medicine cabinet. Then she'd slipped
into her room and changed her T-shirt.

And here she was back in the bathroom again, trying to work up the courage to go out there into the kitchen,
thank Brody for bringing her home and
politely send him packing.

He was moving around out there, running water in the sink, carrying on a

one-sided chat with Winston, his voice set too low for her to make out the words. The tone was chiding, but good-natured.

Most likely, Brody was bent on winning over the cat.

The idea made Carolyn smile, but very briefly, because even *smiling* hurt.

How would she feel when the actual *hangover* kicked in?

Sobering thought. *That's what you get for drinking,* she told herself grimly. *You* know *you're not good at it.*

All this self-recrimination, she realized, was getting her nowhere, fast. So Carolyn drew a deep breath, squared her shoulders, let the air whoosh out of her lungs and forced herself to step out of the bathroom and walk the short distance to the kitchen.

Brody was leaning against one of the counters, sipping what was probably coffee from one of her three million souvenir mugs.

This one bore the image of a famous mouse and was painted with large red letters trumpeting Welcome to Orlando!

"You have quite a collection," Brody

observed, raising the mug slightly for emphasis.

"I've been everywhere," Carolyn said, in a lame attempt at normality. Some of the mugs were from thrift stores and garage sales, actually, but she saw no point in explaining that sometimes she liked to pretend she'd purchased them on family vacations over the years.

Which was pathetic, because to take a family vacation, one needed a *family.*

Brody gave her that tilted grin, the one with enough juice to power a cattle prod, his eyes as soft as blue velvet but with a twinkle of amusement, too. Moving to the microwave, he took out a second cup, this one commemorating some stranger's long-ago visit to the Alamo, in San Antonio.

Carolyn had always wanted to visit the Alamo.

She caught the soothing scent of mint tea with just the faintest touch of ginger. Her throat, still a little sore from being sick, tightened with some achy emotion.

"Good for what ails you," Brody said, setting down the tea on the kitchen table. "Have a seat, Carolyn. I'm not fixing to bite you or anything."

She dropped into a chair, wishing she'd put the sewing machine away before she'd left for Davis and Kim's house to have supper and campaign for fool of the year. Now Brody would probably think she was a *slob* as well as a shameless lush.

Brody waited a beat, then sat down across from her. Watched in easy silence as she took a sip of the tea, sighed at the herbal goodness of the stuff.

"You've been very . . . kind," Carolyn managed to say, after more tea. She was recovering in small but steady increments. "Thank you."

Brody's eyes smiled before his mouth did. "You're welcome," he said. He'd finished his coffee, but he appeared to be in no particular hurry to leave.

"I'll be fine on my own, now that I've had some aspirin and this tea," Carolyn told him, hoping he'd take the hint and hit the road.

Hoping he wouldn't.

He lingered, watching her. "I'm sure you will be," he agreed.

"And your dog is all alone, down there in your truck."

Brody chuckled. "Barney's fine," he replied.

Carolyn let her shoulders slump, and her chin wouldn't stay at the obstinate angle she'd been maintaining since her kitchen reentry. "I'm so embarrassed," she said, in a near whisper, without planning to speak again at all.

"Don't be," Brody said. "It's obvious that you can't hold your liquor, but that's not such a bad thing."

Carolyn bit down hard on her lower lip and forced herself to look Brody Creed directly in the eye. Before, she'd spoken without meaning to—now, she couldn't seem to get a word out.

"You probably should have some soup or something," Brody said mildly. What was it like to be so at ease, so at home, in his own skin? Was this what came of belonging somewhere, being part of a tribe? Even with all those years away, Carolyn reflected enviously, the man's roots went deep into the Colorado soil, curling around bedrock, no doubt. "Might settle your stomach down a little."

Carolyn shook her head quickly. The *thought* of putting food in her mouth—even soup—threatened to bring on a new spate of helpless retching.

"I couldn't," she managed to croak.

"Okay," Brody said.

Oddly, his unflappable solicitude made her feel even more vulnerable to him than that infamous kiss had.

Carolyn steeled herself against what was surely a perfectly normal human need to be reassured, cared for, looked after—normal for other people, that is. Foster kids, no matter how good the homes they were placed in, had to be strong and self-reliant, tough to the core.

Always.

"You could leave now," she suggested carefully.

Brody chuckled again. Sat back in his chair and folded his arms. "I could," he agreed, showing absolutely no signs of doing so anytime soon.

"And as for what Kim said at supper, about my signing up for a dating service . . ."

"Who said anything about that?" Brody asked, when her voice trailed off.

"If I'd known she was going to tell everyone," Carolyn said, "I wouldn't have mentioned it to her in the first place."

"Kim didn't mean any harm, Carolyn," Brody offered quietly. "Anyway, you're a grown woman, sound of mind and . . . body—" He paused, and once more that special *something* sparked in his eyes. "And if you want to date potential con artists, that's your business."

On one level, Carolyn knew full well that Brody was baiting her. On another, she couldn't resist taking the hook. *"Potential con artists?* Well, *that's* cynical," she accused, and never mind the fact that she'd had similar thoughts herself, right along.

"If you're in the market for a man, Carolyn, it's your call how you go about roping one in. All I'm saying is that you ought to be careful. There are some real head-cases out there."

"In the market for a man?" She leaned forward in her chair, incensed. *"Roping one in?"* Being incensed felt like an im-

provement over being embarrassed, at least.

"Will you stop repeating everything I say?" Brody intoned. A tiny muscle bunched in his cheek, then smoothed out again.

"Who else would want to date me, right?" Carolyn ranted, stifling her voice so she wouldn't yell and scare Winston. Or the neighbors. "Only a *head-case* loser who couldn't get a woman the normal way?"

Brody laughed. *Laughed.* He didn't lack for nerve, that was for sure.

Or sex appeal, damn him.

"There you go again, putting words in my mouth," he said, all relaxed and affable. His gaze dropped ever so briefly to her breasts and then returned to her flushed face. "Take a breath, Carolyn. If you want to sign on with Funky Faces, or whatever that outfit calls itself, go for it."

"*Friendly* Faces," Carolyn corrected, hating that she sounded so defensive. Why couldn't she, just once, get the upper hand in one of these sparring matches?

"Whatever," Brody said dismissively, pushing back his chair—at long last—and rising. "You sure you're all right?"

"I'm sure," Carolyn insisted, hugging herself and not looking at him.

Funny, though. Even with her eyes averted, the man was an onslaught to her jangled senses. She was aware of Brody Creed in every part of her; he made everything pulse.

She felt angry triumph at the prospect of his leaving and, underlying that, a certain quiet dejection.

Go, she thought desperately. *For God's sake, Brody, just* go.

Instead of heading straight to the door, however, Brody stepped around the table, paused behind Carolyn's chair and then leaned down to place the lightest of kisses on the top of her head.

"See you around," he said gruffly.

Carolyn clamped her molars together, so she couldn't ask him to stay.

To cajole her about soup and hold her.

She'd said and done enough stupid things for one day, met and exceeded the quota.

A few seconds later, Brody was gone.

The apartment, once her refuge, felt hollow without him.

She sat still in her chair, listening to the sound of his boot heels on the outside stairs, waiting for the roar of his truck engine, the sounds of driving away.

Only then, when she was sure he wasn't coming back, did Carolyn push her teacup aside and bend forward to thump her forehead lightly against the table in frustration.

Once, twice, a third time.

Winston jumped down from the windowsill and padded over to wrap himself around her ankles, purring and offering general cat-comfort.

She bent, scooped him onto her lap and petted his silky back.

Since there was no one but the cat around to see, Carolyn finally gave in and allowed herself to cry.

"Okay, so I was a buttinski," Kim allowed, with a sheepish glance at Brody.

The two of them were standing in the ranch-house kitchen.

"Ya think?" Brody retorted.

In the time he'd been out, Tricia and Conner had gone back to their place— they were probably having slow, sleepy sex at that very moment—and Davis had retreated to his saddle shop, where he was working on a custom order.

Little Bit and Smidgeon must have gone with him, because there was no sign of them.

Except for the lingering scent of homemade tamales, all signs of supper were gone. Dishes washed, leftovers wrapped and put away, counters clear.

Kim Creed ran a tight ship.

Too bad she didn't exercise the same control over her mouth.

"I'm sorry," Kim said, reaching into the laundry basket on the table and pulling out a towel to fold. "I just thought you should know that Carolyn is . . . well . . . *looking.*"

"Why?" Brody asked. "In what universe is that my business, Kim? Or yours, for that matter? Carolyn was nervous in the first place—my guess is, that's why she was swilling wine like she was. And then you had to make everything worse by blurting out something she probably told you in confidence."

Kim stopped folding, and tears brimmed in her eyes.

Brody ached when any woman cried, but with Kim, it was the worst. She was, for all practical intents and purposes, his mom, and he loved her accordingly.

"It seemed like a good idea at the time," she admitted with a sniffle. "I'll apologize to Carolyn tomorrow."

Brody put his arms around Kim, gave her a brief squeeze. "Maybe you could lay off the matchmaking, too, for a while, anyway," he suggested, taking a towel from the basket and folding it.

"Trust me," Kim said, "I've already had this entire lecture from Davis. If you and Carolyn are both too thickheaded and stubborn to see that you're meant for each other, well, it's out of my hands, that's all. You're on your own."

"Thank you," Brody said, smiling. "I'll take it from here."

Kim's eyes widened, and her hands froze in mid towel-folding. "What do you mean, you'll take it from here? Are you . . . ?"

Brody held up one index finger and shook his head, grinning as he turned to head for Davis's shop to bid the man good-night before heading back to the cabin at River's Bend.

The spacious room smelled pleasantly of leather and saddle soap and the wood fire that crackled in the Franklin stove, the flames casting a dancing reflection on the worn planks in the floor. Davis stood at one of several worktables, tooling an intricate design into a strip of cowhide.

At Brody's entrance, he looked up and grinned. Set the rubber mallet and the awl aside and dusted off his hands on the sides of his jeans, a gesture of habit more than necessity.

"Carolyn still feeling peaky?" Davis asked, evidently to get the conversational ball rolling.

"She'll be all right," Brody replied, looking around and recalling when he and Conner were kids, always getting underfoot in their uncle's first shop, a much smaller room than this one, connected to the barn at the other place. Back then, they'd believed nothing and no one could hurt them if Davis was around. They'd grown up feeling safe, and that had fostered self-confidence.

Or arrogance, depending on how you looked at it.

Davis tilted his head to one side, studied his nephew in silence for a few moments, then went back to his worktable, picked up a chamois and began polishing the piece he'd been tooling before.

"How's that fancy house of yours coming along?" Davis asked, at some length. He wasn't a man for chatter.

Brody spotted the little dogs under one of the tables, snuggled up in a bed made to look like a plush pink slipper, and smiled. Dragged back a wooden chair and sat astraddle of it, resting his forearms across the back.

"Slowly," he replied, eliciting a bass note of a chuckle from Davis.

"Pretty big place for one cowboy and his dog," Davis commented. Barney had wandered in behind Brody by then, and lay down at his feet.

"Don't start," Brody warned, leaning to ruffle the dog's floppy ears so the critter would know he was welcome.

"Don't start what?" Davis asked, though he knew damn well what.

Brody merely sighed.

Davis chuckled, shook his head. "My wife did stir something up at supper to-night, didn't she?" he said, polishing away at that hunk of leather.

"You might say that," Brody said dryly.

Davis paused in his work, gave Brody a mirthful assessment before going on. "Conner and Tricia turned out to be a good match," he observed. "Kim put her foot in it, sure enough, but she just wants you to be as happy as your brother is, that's all."

"I know," Brody answered, on a long sigh. Then, presently, he added, "Here's the thing, Davis. Something happened between Carolyn and me, a long time ago, and she'd sooner throw in with a polecat than with me. We're never going to get together, she and I, no matter how much you and Kim want that."

"Is that right?" Davis asked, with his customary note of charitable skepticism. He'd finished with the polishing, and now he was wiping his hands off on a shop towel.

"Take it from me," Brody said. "If it came down to me or a polecat, the polecat would win, hands down. Carolyn wants no part of me, and I can't really say I blame her for it."

Davis laughed. "Is it just me, or was there something mournful in your tone of voice just now, boy?" Smidgeon and Little Bit tumbled out of their slipper-bed and rushed him, scrabbling at Davis's pant legs so he'd bend down and pick them up.

Which he did.

"Mournful?" Brody scoffed, a beat or two too late. "Not me."

"You're taken with Carolyn," Davis said quietly, standing there with a frou-frou dog in the crook of each elbow. "Nothing wrong with that. She's a beauty, and a hand with a horse, too."

Brody chuckled ruefully. Saying somebody was "a hand with a horse" was high praise, coming from a Creed—better than a good credit score or a character reference from a VIP. "Well," he said, "I kind of messed things up with her."

Davis put the little dogs down gently,

and they scampered off, probably in search of Kim. Then the rough-and-tough cowboy pulled up a chair for himself and sat down, regarding Brody solemnly, but with a crook at the corner of his mouth.

"I've messed up with Kim more times than I care to recall," Davis said, once he was settled. "And here we are, married thirty-five years as of next October."

A companionable silence fell; they both sat listening to the fire in the stove for a while, thinking their own thoughts.

Brody's throat tightened a little. "Did you and Kim ever regret not having kids of your own?" he asked, the words coming out rusty.

"We *had* kids," Davis pointed out, with a smile. "You and Conner and Steven."

"Of your own," Brody persisted. Davis's marriage to Steven's mother hadn't lasted.

Davis thought a moment, and there was a twinkle in his eyes when he replied. "We'd have liked to have had a girl," he allowed. "But now that Melissa and Tricia have married into the family,

why, Kim and I feel like we've got everything anybody could rightfully ask for."

Brody stayed silent.

Davis reached out, laid a hand on his
nephew's shoulder, squeezed. "I know
I've said it before," he told Brody, "but
it's better than good to have you back
home where you belong, boy. We all
missed you something fierce."

With that, the conversation appeared
to be over.

Davis stood up and went to the stove
to bank the fire.

Brody told Barney they'd better get
on the road, stepped into the corridor
outside the shop, then remembered
what he'd come for and stuck his head
back in.

"'Night, Davis," he said.

His uncle nodded, smiled. "'Night," he
replied. "You drive carefully now, because we can't spare you."

Brody nodded back.

He didn't run into Kim on his way out.

Twenty minutes later, he pulled up at
River's Bend, near the unfinished barn,
and parked the truck. He and Barney
went inside to make sure Moonshine

was settled for the night—he was—and headed for the cabin.

Brody flipped on the lights and went straight to his computer to log on.

While he was doing that, Barney drank loudly from his water bowl on the floor and then curled up on his dog-bed to catch up on his sleep.

Once he got online, Brody skipped his email—he often went days without checking it—and called up his favorite search engine instead.

Hunt-and-peck style, he typed *Friendly Faces*.

Something like ten thousand links came up.

He narrowed the search to dating services, blushing a little even though nobody was ever, by God, going to find out he'd stooped to such a lame-assed thing.

There it was, the website Carolyn evidently hoped would land her a husband.

Brody's back teeth ground slightly; he released his jawbones by deliberate effort.

Finding her took some doing, but eventually, Brody came across Carolyn's profile. She was calling herself Carol, he soon discovered.

For some reason, that made him feel a little better.

He decided to send her a message.

To do that, he had to sign up for the free trial membership, which was very much against his better judgment.

Having no stock alias to fall back on, as Carolyn evidently did, he used his own name. Since he didn't keep pictures of himself on hand, he uploaded a snapshot of Moonshine instead.

That made him grin. According to Kim, no self-respecting woman would take up with a cowboy unless she'd seen his horse.

He completed the few remaining cybersteps, and the way was finally clear: he could send Carolyn a message.

Right off, Brody hit a wall. Now that he'd gone to all that trouble, he couldn't think of a darn thing to say.

Feeling mildly beleaguered, he sighed, sat back in his chair, frowning at the screen as if something might materialize there if he concentrated hard enough.

Well, slick, he taunted himself silently,

where's all that smooth talk and country charm you've always relied on?

Brody sighed again. Rubbed his chin pensively.

This was ridiculous.

A simple howdy ought to do, even if there *was* some bad blood between him and Carolyn.

Only *howdy* wasn't going to pack it.

"For a good time, call Brody" sprang to mind next, and was mercifully discarded.

He decided on Hope you feel better, and he was tapping that in when the instant message popped up.

Hello, stranger, Joleen wrote. What luck to catch you online—is there a blue moon or something? Anyway, I wanted to give you a heads-up—I'll be back in Lonesome Bend in a few days.

Brody went still. And cold.

Joleen had hit the road weeks ago, swearing she'd stay away for good this time.

"Shit," he muttered. Timing, like luck, was never so bad that it couldn't get worse.

Hello? Joleen cyber-nudged.

Hi, he responded.

Joleen was faster on the draw, when it came to keyboards. I was hoping I could stay at your place. Mom and Dad have room, but they're not too pleased with me these days.

Brody let out a ragged breath. Sorry, he wrote back, using only the tip of his right index finger. Quarters are too tight for a visitor.

Still mad over that little spat we had? Joleen inquired, adding a row of face icons with tears gushing from their eyes.

It isn't that, Brody replied laboriously.

Joleen's reply came like greased lightning. Are you dumping me, Brody Creed?

Brody sighed again, dug out his cell phone and speed-dialed Joleen's number.

"Hello?" Joleen purred, like she couldn't imagine who'd be calling little old her.

"I just think it's time we called it quits," Brody said, seeing no reason to bother with a preamble. "The sleeping-together thing, I mean."

"So you *are* dumping me!" Joleen chimed. To her credit, she sounded cheerful, rather than hurt. One thing about Joleen—she was a good sport.

"Okay," Brody said. "Have it your way."

"If I had things my way," Joleen immediately retorted, "we'd be married by now. With a bunch of kids."

Brody closed his eyes. He could envision the kids all too clearly, but they were all dead ringers for Carolyn, not Joleen.

"We had a deal," he reminded Joleen gruffly. "We agreed from the first that we wouldn't get serious."

Joleen laughed, but the sound had a bitter edge to it. "So it's finally happened," she said, after a lengthy silence. "Some filly has you roped in, thrown down and hog-tied."

"Nice image," Brody said, without inflection. "And for your information—not that I owe you an explanation, because I sure as hell don't—*nothing* has happened."

"Right," Joleen scoffed. "Well, I'm coming back anyway. If you get lonely, I'll be at my folks' house, trying to convince them that I'm a good girl after all."

"Good luck with that one," Brody said, sensing a letup in the tension, however slight. He'd never loved Joleen, and they'd had some wild fights in their time, but he liked her. Wanted her to be happy.

"You and me," Joleen mused, surprising him with the depth of the insight that came next, "we pretty much just use each other to keep everybody else at a safe distance, don't we?"

"Yeah," Brody agreed presently. "I think that's what we've been doing, all right."

"Huh," Joleen said decisively, as though she'd come to some conclusion.

"And it's time we both moved on," Brody added. *You go your way, and I'll go mine.*

"Just tell me who she is," Joleen urged.

"There isn't a specific *she,* Joleen."

"The hell there isn't, Brody Creed. I *know* you, remember? You've been on this path for a while now, coming back to Lonesome Bend, making up with Conner and Kim and Davis, building a house—" She made a moist sound then and, for one terrible moment, Brody feared Joleen was either already crying or about to. "Silly me," she finally went on. "I thought all that talk about not getting too serious was just that—talk. We go way back, Brody."

Brody shut his eyes for a moment, remembering things he'd been doing his best to forget right along. Joleen had been Conner's girlfriend, back in the day, and with plenty of help from him—Brody—she'd driven a wedge between the brothers that might have kept them estranged for a lifetime, instead of a decade.

And a decade, to Brody's mind, was plenty too long to be on the outs with Conner.

"I'm sorry if you misunderstood," Brody said quietly, when the air stopped sizzling with Joleen's ire. "But I never gave you any reason to think whatever it was we had together was going anywhere, Joleen, and I'm not responsible for what goes on in your imagination."

She sighed, calming down a little. "Is this the part where you say we'll always be friends?" she asked, at long last.

"That's up to you, Joleen," Brody said,

wishing he could ask her not to come back, at least not right away, because things were complicated enough already. Trouble was, Lonesome Bend was as much her home as his, and she had every right to spend time there. "We can be friends, or we can steer clear of each other for a while and let the dust settle a little."

"I could make trouble for you, you know," Joleen reminded him mildly.

Was she serious or not? He couldn't tell.

"You could," he allowed.

"You might as well tell me who she is, Brody," Joleen went on reasonably, ignoring what he'd said. "I can find out with a phone call or two, anyway."

"Up to you," Brody reiterated. "Goodbye, Joleen."

She paused, absorbing the finality of his words. Gave another sniffle . . . and hung up on him.

Brody closed his phone and stood there looking at it for a few moments, frowning.

Barney, snugged down over by the stove, raised his head off his muzzle and regarded his master with something resembling pity.

He was probably imagining that part, Brody decided.

"Women," he told the dog, before turning back to the computer and the message he'd been trying to write to Carolyn. "There's no making sense of them, no matter how you try. They say one thing when they mean another. They cry when they're sad, and when they're happy, too, so you never know where you stand."

Barney gave a little whimper and settled back into his snooze.

Grimly, Brody glared at the message box on the screen in front of him. Hope you're feeling better was as far as he'd gotten, as far as he was likely to *get,* if inspiration didn't strike soon.

There didn't seem to be much danger of that.

He rubbed his chin again, aware that his beard was growing in. He'd shaved just that morning—hadn't he?

Brody tried to round up his thoughts, get them going in the same direction, but it was hard going. He was mystified to find himself so confused and at a loss for words. He'd been a smooth talker all his life, he reflected, but when it came to Carolyn Simmons, it seemed, he was about as verbal as a pump handle. Presently, Brody gave up and hit the delete key, logged off of the computer and turned around in his chair.

The bed was still unmade, and there was still no woman in it.

The microwave and the minifridge, inanimate objects posing as some kind of kitchen, presented a sad image of the bachelor life.

The only bright spot in the whole place, Brody decided glumly, after mulling it all over, was the dog.

CHAPTER SIX

Denial, Carolyn decided, as she went through the motions of opening the shop for business promptly at nine the next morning, would be the watchword of the day.

All she had to do was pretend. That she hadn't gotten tipsy on wine at Kim and Davis's tamale supper, in front of Brody Creed.

That she hadn't leaned out the door of a hot guy's truck and thrown up on the side of the road.

That she hadn't made an utter and complete idiot of herself.

Like hell she hadn't. She'd done all those things and more, and the worst part was, she didn't know *why.* It wasn't like her to drink at all, let alone overindulge. She simply didn't have the capacity to assimilate alcohol, never had.

Now, confounded as well as queasy, Carolyn looked up at the Weaver, the art piece gracing the high place on the wall, seeking wisdom in all that quietness and color, but all she got was a crick in her neck and the conclusion that her longtime coping mechanism had failed her.

Without denial to fall back on, she'd be stuck with reality.

Yikes.

There were positive sides to the situation, though. She *had* slept through the night, at least, and two more aspirin, with a water chaser, had made her head stop pounding.

She hadn't been able to manage coffee, though, or even herbal tea.

Breakfast? Forget about it.

Her stomach was still pretty iffy.

So she'd fed Winston, taken a shower and gotten dressed for the day, choosing faux-alligator flats, black pants and a rather prim-looking white shirt over her usual jeans, T-shirt and Western boots. She applied makeup—without blusher, she'd have had no color at all—and even put her hair up in a sort of twisty do she hoped looked casually elegant, then donned her one and only pair of gold posts.

She wanted to look . . . well, businesslike. A woman of substance and good sense.

But she'd settle for looking *sober.*

Tricia breezed in at nine-fifteen, wearing sandals and a soft green maternity sundress and carrying two mega-size cups of coffee from the take-out place down the street. She glowed like a woman who'd spent the night enjoying great sex with her adoring husband.

Carolyn felt a stab of envy. Great work, if you could get it.

Casting a glance at Carolyn before she set the cups on the display counter, Tricia smiled warmly, taking in the slacks and the shoes and the fussy shirt.

"Well, look at you," she observed finally. "All dressed up like somebody about to head over to the bank and ask for a big loan. Or apply for membership in a country club."

Carolyn sighed, and the truth escaped her in a rush. "I think I was trying to change my identity," she said. The scent of the coffee, usually so appealing, made her stomach do a slow tumble backward. "Become somebody else. Lapse into permanent obscurity, disappear forever. Create my own one-woman witness protection program."

Tricia laughed. "You've got it bad," she said forthrightly. "And I'm not talking about the flu, here."

Carolyn's cheeks burned, and she felt her chin ratchet up a notch. "If you mean the hangover, thanks for reminding me. I already feel like four kinds of a fool, after everything that happened last night."

Tricia picked up one of the cups and held it out, and Carolyn shook her head, swallowed hard.

"You had a little too much wine," Tricia said gently, with a shrug in her tone. "It's no big deal, Carolyn—we've all done that at one time or another. And if you do have a hangover—your word, not mine—it doesn't show." She paused while she went behind the counter and stuck her purse into its usual cubbyhole. Then, straightening, she went on. "I was referring, my prickly friend, to the bare-socket electricity arcing between you and Brody all evening. I'm surprised all our hair didn't stand on end, and our skeletons didn't show through our skin."

Carolyn had to laugh, though the sound was hoarse and it hurt her throat, coming out. "*That* was visual," she said. "And what an imagination you have, Tricia Creed. If there was anything 'arcing' between Brody and me, it was hostility."

"Sure," Tricia agreed smoothly, and a little too readily, fussing with a display of sachet packets beside the cash register. Unless a tour bus came through unexpectedly, they probably wouldn't be very busy that day, and Carolyn's heart sank at the prospect of long hours spent making work where none existed.

"I'll check for internet orders," Carolyn said, desperate to change the course of their conversation before it meandered any deeper into Brody Territory.

They kept the shop computer in their small office, a converted bedroom, off the living room. "Maybe we've sold a few more aprons online."

"Maybe," Tricia said, shooting another glance at Carolyn as she was about to turn and walk away. Then she came right out with it. "How come you didn't mention signing up for cyberdates to me, but Kim knew?"

Carolyn wanted to lie, but she simply couldn't. Not to Tricia, one of the first real friends she'd ever had. "I wasn't planning on telling *anybody*," she admitted ruefully, folding her arms. "Kim and I were upstairs, having lunch, and this message just popped up on my laptop screen." She drew in a breath, huffed it out again. "That website—Friendly Faces, I mean—is a little scary. The thing *talks.* If the computer is on, and a message comes in, it just pipes right up with the news. 'Somebody likes you!'" She threw her arms out wide, let her hands slap against her sides. "When that happened, Kim was on to my secret and I had no choice but to explain."

Tricia smiled. "Relax," she said. "It's a

new world. Lots of people connect online before they meet in person."

"Easy for you to say," Carolyn pointed
out. "You don't have to resort to desperate measures—*you're* already married."

Tricia gave a dreamy sigh. "Yes," she
said. "I am most definitely married."

Carolyn barely kept from rolling her
eyes.

Tricia came back from the land of
hearts and flowers and cartoon birds
swooping around with ribbons in their
beaks and studied Carolyn with slightly
narrowed eyes. "I just have one question," she said.

"Of course you do," Carolyn said, resigned. This was the troublesome thing
about friendships—they opened up all
these private places a person liked to
keep hidden.

"Why go online and meet strangers
when the perfect man is right in front of
you?"

Carolyn pretended to look around the
surrounding area in search of this "perfect man" of Tricia's. Arched her eyebrows in feigned confusion and set her

hands on her hips. "He is? I don't see him."

"You know I'm talking about Brody," Tricia replied, going all twinkly and flushed again. She might have been talking about Brody, but it was a good bet she was *thinking* about Conner.

Carolyn reminded herself that Tricia meant well, just as Kim did. She *was* being prickly with her friend, and she regretted it.

"I'm sorry," she said.

"For what?" Tricia wanted to know.

"I might have been a little snappish."

"And *I* might have been meddling," Tricia said. Another long pause followed, then she added, "Was it really so bad, whatever happened between you and Brody?"

Carolyn opened her mouth, closed it again, stumped for an answer.

Tricia touched Carolyn's arm. "There I go, meddling again."

"Could we not talk about Brody, please?" Carolyn asked, after a long time. She realized she was hugging her-self with both arms, as though a cold wind had blown through the shop and chilled her to the bone.

"Of course," Tricia said, her eyes filling. "Of course."

Carolyn turned on her heel and marched off to the bedroom-office, keeping her spine straight.

Was it really so bad, whatever happened between you and Brody?

Yes, answered some voice within Carolyn, too deep to be uttered aloud. *He was the first man I ever dared to love. I gave Brody Creed everything I had, everything I was and ever planned to be. I thought he was different from all the others—Mom, the social workers, the foster families—so I trusted him. In the end, though, he threw me away, just like they did. He left and I watched the road for him for months, hoping and praying he'd come back, and he stayed gone.*

So much for hope and prayer. When had either one of them ever done her any good at all?

Reaching the office, Carolyn booted up the computer, only to be rewarded with an all-too-familiar greeting as soon as she went online.

"Somebody likes you!"

"Imagine that," she muttered.

Why was this happening? She hadn't signed on to Friendly Faces through this computer; she'd used the laptop up-stairs.

It was creepy.

On an annoyed impulse, Carolyn clicked on the Show Me! icon.

And there was a picture of a buckskin horse.

Give me a chance, read the message beneath the photo.

It had been posted in the middle of the night, and it was signed, Brody.

Carolyn put a hand to her mouth. Then, in a shaky voice, she called out, "Tricia?"

Her friend appeared almost immedi-ately. Tricia was light on her feet, for someone so profoundly pregnant.

"Is something wrong?" she asked, from the doorway.

"Am I seeing things?" Carolyn coun-tered, gesturing toward the screen.

Tricia crept forward and peered at the monitor. "That's Brody's horse," she said, very quietly. "Moonshine."

"Apparently," Carolyn quipped, "Moonshine is looking for action."

Tricia giggled, but it was a nervous sound. "*Brody* sent you a message through Friendly Faces?" she marveled. "Wow. He must *really* like you."

Carolyn felt a crazy thrill. "Yeah," she retorted. "That would be why he's hiding behind his *horse.*"

"He knows you like horses," Tricia reasoned. It was a weak argument.

"Oh, for Pete's sake," Carolyn scoffed.

"You registered as 'Carol'?" Tricia asked, frowning a little.

"Never mind that," Carolyn said briskly. "What do I do now?"

"Go out with Brody?"

"Oh, right."

"What can it hurt? The two of you go out for a bite to eat, maybe take in a movie? Harmless fun."

"Nothing about Brody Creed is harmless," Carolyn said, with conviction.

"True," Tricia agreed, wide-eyed. "But is that the kind of man you really want? Somebody *harmless,* who makes zero impact?"

"He scares me," Carolyn admitted.

The words were out before she'd had a chance to vet them as something she actually wanted to say out loud. And Brody *did* scare her, because no one, not even her feckless mother, had ever had as much power to hurt her, to crush her, as he did.

"One date," Tricia negotiated. "You set the terms. How bad can that be?"

"Trust me," Carolyn said, "it can be *really* bad."

"He must have done you a number," Tricia ventured, meddling again and showing no signs of apologizing for it. "You can *tell* me, Carolyn."

"Like I told Kim?"

Tricia made the cross-my-heart motion with her right hand and then held it up in the oath position. "I will tell *no one.* Not even Conner."

Carolyn sighed. She turned to Tricia and, against years of conditioning, took a chance. "Brody was passing through Lonesome Bend," she said wearily, like an old-fashioned record player on slow speed. "It was years ago. I was house-sitting for Kim and Davis, and he—well, he just showed up on their doorstep.

Something happened. Then something *else* happened. The next thing I knew, we'd been sharing a bed for a week and I was crazy in love with Brody Creed. We were making plans for a future together—babies, pets, a house somewhere on the ranch, the whole thing. Brody was going to reconcile with Conner, and with his aunt and uncle, and we were going to get married. Then, one morning, I woke up and found a note. 'Something came up,' he said, and he had to leave. That was it. He was gone."

"Oh," Tricia said, absorbing the story like an impact. "You didn't hear from him again?"

"He called me a month later, drunk out of his mind. It was worse than not hearing from him at all."

"I'm so sorry," Tricia whispered, looking so broken that Carolyn immediately forgot her own pain.

"Don't," Carolyn said. "Don't agonize over this, Tricia. It's ancient history. But you know what they say about history— those who fail to learn from it are condemned to repeat it."

"I love my brother-in-law," Tricia said, "but right now, I could wring his neck."

"The last thing I want is to turn you against Brody," Carolyn told her friend. "He's your husband's brother, Tricia. Your baby's uncle. It would be so, so wrong if what I've told you caused problems within the family. I couldn't bear that—families are precious."

Tricia hugged her, briefly but hard. "Don't worry about me," she said. "You need to do what's right for *you,* Carolyn. When was the last time you put yourself first?"

Carolyn searched her mind, then her soul, for an honest reply. "Always," she said. "And never."

Tricia was quiet for a long, long time. Then she said, "In the beginning, when I was first attracted to Conner, I mean, I resisted my feelings with every ounce of strength I could muster. I was *so* afraid. Nothing in my life had ever prepared me to believe in happy endings—not my parents' brief marriage or, after I was grown up, my own relationships. Nothing worked. Ever. Somewhere along the line, I decided that true love was some-

thing that happened in books and movies, and to other, luckier people, and
that I was better off alone, because that
way, I couldn't be hurt." She stopped,
her eyes searching Carolyn's. "Pretty
stupid, huh? Only one thing hurt worse
than I thought loving and losing Conner
Creed would, and that was not *allowing*
myself to take the risk. And you know
what? No matter what the future holds—
even if, God forbid, Conner dies in his
prime, or he leaves me, or whatever else
the fates might throw at us—it would be
worth it, because once you've loved
someone the way I love Conner, once
someone has loved you the way he loves
me . . ." Tricia's blue eyes brimmed with
tears again, and she swallowed before
going on. "Once you've loved, and *been
loved,* that way, nothing and no one can
ever take it away. Whether it lasts five
minutes or fifty years, that love becomes
a permanent part of you."

Carolyn studied her friend. "It's that
way for some people," she said, at some
length.

"It can be that way for *you,*" Tricia insisted quietly.

"Not with Brody Creed, it can't," Carolyn replied. And she turned back to the monitor, clicked on the appropriate icon and replied to his message, fully intending to turn him down flat.

Instead, she found herself typing Nice horse and then clicked Send.

After nuking a frozen breakfast in the microwave, going out to the barn to feed Moonshine and walking the dog, Brody finally logged on to his computer at around nine-thirty. All the while, he was telling himself it didn't matter a hill of beans if he'd heard from Carolyn, aka Carol.

Barney, having chowed down on his kibble, sat at Brody's feet, waiting patiently for whatever was next on the agenda and probably hoping he'd get to participate.

Brody grinned down at the mutt and flopped his ears around gently, by way of reassurance. "We ought to be on the range already," he confided to the animal. "Davis and Conner will be biting the heads off nails by now, and complaining to each other that some things just never change."

Barney opened his mouth wide and yawned.

Brody laughed and turned back to his computer just as an electronic voice chirped, "Someone likes you!"

"I sure as hell hope so," Brody told the dog, who, by that time, had stretched himself out for a spur-of-the-moment nap.

And there it was.

Nice horse, Carolyn had written.

Brody sighed. It wasn't a yes, but it wasn't a no, either.

He rubbed his hands together and thought hard.

Once again, inspiration eluded him.

Thanks, he finally wrote back. Want to go riding with me?

Brody sighed again, heavily this time, and shoved the fingers of one hand through his hair in frustration. He was a regular wiz with the ladies, he chided himself.

The truth was that he had *lot* to say to Carolyn Simmons, starting with "I'm sorry," but he'd sooner have his thoughts posted on a billboard in the middle of town than send them over the internet.

His cell phone rang.

Distracted, Brody hit Send, and immediately wished he hadn't.

"Hello," he said into the phone.

"What kind of outfit do you think we're running over here?" Conner demanded. "This is a working ranch, Brody—operative word, *working*—and it would be nice if you could drop by and do your part sometime before noon."

Brody laughed. "Now, Conner," he drawled, because he knew slow talking made his brother crazy, "you need to simmer down a little. Take life as it comes. The cattle have a thousand acres of grass to feed on, and the fences will get fixed—"

"Brody," Conner broke in tersely, "this is as much your ranch as it is mine. We split the profits down the middle, and *by God* we're going to do the same with the work!"

"What got up your backside?" Brody asked. "For a man getting regular sex, you're pretty testy."

He could literally feel Conner going

from a simmer to a boil on the far end of that phone call.

"Enough of your bullshit," Conner almost growled. "Get over here, unless you want me coming after you."

"Maybe you're *not* getting regular sex," Brody speculated.

"Brody, I swear to God—"

"Okay, okay," Brody relented affably, logging off of the computer, pushing back his chair and rising to his feet. "Don't get your bloomers in a wad. I'm on my way."

Barney scrambled upright, with a lot of toenail scrabbling against the plank floor, and Brody didn't have the heart to leave him behind. He decided to give Moonshine a day off and drive out to the ranch in his truck.

It was big, that fancy new extended-cab truck, painted a bluish-silver color, and it had all the upgrades, from GPS to video screens in the backs of the front seats. For all the flash the rig had, Brody still missed his old pickup, the one he'd driven right down to the rust.

He hadn't had to worry about denting the fenders or scraping up the bed of the previous truck with feed sacks and tools. And it would have gone anywhere.

Unfortunately, it had finally breathed its last, a few months before, and Brody had been forced to sell it for scrap.

He opened the rear door on the driver's side and Barney leaped through the air like a movie dog showing off for the paparazzi. Settled himself on the far side and stared eagerly out the window.

Chuckling, Brody took his place behind the wheel and started up the engine. He should have been thinking about downed fences and stray calves and generally staying on Conner's good side, but his mind was stuck on Carolyn.

Nice horse? What the devil was *that* supposed to mean?

Fifteen minutes later, he and Barney pulled in at the main ranch house.

He let Barney out of the truck, watched as he and Valentino met in the driveway and sized each other up.

Conner strode out of the barn while the dogs were still getting to know each other, his face a thundercloud with features.

He started right in, tapping at the face of his watch with one index finger. "Damn it, Brody, do you have any idea what time it is?"

Brody didn't wear a watch. Hadn't for years. He went to bed when he felt like it and got up when he was darned good and ready, and old habits were hard to break.

"No," he replied smoothly, "I *don't* know what time it is, and if I did, I probably wouldn't give a rat's ass anyway."

Conner glowered at him, hard, but when it came right down to it, he couldn't sustain his bad humor. Hoarsely, and entirely against his stubborn Creed will, Conner laughed.

Brody grinned and slapped his brother on the shoulder. "That's better," he said. "You're going to be somebody's daddy one day soon, little brother, and that means you've got to stop stressing out about everything. What good will you be to that kid if you keel over from a heart attack?"

Conner shook his head, took his hat off and then plunked it back in place again. Shoved out a loud sigh. "You're impossible," he finally said.

"So they tell me," Brody replied lightly. "What's on the schedule today, boss?"

Conner let the word *boss* pass without comment and arched one eyebrow. "The usual. There are strays to round up, calves, mostly. Davis spotted half a dozen of them down by the river, but he didn't go after them because that gelding of his threw a shoe, and he had to head home to fetch another horse."

"We running low on horses these days?" Brody asked, with a pointed glance at the barn, and the surrounding corral and pasture area. He counted eight cayuses right there in plain sight.

"You know Davis," Conner said. "He wants to ride the roan, and it's up at his place, in the pasture. He's pigheaded and set in his ways, our uncle."

Brody grinned. "You'd think he was a Creed or something," he said.

Conner laughed again, started back toward the barn. "Let's ride, cowboy," he replied. "Calves aren't known for their intelligence, and we'll have a hassle on our hands if any of them take a tumble into the river and get swept off by the currents."

The possibility was real enough; they'd lost plenty of cattle, a few horses and a handful of people to the falls. The plunge was better than a hundred feet, and there were boulders directly below, in the white water.

This probably explained Conner's sour mood earlier, during that phone call.

Brody and Conner saddled their horses at the same pace, with the same motions, and when they rode out, they were side by side.

Barney and Valentino kept up.

Brody enjoyed that ride, enjoyed being with Conner, on horseback, and out in the open air.

But once the brothers reached the ridge overlooking the river, where a narrow trail ribboned off the dirt road and down the steep side-hill to the stony bank, the fun was over.

Five yearling calves bawled in loud dismay at edge, and a sixth was already in the drink, struggling in vain to regain its footing and get back to shore.

"How's this horse in the water?" Brody asked Conner, with a nod to his own mount, resettling his hat as he spoke.

"He's good," Conner said, with grave reluctance. "Brody, maybe you oughtn't to—"

But Brody cut him off with a whooping "Yee-haw" and headed straight down that hill, Snowy-River style, unfastening the leather strap that secured his coiled rope as he went.

Conner yelled a curse after him and followed.

Having gotten a head start, and with the trail barely wide enough for one horse, forget two, Brody reached the riverside first. He and the gelding he'd saddled back at the main barn splashed into the water at top speed.

Back in his rodeo days, Brody's event had been bronc riding, but he was a fair roper, as well. He looped that lariat high over his head, shot a wordless prayer heavenward and flung.

The rope settled around the calf in a wide circle of hemp, and Brody took up the slack. The yearling beef bawled again and paddled furiously, being too stupid to know he'd already been helped.

The current was strong, though, and it was work, for man *and* horse, hauling that noisy critter back to the riverbank.

Conner was mainly dry, except for a few splashes on his shirt and the legs of his jeans, and he'd corralled the other calves into a loud bunch, his well-trained cow pony expert at keeping the animals together.

Brody, of course, was soaked, but he laughed as he brought that calf out of the water, out of sheer jubilation.

"Looks to me like your horse is doing all the work," he called to Conner, swinging down from the saddle to grab hold of the rope and pull that calf along.

"You damn fool," Conner retorted, messing with his hat while that pony danced back and forth, containing the calves in a prescribed area, "you've been away from this ranch—and this river—for too long to go taking chances like that!"

Brody grinned, removed the lasso from around the calf's neck and prodded it toward the herd.

The poor critter didn't need much persuading and, for a bit, the cacophony got louder, while the baleful tale was told.

This time, Conner was in the lead as they drove that pitiful little herd back up the trail to high ground. Valentino and Barney waited up top, their hides dry and their tails wagging.

It just went to show, Brody figured, that they were the smart ones in this bunch.

"What is it with you and rivers, anyhow?" Conner grumbled, as they walked their horses slowly along the dirt road curving along the edge of the ridge.

Brody sighed, took off his hat and wrung the water out of it, leaving it a little worse for wear. "First you bitch because I wasn't here at the crack of dawn, punching cattle. Then, when I get a little wet pulling one out of a river, you complain about *that*. Damned if I know what, if anything, would make you happy."

Conner shook his head. "You always were a grandstander," he accused, though not with much rancor.

"Oh, hell," Brody groused back, "you've

just got your tail in a twist because *you* wanted to show off your roping skills."

Conner let loose with a slow grin. "I can outrope, outshoot and outwrestle you any day of the week," he said, "and you know it."

Brody laughed at that. His clothes felt icy against his skin, and his boots were full of water—again. At this rate, he'd need a new pair every payday. "Keep telling yourself that, little brother, if it'll make you feel better."

"You could have roped that calf from the bank," Conner pointed out, almost grudgingly, after tugging his hat brim down low over his eyes because they were riding straight into the sun. "Instead, you risked your life—and the life of a perfectly good horse—to pull a John Wayne."

"I was safe the whole time," Brody replied, "and so was this horse. It was the *calf* that was in a fix, and I got him out of it. Seems like you ought to be glad about that, in place of griping like some old lady whose just found muddy footprints on her carpet."

Conner's jaw tightened and he looked

straight ahead, as though herding six yearling calves along a country road required any real degree of concentration. When he did speak up, Conner caught Brody off-guard, as he had a way of doing.

"I reckon Carolyn's out to find a husband," he said, with a hint of a smirk lurking in his tone. "And she's not too picky about her choice, as long as she doesn't get you."

The words went right through Brody's defenses, as they'd no doubt been meant to do. Heat surged up his neck, and he glared over at Conner. The two dogs were traveling between them now, both of them panting but otherwise unfazed by the morning's adventure.

"If you're looking for a fight, little brother, you've found one," Brody said. "As far as I'm concerned, we can get down off these horses right now and settle this discussion in the middle of the road."

Conner smiled without looking at Brody and rode blithely on. The main part of the herd was up ahead, grazing on spring grass.

The stray calves seemed to know that, too, because they picked up speed and quit carrying on like they were being killed.

Conner didn't speak again until they'd reached the edge of the range, where the view seemed to go on forever, in every direction.

Even with his hackles raised, Brody couldn't ignore that scenery. The land, the trees, the mountains and the sky, the twisting river—all of it was as much a part of him as his own soul.

Conner raised his hat and swung it in a wide arch, as a greeting to the mounted ranch hands on the fair side of that sea of cattle.

Then he turned to look Brody's way. "You'd better get on home," he said. "Get out of those wet clothes before you come down with something."

Brody just sat there, breathing in his surroundings, letting it all saturate him, through and through. "I'm already half-dry," he argued, "and not the least bit delicate, for your information."

Conner laughed. "I got to you, didn't I?" he said, in quiet celebration. "I do like getting a rise out of the great Brody Creed."

"Why don't you go to hell?" Brody suggested mildly.

Again, Conner laughed. It seemed there was no end to his amusement that morning. "Are you just going to stand back and watch Carolyn order up a husband online?" he asked, a few moments later.

"She can do what she wants," Brody bit out, more nettled than he would have cared to admit.

"What do *you* want, Brody?"

"Me?" Brody asked. "What do I want?"

"That was my question, all right, " Conner replied, implacable and amused.

"Fine," Brody answered, nudging his horse into a trot, figuring the dogs had had time to rest up a little by then. "I want you to stay the hell out of my business, *that's* what I want."

CHAPTER SEVEN

It was time to take action, Carolyn thought, a wicked little thrill going through her as she reread Brody's response to her message earlier that day.

Want to go riding with me?

She bit her lower lip.

Brody had asked her to go riding with him, and she was actually considering it. A sad commentary on her level of intelligence, she figured, since she'd been burned, and badly, the *last* time she played with fire.

And she'd be doing exactly that if she

spent any time alone with Brody Creed, no doubt about it.

That was that, then.

She wasn't getting any younger, and if she ever wanted a home and a husband and children, if she ever wanted to take *real* family vacations, instead of buying souvenir mugs at garage sales and pretending she'd been somewhere, she had to do something, take matters into her own hands.

Prince Charming, if he'd ever been headed in her direction in the first place, had obviously been detained.

"Carolyn?" Tricia appeared in the office doorway, a merciful if temporary distraction from her troubling thoughts. True to Carolyn's prediction, they hadn't had a customer all morning, or since lunch, and the apron orders from the website were wrapped and ready for shipping. "I'm going now. Do you want me to drop the packages off at the post office before I head for home?"

Not wanting Tricia to see that she'd been checking Friendly Faces, Carolyn turned to face her friend with a wide smile, blocking the computer monitor from view.

She hoped.

"That would be great," she said brightly. *Too* brightly, probably. "Thanks, Tricia."

Tricia eyed her curiously, maybe even a little suspiciously. "You'll be okay working alone for the rest of the day?" she persisted.

I've been working alone my whole life. Why would today be any different?

"I'll be fine," Carolyn promised cheerfully. "I'm just tying up a few loose ends online, then I'll go upstairs and start sewing. We're going to need more aprons soon, and I'd like to finish the gypsy skirt before I die of old age."

Tricia hesitated a moment, then smiled and left the doorway. "See you tomorrow," she called, in parting.

"'Bye!" Carolyn sang out, all merry innocence.

Then she turned back to the computer, and Brody's brief message.

If she agreed to go anywhere with this man, even for a horseback ride, she needed her head examined.

In the first note, he'd asked for a second chance.

A second chance to hurt her, to rip her heart out and stomp on it? Was that what he'd meant? Or was she being too cynical? Suppose the man simply wanted to be friends?

That would make sense, wouldn't it, given the way they were always running into each other at social functions, both in town and on the Creed ranch? Maybe Brody was as tired of those awkward encounters as she was.

He'd said as much, just the other day, but then he'd gone and kissed her and confused the issue all over again.

And then there was the fact that Carolyn never felt freer, or more alive—or lonelier—than when she was on a horse's back, riding through wide open spaces.

To have someone riding alongside her out there on her favorite trails, someone who knew horses and was comfortable around them, well, that would make the experience close to perfect.

Adrenaline jolted through Carolyn's system when she made the reckless decision: she would accept Brody's invitation. It was, after all, a horseback ride, not an elopement, or a wild weekend in Vegas, whooping it up in the buff.

Heck, it wasn't even a date, really.

Still, the idea made her nerves leap around under her skin like tiny Cirque du Soleil performers determined to outdo themselves.

What she needed, as she'd already concluded, was some sort of emotional *insurance,* protection against Acts of Brody, and there was only one way to get that—by going out with other guys. As many other guys as she reasonably could.

Not only would they insulate her, create and maintain a safe distance between her and Brody, but she also might actually fall for one of them and forget him entirely.

What began as a defense mechanism could turn out to be the kind of true and lasting love she'd always dreamed of finding.

And wouldn't *that* be something?

Yes, she would make a definite and honest effort.

She finally entered a reply to Brody's

note, a lackluster okay and flashed it off to his mailbox.

She checked her new messages then.

It was sort of gratifying to know she was popular on Friendly Faces—five different men wanted to get acquainted with her, three from Denver and its close environs and two from right there in Lonesome Bend.

Forehead creased with the effort to place the pair of locals, Carolyn studied their photos, one after the other, and came up with no clear recollection of either of them.

Both were moderately attractive, in their thirties.

Richard was tall, if his bio could be believed—wasn't she living proof that people stretched the truth, calling herself Carol?—with dark hair and brown eyes. He was a technical writer, divorced, with no children, and he'd moved to Lonesome Bend only a month before. Since he worked at home, he hadn't made many friends.

He liked to cook, loved dogs, but was violently allergic to cats.

Carolyn, mindful of Winston, gently dispatched Richard to the recycle bin.

The other candidate was named Ben, and he, like Richard, was a fairly recent transplant to the community. He was a widower, with an appealing smile, a nine-year-old daughter and a job that took him all over the western states, fighting forest fires.

He looked like a nice guy, which didn't mean for one second that he couldn't have made the whole story up, invented the daughter, the adventurous career, the dead wife. Stranger things had happened, especially when it came to on-line dating.

Still, if she was going to have any chance at all against Brody Creed and his many questionable charms, assuming he even meant to turn that effortless dazzle on her anyway, she had to do *something,* get the proverbial ball rolling, here.

After drawing and releasing a very deep breath, Carolyn responded to Ben's friendly inquiry with a short, chatty missive of her own. Not wanting to give away too much information—Lonesome

Bend was, after all, a small town—she chose her answers carefully.

Ben's response was immediate. Did the man have nothing better to do than hover over his computer, waiting for his trial membership in Friendly Faces to pay off big?

Hi, Carol, he'd written. Nice to hear from you. So to speak.

Carolyn reminded herself that what *she* was doing could conceivably be described as hovering, and she certainly had better things to do, so she'd better get off her high horse, and answered, I like your picture.

I like that you didn't bail out on your daughter after your wife died.

If you even have a daughter.

If there isn't a current wife, very much alive, innocently cooking your favorite meal or ironing one of your shirts at this very moment, unaware that you're flirting with other women online.

Carolyn reined in her imagination then, but it wasn't easy, and she didn't know how long she could keep it from running wild again.

I like yours, too, Ben responded. I'm new at this computer-dating thing. How about you?

Brand-new, Carolyn confirmed. It's awkward.

Tell me about it, Ben answered.

Carolyn drew another deep breath, rubbed the palms of her hands together. What brought you to Lonesome Bend?

That seemed innocuous enough.

I wanted to raise Ellie in a small town, and my late wife's family lives nearby.

That's nice, Ben. Where did you live before?

Down in L.A. I'm not scared of a wildfire, but the traffic on the 405 is another matter, especially when Ellie's in the car.

Carolyn smiled. Ben was a conscientious father, and he had a sense of humor. She began to warm up to the conversation a little, though she was still wary of the man. I'm not crazy about crowded freeways myself, she replied.

Ben came back right away with Have you always lived in Lonesome Bend?

Carolyn hesitated. I came here eight years ago, she wrote. Before that, I traveled a lot.

You're mysterious, Ben replied, adding a winking-face icon.

Hardly, Carolyn typed. I'm not a woman with a past or anything exciting like that.

Unless, of course, my week-long, red-hot affair with Brody Creed makes me a woman with a past.

The thought of Brody, even in that context, gave Carolyn a twinge of guilt, but she shook it off quickly. It wasn't as if she was cheating on him, for heaven's sake.

So why did it feel that way?

Ellie just came in, Ben told her, and she's trying to get my attention, so I'd better find out what's up. Hope we can chat again soon, Carol.

Me, too, Carolyn wrote in response.

Liar, accused the voice in her head, the one she was always telling to shut up. *You're interested in* using *this guy to keep Brody at arms' length, nothing else. And, admit it, Ben's* other *main attraction is that he has a young daughter.*

"Shut up," Carolyn told the voice.

Then she logged off, wrote a hasty note for any customer who might happen by and taped it to the front door.

Working upstairs today. Just ring the bell, and I'll be right down to let you in, she'd printed, in large letters.

Always better off when she was busy, Carolyn felt pretty chipper as she turned the handle on the dead bolt and headed for the staircase.

Winston, who seemed to be in an unusually circumspect mood that day, scampered after her and, when she entered the kitchen, leaped gracefully onto his usual lookout perch, the windowsill.

Carolyn fussed over him a little, scratching behind his ears and nuzzling his silky scruff once, and washed her hands at the sink, prior to fixing them both lunch.

Winston had his beloved half tin of water-packed sardines, eating off a chipped china saucer right there on the windowsill, while Carolyn nibbled her way through a peanut butter and jelly sandwich, breaking all the food rules by foregoing a plate and standing up while she ate.

Actually, she could have argued that there were sensible reasons for her choice.

Number one, her sewing machine was on the table, and she'd be working there in a little while, and a stray drop of jelly might stain a piece of fabric. Furthermore, who *really* ate sandwiches off a plate?

In any case, the sandwich was soon gone, rendering the whole subject moot. Carolyn washed her hands again, fetched the gypsy skirt from the hook on the other side of her bedroom door and took a few sweet moments just to admire the creation.

It really *was* gorgeous, she thought, loving the way the gossamer ribbons shimmered and shifted. The reds, golds, blues and greens seemed to ripple, like liquid light.

Not for the first time, Carolyn was seized by a crazy urge to *keep* that skirt, alter it to fit her own figure and never let it go. She held it close against her chest for a few moments, as though prepared to defend it against a crazed mob.

"You're being silly," she murmured aloud.

Still, the skirt was so pretty, almost animate with all that subtle motion going on, a true work of art. *Her* art, born of her dreams and her imagination and all the fairy-tale hopes she'd cherished as a lonely child.

She ached to hold on to this one piece, this glorious thing woven with strands spun in the deepest places of her own heart.

Practicality took over quickly.

She'd been over this with herself before, hadn't she? A garment like this should be worn, seen, enjoyed. Where would she, Carolyn Simmons of Lonesome Bend, Colorado, wear such a thing?

Horseback riding?

Sure, there were parties now and then, and she was always invited, but the occasions were never formal—people held cookouts in their backyards, and bingo was big on Wednesday evenings, in the basement of the Moose Lodge, and every year, on the weekend closest to the Fourth of July, there was an amateur rodeo and a visiting carnival.

The closest Lonesome Bend ever got to glamour was when the lodge sponsored a dance the third Saturday of every other month. The music was live, always country-western, and good enough that people came all the way from Denver to dance to it.

Most of the women wore jeans to the gathering, with a slightly fancier shirt than they might ordinarily don, and they fussed with their hair and makeup, too, but that was pretty much the extent of it.

Carolyn would have looked like a fool, just about anywhere she ever went, showing up in that skirt.

She sighed, put the skirt back on its hanger and then back on the hook behind the bedroom door. She'd finish it another day, when she wasn't feeling so much like Cinderella left behind to sweep floors on the night of the prince's ball.

Resolutely, she brewed a cup of herbal tea and got out a stack of fabric purchased on a recent shopping trip to Denver. By then, she'd made so many aprons—frilly ones, simple ones, ones for kids as well as adults—that she no longer needed to measure.

She chose a bluish-lavender calico

from the pile, smiling at the small floral print and the tactile pleasure of crisp and colorful cloth ready to be made up into something useful. She decided to stick with the retro designs that sold so well through the online version of the shop and pictured the end result in her mind's eye.

Then, after eyeballing the fabric once again, Carolyn took up her sewing shears and began to cut.

Sewing, like riding horses, always consumed her, drew her in, made her forget her worries for a while. She got lost in it, in a good way, and invariably came away refreshed rather than fatigued.

The apron came together in no time, a perky, beruffled thing with lace trim stitched to the pockets.

Delighted, Carolyn set it aside, to be pressed later, and delved into her fabric stash again. This time she chose a heavier weight cotton, black and tan checks with little red flowers occupying alternate squares.

She went with retro again, savoring the whir of the small motor, the flash of the flying needle and the familiar scents of fabric sizing and sewing machine oil.

When the doorbell rang downstairs, just as Carolyn was finishing up apron number two, she was so startled by the sound, ordinary as it was, that she jumped and nearly knocked over her forgotten cup of tea, now gone cold.

She glanced at the clock above the stove—three forty-five in the afternoon, already?—and, remembering the note she'd stuck to the front door, in case some prospective shopper happened by, shouted from the top of the inside staircase, "Coming!"

The bell rang again, more insistently this time.

Skipping the normal protocol by not looking out one of the flanking windows first, Carolyn opened the door.

Brody was standing on the porch, his expression so grim that Carolyn felt alarmed, thinking Tricia had gone into premature labor or someone had been in an accident.

She gulped, fumbled with the hook on the screen door that separated them. Through the mesh, she noted Brody's wrinkled clothes, mussed hair and disturbing countenance.

"Brody . . . what—?"

He'd taken off his hat at some point, and now he slapped it once against his right thigh. "Can I come in?" he bit out. Then, almost grudgingly, "Please?"

Carolyn's concern eased up a little then, as she realized Brody was frustrated—maybe even angry—but not sad, as he surely would have been if he were bearing bad news.

She gave one slightly abrupt nod instead of speaking, not trusting herself to be civil now that Brody's irritation had sparked and spread to her, like wildfire racing over tinder-dry grass.

Once the door was open, Brody practically stormed over the threshold, giving Carolyn the immediately infuriating impression that if she didn't get out of his way, she'd be run over.

So she stood her ground, and that proved to be a less than brilliant choice, because they collided and the whoosh of invisible things reaching flash point was nearly audible.

"What?" Carolyn demanded, and found herself flushing.

His nose was half an inch from hers, if that, and fierce blue flames burned in his eyes, and his words, though quiet, struck her like stones. "I. Don't. Like. Games."

Carolyn felt several things then, not the least of which was a slow-building rage, but there was a good bit of confusion in the mix, too, and a strange, soft, *scary* kind of excitement.

"*What* are you talking about?" she asked tartly. It would have been prudent, she supposed, to take a step or two backward, out of Brody's force field, but for some reason, she couldn't move.

"I'm *talking,*" Brody all but growled, after tossing his hat in the general direction of the antique coat tree that dominated the entry way, "about this whole Friendly Faces thing. You trying to scare up a husband online. It's all wrong—"

Carolyn's temper, mostly under control before, flared up. "*Wrong?*" she repeated dangerously.

Brody sighed, but he was still putting

out the same officious vibes. "Okay, maybe *wrong* wasn't the best word," he said.

"Maybe it wasn't," Carolyn replied succinctly, folding her arms and digging in her heels.

"I hate to break this to you," Brody spouted, leaning in again—she kind of liked it when he did that, even though it *was* infuriating—"but you can't just go around trusting people you've never even met. *Men tell lies, Carolyn.*"

Carolyn widened her eyes in mock surprise. "Really?" she trilled, as though she just couldn't conceive of the possibility.

She saw his jaws clamp down, watched with some satisfaction as he relaxed them by a visible effort.

"Men tell lies," she repeated, amazed. Then she stabbed a finger into his chest and said, "Oh, yes, *that's right,* Brody. I remember now. *You* lied to me, through your perfect white teeth!"

"I did not lie to you," Brody lied.

"Oh, no? You said you cared about me—you wanted to stay and make things right with your family. Settle down and start a family. And then you left, vanished, flew the coop!" Carolyn realized she was perilously close to tears, and she was damned if she'd cry in front of the man who had broken her heart so badly that even after more than seven years, she wasn't over it.

So she turned away from Brody, not wanting him to see her face.

He caught hold of her shoulder, his grasp firm but not hard enough to hurt, and made her look at him again.

"I meant everything I said to you, Carolyn," he said evenly.

He had *not,* she recalled, with a terrible clarity, said he loved her. Not in words, anyway.

"But then *something came up,* as you put it in that note you left me, and you hit the road and left me alone to wonder what I did wrong," Carolyn accused, in an angry whisper.

Getting mad, in her opinion, was a lot better than bursting into tears. And it wasn't just Brody she was furious with. She blamed herself most of all, for being gullible, for loving and trusting the wrong man and maybe missing out on the *right* one because she'd wasted all this time loving him. Because she'd so wanted to believe what Brody told her. What his body told hers.

"I regret leaving like I did," Brody said. "But I had to go. I flat out didn't have a choice, under the circumstances."

"And what would those *circumstances* be?" Carolyn asked archly. "Another bronc to ride? Another buckle to win? Or was it just that some formerly reluctant cowgirl wannabe was willing to go to bed with you?"

Brody closed his eyes for a moment. He looked pale, like a man in pain, but when he opened them again, the frustration was back. "If that's the kind of person you think I am," he snapped, "then it seems to me you ought to be *glad* I took off and saved you all the trouble of putting up with me!"

"Who says I *wasn't* glad?" Carolyn demanded. Who *was* this hysterical person, speaking through her? Was she *possessed*?

"You're not going to listen to one damn thing I say, are you?" Brody shot back.

"No," Carolyn replied briskly. "Probably not."

"Fine!" Brody barked.

"Fine," Carolyn agreed.

"Reoww!" added Winston, from the top of the stairs. His hackles were up and his tail was all bushed out and he looked ready to pounce.

On Brody.

Guard-cat on duty.

"It's all right, Winston," Carolyn told the fractious feline. "Mr. Creed is just about to leave."

Brody made a snorting sound, full of contempt, swiveled around and retrieved his hat from the floor next to the coat tree, where he'd flung it earlier.

He wrenched open the front door, looked back at Carolyn and growled, "We're still going on that horseback ride."

Carolyn opened her mouth to protest, but something made her close it without saying the inflammatory thing that sprang to her mind. She didn't like to use bad language if she could avoid it.

"You agreed and that's that," Brody reminded her tersely. "A deal is a deal."

With that, he was gone.

The door of Natty McCall's gracious old house closed hard behind him.

Carolyn got as far as the stairs before plunking herself down on the third step from the bottom, shoving her hands into her hair and uttering a strangled cry of pure, helpless aggravation.

Winston, having pussyfooted down the stairs, brushed against her side, purring.

Carolyn gave a bitter little laugh and swept the animal onto her lap, cuddling him close and burying her face in the lush fur at the back of his neck.

Being a cat, and therefore independent, he immediately squirmed free, leaped over two steps to stand, disgruntled, on the entryway floor, looking up at her in frank disapproval, tail twitching.

"You've decided to *like* Brody Creed after all, haven't you?" Carolyn joked ruefully, getting to her feet. "You've gone over to the dark side."

"Reow," said Winston, indignantly.

Carolyn made her way upstairs, determined not to let the set-to with Brody ruin what remained of the day. She had tea to brew—that would settle her nerves—and aprons to sew for the website and the shop, a *life* to get on with, damn it.

Instead of doing either of those things right away, though, Carolyn went instead to her laptop.

She turned it on and waited, tapping one foot.

Practically the moment the computer connected to the internet, the machine chimed, "Somebody likes your picture!"

"Good," Carolyn said.

While she'd been offline, six more men had taken a shine to her—or to Carol, her recently adopted persona, anyway—and while five of them were definite rejects, the sixth was a contender, right from the instant Carolyn saw his photo.

His name was Slade Barlow, and he hailed from a town called Parable, up in Montana. For the time being, he lived in Denver. Like Ben, the firefighter, he was a widower, with a child. His eleven-year-old-son, Brendan, attended a boarding school there in Colorado but spent weekends and holidays with him.

"Hmm," Carolyn said aloud, clicking on the response link. Tell me about Brendan, she typed into the message box.

Slade apparently wasn't online, but Ben was, as she soon learned, when he popped up with a smiley face and a hello.

Carolyn, jittery but determined, responded with a hello of her own.

How about meeting me for a cup of coffee? he asked. Page After Page Book Store, on Main Street, five o'clock this afternoon?

Carolyn's first impulse was to shy away, but her most recent run-in with Brody was fresh in her mind, too. The *nerve* of the man, showing up at her home and place of business the way he had, and *announcing* that she *would* go horseback riding with him, simply because she'd made the mistake of agreeing to his invitation.

She consulted the stove clock, saw that it was four-thirty.

She would, she decided, *show* Brody Creed that he couldn't go around dictating things, like he was the king of the world, or something.

Okay, she wrote. Page After Page, five o'clock. How will we recognize each other?

Ben replied with a jovial LOL—laugh out loud—and another of those winking icons he seemed to favor. I look just like my profile photo, he responded. Hopefully, so do you.

Right, Carolyn answered. Was there a computer icon for scared to death? See you there.

Half an hour later, having refreshed her makeup and let down her hair, Carolyn arrived at Page After Page. The bookstore was, at least, familiar territory—she spent a lot of her free time there, nursing a medium latte and choosing her reading matter with care.

She spotted Ben right away, sitting at a corner table in the bookstore coffee shop, a book open before him.

As advertised, he looked like his picture. He was a little shorter than she'd expected, but well-built, with a quick smile, curly light brown hair and warm hazel eyes that smiled when he spotted her.

"Carol?" he asked, standing up.

Good manners, then.

Guilt speared Carolyn's overactive conscience. "Actually," she said, approaching his table slowly, "my name is Carolyn, not Carol."

He laughed, revealing a healthy set of very white teeth, extending one arm for a handshake. He wore jeans, a long-sleeved T-shirt in a dusty shade of blue and an air of easy confidence. "And mine is Bill, not Ben."

The confession put Carolyn at ease— mostly. She managed a shaky smile and sat down in the second chair at Ben's— *Bill's*—table. "Do you really have a nine-year-old daughter named Ellie?" she asked.

"Yes," Bill replied, sitting only when Carolyn was settled in her own chair. "Do you really work in a bank, have two dogs and like to bowl?"

"No," Carolyn admitted, coloring a little. "I lied about my job, my hobbies and my pets. Is that a deal-breaker?"

Bill chuckled. His eyes were so warm, dancing in his tanned face.

And as attractive as he was, he wasn't Brody.

Too bad.

"What's the truth about you, Carol—*yn?*" he asked, smiling.

"I sew a lot, I look after a friend's cat and I'm in business with a friend," Carolyn confessed, after a few moments of recovery. She blushed. "And I can't remember the last time I was so nervous."

Ben—*Bill*—smiled. "I don't sew, I'm strictly a dog-person and I fight fires for a living, just as I said in my bio. That said, I'm amazed, because despite all the prevarications, you look just like your picture. You're beautiful, Carolyn."

At that, the blush burned in Carolyn's face. She looked down. "Flatterer," she said.

Bill smiled. "What can I get you?" he asked.

"I beg your pardon?" Carolyn countered, a beat behind.

"Coffee?" Bill said, grinning. "Latte? Café Americano? Espresso with a double-shot of what-the-hell-am-I-doing-here?"

Finally, Carolyn relaxed. A little. "Latte," she said. "Nonfat, please."

Bill smiled, nodded, rose and went to the counter to order a nonfat latte.

Carolyn, desperate for something to do in the meantime, checked out the book he'd been reading when she approached.

You could tell a lot about a person by what they liked to read.

A Single Father's Guide to Communication with a Preteen Girl.

Well, Carolyn thought, trust her to meet up with a guy who was both sensitive and masculine *after* she'd been spoiled for functional relationships by Brody Creed.

Presently, Bill returned with her latte, looking pleasantly rueful. "Confession time," he said, with a sigh, as he sat down again. "I'm on the rebound, Carol—Carolyn. I didn't mention that in my profile."

"No," Carolyn said, oddly relieved. She reached for her latte, took a sip. It was very hot. "You didn't."

"Her name," Bill told her, "is Angela. We're all wrong for each other."

Carolyn considered the foam on her latte for a long moment. "His name is Brody," she said. "Two people were never more mismatched than the two of us."

A silence fell.

"Well, then," Bill finally said. "We have *something* in common, don't we?"

"Are you in love?" Carolyn asked, after a very long time and a lot of latte. "With Angela, I mean?"

"I don't know," Bill replied. "One minute, I want to spend the rest of my life with the woman, the next, I'd just as soon join the Foreign Legion or jump off the Empire State Building."

Carolyn wanted to cry. She also wanted to laugh. "Love sucks," she said, raising her latte cup. Bill touched his cup to hers.

"Amen," he said. "Love definitely sucks."

CHAPTER EIGHT

If Carolyn had had any say as to whom she fell in love with, she would definitely have chosen Bill Venable, brave fighter of forest fires, devoted father of a nine-year-old daughter, all-around good-looking hunk of a guy.

Alas, she *had* no such influence in an unpredictable universe, but she knew early on that she'd found a valuable ally in the man who bought her a latte.

"So, tell me more about Angela," she said, stirring her latte and avoiding Bill's gaze. "Does she live in Lonesome Bend?"

Bill cleared his throat, looked away, looked back. Finally nodded. "She teaches third grade at the elementary school," he said.

"I see," Carolyn answered, without guilt, because in many ways, she *did* see. "So what's the problem between the two of you?"

"She doesn't like my job," Bill answered, after pondering a while. "Fire fighting, I mean. Too dangerous, keeps me away from home too much, et cetera."

"Yikes," Carolyn observed. "How does Ellie feel about Angela?"

"She adores her," Bill admitted. "And the reverse is true. Ellie thinks Angela would make the perfect stepmother. It's a mutual admiration society with two members. Trust me, this is not my daughter's usual reaction to the women I date."

"So the fundamental problem is your job?" Carolyn inquired, employing a tactful tone. While she understood Bill's dedication to his work, she sympathized with Angela, too. Love was risky enough, without one partner putting his life on the line on a regular basis.

Bill thrust out a sigh. "Yeah," he said.

"Maybe you could look into another kind of career," Carolyn suggested, already knowing what his answer would be.

Bill shook his very attractive head. Too bad he didn't arouse primitive instincts in Carolyn the way Brody did, because he was *seriously* cute. "I *love* what I do," he replied. "Flying an airplane. Putting out fires. It is a definite high."

"But . . . dangerous," Carolyn said.

"Well," Bill affirmed, "*yes.* But I'd go crazy doing anything else. The boredom—" He fell silent again, his expression beleaguered. Obviously, he'd been over this ground a lot, with Angela and within the confines of his own head.

Carolyn waited a beat, then went ahead and butted into a situation that wasn't any of her darn fool business in the first place. "What about your daughter, Bill?" she asked gently. "How does Ellie factor into this whole job thing?"

He sighed, shook his head again,

aimed for a smile but missed. "I love that child with all my heart, and I want to do what's best for her," he said. "Keep her safe and happy and healthy. Raise her to be a strong woman, capable of making her own choices and taking care of herself and, if it comes to that, supporting a couple of kids on her own. But—"

Again, Bill lapsed into pensive silence.

"But?" Carolyn prompted quietly, after giving him a few moments to collect his thoughts.

"But," Bill responded, managing a faint grin, "like I said before, I love what I do. Doesn't that matter, too? And what kind of example would I be setting for Ellie if I took the easy route, tried to please everybody but myself?"

Carolyn toyed with her cup, raising and lowering her shoulders slightly in an I-don't-know kind of gesture. It was remarkable, connecting so quickly with another person—a *male* person, and someone she hadn't known existed until she signed on at Friendly Faces.

They were so simpatico, she and Bill, that anyone looking on would probably have thought they'd been close friends for years.

Too bad there was no buzzing charge, no *zap,* between them, like there was between herself and Brody and, it was a sure bet, between Bill and his Angela.

"No," she said, in belated response to his question. "Of course you can't live to please other people, not if you hope to be happy, anyhow." Carolyn paused before asking, "Does Ellie worry about you, when you're away fighting fires, I mean?"

Bill gave a raspy chuckle. "Probably," he acknowledged. "Ellie never lets on that she's scared something might happen to me—she just tells me to be careful. The thing is, even though she's only nine, she seems to get where I'm coming from better than Angela does."

Carolyn took a sip of her coffee, which was finally cool enough to drink without burning her tongue. Now, she thought, with the inevitable rush of reluctance, it was *her* turn to open up.

Sure enough, Bill ducked his head to one side and a quizzical little quirk tugged at the corner of his mouth.

"You're a beautiful woman, Carolyn," he said. "Half the men in the county, if not the state, must be trying to catch your eye. What prompted you to sign up with an online dating service?"

"Curiosity?" Carolyn speculated, blushing a little.

He smiled, settled back in his chair, watching her. "Are you looking for friends, a good time, or a partner for life?" he asked.

There was nothing offensive in his tone or manner, and he positively radiated sincerity. Bottom line, Bill was easy to talk to, perhaps *because* he was a virtual stranger and, therefore, the two of them had no issues, no shared baggage, nothing to get in the way of friendship.

"It's not a new story," she replied, quietly miserable. "I fell for the wrong man, I got hurt—fill in the blanks and you'll probably have it just about right."

Bill arched an eyebrow, waited. On top of everything else working in his favor, the man was a good listener. And all she could drum up was a walloping case of *like.*

He was the big brother she'd never had.

The pal.

And he wasn't even gay, for Pete's sake.

Carolyn squirmed on her chair, not sure how much more she ought to say. This *was* their first meeting, after all, and as genuine as Bill Venable seemed, it certainly wasn't out of the realm of possibility that she was totally, completely, absolutely *wrong* about him.

It had happened before, hadn't it?

Once, she'd been convinced that she knew Brody Creed, through and through. After a long string of shallow, going-no-where-fast relationships, she'd believed in him, been convinced he was The One, taken the things he said and did at face value, only to be burned in the back draft of all that passion when he showed his true colors and lit out.

And there was that other lapse in judgment, too—when she'd thought she'd hit her stride by becoming a nanny. She'd trusted her movie-star boss im-plicitly, admired his down-to-earth manner, his apparent devotion to his wife and small daughter.

Until he'd come on to her, forcing her to abandon a job—and a child—she'd loved.

Carolyn closed her eyes, remembering—*pummeled by*—the rearview mirror image of little Storm running behind her car, screaming for her to come back.

Come back.

Without saying a word, Bill reached across the table and took her hand in a brotherly way. Squeezed it lightly.

Carolyn opened her eyes again, smiled weakly. Enough, she decided, was enough. For now, anyway.

"I should be getting home," she said, bending to fumble under the table for her purse. "My cat will be wondering where I am."

Bill sighed, glanced at his watch and nodded. "I'm sure Ellie's perfectly happy at her grandparents' house," he said agreeably, "but it'll be suppertime soon, and when I'm in town, I try to make sure we're both sitting at the same table for at least one meal a day."

"That's nice," Carolyn said, feeling awkward now.

Supper, for her, was usually a lonesome affair, something she did to stay alive.

She and Bill rose from their chairs at the same moment.

He walked her to the door, opened it for her, waited until she stepped out onto the sidewalk.

It was a balmy May evening, shot through with the first faint lavender tinges of twilight, and there were lots of people out and about, just strolling, or talking to each other under streetlamps that would come on soon, glad to be outdoors.

Winter was long in Lonesome Bend, and good weather was not only savored, it was also celebrated.

Friends smiled and waved, their expressions both kindly and curious as they took note of Carolyn's escort, a man few, if any of them, actually knew.

By the time she went to bed that night, she thought, with a little smile, word would be all over town. Carolyn Simmons was *seeing someone,* and that someone *wasn't* Brody Creed.

Since her car was parked on the street, in plain view of at least a dozen fine citizens, she felt no compunction about letting Bill walk her to it and open the door for her.

"I had a great time," he said, his gaze direct as he waited for her to get settled behind the wheel.

"Me, too," Carolyn said, fastening her seat belt and sticking her key into the ignition.

"Friends?" he asked, with a wry grin.

"Friends," Carolyn agreed.

Bill stepped back, waved and watched from the sidewalk as she drove away.

"Who is he?" Tricia demanded eagerly, when she entered the shop the next morning.

She hadn't even put away her purse yet.

Carolyn, smiling to herself, pretended a keen interest in unpacking the most recent delivery of goat-milk soap.

"And don't say you don't know what I'm talking about," Tricia warned, waggling a finger. Her eyes sparkled with mischievous affection. "Three different people called the ranch last night to ask about the hunk you had coffee with."

Carolyn chuckled. "His name is Bill Venable," she said, "and he fights forest fires for a living. Flies one of those airplanes that spray chemicals on the hot spots."

"Like in that old Richard Dreyfuss movie?" Tricia asked. She was having a hard time bending far enough to stow her purse on its usual under-the-counter shelf. The baby bump seemed to get visibly bigger from one day to the next. "What was it called?" She stopped to stretch her back, her hands resting on either side of what had once been her waist. "I remember. It was *Always.* And Dreyfuss's character went out in a blaze of glory, didn't he?"

"I don't recall," Carolyn lied, still stacking neatly wrapped bars of soap on the counter. The truth was, being a classic movie buff, she'd long since picked up on the similarities.

"Did you meet him through that website?" Tricia persisted. "Friendly Faces?"

"Yes," Carolyn said, making a production of removing the now-empty carton the soap had arrived in and heading toward the storage room. It was company policy to recycle cardboard boxes, among other things.

Tricia was waiting when she came back. "Do you like him? Are you going to see him again?"

Carolyn laughed. "Yes, I like him," she said, with exaggerated patience, "and I wouldn't be surprised if he asked me out at some point."

Tricia's beautiful blue eyes widened. It was hard to tell if she was excited or alarmed by the prospect.

Probably, she was both.

"Will you go? If he *does* ask you, I mean?"

"I haven't really decided," Carolyn said, with breezy nonchalance. She was looking up at the batik of the Weaver now, trying to absorb some of its serenity. "I must say, I was pleasantly surprised by how *normal* Bill turned out to be."

"Normal," Tricia echoed, her tone making it clear that she wasn't planning on dropping the subject anytime soon. "What did you *expect* him to be like, Carolyn?"

Carolyn tilted her head to one side, studying the Weaver, wishing she could afford to buy the piece and keep it forever. There was something so soothing about the thing, about the figure of a woman drawn with indistinct lines, strokes of color and shapes that were hardly more than suggested.

"Carolyn?" Tricia persisted, standing beside her now, giving her a poke with one elbow. Since just about everything on Tricia's body was rounded into soft curves, it didn't hurt. "Talk to me."

Carolyn sighed and turned to look at her friend. "I guess I thought there was the outside chance he might be another Ted Bundy," she confessed.

Tricia rolled her eyes, and then laughed, and then looked serious, all in the space of a few seconds. "Brody isn't going to like this one bit," she said. Tricia wasn't normally given to mood swings, but there were a lot of hormones splashing around in there.

A flash of . . . *something*—resentment? Triumph?—plucked at Carolyn's heartstrings. "Too bad for Brody," she replied.

Tricia studied her face. "Unless, of course, that's *exactly* why you're thinking about going out with this Bill person. To make Brody jealous."

Carolyn's mouth dropped open. She felt an indignant sting race through her, even as she recognized a disturbing quality of truth to Tricia's words. She *hadn't* set out to stir up Brody's envy, not consciously anyway, but there was no denying, in retrospect, that the idea gave her a delicious little thrill.

She gasped, horrified by the insight, and put a hand to her mouth.

Tricia smiled. "Oh, relax," she said, patting Carolyn's upper arm briefly, in a demonstration of feminine solidarity. "I know your intentions were honorable." She paused, looked speculative again. "But what *were* your intentions, exactly?" she asked, her tone and expression kind.

Carolyn sighed, her eyes burned and she swallowed hard before answering, in a small voice, "I just want to—to *get over* Brody Creed. Move on. Have a home and a family of my own."

Tricia gave her a quick, impulsive hug. Awkward business, with that pumpkin-shaped tummy of hers. "Listen to yourself, Carolyn," she said. "You want to *get over* Brody? *You still care for him.* Doesn't that mean something?"

"It means I'm dysfunctional," Carolyn replied briskly, swiping at her cheeks with the back of one hand even though, as far as she knew, she hadn't actually started to cry. "Codependent, a basket case—whatever."

"Poppycock," Tricia said, with a dismissive wave. *"Dysfunctional. Codependent.* Those are just labels, buzzwords, and in my opinion they are overused in our society. You're a smart, strong, talented woman, Carolyn, not some psychological train wreck of a person. Give yourself a little credit, will you?"

Carolyn gave a wavering smile. "And you, Tricia Creed, are a very good friend."

"I'm also right," Tricia said, smiling back.

Having tacitly agreed on that, they both went to work then.

After an hour or so, two vanloads of middle-aged women sporting red hats and purple outfits showed up, and a shopping frenzy ensued.

One of the ladies seemed particularly taken with the Weaver. "That's lovely," she said, looking up at the batik.

Carolyn, busy ringing up purchases at the register, heard the remark even over the cheerful din of oohs and ahhs bubbling up around the shop as the other red-hats examined the merchandise.

So, apparently, did Tricia.

A glance flew between her and Carolyn.

"Isn't it?" Tricia said, edging over to stand alongside the woman who'd spoken first.

"I can't see the price from here," the woman said.

"I'm afraid the piece is already spoken for," Tricia replied quickly, a pink flush rising to her cheeks. "The artist is very prolific, though. I'd be glad to give you her contact information if you'd consider commissioning something—?"

Carolyn frowned. The Weaver was spoken for? Since when?

Several people had admired the batik, but they'd all sighed and shaken their heads when they were told how much it cost.

Tricia gave her another look, as if she thought Carolyn might contradict her.

Carolyn pointedly returned her friend's gaze, though she didn't speak up. She simply turned her attention back to the task at hand.

It was almost lunchtime when the red-hat ladies climbed into their vans and left, leaving the shop pleasantly denuded.

Carolyn was about to ask Tricia why she'd said the batik was sold when the shop door opened again, and Conner strode in, with Brody right behind him.

Carolyn's breath caught, though she tried to look as though she hadn't noticed the man.

Not noticing Brody, she reflected, was like not noticing a meteor big enough to wipe out the dinosaurs.

Still, she had to try. It was a matter of principle.

Conner greeted Tricia with a resounding kiss and then picked her up and swung her around once, in a small, gentle circle, making her laugh ring out like church bells on Easter morning.

Distracted by these goings-on, Carolyn didn't see Brody approach.

He was just *there,* all of a sudden, standing on the other side of the counter.

Carolyn started; every last nerve in her body jumped.

Brody favored her with a slow, unperturbed smile. Either he hadn't heard the gossip about her coffee date with Bill— this option seemed highly unlikely given the nature of small towns—or he simply didn't care.

"That picture up there," he said, indicating the Weaver with a motion of one thumb. "Is that one of Primrose Sullivan's?"

Carolyn cleared her throat, in a way she hoped was subtle, and nodded. "Yes, but—"

Tricia sidled over. Bumped against Brody from one side. "Are you in the market for art?" she asked.

Conner, standing a few feet away, stared at his wife with an expression of baffled wonder on his handsome face. Clearly, to him at least, Tricia was a brilliantly colored butterfly in a black-and-white world.

"I might be," Brody said. "A lot of wall space is going to need filling, once my house is finished."

Carolyn reminded herself to breathe. Told her heart to start beating again, pronto, and no more of that Bambi-on-ice business. After all, this was a perfectly ordinary conversation.

"Primrose would be thrilled if the Weaver found a home right here in Lonesome Bend," Tricia said brightly. "You know how sentimental she is."

Carolyn frowned at her business partner, confused. "Didn't you say it was already spoken for? The Weaver, I mean?"

Tricia smiled. "I was lying," she said, with no apparent qualms whatsoever.

Carolyn opened her mouth, closed it again. Frowned harder.

Brody, meanwhile, got out his wallet, extracted a credit card and set it down on the counter. "I'll take it," he said.

"Don't you want to know how much it costs first?" Carolyn asked.

He gave her that smile again. She was powerless against that smile.

Did Brody know that?

"I reckon I can probably afford it," he said easily.

Carolyn blushed, embarrassed and clueless when it came to the reason. "Okay," she said, and stated the price.

Brody didn't bat an eye. He glanced down at his credit card, and Carolyn recovered enough to swipe it through the machine and push the necessary sequence of buttons.

Conner and Tricia were in the kitchen by then. Carolyn heard their voices, and the sounds of lunch being assembled.

The credit-card machine spit out a slip, and Brody signed it.

"I'll just get the ladder," Carolyn began nervously. "I can have the picture down off the wall and wrapped in no time."

Brody hadn't moved, after putting away his card and wallet. "We're on horseback," he said.

Carolyn blinked. "You're what?"

"Conner and I," Brody said, and she could feel his grin like sunshine against her skin, even though she was still being very careful not to look at him directly. "We rode our horses into town."

"Why?"

He chuckled, and she had to look at him then. He drew her eyes the way a magnet draws metal shavings. "It's what cowboys do," he said simply.

"Oh," Carolyn said, wishing she could shrink, like Wonderland's Alice after a swig from the drink-me bottle, or just fall down any old rabbit hole.

"It would be sort of awkward, hauling that big picture over to my place on a horse, so I'm hoping you'll be so kind as to deliver it for me."

She stiffened her spine. Raised her chin. "I'm sure Tricia would be happy to drop it off for you," she said.

"She can't be carrying heavy things in her condition," Brody answered, with a faint note of disapproval in his voice. He looked around. "Where's that ladder?"

Carolyn told him where the ladder was, and he went and fetched it.

He came straight back, jackknifed that ladder open with a purposeful squeak of metal hinges and climbed nimbly up to the top rung. Lifted the framed batik off its hook and brought it down when he descended, the muscles in his back moving gracefully beneath the fabric of his shirt.

Blood pulsed in Carolyn's ears.

Tricia and Conner were laughing now, their joy in life and in each other bursting out of them between silences. She heard the fridge door open and close, and plates clattering, as if from some great distance, or from fathoms under the sea.

Carefully, almost reverently in fact, Brody laid the Weaver on the round table where Carolyn and Tricia normally displayed handmade papers. She watched his face as he studied the image and knew it would hang in his new house one day soon, a thing he was proud to own.

"You'll bring it by the lodge, then?" he asked, his voice hoarse, as if he'd gone a long time without speaking.

"You could always stop by with your

truck," Carolyn said, because it seemed important—if pointless—to stand up to him.

"I could," Brody agreed. "But I'd like to show you my house, and you did seem taken with Moonshine's friendly face. Here's your chance to say howdy to him in person."

"Moonshine?"

"My horse," Brody said, with a ghost of a grin. "I think he gets pretty lonesome, out there in that unfinished barn. He'd probably like a visitor."

Carolyn thrust out a sigh. She might be able to resist Brody, albeit not with anything resembling ease, but she could not resist a horse. "All *right,*" she said. "I'll bring the picture over. What's a good time?"

"I'm usually there in the evenings," Brody replied.

Of course you are. And what big teeth you have, Grandma.

"I like to sew in the evenings," she said.

Brody was facing her again—and the counter between them wasn't wide enough to suit Carolyn. The whole state of Colorado wouldn't have been wide enough.

He let his eyes drift over her, and she'd have sworn he left her clothes in smoldering rags, just by looking at her.

"And then there's that ride you owe me," he said, his voice low.

Carolyn's face flamed—even after all the talk about horses she managed to misunderstand him right from the get-go—and then he laughed, the sound low again, and raspy.

"The *horseback* ride," he drawled.

Carolyn gulped. "Why are you pushing this?" she whispered angrily, leaning toward him without thinking and then wishing she hadn't.

His mouth was within kissing distance of hers and she couldn't pull back out of reach. She couldn't *move.*

"You said yes when I asked you to go riding with me," Brody reminded her, very quietly, "and that makes it a matter of honor. Either your word is worth something, Carolyn Simmons, or it isn't."

That freed her from the spell he'd cast over her.

Carolyn snapped her head back and

glared. She gripped the edges of the counter so tightly that her knuckles ached. "You're a fine one to talk about honor," she told him, her voice ragged with fury, "after what you did. Furthermore, *my* word has never been in question here. Yours, on the other hand—"

He had the audacity to grin, to raise both hands, palms out, in an ingenuous bid for peace that made her want to slap him silly.

"Carolyn," he said slowly, "you are a hard woman. You are a *stubborn* woman. And you sure do know how to hold a grudge."

"Count on it," Carolyn practically snarled.

They glowered at each other for a long, silent moment.

Then Tricia pushed open the kitchen door and poked out her head, like a turtle peering out of a shell.

"Are you two joining us for lunch or not?" she asked sunnily.

"I'm not hungry," Carolyn said.

"Me, either," Brody agreed.

"Okaaaaay," Tricia replied, singing the word and ducking back into the kitchen.

Carolyn rounded the counter, stormed past Brody toward the front window and dragged a lace curtain aside to look out at the street.

Sure enough, there were two horses, a buckskin and a bay, saddled and standing untethered at the picket fence. They were systematically devouring the leaves of Natty McCall's century-old lilac bush.

Carolyn turned on Brody, full of challenge. And heat.

And things it was better not to identify.

"Two people, two horses," she said tautly. "Let's take that ride right now, Mr. Creed, and get it over with."

"'Get it over with'?" Brody sounded amused—and a little insulted.

"I didn't promise to like it," she reminded him. "All I said was that I'd go." Carolyn indicated her jeans, boots and long-sleeved T-shirt. "And I want to go *now*."

"Fine," Brody said, inclining his head toward the fence, where the horses waited. "We'll go now."

Carolyn didn't even pause to tell Tricia

that she was leaving the shop, because then she'd have had to explain *why* she was leaving, and she wasn't willing to do that. Steam would probably shoot out of her ears if she tried.

So she strode to the door, wrenched it open and crossed the threshold, then the porch.

"Take the bay," Brody told her, when, reaching the gate, she finally hesitated. Ire had carried her this far, but now she was at a loss.

"Great," she bit out.

She gathered the bay's dangling reins, stuck one foot in the stirrup and mounted with an expertise born of outrage as much as long experience.

Brody was standing on the sidewalk one moment, and sitting easy in the saddle the next. Holding the buckskin's reins loosely across one palm, he said, "One hour, Carolyn. Anything less than that doesn't amount to a ride, unless you're on a pony at the carnival."

On the ground, Carolyn was uncertain about a great many things.

In the saddle, she ruled. Her confidence, once she was on the back of a horse—any horse—was complete. Unshakable.

This was something she knew, something that came as easily to her as her breathing or the beating of her heart.

"Let's go," she said.

"See if you can keep up," Brody taunted, with another grin.

"If I don't, it will be this horse's fault, not mine," Carolyn replied, pressing the words through her teeth.

Brody laughed, an exultant, whooping sound, and he turned that buckskin in the general direction of the ranch and took it from a trot to a gallop to a full run in the space of half a dozen strides. The animal fairly flew along that unpaved road, like a butter-colored Pegasus, with Brody bent low over its neck, the two of them melded into one magnificent creature.

Pride swelled in Carolyn, and some emotion fiercer and more intense than joy, and she let Conner's horse have its head. The two geldings ran neck-and-neck then, over vacant lots and across dirt roads, over railroad tracks so long unused that the rails had rusted, and through breast-high brush.

When they both splashed into the river, Carolyn gave a shout of startled jubilation and held on as the waters filled her boots, soaked her jeans from the knees down and then saturated the denim covering her thighs.

Brody turned his head to look at her, and in his eyes she thought she saw the one emotion she'd never expected to inspire in him: respect.

By the time they reached the opposite bank, the horses were wearing out, slowing down. They plodded up the steep bank, laboring for high ground.

Gaining the road that edged the ridge above the river, Brody and Carolyn let the horses set their own ambling pace.

Carolyn knew this road from her own rides on Blossom, knew the direction they were taking would bring them to the main ranch house.

She was wet, and breathless, and thoroughly exhilarated. Only one thing was better than a full-out, hell-bent-for-election ride like the one she and Brody had just shared, and that was the kind of shattering orgasm he'd brought her to, so easily and so often, back when they were lovers.

A shiver went through her, but it had nothing to do with the chill of the river water.

At last, Brody deigned to break the silence. Cocky bastard.

"Tricia probably has some clothes that will fit you," he said. "You need to get into some dry duds, and the sooner, the better."

She looked at him, which was a concession in and of itself. "Did you *plan* that plunge into the river?" she asked. She wouldn't have put it past him—what better way to get her out of her clothes?—but, on the other hand, he probably hadn't, because he couldn't have known whether or not she'd be able to rise to the challenge.

And whatever else she might have believed about Brody, she *didn't* believe he'd deliberately put anyone at risk for any reason.

"Nope," he said, with another easy grin. He was as wet as she was; even his hat was soaked. He leaned to pat

Moonshine's neck affectionately. "I should have seen it coming, though. This horse loves the water." He studied her, a grin in his eyes and playing around, but not quite settling on, his mouth. "You all right, cowgirl?" he asked.

Something in his voice, in the way he sat that horse and the way he looked at her, touched Carolyn in a deep and inexplicable way.

"I'm all right," she confirmed.

"You ride," he said, "like a Comanche."

It was a compliment, and Carolyn took it in. Owned it. Knew she'd bring it out, in future lonely hours, and turn it over and over in her mind, savoring it like some precious heirloom passed down through generations of forbearers.

"So do you," she replied, as they rode slowly toward the ranch house.

"Thanks," he answered.

After that, the horses picked up their pace, probably expecting a rubdown and a flake or two of grass-hay once they got to the barn.

Once there, Carolyn and Brody dismounted, led their tired mounts into waiting stalls and worked in easy concert with each other, grooming the animals carefully, filling their feeders and finally meeting up again in the breezeway.

"Let's get you into some warmer clothes," Brody said, extending his hand.

Like a sleepwalker, Carolyn accepted the offer, let him lead her out into the bright sunlight of early afternoon.

She'd expected Conner and Tricia to be around—they'd had plenty of time to drive from town to the ranch in Tricia's Pathfinder—but there was no sign of them.

Brody tightened his grasp on Carolyn's hand, but only briefly and only slightly.

Entering the house, they were immediately greeted by two dogs, Valentino and Brody's Barney.

"I thought Conner and Tricia would be here," Carolyn said.

Brody smiled. "And miss a chance for some alone-time in that big Victorian house?" he teased. "The place has a lot of meaning for them. By now, they're probably making love."

Carolyn blushed again. Looked away, to avoid Brody's knowing gaze. "I should—" She hesitated, bit down on her lower lip. "I should be getting back to the shop. Would you mind giving me a lift into town?"

"Later," Brody said, taking her hand. He led her across the kitchen, through a doorway into a long corridor. Pushing open a door, he gestured for her to enter.

Carolyn was already in so deep that there was no going back. She stepped into the full bathroom that linked two small guest suites.

Brody had to know he had the advantage, an advantage he could have pressed, but he remained in the hallway, watching her with a sort of grave amusement. "While you shower, I'll rustle up something for you to wear," he said.

Carolyn *was* cold, and the thought of a hot shower was enticing.

Still, to take a shower, one had to get naked. And getting naked in the same house with Brody Creed was asking for trouble. Especially in her present mood.

For whatever reason, Carolyn wasn't her usual self.

"Tricia keeps extra robes for company," Brody went on, as calmly as if the situation were—well . . . a *non*situation. "They're in the closet next to the linen cabinet." He inclined his head, indicating the huge antique wardrobe behind her. "Help yourself."

With that, he walked off down the hall.

Carolyn shut the door quickly, then she turned the lock. *Then* she scurried to make sure the doors leading into the adjoining guest suites were locked, too.

It was silly, she knew, as, shivering, she started the water running in the shower and began peeling away her soggy clothes.

Whatever his other faults might be, Brody wasn't one to force himself on a woman.

But, then, it wasn't what *Brody* might do that worried her.

It was what *she* might do.

CHAPTER NINE

Brody hid out in the laundry room at the main ranch house, keeping his voice down as he spoke into his cell phone.

"Tricia," he growled, feeling his neck turn warm, "cut it out. This isn't funny. Carolyn needs to borrow some of your pre-pregnant clothes *because she got wet while we were crossing the river.*"

"I absolutely believe you," his sister-in-law chimed sunnily on the other end of the call he hadn't wanted to make. "If Carolyn had taken off her clothes for any *other* reason, she would simply put them back on when necessary."

Brody had called for permission to pilfer Tricia's wardrobe, not for a ration. Helping himself to Conner's stuff when he needed it was one thing, and pawing through Tricia's dresser drawers and closets was another.

Tricia went prattling on, without waiting for him to talk again, which was a good thing, because he didn't have a clue what to say. He'd stated his business, and now all he could do was wait.

"One minute," Tricia chirped, in a to-sum-it-all-up kind of tone, "Carolyn was right here in the shop, perfectly dry. The next, she's racing away on a horse and winds up drenched to the skin—"

"Tricia," Brody interrupted hoarsely, getting desperate.

She laughed. Paused to repeat Brody's earlier request to Conner, making *him* laugh, too.

It didn't help one damn bit that his brother's easy, rumbling chortle had a distinctively *satisfied* quality to it. Brody, being Conner's identical twin, and therefore wired the same way, right down to the double helix, knew what that sound meant.

Sure enough, Conner and Tricia had just made love.

Conner, you lucky SOB, Brody thought, too distracted to catch the irony.

Silently, Brody seethed, his body taut with the anticipation of something that wasn't going to happen. Not that he couldn't have had Carolyn—he knew he could. He'd sensed her vulnerability, and the biochemical signals had definitely been traveling both ways.

The lovemaking wasn't going to happen, though, because he wasn't going to *let* it happen. Not yet. It was too soon, the situation was delicate, and while he hadn't learned all his life lessons, or probably even a fraction of them, he *had* learned that one.

Carolyn wanted him, but she wasn't ready.

Oh, she'd respond, all right—she was a responsive woman, as spirited as a wild mare—but when the effects wore off, when the afterglow went out like yesterday's fire in the woodstove, she'd hate him.

Worse, she'd hate herself, too.

So Brody meant to wait—no matter what it cost him.

He shoved a hand through his river-dampened hair—*one* dunk in the water hadn't been enough to do him for a whole day. He'd had to get wet *twice.*

Serve him right if he came down with pneumonia.

While he was thinking all these thoughts, Conner and Tricia were still enjoying the hilarity of it all.

At his expense. And here he was, being freaking *noble,* too.

He deserved better.

At last, Tricia took pity on him. "My skinny clothes are in boxes at the back of the walk-in closet in Conner's and my room," she said, very sweetly. "Feel free to plunder."

Brody had to smile then, even though he was still feeling pretty darned grumpy, all things considered. "Thanks," he said. "I appreciate it." He paused. In the distance, he could hear the water running in the downstairs bathroom. He pictured Carolyn naked, her trim body sluiced with soap suds and spray, and got so hard that the ache practically doubled him over. After a moment spent recovering, he cleared his throat. "You two will be coming home soon, right?" he asked.

Say yes.

Say no.

"Wrong," Tricia said happily. "Conner is taking me out for a very romantic dinner. Would you mind feeding Valentino for us? And the horses?"

"Sure," Brody said, thrown by what ought to have been a perfectly ordinary turn of events. "I mean, no, I wouldn't mind feeding the critters for you. Have fun at dinner."

"We will," Tricia said, and he didn't need to see her smile, because he could feel it, hear it in her voice. This, he dimly recalled, was how a woman sounded, when she was in love. "We'll see you hours—*hours and hours*—from now."

Brody chuckled, shook his head. *If only.* "Suit yourselves," he said.

Goodbyes were exchanged, and the call ended.

Brody rubbed his stubbled chin, sighed as he set the cell phone aside on a counter. Obviously, Tricia thought he and Carolyn were going to spend those "hours and hours" making up for lost time, getting it on.

He was going to have the name without the game, and so was Carolyn.

It just plain sucked.

Carolyn stepped out of the shower, dried off with a thirsty towel and appropriated one of the guest robes from the exquisitely carved antique wardrobe against the long wall. Fleece-lined, the garment brushed against her skin like a whole-body caress.

Don't go there, she admonished herself silently. *Do* not *think about skin and caresses. You are in deep yogurt here, lady. Out of your depth.*

She padded over to one of the two sinks set into the counter, with its custom-painted ceramic sinks, and stared at her image in the mirror, combing her hair with splayed fingers and making eye contact with that other Carolyn.

"Well," she began in a whisper, though she didn't really think Brody had his ear stuck to any of the bathroom doors, "you have done it this time. You are in a real fix, and it won't be easy to get out of this one."

If you even want *to get out of here without giving in to the overwhelming urge to have sex with Brody Creed.*

Carolyn flushed, indignant. "Of *course* I want to get out of here without having sex with Brody," she muttered. She often had these kinds of conversations with herself—what the rest of the world didn't know wouldn't hurt them.

Do you want to make love with him or not?

"Well," Carolyn admitted, deflating a little as she sighed, "*yes.* What healthy, red-blooded woman in her right mind *wouldn't* want to have sex with Brody Creed?" She drew in a deep breath, raised her chin and squared her shoulders under the sensuous fabric of that ridiculously luxurious robe. *"But,"* she went on, "I'm *not* going to give in to temptation. Period. I've already been down this road once, remember, and once was more than enough."

She must have made her case because after that, the argumentative little voice in her head was silent.

A rap sounded at the door leading into the hallway.

"Yes?" Carolyn asked, with only the slightest tremor, finger-combing her hair again.

Brody's low-pitched chuckle penetrated the thick wood of the door. "I've got some of Tricia's things here," he said. "I'll just set them down on the floor and back away real slow."

A smile crooked Carolyn's mouth, but she quickly subdued it. This was a serious situation, she reminded herself, and if she wasn't very, *very* careful, all her drummed-up resolution to take the high road would go right down the old drain.

"Thank you," she called back stiffly.

She waited until she heard Brody walk away, then waited a few moments longer, for good measure. Once she was sure the proverbial coast was clear, she unlocked the door, bent to grab up the untidy stack of feminine garments from the floor and locked herself in again.

Sitting down on the edge of the humungous bathtub because, all of a sudden, her knees had gone squishy, holding the borrowed blue jeans and white cotton shirt on her lap, she considered hiding out in that bathroom until Tricia and Conner got home.

That would be silly, though.

And boring. Who knew how long they'd be gone?

So, with another sigh, Carolyn put on the jeans and the shirt, sans underwear because her own bra and panties were still wet and no self-respecting woman borrows *or* lends lingerie, fluffed out her hair with her fingers one more time and marched out into the corridor.

She found Brody in the kitchen, fiddling with the coffee machine. He'd showered, too, and changed into jeans and a blue chambray shirt, Western-cut with snaps. His boots were old and scuffed, which completed the singularly appealing look.

With a frown, he glanced in her direction. "Do you know how to work this thingamajig?" he asked. "I cannot for the life of me figure out why people can't be satisfied with an ordinary coffeepot."

The question relaxed Carolyn slightly, neutralized some of the charge in the atmosphere. Tricia loved gadgets, and

Carolyn had been with her when she bought the machine. They'd given it a trial run at the shop, studying the instruction book and finally mastering the thing.

It was, in a world thick with enigmas, a problem she could solve.

"Like this," Carolyn said, popping a pod into the top, setting a clean cup under the spigot and pushing the buttons. It was only after the java began to brew that she realized closing the gap between herself and Brody might not have been the smartest thing she'd ever done.

Brody didn't move. Why should he? He'd been there first.

Carolyn didn't move, either. It wasn't pride, or stubbornness, that made her stay put. It was some strange, thrumming kind of centrifugal force.

Brody cleared his throat, an affable sound, but raw at the edges. "Just so there are no misunderstandings," he said, finally, and Carolyn had to strain to hear him over the beat of her heart, "I can't remember when I've ever wanted a woman the way I want you. Fact is, if my conscience would allow it, I'd do my cowboy-best to seduce you, right here and right now."

Carolyn gave a twittery little laugh. "You have a conscience?"

Lame.

The single shot of fresh coffee had long since finished processing itself, but neither of them paid any attention to it.

Brody's mouth kicked up at the corner, but the expression in his eyes was soft. "Believe it or not," he replied, "I do indeed have a conscience. And it's telling me not to screw up." A pause, another quirk of his mouth. "So to speak."

Color flooded Carolyn's face, and heat suffused her traitorous body. "Gee, thanks," she said, somehow keeping her tone level, despite what felt like a million tiny universes colliding within her.

His grin went full-throttle then.

It wasn't the least bit fair.

"A while back," Brody went on, mercifully lowering the wattage on his grin, "I asked you for a second chance. I meant it, Carolyn. Even if this doesn't go anywhere—whatever it is that's happening between you and me—I think we should explore it."

Carolyn couldn't speak. Couldn't even swallow past the lump in her throat. So she just looked up into Brody Creed's damnably handsome, deceptively earnest face, powerless against him. Hoping and praying he hadn't already guessed that.

Fat chance.

He curved his right index finger under her chin, lifted ever so gently, so their gazes locked with an almost audible click, like the tumblers in a lock.

"Carolyn?"

"I'm listening," she whispered. And she was. With her whole being, body, mind and spirit.

Again, the wicked grin flashed. He nodded once. "So do you have an opinion?" he teased. "And, if so, how about letting me in on it?"

"There is—" Carolyn had to stop, clear the frog from her throat, before she could go on. "There is *apparently* something . . . well . . . *going on,* here. And I think, most definitely—maybe—we ought to find out what it is. Sometime."

Mischief danced, cornflower-blue, in Brody's eyes. He arched one eyebrow

and waited, calm as a seasoned fisher-
man with a trout on the hook.

"But not *immediately,* mind you," Carolyn clarified. "I mean, the sensible thing
to do would be to forget the whole stupid idea and pretend we never had this
conversation. But—"

"But . . . ?" Brody prompted, his voice
husky.

He was still standing too close.

"But I'm not feeling very sensible at
the moment," Carolyn admitted, on a
rush of breath.

"Me, either," Brody said, and the twinkle was back in his eyes. "But one of us
has to be strong, here. Somebody has
to be responsible. So I'm telling you flat-
out, Carolyn Simmons—no matter how
badly you may want me, I'm not available."

Carolyn smiled wryly, calm on the
outside, every nerve jangling on the *inside.* "Thanks for straightening me out
on that score," she said, pleasantly surprised that she was able to strike a
breezy note. "What happens now?"

"We do the thing up right," Brody said,

sounding confident. "Starting with a few ground rules."

"Ground rules?"

"Yeah," Brody told her. "No sex, for the time being anyhow. And both of us can see other people if that's what we want to do."

Carolyn hoped the pang that last stipulation gave her didn't show on her face. She was *sort of* seeing Bill Venable, and sort of *not* seeing him, but she already knew he'd never be more than a friend to her, nor she to him.

Bill loved Angela.

And she, God help her, was still hung up on Brody.

"What?" Brody asked, when she didn't say anything.

"If you want to go out with Joleen Williams," Carolyn said loftily, "that's certainly your prerogative."

The twinkle in Brody's eyes turned to temper. "Did I, at any point in time, say I wanted to date Joleen?"

"You didn't have to," Carolyn said. She folded her arms. "It's quite obvious."

"I don't know how you figure that,"

Brody said, clearly irritated. "Do you see Joleen standing around here some-where, waiting for me to help her on with her coat or pin a corsage to her party dress so we can go out on the town?"

It just went to show a person, Carolyn thought, how quickly a spring breeze could turn into an ill wind. Not more than a minute before, she and Brody had had all they could do not to have sex right there in his brother's kitchen. *Now* they were practically at each other's throats.

"You're the one who wanted to keep their options open when it came to dat-ing," Carolyn pointed out, proud of be-ing—okay, *sounding*—so collected and reasonable.

"And *you're* the one who's *already dating*," Brody bit out.

So he *did* know about Bill. She'd won-dered.

"Look at that," Carolyn retorted, fling-ing her hands out from her sides be-cause she had to do *something* with the buildup of energy that wouldn't consti-tute felony assault. "I was already playing by the ground rules before I even knew there *were* any!"

Brody glared at her.

Carolyn glared back.

One of the dogs gave a mournful little whimper, as though the poor creature had just spotted a mushroom cloud billowing on the horizon.

"What kind of guy is so hard up for a date that he joins an outfit like Friendly Faces?" Brody finally demanded. That familiar muscle in his cheek was bunched up again.

"One like you, I guess," Carolyn took great delight in saying. "Or are you going to claim it was your *horse* who signed up for a membership?"

Brody leaned in, his nose nearly touching hers. "*This* is why we need ground rules," he said.

"I think we need a *referee,*" Carolyn replied. "Why don't we just call it a day, Brody? Why don't we cut our losses and run?"

That was when he rested his hands on her shoulders, bent his head and kissed her, lightly at first, then hard and deep, with tongue.

The effect was tectonic, and she was literally breathless when the kiss finally ended.

"*That's* why we're not going to *cut our losses and run*," Brody all but growled. "Get your things, Carolyn. I'm taking you home."

She should have been glad about that, but, oddly, she was stung instead.

She did return to the bathroom, however, collect her original clothing, now rolled up in a soggy clump, and stomped back to the kitchen, where Brody was waiting, with his truck keys already in hand.

Talk about anxious to get rid of somebody.

Carolyn squelched a crazy urge to cry and marched out through the back door, which Brody obligingly held for her.

The two dogs followed, eager, like all their species, for any chance to go *anywhere.*

When Brody reached his truck, he went immediately to the passenger side and opened the door. Once Carolyn was in, he hoisted the dogs, one at a time, into the rear part of the extended cab.

Carolyn fixed her gaze straight ahead, silently noting that the windshield needed washing.

Brody got behind the wheel, slammed his door shut and cranked the key in the ignition, causing the starter to make an ominous grinding sound.

"This is going to keep happening," he told her tersely, "until we go to bed and get each other out of our systems."

Carolyn shifted in the confines of her seat belt and would not look at him. "Way to sweep a girl off her feet," she snapped. "Take me home, Brody. *Now.*"

The truck made another odd noise when he shifted it into gear. "Fine," he replied. "I'll be *glad* to take you home. Of course, there's always the possibility that Conner and Tricia are swinging naked from the chandeliers or something, but I guess that's a risk you'll just have to run."

Carolyn blushed so hard it hurt. What if Tricia and Conner *were* still somewhere in Natty McCall's wonderful old Victorian house, thinking they had the place to themselves and, well, *whooping it up?*

In the next moment, though, Brody's words took root and blossomed into an image—Tricia, six months pregnant, swinging nude from one of the light fixtures, like the daring young girl on the flying trapeze.

Carolyn laughed. She couldn't help it.

Out of the corner of her eye, she saw that Brody was grinning. "What?" he asked.

"I was just thinking about the chandelier thing," Carolyn admitted.

That made Brody chuckle. "It brings one hell of a picture to mind, all right," he agreed. "My guess is, my brother and his lovely bride are probably behaving themselves again by now. Tricia mentioned that they were headed out to dinner."

"Are we crazy?" Carolyn asked, very softly and after long consideration. Every silence that fell between them seemed to throb with things that wanted saying and *couldn't* be said. "The way we go from being this close to having sex to fighting like a pair of feral cats in a back alley—what *is* that, Brody?"

He thought before he answered. Finally said, "I think they call it passion."

With that, he reached over and gave her thigh a squeeze, about midway between her knee and her hip.

Carolyn tilted her head back, closed her eyes and offered up a silent prayer that Brody didn't know he'd turned her insides to molten lava with a single touch.

He'd meant to go straight to the shop— Brody would always think of the place as Natty McCall's house, no matter what they turned it into—but darned if his truck didn't turn in at River's Bend of its own volition.

Carolyn didn't protest, or comment. She just turned her head toward the rising house and since Brody couldn't see her face, he was left to guess at what might be going on inside her head.

The construction crew was finished for the day, loading toolboxes into the backs of pickup trucks, calling to each other, laughing.

For some reason, the sight stirred up some lonesome feelings inside Brody.

That sensation of being on the outside looking in was getting old.

Or maybe it was this confounding woman sitting in the seat just across the console, determined to say as little to him as possible.

The workmen all waved and smiled, and Brody greeted them with nods as he drove up what would one day be a paved driveway. For now, though, it was still a dirt road, thinly peppered with gravel.

"Tricia mentioned that you mean to go on calling the property River's Bend," Carolyn said, her head still turned toward the house, her tone bemused, or maybe wistful. "She seemed pleased by that."

"River's Bend is as good a name for the place as any other," Brody said. "Besides, I liked Tricia's dad. Most everybody liked Joe McCall."

"Tricia misses him," Carolyn observed, finally looking at Brody. He couldn't read her eyes, but it didn't matter, because she was so damn beautiful, in the late afternoon light, a gilded creature wearing somebody else's clothes.

This nobility crap, Brody decided glumly, was overrated. By now, if he'd pressed his advantage earlier, in the ranch-house kitchen, they'd probably be recovered from round one and ready to move on to round two. Or even three.

"That's natural," Brody said, in belated reply to Carolyn's remark.

"Do you miss your dad?" Carolyn asked, as he parked the truck in front of the partially completed three-car garage and shut off the engine.

She sure did have a way of coming out of left field, this woman.

Brody sighed, shook his head. "I never really knew my father," he answered honestly. "Conner and I were just babies when he died, and our mother didn't live long after we were born. When I think of parents, I think of Kim and Davis, and I'm sure my brother does, too."

He opened the truck door and would have gone around to help Carolyn out of the rig—he'd been raised to treat a lady with respect and courtesy, as had Conner and their cousin, Steven—but she was over the running board with her feet planted firmly in the rocky dirt before he could get there.

He took Valentino and Barney from the back and let them circle, as dogs will do when they've been confined for a while, sniffing the ground and looking for a likely place to let fly.

"What about you, Carolyn?" he asked.

"What about me?" she challenged, but mildly, shading her eyes from the sun with one hand.

"You asked me about my dad. I'm asking you about yours."

"Never knew him," Carolyn said, like it didn't matter.

This seemed important, though Brody wasn't sure why. Important enough to press the issue, in fact.

"What about your mother?"

She met his gaze then, and the expression he saw in her eyes was so bleak that he felt it like a punch in the gut. "Just a memory of somebody driving away and leaving me behind," she said.

Brody hadn't wept since the day the Lisa and Justin were buried, side by side, in a windswept little graveyard up in Montana, but he wanted to then.

Didn't, though.

They were both quiet for a few moments, neither one moving.

"This is quite a house," Carolyn said, at long last.

Brody rummaged around inside himself and came up with a flimsy grin. He was proud of that house, saw its conception and construction as the first really grown-up things he'd ever done, and showing it to Carolyn made him feel good.

"Yes, ma'am," he agreed. "It will be, if it's ever finished."

"Show me where you plan to hang the Weaver," Carolyn said, her still-wet boots making a squishy crunch in the gravel as she approached the front door.

He was a few moments remembering what she meant by the term, but then it came to him that she was referring to Primrose Sullivan's picture, the one he'd bought at the shop and insisted she deliver. He'd have to keep it over at the cabin for a while, of course, but he did have a spot picked out for it.

The doors and locks had been installed, and Brody found the key among the others on his ring.

The inside of the house smelled like fresh lumber and new masonry, and the windows were all glassed in. He flipped a switch, expecting nothing, and the track lighting high over their heads came on, throwing the massive living room into an oddly forlorn relief.

He was going to be lonely here, he realized. He was lonely *everywhere.*

Brody shook off the thought, smiled at Carolyn and gestured toward the space over the living room fireplace.

"There," he said. "That's where the picture's going to wind up."

Carolyn seemed to see the piece hanging there. She smiled, albeit a little wanly, her hands resting on her hips. "Perfect," she said.

Brody cupped a hand under her elbow, loosely, wanting her to look at him, not wanting her to turn skittish and spook. "Now that we've established the ground rules," he began, pausing once to clear his throat, "there's the part that comes after."

She held his gaze, and she deserved credit for that, because it was so obvious that she wanted to look away instead. "You're a persistent man," she said, very softly.

Brody had never wanted to kiss a woman—Carolyn or anyone else—as badly as he wanted to now.

At the same time, he knew it might be the mistake of a lifetime if he went ahead and did it.

"*Persistent* doesn't begin to cover it," he said, when he figured he could trust himself to speak. "You've never met a man with more stick-to-it in him than I have, except for Conner, maybe, and he's taken."

"Yes," Carolyn agreed, almost in a murmur, her whole attention focused, it seemed to Brody, on his mouth. Her voice was dreamlike, almost sleepy-sounding. "Conner is definitely taken."

Brody wondered, momentarily, if Carolyn had had a thing for Conner, before he married her best friend. Wondered if by chance her attraction to him was a case of transference.

But that was crazy. Before Lisa's call

that fateful night, seven years back, Carolyn had been in love with *him,* Brody—hadn't she?

This is me *standing here,* he wanted to say. *This is me, Brody Creed. Not Conner.* Brody.

But, of course, he didn't, though the decision couldn't be chalked up to good sense; he was just plain thunderstruck by the possibility.

"What comes after the ground rules, Brody?" Carolyn asked quietly. "After the no-sex pact, and the freedom to see other people if we want to, what happens then?"

At last, Brody found his voice. He even rummaged up a passable grin, one that might even have masked all the catastrophic things happening in the core of his being.

"Maybe," he said, struck by sudden inspiration, "we could start with dinner and a movie?"

CHAPTER TEN

Dinner and a movie.

With Carolyn.

Sounded like a good start to Brody. But *no sex? Had he actually been the one to stipulate that? Was he out of his ever-lovin'* mind *or* what?

"Dinner and a movie," Carolyn repeated thoughtfully, mulling his invitation over. She looked wicked-hot, standing there in the middle of what would one day be his living room. The borrowed shirt was a little too tight across her breasts and a little too short in the bargain, revealing a tantalizing glimpse of stomach skin whenever she moved just right.

Brody shifted uncomfortably, and he was just about to jump in and try to re-negotiate the whole no-nooky thing when Carolyn rocked him with a tiny smile and announced her decision.

"A tame enough evening, I think," she said, and was quick to add, "As long as we don't have to sleep together, of course."

Tame? Was that how she saw him—as *tame?*

Brody gulped. "Of course."

But he was thinking, *You and your big mouth. Brody Creed, you are five known kinds of fool, and a few that haven't been discovered yet.*

"When?" Carolyn asked.

Brody just stood there for a moment, stumped by the question, simple as it was. Then he untangled his tongue and said, "Tomorrow night? I promised Tricia I'd feed their horses and these dogs to-night, and it's getting pretty late any-how."

Carolyn bit her lower lip, thinking

again. Was it really *that* hard to make the decision?

"Tomorrow night isn't good," she said, with a little shake of her head. "I have other plans. How about Friday or Saturday?"

"Saturday would work," Brody suggested, cagey now. Carolyn was probably playing hard to get, and two could ride in *that* rodeo. The only reason he didn't go for Friday instead was that he didn't want to seem too eager.

"Great," she said, looking around. "Is there more?" she asked, with a quirky little grin. "To the house, I mean?"

"Yeah," Brody replied, oddly relieved even though, by his reckoning, Saturday was on the yonder side of forever. He offered his hand, letting her decide whether to take it or not.

She did.

By then, the dogs were already off on an expedition of their own, checking out other parts of the house.

Brody showed Carolyn the kitchen first, with its big stove and center island and its many windows, then the room he planned on using as an office, then

the guest quarters and the family bedrooms and, finally, the master suite.

"Big place," Carolyn said, hesitating
in the double doorway of the main bedroom.

"Carolyn," Brody teased, shaken and,
at the same time, buzzed, "it's okay to
go inside. There isn't even a bed in here
yet."

She blushed a little, stooped to pet
Barney when he doubled back briefly to
brush against her before taking off again.
After that, like a person wandering in a
dream, Carolyn moved to the middle of
the room. Putting her hands out from
her sides, she tilted her head back,
closed her eyes and did a slow, graceful
pirouette.

In that moment, Carolyn seemed impossibly beautiful to Brody, like a sprite
or a fallen angel or a fairy queen. He
wouldn't have been all that surprised if
she'd sprouted gossamer wings. When
she stopped moving and met his gaze
again, she looked embarrassed.

He wanted to tell her it was okay, that
he could watch her dance like that for
the rest of eternity and be perfectly

happy, but he'd sound like a damn idiot if he did, so he held his tongue.

"What do you think?" he asked, just to break the silence. "Of the house, that is?"

She smiled a real smile, practically lighting the place up. "It's *wonderful,* Brody. Did you design it yourself?"

People made plans for houses all the time, but Carolyn made it sound as though he'd personally drawn up the blueprints for Stonehenge, and that made him feel half again his normal height.

He nodded, suddenly modest.

That would have cracked Conner up for sure—his twin brother acting modest. Conner and a lot of other people besides.

"I did," he confirmed belatedly, feeling the backs of his ears heat up. "Got me through a lot of long nights, figuring out the overall floor plan and then the details."

She was silent for a few minutes, absorbing that statement.

"I should be getting home," Carolyn said next, standing in a shaft of silvery

moonlight spilling in through the skylights.

For as long as Brody could remember, he'd wanted to be able to lie in his
bed at night and look right up through
the ceiling and the roof at the stars. In a
couple of months, he'd get his wish.

But what about a woman to share it
all with?

Looking at stars could be lonely business without a partner. Made a man
think how small he was, how small the
whole planet—the whole *galaxy*—was,
specks of dust in all that vastness.

"Okay," he said, finding his voice
again. It came out in a husky rasp, and
he hoped he hadn't caught a cold,
crossing and then recrossing the river.
That would be a hell of a note. "Let's
go."

He whistled for the dogs and they
came promptly, so he sort of herded
them toward the front of the house.
Stepping around Carolyn, Brody grabbed
hold of a fancy brass knob and opened
the door for her.

Valentino and Barney, neither one a
gentleman, bounded out ahead of her

to sniff around in the grass, nearly knocking her off her feet and, at the same time, making her laugh.

Brody loaded them up first, in case they had a mind to take off in all their excitement, and then waited until Carolyn was settled in the passenger seat before he sprinted around the back of the truck and jumped in behind the wheel, not because he was in any hurry to come to a parting of the ways with Carolyn, however temporary, but because he suddenly felt energized, electrified, wired for action, like the dogs.

Carolyn didn't say anything as they drove back to the main road, the one that would take them the rest of the way into town, but this time, she didn't seem annoyed with him. She was relaxed, and maybe a little pensive.

Brody drove her home to Natty's place, noticed right away that Tricia's Pathfinder wasn't parked in the driveway and, knowing that meant his brother and his wife were nowhere around, briefly considered trying to seduce Carolyn after all.

It would have been a fine thing to peel

away those clothes she was wearing, lay her down somewhere soft and warm and lose himself in her, but common sense intervened.

They'd made an agreement, and a deal was a deal.

No sex.

Yet.

Brody parked the truck at the curb, told the dogs to behave themselves and walked Carolyn all the way up the outside stairs to her door.

He waited, his hands wedged into the pockets of his jeans—*Conner's* jeans, anyway—until she'd unlocked the door, stepped over the threshold and switched on the kitchen lights.

While he was still trying to work out whether or not he ought to follow her in, give kissing her a try, that cantankerous cat purred and wound itself around her ankles. Anybody would have thought it had a halfway decent personality, that critter, but Brody knew better—it was demon spawn.

Carolyn smiled fondly down at the animal, said a quick, soft "Good night,

Brody," and shut the door in his face with a gentle click.

Well, that settled the kiss question.

Brody gave an inward shrug, turned and descended the stairs.

He had chores to do at the ranch, and the dogs would be getting antsy soon, shut up in the truck like they were.

Despite these concerns, he took a little detour on the way home, drove past the ticket booth and the snack bar at the erstwhile Bluebird Drive-in Theater and parked, looking up at the peeling hulk of a movie screen.

He'd been meaning to have the thing bulldozed ever since the last of the snow finally melted off back in mid-March, along with the two buildings on the property, but what with the new house and barn going up and his responsibilities on the ranch, he hadn't gotten around to making the arrangements. And, like most residents of Lonesome Bend and the even smaller towns surrounding it, he had fond memories of the place.

He still intended to clear these neglected acres, put in fences, and have it seeded for grass so he could run cattle and horses here, but in the meantime, well, it seemed to him that the Bluebird Drive-in deserved a last hurrah.

Carolyn wanted dinner and a movie?

Coming right up.

After the visit to Brody's house, the apartment seemed not only small to Carolyn—once, she would have said "cozy"—but also out-and-out *cramped.*

"Ingrate," she scolded her reflection in the door of the microwave as she stood at the counter, scraping Winston's half-tin of sardines into one of the several chipped china bowls reserved for his use.

"Reow," Winston said, sounding moderately concerned.

"I didn't mean you," Carolyn told him, setting his dinner on the floor and watching with affection as he gobbled up the stinky fish he loved so much. She washed her hands at the sink, her movements quick with pent-up exasperation. "*I'm* the ingrate around here. I have everything I need, everything anybody could ask for, right here in this apartment." She paused, remembering. "But, Winston, you should *see* that house. It's *huge.* But it's not one of those mansion wannabes, either, it's—it's *homey.* I couldn't help imagining what it would be like to live there." She threw her hands out from her sides, let them fall back. "How crazy is that?"

Winston, busy with his fine dining experience and, after all, *a cat,* naturally didn't reply.

Carolyn, used to carrying on one-sided conversations, didn't let that slow her down. "You're right," she said. "It is *totally* crazy." She dried off her hands, went to the refrigerator, yanked open the door and took out a carton of cottage cheese, the kind with little chunks of pineapple mixed in. After squinting at the expiration date, she decided it would be relatively safe to eat the stuff and lobbed some onto a salad plate with a serving spoon. "The man *cons* me into going for a horseback ride with him, and I end up soaked to the skin and squeezed into clothes that belong to a woman who is at least two inches shorter than I am, and a size smaller, and I'm ready to *get it on* with Brody Creed. I swear, if he hadn't made that speech about responsibility and setting ground rules, I probably would have jumped his bones—"

The landline rang, interrupting her discourse.

Probably for the best, she figured, reaching for the receiver.

"Hello?" she almost snapped. She needed to eat her questionable cottage cheese, put on her own clothes and get her head together, not necessarily in that order—*not* stand around talking on the phone.

She recognized Bill's chuckle immediately. "Am I calling at a bad time?" he asked.

"Who is that?" Carolyn heard a little girl's voice chime in, at the other end of the line. "Is that Angela? It had *better* be Angela."

Carolyn smiled. She remembered what it was to be nine years old. What she *didn't* remember was having a father who, like Bill, was devoted to her.

She'd never met her father. Didn't even know his name, or if he was alive or dead, or if she looked anything like him.

"This is a private call, Ellie," Bill told his daughter kindly, but firmly. "Beat it. Go do your homework or bug your grandmother or something."

"Maybe I'm the one who should be asking if it's a bad time," Carolyn said, still amused. She loved kids, even when they were difficult. *Especially* then. She'd been a handful herself; just ask any one of her fourteen foster families.

"Have dinner with me?" Bill said. "Here, at our place? We'll barbecue on the patio, and Ellie's grandparents will join us, so we shouldn't give rise to a local scandal."

Carolyn felt warm inside. Unfortunately, it wasn't the same kind of warm she felt when she was around Brody, or even thought about him.

Brody.

She'd lied to him, saying she had plans for the following night, simply because she'd needed a chance to catch her breath, regain her perspective, before she stepped into the lion's den a second time by being alone with a man who could melt her with a look, a touch, a word.

"You haven't been in Lonesome Bend long," she joked, "if you think my coming to your place, even for an outdoor meal with your in-laws present, wouldn't be fuel for gossip."

Bill sighed. "Is that a no?"

She watched as Winston licked his bowl clean and then strolled regally away, tail high. "I'd love to come over for a barbecue," she said. If she was going out with Brody, even for an innocuous evening of food and film, it was only reasonable to see other men, too. That way, she'd be in less danger of losing her head and doing something rash.

Keep your options open.

Always know where the exits are.

The foster-kid credo of life.

"Would tonight be too soon?" Bill teased.

"Yes," Carolyn said, with a rueful glance at her cottage cheese. "It would be. Tomorrow night?"

"Perfect," Bill said.

"What shall I bring?"

"Your beautiful smile and all the charm

you can muster. The in-laws will be friendly, but Ellie—"

"I can handle Ellie," Carolyn said, with kindness and humor. *Because I was Ellie, once upon a time, except that I didn't have adoring grandparents and a first-class father.*

"Okay," Bill responded, sounding relieved. "Tomorrow night, six o'clock if that's not too early. Casual dress, of course." He gave her the address, and Lonesome Bend being Lonesome Bend, she knew right where it was. Two-story brick house with green wooden shutters, surrounded by a wrought-iron fence, a block and a half southeast of the public library.

"I'll be there," Carolyn promised, wondering at her bravery.

She could count the dates she'd had, post-Brody, on one hand. And most of them had been at been mediocre at best, disastrous at worst.

The ones in between were highly forgettable.

"Good," Bill said. "I'll be looking forward to seeing you again."

After that, there didn't seem to be

much to say, so they exchanged goodbyes and ended the call.

Carolyn exchanged Tricia's clothes for
an oversize pair of cotton pajamas, ate
the cottage cheese and prayed she
wouldn't get food poisoning.

She wasn't much of a cook, it was
true. She simply couldn't see the point
in fixing elaborate meals when she'd be
the only one around to eat them.

The subject of food brought Brody's
incredible soon-to-be kitchen to mind;
she'd noticed the gigantic professional
stove, with its many burners and a space
for grilling indoors, noticed the subzero
refrigerator, the special built-in cooler
for wine, the two oversize dishwashers
and the extra sink and ceramic stove
top set into the granite covering the island in the middle of the room.

It was the size of Kansas, that island.

All of which meant that Brody either
liked to cook and entertain crowds, or
expected any woman he took up with to
do the same . . . or both of those things.

Smiling to herself—except for helping
out with the chili feed/rummage sale last
fall, she'd never whipped up any dish

more ambitious than macaroni and cheese, the kind that comes in a box— Carolyn went downstairs to make sure everything was in order in the shop. Whatever *else* Tricia had done that afternoon, once she was alone with Conner, she'd remembered to lock up, shut off the computer and wrap the Weaver for delivery to Brody's place.

Carolyn paused, the shop in semi-darkness now, at the base of the inside stairs, already missing the Weaver. Like the gypsy skirt, though, it was a luxury she not only couldn't afford, but also had no real use for.

At Brody's, the magnificent batik would be seen and appreciated, as it should. Perhaps it would even be passed down, a cherished heirloom, through generations of Creeds, the house surrounding it becoming more and more of a testament to family continuity with every passing year. Just like its much older counterpart on the ranch.

Carolyn climbed the stairs slowly, with her head slightly lowered, her heart filled with a sort of bereft enjoyment of the thought.

From her place of honor above Brody's living room fireplace, the Weaver would see newborns brought through the wide front entrance, see those same babies grow up, fall in love, marry and bring home children of their own. She would be a silent witness to whole lifetimes, that woman of wax and paint, there for the joys and the sorrows and the millions of ordinary moments in between those extremes.

Carolyn had coveted many an artwork in her time, but this was the first time she'd ever *envied* the piece itself.

Oh, to *be* the Weaver.

Reaching the top of the stairs, she put the back of one hand to her forehead, checking for fever. There was none, so why was she delirious?

That made her smile again.

She was suffering, she concluded, with glum humor, from a bad case of Brody-itis.

All the more reason to hedge her romantic bets.

Once he got back to the ranch, Brody took the dogs inside and fed them, then headed out to the barn to tend to the horses. He planned on leaving Moonshine right there with the others until morning, when he'd figure a way to get him home to River's Bend.

When he stepped outside, the stars were spilling across the dark sky, and the three-quarter moon looked magnified, hovering just above the rims of the mountains, like it had dipped too low somehow and gotten itself snagged on a tree or the craggy face of a cliff.

Brody sighed and lifted his hat briefly, just long enough to shove a hand through his hair, and stopped right there in the yard to admire the handiwork of a God he wasn't sure he believed in.

God or no God, he figured, and daunting as the expanse of it could be, being there, awake and a part of the whole thing, even for what amounted to the blink of the cosmic eye, was a miraculous gift.

Lisa sure hadn't gotten to stick around long, though, he thought sadly, and little Justin, his boy, hadn't lived long enough to have see two candles blazing on his birthday cake.

Just like that, Brody's throat twisted itself into a painful knot, one he could barely swallow past.

It was true that he wanted a family of his own, wanted to marry a sweet-tempered woman and fill that house at River's Bend with their kids and pack its barn with their ponies, but when he was tired, or felt particularly lonely, like tonight, the idea scared the hell out of him.

Nothing had ever—*ever*—hurt the way losing Lisa and Justin did. What if history repeated itself? What if he had to bury *another* wife, another *child?*

He was Creed-tough, thanks to all those sturdy forbearers of his and a graduate degree from the school of hard knocks, but he'd gone stark-raving crazy after that double funeral in the chapel of a mortuary in a little Montana town. He'd taken to drinking way more than too much, been on the lookout for a reason to fight, 24/7, cut himself off from the people he'd needed most—Conner and Steven and Davis and Kim.

Brody tried to shake it off, this sorry mood, made himself get moving again.

Inside the house, he made sure Valentino had all he needed, told Barney it was time they headed for home and led the way out under all those stars again.

Since it was just the two of them, he let Barney ride shotgun instead of consigning him to the backseat, and drove straight to River's Bend.

There, he remembered that he hadn't eaten, and poked around in his mini-fridge for a minute or so, hoping something tasty might have created itself out of the ether.

Nothing had.

He got out the milk carton, took a sniff to make sure it hadn't soured and was just shaking cold cereal into a bowl when he saw headlights—beams of dusty gold—sweep across the front window.

Barney, having just settled himself on his bed over by the unlighted stove, gave an anxious little whine and perked up his ears.

A car door slammed.

Footsteps crunched along the dirt path leading up to the lodge.

A knock sounded.

"Oh, hell," Brody told Barney, setting his cereal bowl aside on the counter with a bad-tempered thump. "She's back."

Just then, the door opened and Joleen poked her head inside, beaming in the unfounded expectation of a warm welcome. This month she was a blonde, and her contacts turned her eyes an unlikely shade of purple.

Brody had trouble recalling what her real coloring was—Joleen was a chameleon, constantly searching for that perfect look.

"It's me!" she sang, quite unnecessarily, strolling right in and setting a suitcase down on the floor.

"Damn it, Joleen," Brody grumbled, "I *told* you not to come here—"

"It would just be for one night," Joleen chimed, as though that made everything different. "And what kind of welcome is that, anyway, after all we've been to each other?"

"We've been bed partners, and that's about it." Stubborn, Brody folded his arms across his chest. Hardened his jawline. "You're not staying, Joleen."

Joleen tried the hurt expression that had always stood her in such good stead, not just with him, but probably with scores of men. "You know I can't stay with my folks," she said, her mouth pouty and her eyes luminous with on-demand tears. "Mrs. Collins promised I could rent that room over her garage, but it won't be ready until tomorrow and I— It's been a long drive and I'm worn out, Brody."

He took out his wallet, extracted several bills and shoved them at her. "Then I guess you'd better check in over at the Sunset Motel," he said.

"But that's *miles* from here," Joleen practically wailed.

"It's *three* miles, Joleen, and it's not as if you have to hike over there. You have your car."

Joleen eyed the fan of twenties Brody was holding out, hesitated and then took them with a quick, snatching motion, folded them and stuffed them into the pocket of her tight jeans. "I'm almost out of gas," she persisted.

"And I'm almost out of patience," Brody replied.

The threat of tears had subsided, Joleen having figured out that it wouldn't work, but there was a flash of temper behind those tinted lenses. Evidently, she was a member of the contacts-of-the-week club.

"If you won't let me stay here," she said, "then give me the keys to the new house. I'll camp out over there tonight."

"No," Brody said bluntly. "If you don't want to go home to your folks' place or stay with a friend, you can either sleep in your car or check in at the Sunset Motel. Your choice, Joleen."

For a second there, he thought she might throw a hissy fit. Instead, though, she reached down and grabbed the handle of her suitcase again.

"I thought *you* were my friend," she said, sounding not just accusatory but genuinely wounded.

Brody didn't take the bait. In fact, he didn't say anything at all.

"It's Carolyn," Joleen said, with a note of furious triumph. "You're fooling around with Carolyn Simmons. *Again.* Did you think I wouldn't find out, Brody? I have eyes all over this town!"

"I'm not 'fooling around' with any-body—not that it would be any of your business if I were. The point is, *you're not staying here,* Joleen, tonight or any other night, and since you've already been here too long, I'd really appreciate it if you'd get out."

Her lower lip wobbled, and her eyes narrowed to mean slits. "You *bastard,*" she said. "You've been *using* me, all this time, and now that your fancy house is almost ready to live in, and you're plan-ning on settling down with a wife, hav-ing some kids, *starting a life,* you have the nerve to throw me over for that— that movie star's *castoff?*"

Brody went around Joleen, pulled open the door, was grateful for the cool breeze that blew in from outside. His temper was at flash point.

"Get out," he said.

Joleen crossed the threshold with her suitcase, stood with stiff pride on the step and glared back at Brody over one shoulder. "If my car runs out of gas and I get murdered by some serial killer be-cause I'm forced to walk in these shoes, *in the dark,* it will be *your fault,* Brody Creed."

"You have a cell phone," Brody reminded her. "And a hundred dollars of my money. If you get stranded on the road, call the auto club."

With that, he closed the door.

He heard Joleen give a furious, strangled scream of frustration on the other side.

But then she stomped away.

Her car door slammed again.

The motor started with a roar.

Brody flung a meaningful look at Barney, who was calm again, now that Hurricane Joleen had changed course.

She laid so much rubber getting out of there that Brody could smell burning tires, even through the closed door and the walls.

"I have always had a way with women," he told Barney.

Barney lay down, shut his eyes and dozed off.

Well, at least *somebody* would get some sleep that night, Brody thought.

*   *   *

Carolyn rooted through her closet the next morning until she found a breezy pink cotton sundress she'd made years ago, in one of her I-enjoy-being-a-girl moods.

The garment was wrinkled, from hanging for so long, and it could use freshening, too.

Carolyn took it downstairs to the laundry room, tossed it into the machine, added a little soap and set the washer to the gentle cycle, with cold water.

She had a date that night, after all, and even if Bill *had* said to dress casually, she wanted to look her best.

She nearly tripped over Winston, who had trailed her from upstairs.

"What?" she asked archly, meeting the cat's thoughtful amber gaze. "I *do* wear dresses sometimes, you know. Of course, this means I'll have to shave my legs—"

"Reoww," Winston said, stepping out of her path.

"I know," Carolyn replied. "It's a major bummer."

"Hello?" The voice was Tricia's, coming from the main part of the house, where the shop was. "Carolyn? Are you here?"

Carolyn crossed the kitchen and pushed open the door leading into the shop. "I'm here," she confirmed cheerfully, with a glance at the antique clock on Natty's front-room mantel. "And you're early. We don't open for another hour, remember?"

"Oh, we'd better open right now," Tricia said, stashing her purse under the counter and smiling at Winston, who went purring to greet her. "Primrose Sullivan called me while I was making breakfast. She wanted us to have a heads-up—seems she spotted three tourists' buses in the parking lot out at the Roadside Diner."

"Yikes," Carolyn said. There went a new batch of goats' milk soap. Then, speculatively, "Maybe they'll just go right on past."

"Nope," Tricia answered matter-of-factly, picking up the telephone receiver to check for voice mail. For a watermelon smuggler, she looked very businesslike, especially after she popped her reading glasses on and began scribbling down notes. "You know Primrose. She stopped and snagged one of the travelers and asked where they were headed. Ultimately, the casino up at Cripple Creek, but the next stop? Us. Primrose is rushing over with a few new pieces just in case there are some big spenders in the crowd."

Carolyn looked at her friend in wonder. How could she listen to voice mail, carry on a conversation *and* take down names and call-back numbers, all at the same time?

"Don't just stand there," Tricia commanded good-naturedly. "Thank heaven there were some deliveries from our suppliers yesterday afternoon, so we'll be able to stock the shelves properly. I had Conner stack the boxes in the small parlor."

Said parlor stood just to the left of the front door.

Carolyn hurried in that direction and, when she got there, immediately started ripping open cartons. She and Tricia sold handcrafted items from all over the

United States, made by talented people they usually referred to as "cottage industrialists."

Today, there were chenille bedroom slippers in one box, and Victorian tea cozies in another.

Tricia arrived to help, unpacking exquisitely made art dolls, personal journals and all manner of scented bath salts.

Primrose showed up with a pair of canvases, both mixed-media abstracts in colors that roused a yearning in Carolyn.

"Oh, Primrose," Tricia said, stopping to look at the pictures. "Those are *lovely.*"

Primrose, bespectacled, with gray curly hair and owner of the largest and most colorful collection of muumuus that side of Hawaii, beamed with pleasure. "They're not batiks, like the Weaver, but—"

"They'll be sold in no time," Carolyn said, almost sadly.

Tricia and Primrose both looked at her with curious concern, but neither one commented.

For the next twenty minutes, which

was all the time they had before the first of the three jam-packed buses pulled up outside, the three women were far too busy to chat.

CHAPTER ELEVEN

By the time the third tour bus pulled away, an hour and a half later, Carolyn and Tricia were so low on merchandise that they had to close the shop in order to regroup.

Primrose's two new works of art had been sold immediately, as had the last of the aprons, the most recent batch of goats' milk soap and the contents of most of the boxes they'd unpacked earlier.

"That was *incredible*," Tricia marveled, sitting wearily at the table in the downstairs kitchen, a cup of tea steaming in front of her. "Like a plague of locusts, but in a good way."

"Beyond incredible," Carolyn agreed happily. "Of course, we still have to pay all our consignment people, cover basic expenses and all that, but—drum roll, please—*we definitely turned a profit!*" She'd just taken her pink dress out of the washer and was about to hang it outside, on the clothesline.

Tricia was focused on the dress. "That's pretty," she said. "Is there a special occasion coming up?"

Pleased, Carolyn nodded. "I have a date tonight," she confided.

Interest sparked, Tricia asked hopefully, "With Brody?"

Carolyn paused at the back door, shook her head. "Brody and I are going out Saturday night," she said, blushing a little.

Tricia's face lit up. "Really?"

"It's only dinner and a movie," Carolyn said. Then, with a gesture of one hand that meant "hold on a moment," she dashed outside, pegged her sundress carefully to the line and drew in a breath of that thin high-country air, full of blue sky and budding flowers and freshly cut grass.

When she returned to Natty's kitchen, Tricia went right on, as though there had been no interruption in the conversation. "But you *are* going out with Brody?"

Carolyn got out a cup and poured tea into it from the china pot on the counter. Sat down at the table, across from Tricia.

"We have ground rules," she said, treading carefully. *"Responsibilities."*

"Who does?" Tricia asked, raising one eyebrow.

"Brody and I. For one thing, we have agreed not to have sex."

Tricia twinkled as she smiled. "Is that a ground rule or a responsibility?" she teased.

Carolyn made a face at her.

Tricia laughed. "And tonight?"

"Bill invited me over to his place for a barbecue," she said.

"Bill?" Tricia pretended to muse over the name. "That would be Mr. Coffee, right? The death-defying firefighting pilot?"

Carolyn sighed. "Yes," she said.

"Does Brody know?"

"He does."

"I love it," Tricia enthused. "My brother-in-law must be beside himself."

"He was actually pretty unconcerned," Carolyn recalled, concerned.

"Maybe he wanted you to *think* he was," Tricia said, with utter confidence in her own powers of discernment.

Carolyn wished she could be that sure of herself and her perceptions, but certainty didn't seem to be part of her personal makeup.

She stiffened, reminded of the original conversation with Brody, in Tricia and Conner's kitchen, when the whole situation had come dangerously close to circuit-blowing, spark-throwing over-load. "You didn't hear him setting his stupid ground rules," she said, revealing more than she'd ever intended by that statement.

"No sex?" Tricia asked, visibly battling back a laugh.

"*And* we can both see other people if we want to."

Tricia's expression changed in an instant. "Brody said that?"

Carolyn nodded.

"That stinker," Tricia muttered.

Carolyn peered at her in a don't-stop-there kind of way. "If you know something I don't, Tricia Creed, you'd better tell me," she challenged.

"There's probably no connection," Tricia said.

"Spill it," Carolyn persisted, her tea entirely forgotten.

"Well," Tricia replied, squirming a little, "Joleen is back in town, that's all."

Joleen is back in town—*that's all?*

Although she knew she had no right to bristle at this news, Carolyn did indeed bristle. Like a porcupine.

Tricia smiled again and reached over to pat Carolyn's hand. "I'm sure one thing has nothing to do with the other," she said.

Carolyn just looked at her.

"Joleen grew up in Lonesome Bend," Tricia explained quickly. "Her family is here. I'm sure that's the reason she came back—and you know she never stays around for long."

"I should have known what he was up

to," Carolyn said. "In fact, I *did* know, but I chose the luxury of denial."

This time, it was Tricia who didn't respond. She seemed to be at a complete loss for words.

"Brody knew Joleen was on her way," Carolyn went on. *"That's* why he said what he did about both of us seeing other people. I wonder if *he and Joleen* have set any ground rules? No sex? I doubt it!"

Tricia looked pained. "Carolyn—"

"If that's the way Brody wants to play the game," Carolyn interrupted, *"fine."* She pushed back her chair, stood up again. "As a matter of fact," she continued, "I think I'll go upstairs, log on to my laptop and check my mailbox at Friendly Faces."

"Carolyn, you shouldn't— Brody wouldn't—" She fell silent, after uttering a long sigh, and covered her face with both hands.

Carolyn left her friend sitting at the table and practically sprinted toward the inside staircase.

She was behaving like a crazy person, she knew that.

It was just that knowing didn't seem to make much difference.

While the laptop booted up—it was old and therefore slow—Carolyn paced back and forth across the kitchen. Winston, meowing, kept weaving his way back and forth between her feet.

She finally sank into the chair in front of her desk to wait for the computer to grind through all its mysterious electronic sequences. Better to sit down than to squash the cat, or trip over the fool critter and break her neck.

Spookily, the Friendly Faces website opened on its own.

Carolyn's eyes widened. The mailbox icon—a yellow one, rural-style, with a red flag—pulsed like a heart. Cartoon letters spewed from its opening in bursts like erupting fireworks.

She drew a deep breath, let it out slowly and clicked on the mailbox.

Robert, from Telluride.

Buck, from Colorado Springs.

Sam, from Aspen.

All in all, there were an astounding forty-three messages.

Rattled, Carolyn looked down at Winston, who was now sitting on the floor next to her chair, as attentive as ever.

"It wasn't even a very good picture of me," she complained to him.

Downstairs, she could hear Tricia moving around Natty's kitchen.

Carolyn sighed, got up from her chair and went back down to find her friend.

"I'm sorry," she said, from the kitchen doorway. "For the way I acted just now, I mean."

Tricia, having washed their tea cups and set them in the drainer to dry, turned to smile at her. "Breathe, Carolyn. Everything will be all right."

Carolyn hunched one shoulder, let it fall again. "I have forty-three messages on my Friendly Faces page," she said weakly. "*Forty-three.* Tricia, what am I going to do?"

"Read them?" Tricia asked mildly, re-hanging the hand towel she'd just used. "Answer some and delete others?" She pressed her hands to her back, stretched contentedly. "It's an embarrassment of riches, Carolyn. *Enjoy* it. You might meet the perfect man for you." A pause, accompanied by another smile. "Of course, there are those among us who believe you already *have* met the perfect man for you and can't bring yourself to admit it."

"What do you want from me?" Carolyn asked, in a burst of friendly frustration. "I'm going out with Brody on Saturday—against my better judgment, I might add."

Tricia's eyes danced. "Ah-ha," she said.

"I didn't name names, Tricia," Carolyn pointed out. "I didn't say *Brody* was the perfect man for me. If there even *is* such an animal."

"I didn't name names, either," Tricia said, her tone sunny. "Interesting that you made the leap, though. From *perfect man* to *Brody*."

"Stop it," Carolyn said. "Nobody made any *leaps* here."

"Whatever you say," Tricia replied, heading for the shop. Taking a sheaf of receipts from the drawer of the cash register, she waggled them at Carolyn. "I'll do the books this time," she said. "Do you want me to order more goats' milk soap? And those beeswax candles went fast, too, especially for this time of year—"

Carolyn felt a surge of affection for her friend. "It's a lot of paperwork, Tricia. It might take all evening—"

Tricia extracted her purse from under the counter and shouldered it on, like one of those old-fashioned plow harnesses. "Carolyn," she said, "it's the least I can do. Aren't you always sewing aprons and filling orders from our website? Excuse me, but even *you* can't do everything."

With that, she waddled over, kissed Carolyn on the cheek, bid Winston a fond farewell and headed for the back door.

Carolyn followed her.

The pink dress looked like a swath of cotton candy, billowing in the fresh breeze.

"What am I supposed to do for a whole afternoon, if you're taking all the work home with you?" Carolyn called, as her friend opened the door of her Pathfinder to get behind the wheel.

"Get ready for your date?" Tricia responded merrily. "Soak in a bubble bath.

Give yourself a facial. Take a nap. You're an intelligent woman—you'll think of something."

Carolyn wanted to offer a parting protest, but she didn't have one ready.

There were, however, plenty of things to keep her occupied for the rest of the afternoon, she soon realized, even without Tricia's decadent suggestions.

She could work on the gypsy skirt.

She could make more frilly aprons, with zigzag trim and ruffles.

She could deal with all those emails in her Friendly Faces box.

She could even shave her legs.

"So," Conner said, as he and Brody and Davis hoisted a sick calf off the ground and into the bed of one of the work trucks, "I hear Joleen blew back into town last night."

Once upon a time, Joleen had been a sore subject—a *real* sore subject—between the brothers. Now she was just another way for Conner to get under Brody's hide. He couldn't seem to go more than fifteen minutes without making the attempt.

"Is that right?" Brody asked, dusting his hands off on the thighs of his jeans. "I hadn't heard."

The mama cow was bawling her head off, worried over her baby being hauled away. Davis patted her flank and said, "We'll fix your little one up for you, Bessie. Good as new."

The range cattle didn't have names, as such, but Davis called all cows Bessie, and all bulls Ferdinand.

Conner cocked a grin at Brody as he stepped up onto the running board of the pickup, about to get behind the wheel. "You're a pretty bad liar for somebody with a rascal's history," he joked. "Word is, Joleen went straight to your place and you threw her out with a hundred dollars and a speech about taking the moral high road."

"Drive slow," Davis advised, hoisting himself up onto the tail gate to ride with the calf. "Bessie here will be following after us, and I don't want her worn out from trying to keep up."

Conner nodded—he'd been through this process many times, and so had

Brody and Davis—and Brody got in on the passenger side.

"Small-town gossip is one of the few things I *didn't* miss while I was away from Lonesome Bend," Brody said immediately.

Conner chuckled, checked the rear-view mirror to make sure Davis was ready to roll and put the truck in gear. "Folks talk about you," he said. "It means they care, that's all."

"It *means*, little brother, that they have small minds and too much free time."

That made Conner laugh.

Bessie ambled behind them, still carrying on like a sinner on his first day in hell. Even over the roar of that old truck's old engine, she was audible.

Back at the barn, they'd settle Bessie and the calf in a stall, keep an eye on the little one for a day or two, bring the vet if necessary. They'd found the calf lying with his head downhill, probably suffering from sunstroke and mild dehydration, but the worst danger—being vulnerable to predators—was over.

Usually in these cases, a little TLC did the trick.

Bessie and her baby boy would be back out on the range, with the rest of the herd, in no time.

All of a sudden, his jocular mood vanished, and Conner turned serious as all get-out. "Be careful, Brody," he said. "Carolyn is a good woman, and she's had a hard row to hoe almost since the day she was born. It wouldn't be right to hurt her."

Again.

Conner hadn't actually said the word, but it hung in the air between them.

"You think I *want* to hurt her?" Brody asked, nettled. He shifted around on the seat, which was cracked leather, with springs and stuffing showing in places. Davis believed in using equipment until it disintegrated back to the particle state.

"I didn't say that," Conner replied, shifting again. "Didn't mean to imply it, either."

Brody heaved a sigh. "I know," he said. "Maybe I'm a little touchy when it comes to Joleen. She's got some wild hair about my being involved with Carolyn, and I'm afraid she's going to make trouble."

"Did she say she would?"

"In so many words," Brody answered wearily, "yes."

Conner considered for a while before asking, "Are you, Brody? Involved with Carolyn, I mean?"

Brody glanced over at his brother, at the profile so remarkably like his own that he might have been looking into a mirror. "Let's just say I'd *like* to be," he finally said. "But she doesn't trust me, and I can't blame her for that."

"Amen," Conner agreed.

They were quiet for a while, except for the truck engine and old Bessie.

"What did you mean before," Brody ventured, "when you said Carolyn has had a hard time from when she was little?"

Conner was silent for so long that Brody didn't think he was going to answer. "She grew up in foster homes," he said. "There are a lot of good ones out there, caring people trying to make a difference in kids' lives, but there are also a few whose hearts just aren't in it. From what Kim and Tricia have told me,

Carolyn got more than her share of the second variety."

Brody pictured Carolyn as a skinny, coltish little girl, tall for her age, with freckles and clothes either handed down or bought cheap, probably smarter by half than the other kids in her class, and the image bruised the underside of his heart. The secondary emotion, though, was anger.

"Was she abused?"

"More like neglected, from what I gather. And then there was the thing with that movie star, after you left."

Something quickened inside Brody at the reminder. What had Joleen called Carolyn last night?

A movie star's castoff.

"What happened?" Brody asked carefully. The barn was in sight now; soon, poor Bessie could relax, and the calf could start recovering from whatever ailed it.

And that god-awful caterwauling would stop.

"Don't know," Conner said, turning his head long enough to give Brody the kind of level look that always meant he was telling the truth. "There were lots of rumors flying around at the time, of course. Carolyn was the live-in nanny, and some people said she was having an affair with Gifford Welsh while his wife was away on some movie set."

Brody's back molars clamped together, unclamped again. As the lifelong resident of a glass house, he couldn't go around throwing stones, but it galled him, just the same, to think of another man—*any* other man—touching Carolyn in all the intimate ways he once had.

And wanted to again.

"If you had to hazard a guess as to whether or not the gossips had it right," he began, watching Conner, who was watching the bumpy range trail by then, "what would you say?"

Again, Conner was thoughtful. He liked to take his time when he answered a question, especially one he considered important. "I'd say," he finally replied, "that Carolyn wouldn't take up with a married man, and not just because she'd figure it to be wrong. She's got too much pride for that."

Brody laughed, out of relief and not

because anything was funny, and reached over to clasp his brother briefly by the nape and give him a good, squeezing shake.

"Bull's-eye," he said. "Give the man a Kewpie doll."

"A what?" Conner asked, with a frown that made Brody laugh again. And this time, it *was* funny.

"Figure of speech, little brother," he said, when his amusement had ebbed away a bit. "Back in the day, when somebody won a prize at a carnival booth, they'd get a Kewpie doll."

"Whatever," Conner said, comically indignant.

By then, they were home, with the task of unloading the sick calf before them, and poor Bessie panting and huffing from the exercise.

"Everything will be all right now, girl," Brody heard his uncle tell the cow. "Your baby is safe, and so are you."

Legs shaven, hair clean, Carolyn stepped out of the shower and wrapped herself in a towel.

Winston sat on the lid of the toilet,

waiting for her to emerge from what probably seemed, to him, to be a chamber of horrors.

"See?" Carolyn said, patting his head. "It *is* possible to get wet and survive."

"Reow," Winston objected, and leaped down off the commode, tail fluffed out in annoyance. The top of his head was damp where she'd touched him.

Carolyn laughed. "Okay," she said, waiting for the fogged-up mirror over the sink to clear up so she could apply moisturizer. The makeup—she didn't plan on wearing much—could wait. "That's two things off the predate checklist. Legs shaved, hair washed. Now, for the facial."

She opened the medicine cabinet and peered inside.

A box of stick-on bandages. A bottle of mouthwash, nearly empty. Toothpaste, a brush, a box of cotton swabs and three tampons trying to escape from their paper wrappers.

Not one single component of a facial. Oh, *well.*

That left the nap.

Carolyn left the mirror to defog on its

own and went into her bedroom. Flung herself down on the bed and lay there, spread-eagle.

Nope.

Sleep was not going to happen.

She was too keyed up to get any shut-eye and, anyway, it was the middle of the day.

And it was too early to take the pink dress from the clothesline, give it a quick spritz of spray starch and a few licks with a hot iron.

She arose, with a sigh, and put on her bathrobe, but that was too warm, so she replaced it with an oversize T-shirt.

For now, that would have to do.

Carolyn took the gypsy skirt down from its hook on her bedroom door and held it out for inspection. She'd expected to be over wanting to keep it by now, but she definitely was not over it.

She could fit it to her own dimensions in a trice, but that was beside the point. The skirt definitely would not work at a backyard barbecue—or when Brody took her out on Saturday night, either.

There was only one movie theater in that part of the county, and it was in the next town, Wiley Springs. The nearest fancy restaurant, where one might presumably wear a magical concoction of ribbons and beads, was just outside of Denver.

Carolyn put the skirt back on its hook, suddenly dispirited. She'd planned to fuss with it a little, but now the prospect had zero appeal.

There were always the aprons. They could barely keep up with the demand.

Yee-haw, she thought sourly. Aprons.

Carolyn decided to give the nap another shot.

This time, it worked.

When she woke up to the cold, nuzzling nose of a cat wanting his supper, it was after five o'clock.

Hurriedly, Carolyn doled out Winston's sardine ration, then rushed downstairs, still in the T-shirt, to collect the pink dress from the clothesline.

The smell of the fabric was delicious.

Back upstairs, she wielded the iron, keeping one eye on the kitchen clock the whole time, and then went into the bathroom to put on mascara, minimal foundation and lip gloss to match the dress.

Since she'd gone to sleep with her hair still damp from the shower, it stood out around her head like the mane of a lion named Frizzy, and bringing it under control practically called for a whip and a chair.

Pinned into a loose knot at the back of her head, it looked passably good, Carolyn decided. Although there might well be wide-spread injuries if it escaped its pins at an inopportune moment.

"Now you're just being silly," Carolyn told her reflection, in the fog-free mirror. "Get a grip, okay?"

Carolyn's reflection looked indignant.

"Well," Carolyn told the familiar image, "it's your own fault for not blow drying before you took your nap."

"Reow," said Winston, now sitting in the bathroom doorway, licking his chops.

Nothing like a good sardine.

Carolyn laughed, at the cat and at herself.

She was going to a barbecue in Bill Venable's backyard. His late wife's par-

ents would be there, along with his nine-
year-old daughter.

What was there to be nervous about?

Plenty, as it turned out.

When Carolyn pulled up in front of
Bill's very nice house, in her very old
car, a child who had to be Ellie was waiting on the sidewalk.

With a big sign, hand-lettered in colorful markers and stapled to a stick.

It read "Go Away. We Don't Want You
Here Unless You're Angela."

The greeting gave Carolyn pause, of
course, and so did the glower on the
child's face. She was as pretty, this kid,
as a Victorian rendering of *Alice in Wonderland*.

And if looks could kill, Carolyn would
have been incinerated on the spot.

She was debating—go or stay—when
Bill suddenly appeared, bursting through
the front gate and gently but firmly taking the sign from Ellie's hands before
pointing a stern index finger toward the
house.

Ellie obeyed, shuffling her feet, her
head lowered.

Bill tossed the sign into the yard, summoned up a sporting smile and approached Carolyn, opening the car door for her.

"Maybe this isn't a good idea," Carolyn fretted. Despite the child's behavior, she'd taken an instant liking to Ellie. The munchkin definitely had spirit.

"Nonsense," Bill said. "It's a *great* idea. Come along—the steaks are on the grill, and I want to introduce you to Ellie's grandparents, Charlie and Stella. They're excited to meet you."

Privately, Carolyn doubted that. Most likely, Charlie and Stella were Angela supporters, like Ellie. They, being grownups, would just be a bit more subtle about it, that was all.

"I don't know—"

"Carolyn," Bill said, smiling, "it's *supper,* not the coronation of King William."

Carolyn laughed, reminded of how much she liked this man.

If only she could muster up something more.

Bill offered his hand. "Let's go," he said quietly. "I promise you, Ellie isn't a monster. She just acts like one sometimes."

"Don't we all," Carolyn responded, her smile genuine now, comfortable on her face.

Bill led her around the side of the big house and into a wonderful, shady backyard, with flowers and an arbor and a swinging bench.

Charlie and Stella were both attractive, a well-matched couple in their sixties. As Bill and Carolyn approached, Charlie, a big man with a full head of snow-white hair, rose from his seat on the bench at the picnic table. Stella, also white-haired, looked like a slender pixie, and her smile was warm.

Bill made the introductions and, once Carolyn was settled at the picnic table, with a glass of fresh lemonade, excused himself to duck into the house, presumably to deal with Ellie.

Stella, seated beside her handsome husband, watched Bill disappear through the back door, a wistful smile lingering on her lips but not quite reaching her eyes. "I take it our granddaughter has been acting up again," she remarked.

Carolyn chuckled, took a sip of the tasty lemonade and set her glass down on the red-and-white checked oilcloth covering the top of the picnic table. "She certainly doesn't lack for imagination," she replied.

Charlie raised bristly white eyebrows. "What happened?"

Carolyn hesitated, then described the sign incident.

"Oh, dear," Stella breathed.

"It might have been an imaginative thing to do," Charlie began, "but it was also rude. Bill needs to stop fooling around and get married again, give that child a mother to guide her before she turns into a complete mess."

Stella elbowed him in the ribs. "Charlie!" she scolded, but there was so much love in her voice that Carolyn choked up a little, just hearing it. What a beautiful thing it was, the two of them growing older together, and still frisky.

Charlie ignored his wife, but his love for Stella, like hers for him, was clearly visible to Carolyn, who was feeling oddly detached from the scene now, an observer, not really part of things.

"Don't get me wrong," Charlie went on, quietly earnest. "We love our granddaughter. Ellie's a force of nature—the spitting image of her mother, our daughter, Connie—and we wouldn't want to see her change too much." He paused, sighed. "However, it *will* be a relief when the brat phase passes."

"Ellie," Stella said firmly, "is *not* a brat."

At that, the screen door swung open, and the little sign-bearer stepped out onto the back porch, looking like a recalcitrant angel in her pink cotton shorts, matching top and purple flip-flops.

Bill, standing behind her, gave her a little nudge to the shoulder. "March," Carolyn heard him say.

Ellie sucked in a dramatic breath and let it out as a huge and wobbly sigh. She looked back at Bill.

Bill gave a brief nod, part encouragement, part impatience.

Carolyn, looking on, felt another sweet stab of affection for little Ellie Venable.

Stalwartly, Ellie faced forward again, high-stepped it down the porch stairs and walked over to stand near the picnic table, next to Carolyn.

Putting out one small and probably sticky hand, the child said, with an utter lack of conviction, "I'm sorry for being impolite. After all, you can't help it if you're not Angela."

Muted groans from the other adults greeted this pronouncement.

But Carolyn merely smiled and took the small hand, shook it. Sure enough, it was sticky.

"You're right," she replied, after a moment, "I have my hands pretty full just being *Carolyn* these days."

Ellie narrowed crystalline blue eyes, studying Carolyn. "Are you willing to start over?" she asked.

Carolyn was struck by the wisdom of that question, especially coming from a nine-year-old. "I'd like that," she said.

The little girl indicated that she wanted to sit down, and Carolyn scooted over to make room.

"My dad says when I grow up, I'm either going to be the first woman president or the head of my cell block," Ellie said, quite seriously. The tiniest smile peeked out from the clouds of caution veiling that lovely little face, and she dropped her voice. "My dad kids a lot.

He doesn't *really* expect me to wind up in prison."

"I don't know, kiddo," Charlie teased, grinning at his grandchild from the opposite side of the picnic table. "It seems to me that you're developing criminal tendencies."

"My grandpa makes jokes, too," Ellie confided to Carolyn.

"I *am* a retired cop," Charlie insisted, with a twinkle, picking up the lemonade pitcher and pouring a glassful for Ellie. "I know a troublemaker when I see one."

"All you have to do is look in the mirror," Stella supplied, singsonging the words and, at the same time, beaming at Ellie like a golden sunrise. "You'll be *president,*" she told the child, without a hint of doubt.

"I'm not sure I'd want the job," Ellie replied, with the solemnity of a very intelligent and precocious child. "No matter what the president does, somebody pitches a fit about it. I'd rather fly airplanes and put out big fires that cover whole states, like Dad does."

Bill, who had been turning steaks on the grill until then, joined the others at the table, sitting at Carolyn's right, not too close, but not too far away, either.

Yet again, Carolyn silently lamented her lack of passion where he was concerned. Why couldn't she have these brotherly feelings toward *Brody,* and want Bill with an intensity that was getting harder and harder to deny with every breath she drew?

It was *perverse,* that was what it was.

She did enjoy the remainder of the evening, though. The steaks were delicious, Bill was attentive without coming on too strong, Charlie and Stella were chatty and cordial, without asking any questions more intrusive than, "Did you grow up in Lonesome Bend, Carolyn?"

Even Ellie warmed up considerably, though it was clear that she still had her reservations about her father's new friend.

When the air got chilly and the mosquitoes came out, it was generally agreed that the party was over.

Carolyn offered to help clear the table and carry in the leftovers and the dirty dishes, but Stella and Charlie insisted that this was their job. Ellie could be their assistant.

Bill walked Carolyn back to her car, stood on the sidewalk looking down at her with an expression of friendly regret in his eyes.

"This airplane isn't going to lift off the runway, is it?" he asked.

Carolyn sighed, smiled up at him and shook her head. "No," she said. "I don't think so."

"Can we still be friends?" Bill wanted to know. "Because here's the thing, Carolyn Simmons—I really *like* you."

"I like you, too," Carolyn said truthfully.

He lowered his head then, and brushed his lips lightly against hers, but there was no charge.

Both of them sighed in resignation.

"I had to try," Bill told her, smiling when she laughed.

"I understand," Carolyn replied, feeling sad but kind of relieved, too. "Did you mean what you said just now, about our still being friends?"

"I meant it, all right," he said.

Carolyn rocked back on her heels

slightly, something she did when she was thinking. "It would have to be take-out food or something," she mused, "because I don't cook very well. But I'd love it if you'd come over to my place for dinner one night soon."

Bill's expression was one of pleased surprise. "Sounds good," he said. "But if we're not going anywhere, the two of us—?"

Carolyn's smile broadened. "If we're not going anywhere," she finished for him, "we can relax and have fun."

"I like that idea," Bill said. "How would you feel about taking a spin in my airplane?"

CHAPTER TWELVE

"I'm going to be a little late getting to the ranch today," Brody said into his cell phone.

"What else is new?" Conner retorted from his end of the call, but there was a grin lurking in his voice. "You're about *ten years* late already, not that I've been keeping track or anything."

"Of course you haven't," Brody said wryly. He stood outside the old snackbar/projection house at the Bluebird Drive-in that sunny May morning, watched as his contractor and another member of the crew unloaded the gas-powered generator that would, hope-fully, provide the necessary juice to run the movie on Saturday night.

The original projector was useless; over the years, it had been converted to a mouse-and-spider condominium com-plex. Brody had rented the necessary equipment from an outfit in Denver, and a friend of his, a film distributor by pro-fession, was overnighting a couple of first-run movies. An electrician was due any minute to check the antiquated speaker boxes, on their rusty poles, and run a line out to whichever one worked best.

If *any* of them worked.

Inwardly, Brody sighed.

"Brody?" Conner prompted. "Usually, when people are on the phone, they *talk* to each other."

Brody chuckled. "Yeah," he agreed. "Guess that's an indication that the call is over. I've said my piece, and I have things to do."

"What things?" Conner wanted to know. Usually the classic man of few words, impatient with telephones, he was being downright chatty.

"Who pulled your string?" Brody countered, giving the contractor and his helper a thumbs-up when they were ready to set the generator down.

Conner sighed. "It's like you to be late," he said. "It *isn't* like you to call and explain. What's going on, Brody?"

"It's none of your business, little brother," Brody replied affably, "but I'll tell you anyway. I'm getting ready for a big date."

Silence.

Now it was Brody's turn to do the prompting. "Conner? You still there?"

"I'm here," Conner said. "What *kind* of 'big date,' Brody?"

"How many kinds are there?" Brody countered, amused.

Conner didn't say anything right away, but the two-way twin radar was functioning just fine, and Brody knew what he was thinking.

"I'll tell you all about it later," Brody assured his brother. "Provided you don't keep me on this damn phone all day, that is. In that case, I'll be rolling out there sometime tomorrow."

Conner broke down and gave a raspy

chuckle then. "See you when I see you," he said. "Davis and I will be on the range for most of the morning, rounding up strays, if you want to look us up."

Brody grinned. "*Goodbye,* Conner," he said pointedly, before shutting down the call. They'd had their share of long conversations, he and Conner, back when they were boys, yammering on about everything from girls and fishing tackle to what their lives might have been like if their folks had lived to raise them.

They'd traveled their own separate broken roads for a long time after that, though, and, and despite all the progress they'd made, opening up to each other still took an effort.

Maybe, Brody thought, his throat tightening even as his spirits rose, the worst was over, and those winding roads were finally going to converge.

Carolyn had the shop all to herself that morning, except for Winston, of course. Tricia was at home resting. Over the phone earlier, she'd insisted she felt fine, and there was nothing to worry about—

it was just that her ankles were swollen, she felt like an elephant and she was *so tired.*

Carolyn couldn't help worrying, at least a little bit, because Tricia was her friend, but she kept herself busy, and that helped.

Not that there were a lot of customers, because there weren't.

Primrose brought in more art pieces—she apparently had a stockpile of them stashed in her home studio—and she and Carolyn decided on prices and hung the series of small batiks, all featuring Native American women, on one wall of the shop.

After Primrose had gone, Carolyn took digital pictures of the arrangement and posted the best images on the website, since a lot of their business came via the internet.

More boxes full of merchandise were delivered, thankfully, and Carolyn made the necessary changes to the inventory list she and Tricia kept on the downstairs computer, ignoring the pesky little blitzes from Friendly Faces—*somebody likes your picture!*—as best she could, given how intrusive they were.

Once that was done, and the items had been tagged with prices and set out on shelves and display tables, it was lunchtime.

Upstairs, in her apartment kitchen, Carolyn shared a couple of hard-boiled eggs with Winston and contemplated the long afternoon that lay ahead. To be followed, alas, by an even *longer* evening.

Determined to make good use of what would otherwise be idle time—she didn't want to close the shop early again that day, lest it become a habit—Carolyn lugged her portable sewing machine downstairs and set it up on one of the display tables. She carted down stacks of fabric next, along with various sewing notions, and settled in to run up a new supply of aprons.

Two local women came in around 3:00 p.m., looking for birthday gifts for a friend, and bought up the pair of aprons Carolyn had just finished making, sending her happily back to square one.

It looked like the rush was over, as far

as customers were concerned, and Carolyn, with tiny threads stuck to her clothes and eye strain setting in, decided four-thirty wasn't too early to close.

She was at the door, in fact, just about to turn the dead bolt, when she saw someone step up onto the porch, hesitate and then reach for the knob.

Carolyn swung the door open, never one to turn away a potential sale, and nearly gasped.

The woman standing on the other side of the threshold was about her own age, and outlandishly beautiful, with copper-blond hair and striking brown eyes. Except for her modern clothing, a trim tan pantsuit, she might have stepped out of a Renaissance painting, she was that regal.

Instantly, Carolyn knew who she was.

"Angela?" she said, stepping back and holding the door open wide.

"How did you know?" Angela asked, after a short and rather nervous nod of acknowledgment.

"Wild guess," Carolyn said, with a smile. "Come in."

"I—I didn't really come here to shop. I just wanted—"

Carolyn touched the woman's arm. "Come in," she repeated. "I'll make tea."

Angela finally stepped into the entryway, and was instantly greeted by a purring Winston.

The Botticelli face lit up, and she bent to pet the cat. "Hello, there," she said.

Winston, the diplomat, Carolyn thought, with a tender twist to her heart. Except when it came to Brody, the animal was a one-cat welcoming committee.

"This way," Carolyn said, and moved through the entryway, then through the shop and into Natty's big kitchen.

Angela followed, politely reluctant. She was probably wondering what had possessed her to drop in on the woman Bill Venable was dating, though she gave no outward indication of that.

Carolyn liked to brew tea the old-fashioned way, especially when she had guests, and she warmed the china pot with hot water while putting the kettle on the stove to boil, got out the canister of fresh tea leaves.

Angela, meanwhile, took a seat at the table.

"I'm so sorry," she said, after long consideration and a shake of her head. She wore her hair in a tidy, upswept style, accented with a braid across her crown. That probably accounted for the Renaissance look. "I never do things like this."

"Things like what?" Carolyn asked, determined to put her visitor at ease.

"I needed to see what you look like," Angela confessed, in a little burst of self-exasperation.

Carolyn laughed softly, mindful of her blue jeans, baggy T-shirt and the coating of tiny threads clinging to her clothes and probably her hair, too. She spread her hands, while waiting for the tea water to boil, and joked, "Here I am. Are you impressed?"

A little smile flicked at one corner of Angela's Cupid's-bow mouth, but her eyes were sad. "Actually," she said, "yes. I *am* impressed."

Carolyn didn't know what to say to that—"thank you" wouldn't sound right—so she went to the breakfront, another of Natty's belongings, passed down to Tricia, and took out china cups and saucers. Silver teaspoons. And where were the sugar bowl and the little milk pitcher?

"I shouldn't have come here," Angela said.

The teakettle began to wobble on the burner.

Carolyn crossed to the table and sat down across from Angela. Trying to project friendly receptivity, she simply waited for the other woman to speak again.

Tears swam in Angela's eyes, but she quickly blinked them back.

Ah, Carolyn thought, *another tough cookie, like me, holding it together.*

"Bill has a perfect right to go out with other women," Angela announced.

Carolyn let her mouth quirk at one corner, but held her peace. The ball was, after all, still in Angela's court.

"Do you like him?" Angela's voice was small now, almost timid.

"Yes," Carolyn said. *Not in the way you think, but, yes, I definitely like Bill Venable. I like him a lot.*

Angela gave a little sigh. "Help me out, here," she said, her eyes glistening again. "Please?"

"What do you want to know, Angela?"

The teakettle came to a whistling boil. Great timing.

Carolyn hurried to the stove, took the kettle off the heat and poured hot water into the china pot, over the waiting leaves of orange pekoe, left the works to steep for the requisite five minutes.

"Is it serious?" Angela asked. "Between you and Bill, I mean?"

Carolyn considered her answer carefully. Obviously, Angela cared for the man, whatever her reservations might be concerning his work as a flying firefighter, but this was dangerous ground.

She meant to tread lightly.

"I guess that depends on your definition of *serious*," she said, at last.

"I know I don't have any right to ask," Angela said, shaking her head and looking baffled, as if she just didn't understand herself sometimes.

God knew, Carolyn could relate to *that* feeling.

"I like Bill," she reiterated, albeit gently, "but I wouldn't feel right trying to explain *his* feelings. If you have questions, Angela, you need to ask him."

Angela was quiet, thoughtful. But, thank heaven, no longer tearful.

Carolyn brought the teapot to the table, giving her unexpected company a few moments to collect herself. She poured for Angela, then for herself and shushed Winston, who was lobbying for his sardine ration. Not trusting the milk she had on hand, she retrieved the sugar bowl but not the matching creamer.

Angela, somewhat recovered, actually smiled—and went from beautiful to dazzling. "Ellie was right," she said. "You're a 'nice lady,' Carolyn."

"I try," Carolyn said, spooning sugar into her tea. Silver rattled against the inside of her cup. And, of course, the conversation lagged. To get it going again, Carolyn added, "I hear you teach school."

"Third grade," Angela said, with pride.

"Is Ellie in your class?" Did nine-year-olds go to third grade? Carolyn couldn't recall.

Angela's hand trembled slightly as she lifted her teacup to her mouth, took a sip and shook her head, but she was more relaxed than before.

Not that that was saying a whole lot.

"She was last year," Angela replied. "That's how—" She paused to blush. "That's how Bill and I met. At a parent-teacher meeting."

"I see," Carolyn said.

Angela spoke reluctantly. "Did Bill tell you about me?"

"Yes," Carolyn answered, in a tone that said she'd go that far, but no further. As she'd told Angela before, if she wanted to know how Bill felt about her, she was going to have to ask *him.*

Angela sighed. "There I go again," she said. "You must think I'm on the short list for my own reality show—they could call it *The Real Crazies of Colorado.*"

Carolyn laughed. She liked Angela, hoped they might become friends at some point. "Do you like teaching?" she asked. "I used to want to be a teacher, once upon a time."

Again, Angela lit up. "I *love* teaching," she said. "Make that, I love *children.* The job itself can be really discouraging—the pay is bad, and the parents can be impossible. But the kids, well, they make it all worthwhile."

Carolyn had been blessed with several insightful, compassionate teachers while she was doing her best to grow up, and their kind guidance had made all the difference. They'd told her she was bright, and talented, and she could be anybody she wanted to be, if she was willing to put in the effort.

"What stopped you?" Angela asked, breaking into her thoughts, bringing her back to the here and now.

Carolyn must have looked puzzled, because Angela immediately clarified her question. "From being a teacher, I mean."

"I didn't go to college," Carolyn said, off the top of her head.

"Oh," Angela said, and took another sip from her elegant teacup. Now *she* was the one doing the waiting.

"Which means," Carolyn went on presently, "that I didn't want to teach badly enough to go the scholarship, student-loan route. When I did manage to take a few night courses, they were all design-related. Color theory. Perspective. Things like that."

"You're an artist?" Angela asked, with genuine interest.

"No," Carolyn hastened to say. "I sew a little, that's all."

She thought of the gypsy skirt, hanging on its hook upstairs, behind her bedroom door, and she felt a twinge of guilt, as though she'd been disloyal to a trusting friend.

"Sewing is an art," Angela said.

To Carolyn, sewing was a craft, not an art, but it was also sacred. There was no magic quite like making something useful and pretty from a bolt of cloth; for her, the process was almost mystical, a form of active prayer. "I guess for some people, that's true," she said. "I've seen some quilts that belong in museums."

Angela nodded in agreement. "I'd like to see something you've made," she said. Then she blushed. "I'm not good at sewing myself. I could never set a sleeve, or put in a zipper that didn't look as though it was the work of a chimpanzee."

Carolyn, smiling, thought of the aprons she'd been working on, but immediately dismissed the idea. She had the oddest desire to show Angela—a woman she barely knew—her masterpiece, the gypsy skirt. So far, only Tricia had seen it.

She bit her lower lip, thinking.

"I've overstepped," Angela said. "Again."

"Wait here," Carolyn told her, pushing back her chair. Before she could change her mind, she hurried upstairs, grabbed the skirt and brought it back down to Natty's kitchen.

Shyly, she held the garment up for Angela to look at.

Angela's eyes widened. "Oh, *my*," she said, setting her teacup in its saucer with a little rattle. "You *made* that?"

Now that she'd done the deed, Carolyn was suddenly flustered, even a little embarrassed. The skirt probably seemed gaudy, with all those shimmering beads and ribbons.

Oh, but the way they captured the light, those beads and ribbons. The sight made Carolyn's breath catch in her throat, just like always.

"It practically makes *music*," Angela said, with what sounded like wonder. She stood up, approached and examined the skirt carefully, though she was careful, Carolyn noticed, not to touch it.

It practically makes music.

Carolyn felt quietly joy-stricken by the comment.

"You *are* an artist," Angela pronounced, her voice taking on an insistent note now. "Do you take orders? For custom-made things, I mean?"

Carolyn was thrown by the question, which was really strange, considering that she'd been making clothing for other people since that first sewing class in high school. "I . . . yes, sometimes," she managed to reply.

"Of course, something like this would cost the earth," Angela said, looking thoughtful. She sighed. "But a girl can dream."

That remark sealed it. Friends. She and Angela were going to be *friends.*

And that was bound to complicate things.

"I know what you mean," Carolyn said. "I can't afford this skirt, either."

That made Angela laugh. "But you *made* it," she said, after a few moments. "You don't have to buy your own work."

Oh, yes, I do, Carolyn thought. "I need to recover the cost of supplies," she said, feeling very young all of a sudden, and very *poor.*

For Carolyn, that was a watershed moment. It was time to stop fiddling around with the skirt, finish it and put it up for sale. Holding on to the thing, wishing she had a place and a reason to wear it, was just a way of putting off the inevitable.

It was getting too painful.

"I guess you could make another one to keep for yourself," Angela said, faltering. She was reaching for her purse, preparing to leave.

Carolyn shook her head. "I couldn't duplicate it, even if I tried," she said, thinking how peculiar it was that Angela had come here to size up a rival, and Carolyn, famously independent, had ended up confiding in her.

A virtual stranger.

"I suppose not," Angela agreed sadly. "It's definitely one of a kind." She smiled. "Thank you for the tea, Carolyn, and for showing me this amazing work of art and, especially, for overlooking the fact that I acted like a maniac by coming here in the first place."

"I'm *glad* you stopped in," Carolyn said warmly, draping the skirt over the back of one of Natty's kitchen chairs, wishing there was more she could say, or do, to reassure Angela that things would work out for her and Bill.

Unfortunately, that might not be the case, given the impasse the two of them had reached over the perils of Bill's job.

"I think you really *are* glad I came over," Angela said, in good-natured surprise. "You're a hard woman to hate, Carolyn. I can see why Bill is taken with you—not that I like the idea."

Carolyn wished she could tell Angela that Bill loved her but loved his job, too, and wouldn't feel like himself without it. Since this would amount to a betrayal of Bill's confidence, though, she would do no such thing.

"I hope you won't work too terribly

hard at hating me," Carolyn said, with another smile, accompanying Angela as she started toward the front door.

Angela held her reply until they reached the entryway. "You'll be patient with Ellie?" she asked quietly. "She's a wonderful child, bright and funny and every other good thing. It's just that she had her heart set on Bill and me getting together."

Carolyn nodded. "Ellie," she agreed, "is a delight."

Angela opened the door, stepped over the threshold and onto the porch and would have gone down the steps and along the walk to the gate—her car was parked at the curb—except that Carolyn stopped her with a word.

"Angela?"

Angela paused, turned to look back at Carolyn. Waited.

"Talk to Bill," Carolyn said.

Angela's brow knitted with pretty puzzlement, and the nod she gave was hesitant. With that, she walked away.

Carolyn watched her for a few moments, then closed the door, turned the lock and returned to the kitchen.

It was time to serve up Winston's plate of sardines.

The calf they'd brought in off the range the day before was back on its feet, Brody was glad to see, when he and Barney arrived at the ranch a little after noon and headed straight for the barn.

"He's lookin' good," Brody said to Davis, after inspecting the calf in the stall it shared with Bessie. Conner was probably around somewhere, but he wasn't in sight at the moment.

Davis, having backed one of the ranch trucks in at the rear entrance to the barn, was standing in the bed of the pickup, about to start unloading sacks of horse feed. He grinned and gave Brody a thumbs-up. "Bessie and her boy will be ready to go back to the herd in another day or two," he said.

Brody approached the truck and reached in for a feed sack. The things weighed fifty pounds, and he didn't think Davis ought to be doing such heavy work at his advanced age, but he wasn't stupid enough to say as much. "Where's Conner?" he asked.

The unspoken subtext was, *And why isn't he out here helping unload this truck?*

"Tricia's feeling a mite flimsy," Davis replied, hoisting another bag and waiting to hand it down to Brody. "Conner's been checking on her at regular intervals. Truth is, he's probably driving her crazy, running in and out like that, but he's a Creed, after all, and that means you can't tell him a damn thing."

Brody took the second bag and stacked it in the storage room while Davis picked a new one up. "Tricia's all right, though?" he asked, worried.

"She told Kim she was fine, and we see no reason not to take her at her word," Davis replied. Then, probably not the least bit fooled by Brody's attempt to be casual, he added, "Pregnant women get tired, Brody. That doesn't mean they're ailing, or about to lose the baby. But Tricia's got a genuine human being taking shape inside her, and that takes some doing."

The past had a way of ambushing Brody when he least expected, and suddenly, his knees wanted to buckle and he felt as though he'd had the wind knocked out of him.

"Babies die, Davis," he told his uncle, without looking at him. "And so do their mothers."

Davis, in the process of handing down another sack of feed, stopped, gave a low whistle of exclamation through his teeth.

Barney, busy smelling every corner of the barn he could get to, paused at the sound, and trotted to Brody's side.

Brody acknowledged the dog with an ear-rub, but he looked up at Davis, who was standing motionless in the bed of the pickup, watching him.

"Can we just forget I said that?" Brody asked. He'd tried for levity, but the words came out sounding husky and a little raw, just the same.

"Nope," Davis replied, in his taciturn way, after climbing down out of the truck to stand facing Brody. "We can't."

"I'm not sure I'm ready to talk about this, Davis," Brody said.

Davis squeezed his shoulder briefly, then vaulted himself up to sit on the extended tailgate of the truck. "I'll wait," he said, with a kindly twinkle and a brief quirk of a grin.

Brody sighed, and then laughed. At least, he'd *meant* to laugh—the sound came out sounding like something else. "I wasn't born yesterday," he told his uncle grimly, and with another failed attempt at humor. "I know Conner told you and Kim about my wife—my *late* wife—and the baby boy we had together."

"Whatever Conner did or didn't say, he had the best of intentions," Davis replied, in the same deep, solid voice he'd used to tell three young boys they'd be all right when they'd scared the hell out of themselves watching rented horror movies for hours on end. After all that on-screen blood and gore, a summer thunderstorm or mice in the rafters had them instantly convinced that they were about to experience wholesale slaughter, right there in their ranch-house bedroom.

Davis had always been able to put those fears to rest, though, just by reminding them that he was right there, under the same roof. His presence was enough, though his words were a comfort, too. It went without saying that anything or anybody out to hurt any member of his family would have to get past Davis Creed first, and that would take an army or two.

These days, Brody's demons didn't come from any movie. They came from the hidden caverns of his heart, from the darkest parts of his mind, lying in wait until something triggered them to spring.

True to his word, Davis waited.

Brody tried to reach past him, unload another feed sack, go on as if nothing had been said, but his uncle stopped him by taking a hold on his upper arm. Davis might have been in his fifties, but he still had a hell of a grip.

Just then, Conner stepped into the barn. Brody didn't see or hear his brother—he just felt a tug on that unseen cord that connected them to each other.

Davis had let go of Brody's arm by then—he'd only been out to make a point by taking hold in the first place—and there was a silent message in his eyes as he looked past one nephew to the other.

"Is Tricia okay?" Brody asked, without turning around.

Conner was silent for a charged moment before he responded gruffly, "She claims she'll be fine if I just let her alone long enough to close her eyes for an hour or two."

Brody nodded, but still didn't move to face his brother.

"Is this what I think it is?" Conner asked, stepping up to stand next to Brody. He'd brought his dog along, and Valentino and Barney, evidently nonplussed by all that human drama, trotted through the rear entrance to the barn and disappeared into the dazzling sunshine.

"Now, what the hell kind of lame-assed question is *that?*" Brody wanted to know, glaring sidelong at his twin and hoping the subject would change course, like some river blasted into a new direction with dynamite.

"Brody, here," Davis drawled, looking at Conner, "is about to jump right out of his own hide. Make no mistake about it, though—he *doesn't* want to talk about the wife and the little boy."

Conner moved to lay a hand on Brody's shoulder, and then, wisely, thought better of the gesture. "I told Davis and Kim what you told me," Conner said, quietly forthright and with no trace of regret or apology. "About Lisa and Justin, and the way you lost them."

It was no good pointing out that he'd told Conner the story and trusted him to keep it a secret. On some level, Brody had known Conner would confide in their aunt and uncle, if no one else. Maybe he'd even hoped, somewhere down deep, that his brother *would* let the cat out of the bag. That way, Davis and Kim would know the bitter truth without Brody having to tell them what happened.

Feeling cornered, Brody looked from Davis to Conner and back again. "If you already know," he began tautly, reasonably, "what's the point of my repeating it all?"

"Because you need to," Davis said, solemn and certain. "It's festering inside you like a wound, son. Holding that secret corralled up inside you kept you away from your home and your people and a lot more for too long. Don't you think it's time you turned it loose?"

Brody shoved a hand through his hair, barely noticing that he'd knocked his hat to the floor in the process. He didn't move to retrieve it.

"Lisa said she'd put the baby up for adoption if I didn't marry her," Brody said, sounding, in his own ears, like a man ranting from the depths of some consuming fever. He didn't see Davis, didn't see Conner—just a blurry rush of scenes from years gone by. "If I'd let her, if I hadn't bailed out on Carolyn in the middle of the night and rushed off to put a golden band on Lisa's finger, then Justin would still be alive, a growing kid with parents and maybe brothers and sisters—"

Brody's voice ground to a painful stop. It was as though the gears running his speech had rusted and then seized up.

"I used to think my brother, Blue, would have lived," Davis said evenly, "if I'd done some small thing differently the morning your dad tried to ride that crazy horse. If only I'd called him out of bed a few minutes later, or stretched breakfast by another cup of coffee or two, or even started some kind of row with him. *Anything* to keep him off the back of that stallion. But he was bent on making that ride, Brody, and if he hadn't gotten himself thrown that day, he'd have done it some *other* day. What I'm trying to get at here is that folks seem to come into this life with a list of things they need to get done while they're here inscribed on their souls. Old or young, when their work is done, they leave."

After that, nobody said anything.

There was no need for words.

CHAPTER THIRTEEN

Carolyn had slept fitfully the previous night, and she was awake early, feeling jittery, rather than rested.

She fed Winston, brewed herself a cup of instant coffee and peeked out at the beginnings of a blue-gold day in May. In the neighbor's yard, as well as the distance, the ever-lovely cottonwood trees shimmered and shifted, like the ribbons on the gypsy skirt.

Of all the places she'd lived, she liked Colorado best. Especially when spring evolved into summer so quickly, as it seemed to be doing this year.

With her head cloudy from lack of sleep and hectic dreams she couldn't quite remember, Carolyn imagined herself on horseback, riding the crooked trail on the rim of the ridge on the Creed ranch, or along the banks of the river. The air was thin there in the high country, but once a person got used to it, every breath of fresh air was exhilarating.

Carolyn bit her lower lip, pondering her options.

Today was a workday, and she had to open the shop by nine-thirty at the latest, but that still left her with a couple of hours of freedom. If she hurried, she could drive out to Kim and Davis's place, saddle up old Blossom and quite literally head for the hills.

Or the trail that followed the wandering line of the river.

A ride would clear the cobwebs from her brain and maybe even ease the anxious little ache in her heart, the one she'd awakened with some tattered remnant of dreams forgotten.

Or denied.

Hastily, before she could change her

mind, Carolyn showered, dressed in the usual jeans and T-shirt and, because of the inevitable morning chill, a long-sleeved flannel shirt. She donned socks, hauled on her boots and said goodbye to Winston, promising she'd be back soon.

The drive to the Creed ranch was refreshing in itself—Carolyn kept her car window rolled halfway down and listened to a Keith Urban CD while she drove. By the time Davis and Kim's rambling house and barn came into view, she was singing along at the top of her lungs.

Kim came out of the house when Carolyn pulled in, smiling a warm welcome, the little dogs frolicking at her feet.

"Come in and have coffee," Kim called. "I have something to ask you."

Kim Creed was a dear and treasured friend, but Carolyn didn't want to sit and drink coffee—she wanted to ride.

"I was hoping to take Blossom out for a little spin," she answered, pausing to smile at the comical antics of the dogs. "What did you want to ask me?"

Kim scooped the Yorkies up into each hand and walked over to where Carolyn was waiting. "Davis and I have a hankering to head down to Stone Creek for a week or two, and spoil our grandchildren," Kim said. "Run interference for Steven and Melissa a bit, so they can go off somewhere by themselves for a couple of days. We need somebody to stay here and look after the house while we're away, though. Can you do it?"

"I'd be glad to," Carolyn said, pleased. As much as she loved her apartment on the second floor of Natty McCall's house, she enjoyed a change of scene once in a while, too. And while other people's houses usually left her feeling rootless and more adrift than ever, this was the Creed Ranch; for whatever reason, she'd always felt at home here. "Would it be okay if I brought Winston along?"

"That would be fine," Kim answered, nuzzling the top of one tiny dog's head and then the other. Early as it was, Smidgeon and Little Bit's carefully trimmed coats were already brushed to a high shine, their topknots tied with little yellow ribbons. "Brody will stop by twice a day to tend the horses—just call him or Conner if there's any sort of emergency. You're more than welcome to ride Blossom anytime, but Davis doesn't want you going near that Thoroughbred. Firefly's too dangerous."

The *Thoroughbred* was dangerous?

He couldn't hold a candle to Brody when it came to making trouble.

"Kim Creed," Carolyn reasoned, in fond irritation, "if Brody is set to take care of your horses, why can't he simply sleep here at night, too, and keep an eye on the property?" She paused, enjoying her friend's sheepish expression. "Is it just my imagination, or are you trying to throw the two of us together?"

Again.

Kim's cheeks were pink, but her eyes smiled even before her mouth did. "Would I do a thing like that?" she challenged.

"In a heartbeat," Carolyn said, with smiling conviction.

Kim was not only thinking fast, she was thinking *visibly.* The gears behind that still-lovely face were turning for sure. Finally, she drew a deep breath and huffed it out.

"Brody can't stay here because he's got to take care of his own place, the new construction, I mean. There's always a chance of theft or vandalism, you know, particularly after the sun goes down."

Carolyn laughed and rolled her eyes, wondering if Kim knew about the Saturday night date she and Brody had scheduled.

She decided not to mention it, in case the gossip hadn't reached Kim's ears yet. There was no sense in pouring fuel on the fires of speculation, especially when the evening with Brody would probably turn out to be a nonevent.

Or the mother of all rows.

When it came to herself and Brody, there seemed to be no middle ground.

"You'll do it, then?" Kim persisted. "Stay here at the house while Davis and I are in Stone Creek? I know you have the shop to run, but other than that—"

Silently, Carolyn completed her friend's sentence. *Other than that, you have no life.*

"I'll be here, Kim," she said gently. Kim and Davis had always been kind to her, and their trust was something she prized. She couldn't have refused the request without a much better reason than her compulsive need to avoid Brody whenever possible. "When are you leaving for Stone Creek?"

"Sunday morning," Kim answered, with a glance in the direction of the barn and a crooked little smile. "Go ahead and saddle Blossom. I know your time is limited, and I won't insist on the coffee klatch."

On impulse, Carolyn hugged Kim, being careful not to squash the little dogs.

"What was that for?" Kim asked, blinking even as she smiled.

"You're a good friend, Kim," Carolyn answered, turning to walk away, but looking back over one shoulder. "And I'm grateful to you and *for* you."

The majestic Thoroughbred, king of all he surveyed, nickered a greeting to Carolyn as she moved past the corral fence, heading for the barn.

"Good morning, handsome," she told the gigantic gelding. What an amazing creature he was, standing there with his head high and his ears pitched forward, his whole frame rimmed by morning sunlight.

A few moments later, Carolyn reached the door of Blossom's stall.

The little mare seemed ready for an excursion and submitted happily to all the customary preparations—saddle blanket, saddle, bridle, cinch-tightening and, finally, a quick check of her hooves.

"You're getting fat from standing around in this barn or out in the pasture all the time," Carolyn told the animal, leading her out into the unusually warm morning air. "Let's get some exercise."

Carolyn chose the route that led along the ridge, as opposed to the one next to the river, mainly because she didn't want to look over the waters and see Brody's fabulous house, nearer to completion with every passing day.

Would he end up marrying Joleen?

Or would it be some other woman who wasn't even on the scene yet?

Brody had taken out a trial member-ship on Friendly Faces—and even though he'd posted his horse's picture instead of his own, he wouldn't lack for prospective dates—or *mates.* He was, after all, a real catch—young, single, good-looking and financially secure, if not downright rich.

Strangers might not know these things, but plenty of available Lonesome Bend women *would,* and they wouldn't hesitate to lobby for a date.

What if Brody fell for one of them?

Then he *fell for one of them,* Carolyn thought, in rueful answer to her own silent question.

She stuck a foot into the stirrup and swung herself up onto Blossom's wide back. A glutton for punishment when it came to Brody Creed, Carolyn imagined a wedding, crowded with well-wishers. A beautiful bride, with one hot groom—Brody—promising to love, honor and cherish.

One thing led to another. She pictured the two of them—Brody and the faceless woman—leaving on their honeymoon.

In her mind's eye, she witnessed their return to Lonesome Bend. Brody would carry his new wife over the threshold of

that amazing house—she could probably even *cook,* the bitch—and there
would be a baby on the way in no time
at all.

Carolyn, leaving Blossom to choose
their path, blushed at the thought.

The new Mrs. Creed would probably
stop by the shop often—after all, she'd
be Tricia's sister-in-law and, therefore,
need no excuse to visit—and Carolyn
would have to watch as the woman's
belly swelled with Brody's child. . . .

"Stop it," she told herself out loud.

Blossom, no doubt thinking Carolyn
was speaking to her, stopped and looked
back in comical equine curiosity.

"I'm sorry," Carolyn told the horse
gently, patting the mare's neck. "I wasn't
talking to you."

Blossom, seemingly satisfied, plodded on.

Carolyn, in the meantime, went right
on daydreaming, paying no attention
when Blossom left the ridge trail and
meandered through a copse of cottonwood trees to the banks of Hidden Lake.

Hidden Lake.

Carolyn's heart almost stopped when

she realized where they were. She'd been careful to avoid the place since her last visit, years ago—with Brody.

They'd camped on the shore, sharing a single sleeping bag inside an insulated pup tent made for one.

They'd fished, and fried the catch over a fire in the open air.

And, oh, how they'd made love.

Carolyn had never been happier, before or since.

"Let's get out of here," she said to the horse, tugging lightly on the reins.

But Blossom waded into the water instead, lowered her head and began to drink noisily of the crystal-clear water.

With a sigh, Carolyn backed the mare onto the shore and dismounted to walk around a little, and work the kinks out of her legs. Lately, she'd gone too long between horseback rides, and she felt the omission in the insides of her thighs and in her lower back.

Blossom waded in again, bent her head to satisfy her thirst.

Carolyn looked around, stricken anew by the beauty of the place. With the trees filtering the light of the sun and causing it to dance with leaf shadows on the surface of the lake, it seemed sacred, almost cathedral-like.

It was ridiculously warm, for a morning in May, and she shed the flannel shirt, draping it over a nearby boulder, and enjoyed the feel of soft heat on her shoulders and arms. She shouldn't be dallying out here, she thought—the shop was supposed to open in an hour, and she'd need another shower and a change of clothes before then.

But the silence, the trees, the muted birdsong, all of it was solace to her soul.

Eventually, the sensual pull of the water proved to be more than she could resist. Carolyn, so rarely impulsive, resolutely kicked off her boots, peeled away her socks and waded into the sky-tinted waters of Hidden Lake.

The water was warm, and soft as liquefied silk.

Carolyn rolled her jeans up to her knees and waded in deeper. The lake bottom was covered in tiny, smooth stones, and those stones worked the flesh on the bottoms of her feet like the fingers of a gifted masseuse.

Tilting her head back and closing her eyes, Carolyn gave herself up to sensation—peace, the deliciousness of water, the smooth caress of the little rocks under her soles, the sunshine spiking between the branches of the cottonwoods that arched overhead like great pillars supporting the sky.

For all the things she would have changed about her past, her present and her future, if that had been possible in the first place, in the here and now, Carolyn counted only the good things.

She was young, she was healthy and she loved her life.

She loved working in the shop. She loved sewing, and riding horses, and taking care of Winston. She loved her friends and her modest apartment and the town of Lonesome Bend, Colorado, which *felt* like a family, even if it wasn't.

She was blessed among women.

Blossom nickered, attracting Carolyn's attention.

She turned, watched as the mare moved farther up the sloping bank to graze happily on sweet grass, the reins still looped loosely behind the horn of the saddle.

The urge to strip to the skin and swim in that lake came over Carolyn suddenly, and it was all but overwhelming.

Carolyn got out of the water, intending to get back on Blossom and ride away, but instead, she found herself peeling off her clothes, piling them on the dry boulder, with the flannel shirt she'd doffed earlier. She plunged back into the lake, gasping at the initial chill but adapting quickly. She swam out into deeper water and then turned onto her back to float and gaze up at that painfully blue sky.

It was a time out of time; she'd drifted, somehow, into a magical world, parallel to the one she usually inhabited.

Then she heard the sound—another horse, somewhere very nearby.

Heart pounding, Carolyn stopped floating to tread water, her eyes narrowed as she scanned the trees for any sign of an intruder.

All was silent now—even the birds had stopped singing.

Carolyn was convinced of it: she had

definitely heard a horse, and it hadn't been Blossom. The mare was still grazing.

"Who's there?" Carolyn called, somewhat shakily, as terrible headlines flashed through her mind.

Woman Found Dead Near Remote Lake . . .

Local Shop-owner Perishes in Brutal Attack . . .

There it went again, that imagination of hers.

She'd probably heard a deer, or, since livestock ranged all over the Creed ranch anyway, a cow or a horse.

Then Brody appeared, riding through the cottonwoods and swinging down off the back of his buckskin gelding, Moonshine. He smiled, took off his hat and hung it on the saddle horn. Soothed a fretful Blossom with a muttered word and a few pats on the neck.

Carolyn's heart seized and moved up into her throat. Things like this only happened in books, or in old movies.

They did *not* happen to her, not in real life, anyway. There might have been a fantasy or two, but those were just—well—*fantasies.*

"These your clothes?" Brody asked mildly, inclining his head toward the boulder and the pile of discarded garments.

Carolyn felt a surge of true annoyance and her cheeks burned. "Who *else's* clothes would they be?" she demanded. "And what are you doing here? Did you follow me?"

"Davis sent me out to ride the fence lines," Brody replied, kicking off one of his boots. "That's one of his prescriptions for a case of what he calls 'the moody blues.' Hard work or a long ride. I happened to spot you and Blossom leaving the trail, so I decided to follow, make sure the both of you were all right."

Off went the other boot.

Carolyn was gripped by memories of the last time she and Brody had been here, together. It had been too cold to swim then; now, she was surprised the lake didn't start to simmer.

"What are you doing?" she snapped, still treading water but moving away from shore, away from *Brody.*

"It's a nice day," he said, neatly evading the question, tossing his hat down on top of his boots. "Unusually warm for May, wouldn't you say? Perfect for skinny-dipping."

"Brody Creed, don't you dare—"

He hauled his shirt off over his head, tossed it.

His chest was sculpted, sprinkled with gold; time had been good to Brody Creed.

Damn it.

"It's a free country," he told her, his belt buckle making a jingling sound as he unhooked it. "And this lake *is* on Creed land."

"I'll leave," Carolyn said, on a rush of breath. "Just turn your back, so I can get out of the water and put on my clothes, and I'll be gone—"

Brody unfastened his jeans.

That was no answer, Carolyn thought frantically.

Or was it?

She squeezed her eyes tightly shut, trying to think. Her breath was shallow, and her heart was thudding against her rib cage.

She wanted to be anywhere but here.

She wanted to be *nowhere* but here.

There was a splash, and Carolyn felt a subtle, sensual movement in the water, and when curiosity forced her to open her eyes again, Brody was right in front of her.

Crystal beads glimmered in his eyelashes, and his grin was as obnoxiously winsome as ever. Maybe more so.

From the neck down—Carolyn *did* try not to look—he was a moving shadow. Sunshine, filtered by cottonwood leaves, glimmered in his tarnished-gold hair and that grin—well, *that grin.*

"Relax," he drawled, his blue eyes percolating with mischievous delight—and something else that might have been desire. "I'd never force you or any other woman to do anything you didn't want to do."

This, Carolyn knew, was a perfectly true statement.

It was also no comfort whatsoever.

"Don't," she murmured, not knowing if she was addressing that single desperate word to Brody, or to herself.

He raised one eyebrow. "Don't what?"

He knew damn well *don't what*.

But did she?

With a great sigh of lusty contentment, Brody tilted his head back, closed his eyes, breathed in the blue-sky air with the same relish Carolyn had earlier.

Carolyn, though still flustered, used those few stolen moments to admire him—the strong line of his jaw, the long eyelashes, the hair bejeweled with droplets of lake water.

When he opened his eyes again, and caught her looking at him, she actually gasped, startled.

That made Brody chuckle, and Carolyn blushed.

"Remember the last time we were here?" he asked, his tone slow and almost sleepy. "It was a lot colder than it is now, and we kept the bonfire going long into the night. Not that we needed it to keep warm."

Now it was Carolyn who closed her eyes, tangled in the vision like a fish in a net. They'd *hadn't* needed a fire—their lovemaking had set them both ablaze.

"I remember," she murmured softly.

"Carolyn," Brody said, "open your

eyes and *relax.* I'm not trying to seduce you, here."

"You could have fooled me," Carolyn protested, getting angry again. "Taking off your clothes and jumping right into this lake when I *specifically* asked you not to—"

He laughed—threw back his head and *laughed.* He certainly didn't lack for nerve.

Carolyn seethed.

When Brody's amusement abated a little, he said, "You were naked when I got here, remember? How was I to know you weren't *hoping* I'd show up and seduce you?"

If the water hadn't limited her momentum, Carolyn swore she would have broken all her personal rules about violence and slapped him, hard.

"How was *I* to know," she countered, quietly furious, "that you were *following* me, like some—some *stalker?* Do you honestly think I would have *taken off my clothes* if I'd had the faintest glimmer that *you* were going to show up?"

This time, Brody didn't laugh. His gaze was solemn, with just the faintest sparkle of mischief, as he regarded her. "I wouldn't have thought you'd take off your clothes for *any* reason," he drawled. "Especially to take a swim in a mountain lake that doesn't generally warm up until the middle of August."

When had he gotten closer? Carolyn wondered distractedly, moving back a little, scanning the lakeside for Blossom

No Blossom.

The mare must have wandered off at some point.

Which was just terrific, because now Carolyn wasn't just naked and embarrassed and alone with Brody in what basically amounted to the Blue Lagoon. She was all of those things *and* stranded.

"Blossom!" she called out, going around Brody and heading for shore, but pausing when she realized she was about to reveal herself in the altogether. "Blossom, where are you?"

Nothing.

Brody appeared beside her.

Carolyn crouched a little and crossed her arms in front of her breasts. Her nipples felt hard and tight, and it wasn't just because there was a slight nip to the water.

"That's one thing about Blossom," Brody said easily, evidently enjoying this new development in an already impossible situation. "She's always been kind of flighty. As likely as not, she's halfway home by now."

"Don't say that," Carolyn sputtered. "Don't even *think* it."

"You and I can ride double, on Moonshine." He paused, sighed. "We'd better get going. Kim will freak out when that horse trots into the barnyard with her saddle empty."

"I *have* to get my clothes first," Carolyn said. All she needed was for Kim to call Davis when Blossom came home without a rider, and the two of them to come searching for her.

Brody chuckled again, but very slowly he turned his back. "I won't look until you tell me it's all right," he promised.

Tugging dry clothes over wet skin, especially in a hurry, had frustration singing through Carolyn's veins by the time she was decent.

"Okay," she said begrudgingly.

Brody turned around and started out of the water, no more concerned with his own nakedness than Adam in the Garden.

Carolyn whirled to give him her back and folded her arms tight against her chest.

Brody muttered the occasional cheerful curse as he dressed himself, and when he was ready, he whistled for Moonshine.

The buckskin came right to him, docile as a dollar-a-ride pony at the state fair.

"Need a boost?" Brody asked, his voice like the flick of a feather across the sensitive skin at her nape.

Carolyn cast one last look around for Blossom, didn't see a sign of that fickle critter, and climbed into Moonshine's saddle like the skilled horsewoman she was.

For a second or so, she actually considered riding off and leaving Brody to *walk* home from Hidden Lake, but of course she couldn't do it. The Code of the West went way back and ran deep. And one of its tenets was that you never took off on somebody else's horse and left them afoot.

Even now, in this modern day and age, there were too many bad things that could happen to a stranded rider.

Brody chuckled, reading her expression accurately, it would seem, and sprang up behind her, nimble as a Native warrior. "I knew you weren't a horse thief," he teased, leaning around her, *into* her, to take up the reins.

"H-how?" Carolyn asked. Damn Brody for suggesting that the lake was too cold to swim in at this time of year. Now her teeth were starting to chatter, and she could feel a wicked sneeze building up in her sinus passages.

He nudged Moonshine into a fast walk. "Well, for one thing," he replied, "you're missing the big handlebar mustache."

Carolyn did not—*would* not—laugh.

But she wanted to, and Brody probably knew that.

They rode out of the cottonwoods and onto the trail, picking up speed as they went.

Carolyn tried not to notice that Brody

felt as hard-chested as a statue behind her, that the heat of his body was leaching past the chill of her damp flesh, warming her, making her heart race a little.

She should have been relieved that they hadn't made love, she supposed, and she *was,* mostly. She was also somewhat disappointed.

Like before, he seemed to know what she was thinking.

Which just went to prove how arrogant he was.

And how right.

He bent his head, touched his tongue to the back of her neck, made a chortling sound when she reacted with a little groan.

"Back there at the lake," he told her, his voice throaty and almost hypnotic, but audible even over the clatter of Moonshine's hooves on the hard-packed dirt of the trail, "I wanted to lay you down in the grass and have my way with you. Know why I didn't try?"

A tremor, as involuntary as the groan, shuddered through Carolyn. "You didn't try," she managed to reply, "because you knew I'd scratch your eyes right out of your head if you did."

Brody laughed. "I didn't try," he said, "because I didn't have a condom handy."

Carolyn was still in way over her head, lake or no lake, but she *had* had the presence of mind to wonder why Brody hadn't even attempted to make love to her, when he had the chance.

"You wouldn't have succeeded anyhow," she said stiffly, and maybe a beat too late.

"Are you challenging me?" Brody wanted to know. Managing the horse, even with another rider in front of him, required no discernible effort on his part. He might have been part of the animal, he was so at ease. "If you are, I'm up to it—so to speak."

Hard need went through Carolyn's entire being in that moment. She was half again too stubborn—and too rattled—to come up with a response.

Brody laughed, and one of his hands rose to slip inside her loose-fitting flannel shirt to cup her breast. Even with a bra and a T-shirt in between, he must have felt her nipple tighten against his palm.

It took all of Carolyn's considerable self-control to grab his wrist and jerk his hand away. "We have an agreement, Brody," she reminded him tersely. "*No sex.* Remember?"

"That might have been a little rash of us," he said. "Deciding to save ourselves, I mean." His breath brushed her right ear, and then he nibbled briefly at the lobe.

Carolyn bit back another groan. Gave him a quick jab with her elbow. "*Stop it,* Brody," she said.

He sighed again. By then, Moonshine was traveling at a smooth lope, and the motion of that horse, and Brody at her back—well, it was beyond sensual. It was very nearly climactic.

"Is this agreement of ours . . . open-ended?" he finally asked.

Up ahead, Carolyn spotted Blossom, placidly munching on grass alongside the trail.

"Wh-what do you mean?" Carolyn asked, glad to see the runaway mare within catching distance, and unhurt.

"I mean," Brody almost breathed, making no comment on Blossom's reappearance, though he'd surely seen her, "that the no-sex deal isn't working for me. We need to discuss it, Carolyn."

"*Discuss* it?" Carolyn echoed. "That isn't what you mean at all, and you know it."

They drew up alongside Blossom, and Carolyn swung one leg over Moonshine's neck and jumped to the ground while Brody leaned to take hold of the mare's bridle strap in case she took a notion to run off again.

"What *do* I mean, then, since you seem to know?" Brody countered, wielding that grin again. He let go of the bridle when she was mounted on Blossom, but he didn't make Moonshine turn, didn't give her so much as an inch of space, so his left leg was pressing into her right.

"It's working fine for me," Carolyn said, ignoring the question.

"What's working fine for you?"

She flushed. "The no-sex agreement," she said. She pointed Blossom toward home and gave the animal a light nudge with her boot heels to get her going.

Brody kept up. "Now, that is a peculiar statement, Carolyn," he observed mildly, "because the nooky-ban obviously *isn't* working any better for you than it is for me—which is to say, not at all."

"*Nooky-ban?*" Carolyn shot back. "Isn't *that* colorful?"

"Oh, I just ooze *colorful,*" Brody teased.

"Shut up, Brody."

He didn't, of course. "Why can't you just admit it, Carolyn? Wherever else we might have dropped the ball, we had a real good thing going in bed."

Even she, the queen of denial, couldn't refute that one. "Not good *enough,* obviously," she said, glaring over at him. "It didn't keep you in Lonesome Bend, now did it?"

Now that they'd recovered Blossom, and Kim and Davis wouldn't be sending out a posse to look for her, Carolyn had time to be mad at herself.

She should be at the shop right this

minute, have the door unlocked and the Open sign facing the porch.

Instead, Tricia was probably there by herself, wondering where the heck Carolyn was.

She was so engaged with this thought, and others like it, that she didn't immediately notice the strange stillness that had descended over Brody.

A glance in his direction verified the intuition.

His jawline was tight, his backbone was straight as a ramrod, and he was looking directly ahead, between Moonshine's ears. Both horses were ambling along at an easy pace now.

"Like I said before," Brody went on, without looking at her, "it's time we talked."

"I'm not sure we have anything to say to each other," Carolyn said, hoping those words hadn't come out sounding as sad as they *felt*.

At last, he caught and held her gaze. His expression was grim. "I have plenty to say to you, Carolyn," he answered, "and I mean to get it all said."

Panic took wing behind Carolyn's rib cage, like some crazed little bird. "Brody, I have to get back to the shop—I never planned on being gone this long and—"

"Later will be fine," he said, when she finally fell silent. "Your place or mine?"

Your place or mine?

Risky business, either way.

Still, Brody wasn't going to let her put him off, that much was plain.

"How about the coffee shop?" she asked, too brightly. "We could meet after I close the shop at five."

"Too public," Brody said, looking as though he'd never grin that trademark grin of his again, he was so solemn.

Carolyn tried to think. If they "talked" at Brody's place, he'd have condoms handy, so why not go ahead and seduce her? Essentially, she'd be helpless against him, and he knew that.

If, on the other hand, they got together at the apartment, all he'd have to do was kiss her, or cup her breast in his hand again, and she wouldn't *care* whether or not they used a condom.

"My place," she finally said. "Six o'clock?"

Brody nodded, and Kim and Davis's barn came into view, and the conversation was over—for the time being, anyway.

CHAPTER FOURTEEN

In front of Kim and Davis's barn, Brody dismounted and left Moonshine at the hitching rail to take hold of Blossom's bridle strap. Carolyn was still in the saddle, flustered and so delicious that just looking at her sent a whole new charge of desire grabbing its way through him like wildfire.

"I'll tend to the mare," Brody told her quietly. "You go on into town and do whatever it is you figure you should be doing right now."

Carolyn bit her lower lip, nodded once, got down and practically sprinted to her

car. Next thing he knew, she was speeding down the driveway in the proverbial
cloud of dust.

One corner of Brody's mouth quirked
up at the sight, but there wasn't much
juice behind that grin. If only he hadn't
run off at the mouth before about how
he and Carolyn oughtn't to have sex, he
might be making love to the woman in
the tall grass back there at Hidden Lake
right now—condom be damned—instead of watching her rush off like the
devil himself was on her trail.

He heard the creak of screen-door
hinges, and Kim stepped out of the
house, sans her usual yappy little side-
kicks, to stand on the side porch, shading her eyes from the sun with one hand.
"Brody?" she called, casting a concerned look in the direction of Carolyn's
still-billowing dust-plume. "Did something happen?"

"Nothing happened," Brody replied.

And I mean nothing. *Damn it all to
hell.*

He led Blossom inside the barn, hoping Kim would leave him in peace, so he
could unsaddle the mare, give her a

flake of hay and a quick brushing and get on with his day.

No such luck.

"It's not like Carolyn to rush away like that," Kim said, standing in the breeze-way now, watching him over the door of Blossom's stall. "She didn't even say goodbye."

She'd always been as light-footed as a Sioux scout, Kim had. Back when he and Conner and Steven were kids, she'd had an uncanny way of showing up out of nowhere, without any sound to warn of her approach, just when they were about to get into some kind of mischief.

"She's in a hurry to open the shop," Brody said offhandedly.

He'd spilled his guts to Davis and Conner, back at the other barn, going over all that bitter ground, and he meant to do the same thing all over again when he went to see Carolyn at her place, later in the day. In the meantime, he preferred to enter into as little conversation as possible.

"You made Carolyn mad again, didn't you?" Kim persisted.

Inwardly, Brody sighed, wondering if

the whole universe was out of whack, or if it was just him. There had to be *some* reason why nothing had gone his way since he'd opened his eyes that morning.

"No," he said, returning the grooming brush to the high, rusty nail where it was kept, dangling from a small leather loop. "I didn't."

Kim narrowed her eyes at him as he opened the stall door and eased through the gap to stand there in the aisle, facing her. "*Something* upset her," she said.

Brody ducked his head, rubbed the back of his neck. It wasn't until then that he realized he'd left his hat in his truck, down at the main ranch house. These days, he figured, he probably would have forgotten his right arm if it wasn't hooked to his shoulder.

"Carolyn doesn't need me to upset her," he said reasonably. "She can handle that one all on her own."

Kim sighed and folded her arms. She was dressed about normal for her, in a pink Western-cut shirt with pearly snaps, worn jeans and boots. "Maybe you ought to go after her. The two of you could talk. . . ."

"We've already made plans to do that," Brody answered, willing to give Kim that much information but no more.

Kim opened her mouth, closed it again, evidently deciding she had nothing more to say. It was a rare phenomenon, but it happened.

Brody grinned, kissed her on the forehead and headed for the barn door.

Moonshine, ever patient, waited at the hitching post. Brody released the loose slipknot he'd made with the reins and hauled himself up into the saddle.

Kim, on her way back to the house by then, waved a farewell.

Passing the corral on Moonshine, Brody paused to look over at Firefly, the Thoroughbred Kim and Davis had adopted some time before. While he understood their concern about the animal's welfare, he had serious reservations where Firefly was concerned.

This was no ordinary saddle horse. The Thoroughbred was fifteen hundred pounds of raw power, with the blood of champions running hot in his veins. He was still sound physically, but famously temperamental—according to Davis, even the most seasoned jockeys in the business had refused to ride him, there at the end of his mostly unremarkable career.

Brody was a cowboy, not a jockey, and for that very reason, he was tempted to throw a saddle and bridle on that gelding and see for himself just how fast the sucker could run.

Of course, Davis would kill him if he tried. Provided the horse didn't kill him first, that is.

Still, the idea burrowed into Brody's already beleaguered brain, germinated and took root there, like a magic bean.

But he was, as Davis would say, burning daylight; he had fence lines to ride, if he didn't want a lecture from his uncle about pulling his weight on the ranch.

At the moment, Brody didn't want a lecture from *anybody.*

What have I done? Carolyn asked herself, as she drove toward town.

Well, duh, that self answered. *You practically offered yourself to Brody*

Creed on a silver platter, that's *what.*
You invited him to your apartment, know-
ing full well what's going to happen.

A smile broke over Carolyn's face, and
a thrill went through her, lodging squarely
between her pelvic bones. "God, I hope
so," she said, right out loud, the an-
nouncement rising, it seemed, from the
very ground of her being, as though her
body had somehow summoned all its
resources to be heard over the voice of
common sense.

Brimming with crazy emotions she
couldn't begin to untangle, let alone
name, Carolyn wondered if she really
was losing her mind.

When she arrived at the shop, Tricia
was there, as she'd expected.

What Carolyn *hadn't* expected was a
store full of customers.

Where had they all come from? She
hadn't seen a bus outside, or even a
car.

"Glad you could make it," Tricia told
her sweetly, looking her over with an expression of knowing amusement frolicking in her eyes.

Carolyn, unprepared for a crowd,

blushed. She smelled like a horse, her hair probably looked like a fright wig, and her friend seemed to know precisely what she'd been up to that morning, up at Hidden Lake.

Or *almost* up to, anyway.

Probably impossible, she thought, with considerable relief. Tricia was smart, but she wasn't psychic, for pity's sake.

"I'll be right back," she told Tricia, racing for the inside stairs.

Reaching her apartment, Carolyn took the world's fastest shower, threw on fresh clothes, blow-dried her wild tresses into a semblance of submission and practically broke her neck getting back down to the shop.

All the shoppers had gone by then, and Tricia, perched on a high stool behind the counter, eyed Carolyn with good-natured suspicion.

"And where have *you* been, pray tell?" she asked warmly.

Carolyn knew what Tricia was thinking—that she'd been out the whole night and not just for part of the morning—and she teetered on the edge of protesting too much.

"Out," she replied pleasantly, as Winston meowed and curled himself around her ankles. "Where did all those *people* come from?"

"Around," Tricia said airily. "Word seems to be getting out that we carry unique merchandise. Two of them had seen the gypsy skirt online, and they wanted to know if they could make offers. I told them they'd have to go to the auction site and bid."

Carolyn felt the usual pang at the thought of selling the skirt. It would be better if it went to a stranger, though, someone who lived far away from Lonesome Bend. Seeing some local woman wearing it would be like catching regular glimpses of a child she'd given up for adoption in the company of another mother.

"Good call," Carolyn said, and began straightening a display table. She needed, in that moment, to look busy.

"Carolyn," Tricia said firmly, but quietly.

Carolyn stopped cold, like a Londoner during the Blitz, hearing the telltale whistle of a dropping bomb.

"We need to talk," Tricia told her.

Brody had said pretty much the same thing, just that morning.

Why did everyone suddenly want to *talk?* Whatever happened to leaving well enough alone?

"O-o-okay," Carolyn said warily, stretching out the word. She stopped pretending to work and turned to meet Tricia's gaze. "You start."

Tricia sighed. "You've probably noticed that I've been leaving the shop early a lot lately," she began. "And I don't think that's fair to you. We're supposed to be partners."

"Tricia," Carolyn reminded her friend softly, "you're *expecting a baby.* I don't mind covering for you once in a while."

"That's just it," Tricia answered, "it hasn't *been* just *once in a while.* I feel perfectly fine—honestly, I do—but some days I just feel so *tired.* My doctor says that's pretty much normal, but that doesn't change the fact that you're doing more than your share." Another sigh. "Which means something has to give."

Carolyn swallowed hard, suddenly aware, and keenly, of what was coming.

She should have anticipated that Tricia would want to quit the business, she supposed, but she hadn't. The decision made sense—while Tricia would have lots of help at home after the baby came, the new arrival would take up more of her time and energy, not less.

"I'm not asking you to buy me out," Tricia went on. "I know that isn't possible right now. Maybe, once the baby is older—"

When the baby was older, Carolyn thought, with a mixture of understanding and affectionate envy, there would probably be *another* baby. If not several.

"Carolyn," Tricia urged, "*say* something."

Carolyn rummaged up a smile. "Everything has to change sometime," she said, looking wistfully around at the shop, with all its colorful and many-textured handmade offerings. It was a haven of grace, a virtual celebration of creativity, and Carolyn hadn't realized how much she loved the place until now. "But it was good while it lasted."

Tricia eased down off the stool then and sort of waddled over to Carolyn. A worried frown creased her forehead. "While it lasted?" she echoed. "Are you saying you don't want to keep the shop open?"

Carolyn spread her hands wide for a moment. "How would I do that, Tricia?" she asked. "I can't afford to hire help, and running this place alone would be too much, considering all the sewing I need to do in addition to stocking shelves, keeping the books, waiting on customers and all the rest."

"Carolyn," Tricia said, her voice taking on a note of quiet urgency, "I don't think you understand what I'm saying here, and it's no wonder, I guess, given all I've left out." She drew a deep breath, let it out and rested her hands on the sides of her protruding belly. "I was hoping to become a sort of silent partner—you know, pump some cash into the business and maybe help out in an advisory capacity once in a while. Track down new artists online. If I invested in the shop, well, then you *could* hire some help—maybe a couple of part-timers?—and still have more time for the creative stuff."

Always wary of anything that sounded too good to be true, Carolyn plunked her hands on her hips, in an unconscious reflection of Tricia's stance, and considered the situation. Finally, she blurted out, "Is this charity?"

"Oh, for heaven's sake," Tricia replied, "*of course* it isn't charity. It's a business proposition." She looked thoughtful for a long moment. "I suppose I could buy *you* out, though, and hire a manager and some salespeople—but what would be the use in that? It's things like those aprons you're always whipping up, and your eye for unique merchandise, that sets us apart from other stores and galleries."

"No," Carolyn said, very quickly, and then blushed.

"Huh?" Tricia asked, clearly confused.

"What I meant was, I don't want you to buy me out," Carolyn explained, with a nervous laugh and a shake of her head. "Kim asked me to house-sit for her and Davis, this coming week, while they're in Stone Creek visiting the grandchildren, and if I put the word out, I could probably get right back into the groove with all my former clients—"

"But you love this shop," Tricia interrupted. "And the apartment. And what would happen to Winston?"

"Winston," Carolyn reminded her friend tenderly, "belongs to your great-grandmother. And once Natty gets all this world travel out of her system, she'll want him back."

"Natty is *never* going to get world travel out of her system," Tricia argued. "When her time comes—and that won't be for a long while, God willing—she'll probably be in a state room on some cruise ship, or riding a camel or shopping for exotic spices in some distant marketplace. She knows Winston is happy with you, Carolyn, and she doesn't plan on reclaiming him. Why do you think she charges you so little rent for the apartment?"

Carolyn, busy wondering how she'd ever bear being parted from that silly, spoiled, sardine-eating cat, was brought up short. She simply looked at Tricia, at a loss for words.

"And besides," Tricia went on, evidently suffering no such difficulty, "Natty's planning on signing the house over to me ahead of time, on the advice of her lawyer—something about avoiding probate when she passes—which means, for all practical intents and purposes, that *I'm* your landlady. And I'm lowering your rent—to zero."

"That *would* be charity," Carolyn protested.

"No," Tricia replied pointedly, but with a hopeful little smile, "it would be good business sense. Part of the compensation package for running the shop while I concentrate on giving this baby the best possible start in life. Think of it as just another house-sitting job, if it makes you feel better."

Carolyn's eyes widened, even as her throat constricted. "You don't have to do this, Tricia," she almost whispered. "Really. I'll be fine. I can make my own way—"

"Stop being so stubborn and so proud and listen to me," Tricia said. "Right now, I want to be at home. I want to be Conner's wife and this child's mother, fulltime. But I'm still *me,* Carolyn. I still love arts and crafts, and I want to promote them—the world needs beautiful things that don't come in blister packs. *Please,* say you'll stay. Say you'll keep Creed and Simmons going." She stopped long enough to draw breath. "Don't you want to see what our little company could become? I know I do."

Carolyn blinked. She'd had a few thoughts along those lines herself—fanciful ones, about expanding the selection of merchandise, building a stronger presence on the internet, maybe even trying mail order—but she'd never taken them very seriously.

But she could start small, virtually on a shoestring. Carry greeting cards and regional cookbooks and the like. And what about scrapbooking supplies and whimsical rubber stamps?

It was even possible that Primrose, along with other talented locals, might be willing to teach art classes, share their knowledge and skill.

All these thoughts were still tumbling into Carolyn's mind when Tricia's face, plump with pregnancy, lit up with excitement. She took both Carolyn's hands in hers and squeezed. "You're seeing it, aren't you?" she guessed, with amazing accuracy. "You're seeing all the wonderful possibilities, just like I do."

Carolyn's eyes burned then, and pride dictated that she had to turn away, sniffle. "Suppose it's all a big mistake?" she murmured.

There was nothing wrong with Tricia's hearing. "Everything worth doing involves risk, Carolyn," she said.

Everything worth doing involves risk.

"I'll think about it," Carolyn said, very carefully, and then, after squaring her shoulders and straightening her spine, she headed for the small office where the shop's computer lived.

She logged on, ignoring another onslaught of enthusiasm from the Friendly Faces website, and clicked over to the auction page, where she'd put the gypsy skirt up for sale.

What she saw there nearly took her breath away.

The bidding was over the four-figure mark already and, judging by the number of people competing for the item, it was bound to go higher still.

That was when Carolyn began to imagine what it would mean, having help around the shop, so she could spend more time on creative work, like designing and sewing *other* one-of-a-kind wonders.

Maybe, she mused, her heart beating a little faster, Tricia was right.

Maybe it was time to stop being so careful and take a chance on something.

And some*one*.

The express package was waiting on Brody's doorstep when he and Barney got back to the lodge at River's Bend, around five o'clock that afternoon, and he picked it up, smiled at the return address and bounced it once in his hand before tossing it onto the counter.

The DVDs he'd cadged from his film-distributor friend had arrived, with time to spare. When Saturday night rolled around, and it was finally time for his drive-in movie date with Carolyn, he'd be ready.

He shoved a hand through his hair, got out some clean clothes and made for the bathroom, where he took a very quick, very hot shower, shaving and washing the dust and sweat out of his hair while he was under the spray.

Once he was dressed again, Brody fed Barney, made sure his water bowl was full and fresh and walked to the door. Barney, exhausted from playing ranch-dog with Valentino all day, out at the other place, went straight to his bed and collapsed onto it with a contented sigh.

Brody locked up, glanced over at the new house to note any visible progress and climbed into his pickup. He was due at Carolyn's place at six, and it was almost that now, but she was probably still in the process of winding down from the day anyhow, so a few more minutes probably wouldn't matter.

He pulled into the lot at the super-market, hurried inside, bought two dozen bright pink roses and a box of condoms and hurried out again.

Fortune, he reminded himself, with a grin, *favors not only the bold, but also the well-prepared.*

When he pulled up in front of the Mc-Call house, Tricia was just coming down the porch steps. They met in the middle of the walk, and she took pointed notice of the roses—thank God, the box of condoms was in a paper bag, under his elbow—raised one eyebrow, and smiled even more brightly.

"Fancy meeting *you* here, Brody Creed," she said.

Brody laughed. "Fancy that," he replied.

He turned around, walked Tricia to the Pathfinder and waited while she climbed inside. He hoped she wasn't planning on stopping off at the supermarket before she went home, because somebody was sure to tell her about the purchases he'd made there a few minutes before. If word got back to Conner, there would be no end to the ribbing he'd have to endure.

"Drive safely," he told Tricia.

She smiled. "You, too," she answered.

And then she started up the rig and drove away.

Brody watched her out of sight, then took his roses and his box of condoms and headed for Natty McCall's front door.

It opened before he could shuffle the flowers and the paper bag around enough to knock.

Carolyn stood just inside, her eyes luminous, her cheeks flushed. She was wearing jeans, as usual, along with an oversize white shirt with the top three buttons undone.

She was so beautiful that Brody very nearly lost his nerve.

Sure, he hoped they'd finish what they'd started that morning, at Hidden Lake, but before the evening was over, he'd *also* have to explain why he'd gone off and left her nearly eight years before. That was going to be hard, because talking about Lisa and Justin twice in one day was bound to hurt twice as much as doing it once.

And that was a lot.

"Come in," Carolyn said quietly, her eyes dropping to the roses and then rising to his face again. The flush in her cheeks deepened.

The entryway was quiet and cool, and there was a faint, flowery scent in the air, though Brody couldn't tell if it was coming from her or from all the candles and bath salts and stuff she and Tricia sold in the shop.

He handed her the roses but held on to the bag with the condoms inside.

"Thank you," she said, her tone revealing exactly zip about what was going on in her mind. She turned and led the way toward the staircase, and Brody followed.

He half expected that schizoid cat to pounce on him the moment they reached Carolyn's kitchen, but it didn't happen. The feline was on the windowsill, busily snarfing up sardines from a saucer, and he didn't spare Brody so much as a glance.

"Have a seat," Carolyn offered, laying the bundled roses down on the counter. She rummaged through cupboards until she found a plain glass vase and got a pair of shears from a drawer.

"I'd rather stand awhile, I think," Brody heard himself say. At least, he *thought* he'd been the one to say it. He hadn't recognized the voice.

Carolyn glanced back at him, but she didn't reply. Her actions over the next few moments were ordinary enough, he supposed—she filled the vase with water, removed the roses from their cellophane cones, trimmed their stems with the scissors and arranged a fetching bouquet.

And watching her left Brody spellbound.

Even speechless.

When she turned around to face him, he was right there in front of her—he honestly didn't remember the strides that had brought him from one place to another—and he *had* to kiss her.

It was as vital as his next heartbeat, his next breath.

She stiffened briefly, and he felt a tremor go through her, but then she slipped her arms around his neck and kissed him right back.

The floor seemed to pitch under Brody's feet, as if he were out log-rolling on the river or something, and he deepened the kiss, leaning into Carolyn, feeling that free-fall kind of exaltation when she opened for him, responded to his embrace.

"Inevitable," he rasped, when their mouths finally parted.

"Yes," Carolyn agreed.

He scooped her off her feet and kissed her again, this time softly.

It wasn't a big apartment, so he hazarded a guess as to which door led to the bedroom and got it right.

Unfortunately, he'd left the condoms in the kitchen, still in their discrete little brown bag.

Brody swore under his breath, set Carolyn on her feet and fumbled for the buttons on her shirt.

Only her hands were there ahead of his, unfastening the buttons first.

He watched, stricken with need, as she shrugged out of the shirt, revealing her perfect, lace-covered breasts, her flat, silken stomach, the rounding of her hips. When Brody reached out to unfasten her bra, he felt like a slow-motion figure in a movie, or a deep-sea diver without a tank and a mask.

And then Carolyn's breasts spilled into his hands, the nipples already hard. Ready for him.

She sighed and tilted her head back in surrender as he caressed her, roused her, told her, in all truth, that she was beautiful.

Standing there in her quiet bedroom, Carolyn gave herself up to the commands of her body, gave herself up to Brody.

It had been so long, and she needed him so much.

Tears of amazement burned her eyes when he bent his head to take one of her nipples into his mouth, his strong hands splayed across her lower back, his touch a tacit promise that he wouldn't let her fall.

Staggering sensation rocked her as Brody attended to her breasts, nibbled at her earlobes, traced the length of her neck with his mouth, all the while unfastening her jeans, but, like before, this was something way beyond physical response.

Everything about Brody, from the scent of his hair and skin to the touch of his hands to the warm moistness of his mouth on her, seemingly everywhere, stirred emotions in her that had no names.

He laid her down on the bed sideways, tugged off her boots and, over the tingling flesh of her legs, brought her jeans and underpants down and discarded them. She was completely, wonderfully naked, while Brody, she thought dimly, was still partially clothed.

She groped for his shoulders, his bare chest, heard the jingle of his belt buckle.

"Hold that pose," he murmured, with a hoarse chuckle just beneath the surface of his voice. "I'll be right back."

Carolyn, already dazed, could only moan in reply.

It was a despairing sound, full of yearning.

Brody wasn't gone long, but Carolyn felt his absence as a shadowy chill, his return as the lovely, bone-saturating warmth of a tropical sun.

When he knelt next to the bed and eased her thighs apart, she uttered a sob, not of sorrow, but of wanting and of welcome.

When he took hold of her, she gasped his name, plunging both hands into his hair and gripping his scalp, pressing him closer and closer still.

His chuckle vibrated through her and that—only that—caused her to climax so fiercely that she arched her back high off the mattress and gave a long, throaty cry of pure lusty release.

Brody caressed her hips with his hands as she descended slowly, so slowly, from the heights, but he was still using his mouth on her in an easy, insistent way that immediately sent her rocketing past the last seizures of satisfaction into an even more ferocious state of arousal.

"Brody," she whimpered, when she found the breath to speak at all, "oh, Brody—don't make me wait—take me, please. . . ."

She felt him shake his head, felt the silk of his hair brushing the tender insides of her thighs. Felt her need to have him inside her ratchet up to an almost unbearable peak.

And still he drew on her, now nibbling, now flickering her with the tip of his tongue, now sucking without mercy.

She exploded, with a low shout of ecstasy, her body straining like a bowstring drawn tight as volt upon volt of pleasure seared through her.

Brody didn't let her go until she'd given the last, shuddering gasp of surrender. He murmured to her, soothed her as all her muscles melted like wax under her still-pulsing flesh.

He shifted her to the center of the bed, kneeling astraddle of her thighs, and she knew he was putting on a condom.

"Decision time, pretty woman," he said gruffly. "Yes or no?"

"Yes," Carolyn managed to respond. "Oh, Brody—Yes—"

He entered her with a long, slow stroke and, that easily, set her ablaze all over again.

They moved in rhythm from the first, pacing themselves, their joining as graceful as a waltz.

Carolyn felt every nuance of pleasure, not only in her body, but also in her heart and her mind and her spirit as well. She experienced Brody's lovemaking with her entire self, and deemed it sacred.

When she knew Brody was getting

close to the pinnacle, she ran her hands over his shoulders and his back and his firm buttocks, whispering to him, comforting him and, at the same time, inciting him to let go.

And when he finally did give in, Carolyn herself was drawn back into the maelstrom of release, as powerless against the seemingly ceaseless, racking joy as a robin caught up in a hurricane.

The sunlight at the window turned pink and then pale lavender as they lay there afterward, both exhausted, waiting, arms and legs entwined, for their breath to return and their hearts to stop pounding.

The room began to darken.

Winston meowed at the closed door, but neither Brody nor Carolyn moved, except to settle into each other's warmth. When they'd both recovered enough, they made love again, more slowly this time, and less frantically, but with the same shatteringly glorious conclusion.

When it was over, Carolyn was lying on top of Brody, her face buried in his neck, her senses full of him, of his scent and the texture and shape and strength of him. She drifted into a sated sleep and awakened, sometime later, with his fingers driving her straight into the throes of yet another earth-shaking orgasm.

She sighed when it was finally finished. Rolled onto her side, resting in the curve of Brody's left arm.

"Are we going to regret this?" she asked presently.

"Probably," Brody said, in a sexy murmur. "But I'm a great believer in living in the moment."

She giggled at that. Knotted up her fist and thunked him lightly on the chest. "Brody Creed," she said, "you are incorrigible."

He kissed the top of her head. "And hungry," he answered.

"I could whip up some scrambled eggs," Carolyn said, and wondered who this woman was who'd taken her over. The same one, apparently, who had dashed out to the convenience store earlier to buy bread and eggs and milk.

"Sounds good," Brody said. His voice was sleepy now.

Carolyn crawled over him to get out

of bed. After a brief shower, she put the white shirt back on and went into the kitchen.

Winston eyed her reproachfully from the windowsill.

"Don't give me that look," Carolyn told the cat. "You had your supper, remember?"

"Reow," Winston said, and, with an air of elegant resignation, began to groom his right paw.

My cat, Carolyn thought, flashing on her conversation with Tricia that afternoon. *My cat, my apartment, my shop.*

Look who suddenly has a future.

And all I have to do now is find a way to get over Brody Creed before he breaks my heart all over again.

CHAPTER FIFTEEN

Damn but Carolyn looked good, standing there in her apartment kitchen, cracking eggs into a pan and wearing nothing but some guy's shirt.

Brody frowned. Kim sometimes wore Davis's old shirts to paint or garden or clean house, and Tricia had been known to throw one of Conner's on once in a while, until the baby bulge got away from her. So who was the yahoo who'd left *this* one behind?

"What?" Carolyn asked, with a shy little smile curving her well-kissed mouth.

"Nothing." Brody sighed and hauled

back a chair so he could sit down at the table. The lovemaking was over, for now, at least, and maybe forever, once she'd heard what he had to say.

It was past time to set things right between the two of them, though, one way or the other. He owed her the truth about a lot of things—first and foremost, his reason for abandoning her that long-ago night, leaving her with nothing but a brief note, a lot of anger and pain, most likely, and a whole slew of unanswered questions.

Evidently, Carolyn wasn't ready to move on. She peered down at the shirt, then looked up at him with wide, laughing eyes, as though she suspected what was bothering him, but wasn't quite sure. Her eyebrows rose in humorous inquiry. "Why the strange look, Brody?"

"I was just wondering who that shirt belongs to," he admitted, embarrassed but still feeling mighty territorial, too. "I'm over it now."

"It's yours," she told him, taking a mischievous delight in her answer. "You left it behind when you—"

The joy drained out of her eyes as she fell silent, remembering.

"I left it behind when I left *you*," Brody said quietly, leaning to push back a second chair. "Carolyn, take that pan off the burner and sit down."

She turned away instead, though, shaking her head and shoveling a spatula under those eggs like she was trying to scrape road-tar off a hot surface. "That was a long time ago," she said, her words coming out rapid-fire, seeming to bounce off the cupboard doors and ricochet back at him. "Let's forget it, okay?"

Brody sighed again, shoved a hand through his hair. "If I could forget it," he said solemnly, and in all truth, "believe me, I would."

Carolyn looked back at him then. A scorching smell wafted over from the stove, and she quickly glopped the scrambled eggs onto two plates, brought them to the table, went back to the counter for silverware.

"For God's sake, Carolyn," Brody said, "sit down. Please."

"You *said* you were hungry," she retorted, going bright-cheeked again, but she finally sat down.

Neither of them picked up a fork, or even looked down at their plates. Their gazes had locked, and Brody saw plenty of pain in hers. Maybe, he thought, it was a reflection of his own.

"Her name was Lisa," he ground out. Even that much was damnably hard to say, but it was a beginning.

Bless her, Carolyn didn't come back with a flippant "Who's Lisa?" the way he'd half expected her to do.

"The woman who called that last night," Carolyn said softly. "The one you wanted to be with—"

Instead of me. The unspoken words hung between them.

"Yes," Brody replied, plowing a hand through his hair. "We met while I was rodeoing, Lisa and me, and we had sort of an affair—"

Color flared in Carolyn's cheeks, and her eyes flashed. "How do you have *sort of an affair?*" she asked.

"If you feel some need to make this harder, Carolyn," Brody said, "go right ahead."

She pressed her lips together into a hard line.

He flashed back to the taste of those lips, the feel of them against his.

Hot need struck him like a meteor blazing down from a clear blue sky.

"Lisa and I had an affair," Brody went on, putting a slight emphasis on the last word. "Nothing *sort of* about it. Then we broke up—I wanted to keep on following the rodeo circuit and she wanted to stay put, get married and buy a house, and there was no way either one of us was going to compromise, so we said our goodbyes and I left."

Carolyn waited. She looked pale now, rather than flushed, and very small inside that white shirt. Her throat worked, but she didn't say anything.

"I knocked around the Southwest for a while, then I ended up here. I was going to try and work things out with my family, but, as you know, when I showed up at Kim and Davis's place, they were nowhere around. I think Conner was away, too, at the time. Anyway, once I got that first glimpse of you, standing there in my aunt and uncle's doorway, framed in light, I couldn't think of anything *but* you, Carolyn."

He saw disbelief in Carolyn's face, along with something that might have been hope. Memories haunted her eyes like ghosts and she bit down on her lower lip.

"I wasn't sure what I felt for you was love," Brody went on, "but whatever it was, I'd never come across anything like it before."

She raised one eyebrow, but still held her peace.

"That last night, Lisa called," Brody said wearily. "She told me she was pregnant with my baby, and if I didn't marry her, she was going to put him up for adoption. I freaked right out—everything was going in forty different directions, and I couldn't seem to find the center."

Very slowly, Carolyn reached over and put her hand in his, but her eyes were still watchful, wary.

"Now," Brody said, with a ragged sigh, "I wish I'd *let* her have Justin and give him to some nice family to raise, because both of them might still be alive if I had. Most likely, Lisa would have found a man who loved her in ways I couldn't, no matter how hard I tried, and Justin, well, he'd be seven now. A normal, healthy kid. Starting second grade in the fall."

Carolyn swallowed, squeezed his hand, an I'm-listening sort of gesture. Some, but by no means all, of the ache in her eyes leaked away.

"Instead, they died in a car accident," Brody told her, when he felt like he could go on. After that, it was like somebody else was telling the story, while he stood apart, like a silent witness, listening, watching, remembering.

But detached from the pain.

Carolyn heard him out without interrupting, and, by the time he'd finished, she was sitting on his lap, her arms around him, her head resting on his shoulder.

Brody felt broken inside, torn apart, as though he'd used himself up, not just emotionally, but physically, too. The old grief, which could only be held at bay for so long, washed back over him and a steely force wrenched him back inside himself.

Without a word, Carolyn held him . . . for a long, long time. Then, presently, she stood up, took hold of his hand and led him back to her bed, where she proceeded to put him back together again, piece by piece.

Brody left a little after midnight—he didn't feel right leaving Barney alone for too long at a stretch, he said—and Carolyn, after locking the door behind him, went straight back to bed and slept a deep, healing sleep.

The next morning, yawning, she padded into the kitchen and immediately spotted the two plates of scrambled eggs, now congealed, still sitting on the table.

Making a face, she scraped the food into the sink and washed it down the disposal.

By that time, Winston was making give-me-breakfast-now noises, so she gave him kibble, which he disdained at first, probably angling for sardines.

Carolyn filled a cup with water, dropped in a tea bag and set the works in the microwave. While she was waiting for the timer to ring, signaling the end of two minutes, she thought about Brody. After last night, *not* thinking about him would have been quite a trick.

The lovemaking still reverberated throughout her body, in small, intermittent aftershocks, but that wasn't something to think about, it was something to *feel.* To savor and enjoy, in secret.

No, it was all that Brody had told her about Lisa, about their little boy, about that terrible accident and how he'd lost his way after it happened, that occupied her mind now.

She'd known intuitively that he was telling the truth, so it wasn't a question of believing or not believing what he said. Instead, it was a matter of personal damage.

How could a person ever come back from a tragedy like that?

Could *she* come back from what she'd so thoroughly believed was a cruel betrayal, even knowing the truth?

Some wounds, after all, never healed.

For Brody, the experience was beyond horrific; he'd been on the phone with Lisa when the collision *happened;*

he'd heard the deafening crash and then the silence that followed. On top of that, he blamed himself—if only he'd let Lisa put their baby up for adoption, if only he'd been at home on that wintry night instead of on the road, driving an eighteen-wheeler, he'd have been at the wheel, not Lisa.

He might have been able to steer clear in time to avoid impact.

If only, if only.

Carolyn knew that phrase well. If only her mother had cared enough to stick around instead of dumping her into the foster-care system and taking off for good. If only her dad had been the strong, steady, reliable type, like Davis Creed, willing to raise his child.

If only pigs had wings and chickens could tap dance, Carolyn thought. One of her foster moms had said that every time she dared to express the slightest dream for the future.

Soon, she'd stopped telling anyone what her hopes were.

Emotionally saddened but still jubilant physically, from making love with Brody, Carolyn switched on her laptop so it would boot up while she was in the shower.

Once she'd washed and dried herself off and gotten dressed, the computer was wide awake, icons flashing, robot voice repeating, over and over, "Somebody likes your friendly face!"

The thing was the auditory equivalent of stone soup, like in the children's story. It just kept right on pumping out noise. So over the whole idea of hooking up online, Carolyn zipped over to the control-panel page and blocked all further communication from the dating site.

And then there was sweet, blissful peace.

"That's better," she told Winston, who didn't offer an opinion, one way or the other.

A few clicks of the mouse took her to the auction site, where she'd posted the gypsy skirt. The bids were still pouring in, and the current number had Carolyn rubbing her eyes, sure she must be misreading it somehow. Nobody paid *that* much for a skirt, however beautiful it was—did they?

She squinted at the high bidder's

screen name, in case it was someone she knew, or maybe one of her regular customers, but she didn't recognize the moniker. Still, a prickle in the pit of her stomach insisted that something was amiss.

Carolyn stared hard at the screen, as though that would unveil the mystery, but she remained in the dark.

She was still at the computer, catching up on legitimate email, when she heard the knocking downstairs, at the front door.

Tricia? No, she had a key, and it was still too early for her to be there, anyway.

Brody? A little OMG thrill riffed through Carolyn, but she quickly quelled it. He'd told her he had a lot to do on the ranch, and they'd agreed to take a few days to catch their breaths.

They had a date for Saturday night, dinner and a movie.

In the interim, they'd play it cool.

The knocking continued, polite but insistent.

"Hold your horses," Carolyn muttered grumpily, nearly tumbling headfirst down the inside stairs because Winston ran past her to be on hand for the welcoming ceremony.

By the time she reached the entryway and opened the front door, Carolyn had assembled a smile and pasted it on her mouth.

It fell away when she got a good look at her visitor. Bill Venable was standing there on the porch, looking worried and uncomfortable and, as always, very attractive in his jeans and sleeveless T-shirt. His biceps were almost as impressive as Brody's.

"Bill," Carolyn said, unable to hide her surprise.

"I'm sorry," Bill said. "I know I should have called before I came over."

Carolyn stepped back to admit him. What on earth was he doing there, at that hour of the morning? The newspaper hadn't even been delivered yet.

"Is something wrong?" she asked. "Ellie's all right, isn't she?"

Bill nodded. His beard was growing in, a sign of anxiety, maybe, since he was normally clean-shaven. "Ellie's fine," he said quickly. "It's just that—well—

there's a fire, a big one, down in New Mexico, and I have to leave right away."

They stood in the entryway, with Winston meowing and curling between their ankles, as sleekly sinuous as a snake with fur.

Carolyn waited, still without a clue as to why Bill was there.

He gave a tentative smile. "We were planning on going up in my plane together, sometime soon?" he reminded her. "I didn't want you thinking I'd forgotten. I'm not sure how long I'll be gone, and I'll probably be too busy to call and, anyway, the fire's pretty remote, so there might not be cell service out there—" He appeared to be struggling, and Carolyn felt a stab of empathy for him. When he finally went on, what he said alarmed her a little. "There's always a chance I won't— I just needed to tell you face-to-face that I won't be around for a while."

Carolyn's spirits sank. It was almost as if Bill had come to say goodbye—forever—as he had reason to worry. She'd heard of pilots having premonitions of a crash or some other fatal disaster, of course.

Was Bill telling her that he thought he might be *killed* fighting this fire?

Her eyes filled and, for a crazy moment, she wanted to beg him not to go, to think of Ellie, and of Angela, and all the other people who must have loved him.

"Will Ellie be staying with her grandparents while you're gone?"

Bill shook his head, still looking miserable. "Not for the next few days. A friend of theirs passed away unexpectedly, so they've gone to Houston for the funeral. Ellie's staying with Angela until Charlie and Stella get back."

"Oh," Carolyn said, hopeful that this meant Bill and Angela were reconsidering their breakup. They belonged together, in her opinion.

"It's not what you're thinking," Bill said quickly. "Angela's feelings about my job haven't changed. She hates it, and she's furious because I refused to turn down this assignment." He sighed, thrust a hand through his hair. "But I know she'll take good care of Ellie, and that's what matters most. The two of them are close."

Carolyn thought of her friend soaring above a burning forest in a small plane, spraying fire retardant on flames clawing at the smoky sky like gigantic red-orange fingers, and she was afraid for him. The words *don't go* scrambled up into her throat and got stuck there, making her eyes sting.

Seeing her expression, Bill smiled sadly, gripped her shoulders gently and kissed her forehead. "Think good thoughts," he said hoarsely, in parting, and then he was turning away, walking out, closing the front door behind him.

Carolyn didn't move until several moments after he'd gone.

If only she'd had the power—or the right—to call him back, make him stay right there in Lonesome Bend, where he'd be safe.

But was anyone ever really safe, anywhere?

The answer, unfortunately, was no.

Bill's plane *could* crash, plummet right into the raging, hellish heart of a forest fire, leaving Ellie an orphan and Angela—sweet, well-meaning Angela—in a state of permanent grief. But he could just as easily drop dead from a heart attack, contract some fatal disease, or be run down in a crosswalk by a speeding car.

No one was getting out of here alive, no one had a guarantee that there would be another tomorrow, and another after that.

Living wasn't safe. Look what had happened to Brody's wife, Lisa, and their baby son. They were alive one moment and gone the next.

And as for laying the heart bare by loving another person? Why, that was the biggest, most deadly risk of all.

The starch drained out of Carolyn's knees, and she took a few groping steps backward and plunked herself down on one of the stairs, propping an elbow on one knee and resting her chin in her palm.

Winston approached, purring, and snuggled against her hip, either offering comfort or seeking it—or both.

Numbly, Carolyn stroked his glossy back with her free hand.

Yes, indeed, she'd been right all along—it was downright dangerous to love a person, or a pet, or even a house or a town or a job. Everything could change with a single turn of the steering wheel, or a phone call, or a policeman knocking at the front door.

But in the end, what choice did anyone have?

Could a person choose *not to* love?

They could try, of course, maybe even succeed to some degree.

But they might as well buy a plot and a tombstone, Carolyn reflected, and stretch out prone on the grass to wait for death, while others marched on in the parade of life, laughing and crying, loving and hating, knowing triumph and defeat and everything in between.

She might be able to kid herself that she was safe, but she'd also miss out on the party.

"You're pretty chipper today," Davis observed, that morning, with a slight twinkle, as he and Conner and Brody rode out to mend the broken fence lines Brody had taken note of the day before, while riding the lines. "Yesterday, you were traveling a rocky road."

Brody didn't answer right away, but he was poignantly aware of the value of ordinary moments. Conner was in the back of the pickup, with Valentino and Barney, hoops of new wire and the communal toolbox, while Brody drove and Davis rode shotgun.

They were working together, he and his brother and his uncle, just the way they ought to be.

Another part of Brody wished he was back in bed with Carolyn; it was too bad a man couldn't be in two places at once.

"That was yesterday," he finally replied, "and this is today."

Davis kept his face turned toward the windshield as they bounced and jostled over rough ground, but Brody knew his uncle was watching him from the corner of his eye. "We all racked up a whole lot of 'yesterdays' before you decided to go on ahead and tell me about Lisa and Justin. Why was that, Brody?"

Brody raised and lowered one shoulder, looking not at Davis, but ahead, at the cattle-speckled terrain of the ranch that had been home to generations of Creeds. Some branches of the family tree bore good fruit—solid, honest men and women committed to giving the best of who they were and what they had to building a lasting legacy for their children and grandchildren, right on down. Here and there, though, a rotten apple cropped up, a rascal or even an outlaw.

Most likely, by his own reckoning, he fit into the second category better than the first.

"It was a hard thing to talk about," he finally said.

"Life is full of things that are hard to talk about," Davis countered matter-of-factly. "Seems to me, if a man's lucky enough to have a home and kinfolks who care about him, it would be better to run *to* them when he had troubles, rather than *from* them."

Brody glanced at his uncle, un-clamped his jawbones. "What do you want me to say, Davis? That I was wrong to stay away all those years?" A pause. "Well, fine. I was wrong."

"It's not a matter of what's right or

wrong," Davis countered quietly. "What bothers me is that you must not have known you'd be welcome here."

"There was that blowup between Conner and me, over Joleen—"

"Don't bullshit me, boy," Davis broke in, sounding gruffer and more annoyed now. "That could have been settled over a couple of beers after supper, and you damn well know it." He gave a deep, ragged sigh. "Here's how I figure it . . . correct me if I'm mistaken—you were *ashamed* to come home. You figured it was your fault, what happened to the wife and the boy, and you wouldn't *let* yourself turn to your family and your friends."

Again, Brody's back teeth ground together. He had to consciously relax his whole face, and that made it damn near impossible to keep the devil-may-care mask in place.

"I never loved Lisa," he heard himself say, straight out.

It was crazy, because he'd never intended to say anything of the sort.

"You tried to do right by her, Brody. When you found out she was carrying

your baby, you went to her. You took responsibility. That might not amount to
the kind of love they print up inside Val-
entine cards, but it *is* love. It's the practical, take-hold, buckle-down-and-get-
it-done kind of love that pretty words
can't hold a candle to."

Conner thumped on the roof of the
cab with one fist, signaling that they'd
reached a place where the fence needed
mending. Brody stopped the pickup
with a lurch that made his brother shout
a swear word.

Brody grinned over at Davis. "You
missed your calling, cowboy," he said.
"You ought to sign on with a greeting
card company and write poetry."

Davis didn't crack a smile. "You think
about what I said, son. What happened,
happened. No getting around it—that
kind of loss is an awful thing, but it's
over. Your wife and your little boy are
gone, and that's a shame, but you're
alive, and that's counts for something.
Make use of the time you have, Brody."

Just then, Conner stepped onto the
driver's-side running board and banged

at the window once, with the flat of his hand. He looked seriously pissed.

"Are you trying to kill me *and* these dogs, driving like that?" he demanded. "First you're doing fifty, then you stop on a damn dime!"

Brody shoved the truck door open, forcing Conner to scramble clear. "Hell, no," Brody mocked, grinning. "If that were the case, I would surely have succeeded."

Davis rolled his eyes. "Don't start, you two," he warned. "We've got work to do."

The bids on the gypsy skirt were still climbing, Carolyn learned, later in the morning, when she checked the auction site again. Tricia had a routine doctor's appointment, so she wouldn't be in for a couple of hours.

Meanwhile, Carolyn couldn't seem to concentrate on the task at hand long enough to get anything done.

Ideas for more one-of-a-kind garments had been pouring into her head in such plentitude that she had to keep stopping whatever she happened to be doing at the time to rough out a sketch, lest, in her scatterbrained state of mind, she forget.

A few customers stopped in, and she boxed and addressed several orders for shipping.

Every time she passed through the main part of the shop, her gaze went straight to the large square package containing the Weaver. She hadn't given the batik a thought the night before, for obvious reasons, and Brody probably hadn't, either.

Too bad, because he could have taken it with him when he headed home, and saved her a trip.

On the other hand, Brody Creed had a stubborn streak as wide as the river, and he might have refused to take the piece with him just because he wanted her to deliver it.

Carolyn ran a fingertip over the wrapping, a little smile playing around her mouth but never quite coming in for a landing.

When the time was right, she would take the batik to Brody's place, as agreed, but there might be more to the delivery than a piece of art.

She was thinking this lascivious thought, and flirting with a few others, when the door of the shop opened, bell jingling, and she braced herself for another onslaught of unexpected customers.

Instead, Primrose Sullivan swept in, wearing one of her brightly colored caftans and lugging more paintings.

"I've been working like a crazy woman," she enthused. "Any time you want me to stop bringing in artwork, you just tell me."

Carolyn laughed, glad to see her friend. And the paintings.

The last batch was selling fast, via the website.

Primrose set down her burden with the gentleness of a mother putting a child down for an afternoon nap and beamed at Carolyn, her blue eyes huge behind the lenses of her leopard-skin glasses.

"It's all over town," Primrose announced gleefully.

This was another OMG moment for Carolyn, but not the pleasant kind. She felt her ears burning and her throat closed up tight. Which was a good thing, as it turned out, because she'd been on the verge of blurting out that Brody *hadn't* stayed the whole night, which was true, and that nothing had happened—*not* true—and that, frankly, she was getting sick of being gossiped about.

"You're planning to expand the shop," Primrose rushed on, making Carolyn almighty thankful that she hadn't been able to speak before. "I think that's so exciting! Is it true that you're planning to hire help?"

"Y-yes," Carolyn managed to respond, somewhat weakly. "It's true. Tricia and I are hoping you might consent to teach some classes . . . ?"

Primrose rubbed her many-ringed hands together in anticipation. "You bet I will," she said. "And you might consider bringing Mavis Pawlings in to teach sometime—she knows everything there is to know about scrapbooking and rubber stamps and all that sort of thing. Then there's Lily Wilde—one of her quilts won best of show last year at the state fair—"

Carolyn smiled, held up both hands, palms out. "Whoa, Primrose," she said good-naturedly, "give me a minute to catch up."

But Primrose was too excited to be still, even for that long. "Scrapbooking is very big, you know," she blurted. "And quilts? Heavens, that's become a regular *industry,* all by itself." She looked around speculatively, a comical sight with her magnified eyes. "Knock out a wall or two," she mused, "and you could sell fabric. This town needs a fabric store—folks have to drive all the way to Denver for a few yards of cotton and spool of thread as it is now."

"Primrose," Carolyn pleaded, grinning, "take a breath."

Primrose *did* take a breath, but the respite was brief. "Handmade items are great," she continued, "but most of your business comes in over the website, doesn't it?"

"Most of it," Carolyn agreed cautiously. "Why?"

Primrose was on a real roll. "The sachets and the doilies and all the rest of it are *fine*—and heaven *knows* I'm grateful to you and Tricia for selling so many of my batiks—but it might be a better use of floor space to display things people would come in purposely to buy. Like quilting fabric. Maybe even a sewing machine or two."

Carolyn smiled. "Primrose?"

"Yes, dear?" The older woman beamed.

"How would you like a part-time job?"

Primrose all but clapped her hands. "Are you offering me one? My friends all say I spend too much time in my studio, and I'm bound to get stale or even burn out, and I'd just love a change of scene for a few hours a day."

"I'll have to double-check with Tricia, of course," Carolyn said, "but I can't think of anybody I'd rather hire to help out around here, and I'm sure she'll agree."

Primrose looked around, her expression dreamy now. "Oh," she said, "I can just *see* it all, in my mind's eye."

"Me, too," Carolyn agreed.

It was then that Primrose noticed the parcel containing the Weaver, still resting on top of a display table. There was something of a caress to the way she touched the wrapping. "I could drop this off at Brody's place on my way home," she offered.

Silently, Carolyn called herself three kinds of crazy—here was her chance to cross an errand off her to-do list *and* a way to show Brody that she wasn't about to dance to his tune—but she shook her head. "He's out at the ranch, working with Davis and Conner," she said. "And the Weaver is much too valuable to be left on his doorstep."

Primrose watched Carolyn closely for a moment, a happy light dancing in her eyes. "You know right where Brody Creed is, at this very minute," she observed, in a teasing tone. "Now, isn't that interesting?"

Carolyn blushed slightly. "I just assumed that's where he'd be," she said lamely.

Primrose chuckled. "It does my old

heart good," she said. Like many older people, Primrose didn't do segues.

Carolyn didn't ask what the woman meant, because she already knew.

Segues weren't always necessary, now were they?

Primrose went on to show Carolyn each of the new pieces she'd just brought in, and Carolyn's admiration was sincere.

"What's it like, to be able to bring people and animals to life on cloth or a canvas, the way you do?" she asked wistfully.

Primrose patted her gently on the back. "I imagine it's about the same as being able to sew up something beautiful in no time flat, the way *you* do," she replied. "I've seen your work, Carolyn. You have an eye for line and color and movement—stop being so all-fired humble all the time and own it."

Own it.

What did that mean, exactly?

All her life, it seemed to Carolyn, she'd been trying to prove something—she was a foster kid, *but*— She'd never gone to college, *but*— She'd fallen head over heels for Brody Creed, back in the day, *but*—

But what if everything she'd ever wanted was within her grasp—and all she had to do was own it?

CHAPTER SIXTEEN

Saturday took its sweet time rolling around, as far as Brody was concerned, and staying away from Carolyn in the meantime was only possible because he'd been putting in twelve-hour days on the ranch, along with Davis and Conner. There were fences to mend, strays to round up, sick cows to dose with medicine, stalls to muck out and horses to shoe, deworm and exercise.

A rancher's work is, quite literally, never done.

Since he and Kim and the minidogs were heading out to Stone Creek Sunday morning, Davis whistled a lot, and there was a spring in his step. He was a born grandfather, and Brody knew his uncle could hardly wait for Tricia and Conner's little one to be born so he'd have a Creed youngster readily available for spoiling.

Conner was in a fairly good mood, too, now that Tricia had agreed to stay home, let Carolyn be in charge of things at the shop and take it easy until after the baby came.

As for Brody himself, well, he was as jumpy as ice water on a hot griddle. His moods ran the gamut from woe-is-me to yee-haw, and he never knew when one mood would give way to the other.

He worked a half day on Saturday, appropriated a horse trailer to bring Moonshine back from the ranch to the new barn and, with Barney's questionable assistance, got the gelding settled in his own stall.

To Brody's way of thinking, Moonshine looked a bit on the lonely side, all by himself in that big place, fancy as it was shaping up to be. The stalls were finished and the water and electricity were hooked up, which was more than could be said of the house. The corral fence stood straight and sturdy, too.

"Maybe you and I ought to move in with Moonshine," he told Barney, only half kidding. It wasn't even June yet, and the house wouldn't be ready to live in until mid-August, according to the contractor.

Barney trotted happily at his side, panting, as they headed toward the log cabin where he'd been living since he'd bought the River's Bend property from Tricia.

He hated the lack of elbow room, the counter running through the middle of the building, the jury-rigged bathroom and the borrowed bed and making do with a knee-high fridge and a microwave the size of a shoebox.

Most of all, he hated that he was always alone in the place. That definitely sucked.

But, hallelujah, it was finally Saturday.

He'd had part of the contractor's crew up at the Bluebird Drive-in for a couple of days now, cleaning up the snack bar and hooking up a popcorn machine, rented, like the projector, and he'd hired a caterer from Denver to whip up and deliver a fancy meal for two, complete with wine and candlelight.

Oh, he had definitely outdone himself this time, Brody thought cheerfully. Not that he went around revamping old drive-in theaters for one dinner-and-movie date—there had been a lot of women in his life, and he'd given some of them expensive presents, or paid their bills a time or two, but he'd never done anything quite like this before.

However things shook out between him and Carolyn, when it was all over but the shoutin', he'd have this night to remember, and so would she.

Brody ducked into his makeshift bathroom, stripped off his work clothes and showered.

After that, he put on clean jeans, a pale blue Western shirt, socks and his second-best boots. It was still too early in the day to go with the custom-made pair, the ones he usually broke out only for weddings and funerals with the Creed brand subtly embossed into each shaft.

He ran a comb through his hair—he

needed barbering, he guessed, but the more clean-cut he was, the more he could have passed for Conner, and something about that chapped his hide a little. Love his brother though he did, Brody figured it was enough that he and his twin had the same face, coloring and build.

They didn't need the same haircut and close shave, too.

Hungry, but downright averse to the idea of yet another half-assed concoction made up of the strange assortment of stuff in his refrigerator, he decided he'd treat himself to a hamburger and a milk shake for lunch.

With that in mind, he left Barney to snooze on the dog bed, while he drove over to the Birdcage Café for a generous helping of fat, sugar and preservatives.

The hole-in-the-wall restaurant had been a mainstay in Lonesome Bend since before his dad and Davis were born, and while everybody wondered, nobody recalled why any sensible person would give a food-service establishment—even a greasy spoon like that one—such an unappetizing name.

For all that, the Birdcage served a mean burger, made from scratch, and they grilled the buns in real butter before slapping a thick patty of ground beef between them. They changed the oil in their deep-fat fryer once a week whether it needed doing or not, and the only thing better than their potato salad was Natty McCall's secret-recipe chili, available only at the annual rummage sale in late October.

The parking spaces on the street were full, as usual, so Brody pulled into the dusty gravel lot next to the café, driving slowly so he wouldn't get his truck too dirty before it was time to pick Carolyn up for their get-together that night.

He had some high hopes for the *together* part.

"Way you was drivin' two miles an hour, I figured some maiden schoolmarm was fixin' to get out of that truck," boomed Will Carlson, one of several old-timers who took turns holding down the peeling wooden bench under the

Birdcage's front window, as Brody walked toward him.

"How many maiden schoolmarms drive extended-cab pickups, Will?" Brody retorted with a good-natured grin and a tug at the brim of a hat he wasn't wearing.

Will eyed him from beneath the bill of a ratty old cap, his face beard-stubbled and loose-skinned. He shifted his jaw around, most likely in an effort to realign his ill-fitting dentures. "You come here to see Joleen?"

The old man's question didn't register with Brody until it was too late—by the time it did, he'd already pushed open the front door and stepped inside.

And there was Joleen, wearing a waitress uniform and flirting shamelessly with some out-of-towner in a business suit while she took his order.

Brody briefly considered bolting, but one, that would be a chickenshit thing to do, since this was still a free country the last time he checked and he had as much right to be there as anybody, and two, he wanted a grease-burger.

So he stayed put, feeling his neck

warm up as everybody in the café turned to look at him.

Including Joleen.

Brody nodded a greeting to her and took the last stool at the counter, between two grizzled ranchers who'd lived around Lonesome Bend since the fifth day of Creation. That pair of old buzzards hadn't spoken to each other in fifty years, it was said—something about a hand of poker and a girl—which was the only reason there was a single place to sit down.

Joleen, sly-eyed, finished writing up the suit's order and sashayed behind the counter to stand directly in front of Brody.

"Well," she said, almost purring. "If it isn't Brody Creed."

Brody reset his shoulders, set his hands on the counter, fingers interlaced. "Hello, Joleen," he said casually. "How about a burger with everything and a chocolate milk shake?"

Joleen made no move to write down the request or relay it to the fry cook back at the grill. All the chatter had ceased, and even the jukebox fell silent.

Evidently, the folks who patronized the Birdcage had free time aplenty, if they could sit around gawking like they were, with their ears practically tilting forward, like Moonshine's did when he was trying to decide whether or not he ought to spook.

Joleen folded her arms, underscoring her ample breasts. "You probably thought I'd be long gone by now, didn't you?" she asked, with acid sweetness.

"A man can always hope," Brody replied mildly.

This brought a few snickers from the onlookers and made Joleen's green eyes flash with temper.

Brody wondered idly if her eyes were really green, or if she was wearing another set of contact lenses. He didn't plan on getting close enough to find out.

Quietly, he repeated his order.

Joleen turned around and fairly screeched it at Manuel, the fry cook.

Manuel winced, tossed Brody a glance of amused sympathy and commenced to building his famous two-thousand-plus-calorie gut-buster.

After that, Joleen steered clear of

Brody to such an extent that Manuel had to bring out the burger and fries himself when they were ready. As for the milk shake—well, Brody decided not to remind anybody of that, because it was too easy to picture Joleen upending the thing over the top of his head.

Gradually, folks lost interest, probably disappointed that there hadn't been some kind of donnybrook, and went back to their own food and the conversations they'd suspended when Brody and Joleen first faced off.

Brody ate most of his meal, though he'd mostly lost his appetite, and he even pretended to enjoy it. When he couldn't face another bite, he estimated the total for his check, since Joleen didn't bring one, and left the money on the counter, next to his plate.

He headed for the parking lot and was just opening the door of his truck when Joleen shot out of a side door and stomped over to him.

"What about my tip?" she demanded.

Brody grinned affably. "You've got to be kidding," he said.

"It just goes to show I was absolutely

right to dump you, Brody Creed, because you have *no class* whatsoever!"

Brody folded his arms. If Joleen
wanted to rewrite history, it was okay
with him. Especially if it meant she'd let
him be from now on. "I guess you did
the right thing for sure, that being the
case," he said. He set one foot on the
running board, fixing to climb behind
the wheel. "But since you wanted a tip,
here it is, Joleen—move on, find yourself a big city with bright lights, because
Lonesome Bend, let alone the Birdcage
Café, is never going to be enough for
you."

An impish smile played on Joleen's
mouth. Some people would have been
surprised by that reaction, Brody supposed, but he wasn't. The word *mercu-
rial* didn't begin to describe the woman's
temperament.

"I would, if I had, oh, say, five thousand dollars to travel on," she suggested
coyly.

"Then you'd better find yourself a
sucker pronto," Brody replied easily,
"because if I fork over the money, it's

going to look like a payoff, and that kind of thing doesn't set well with me."

The smile turned to ice, a thin layer over poison. "Since when do you care how anything looks to other people, Creed?"

Since Carolyn, Brody thought, just then realizing it was true.

He didn't give a rat's ass about the town's opinion of him, or Joleen's. Never had, really. But it mattered what Carolyn saw when she looked at him—Conner and Davis, too. Moreover, it mattered what he thought of *himself.*

"Well?" Joleen prompted, angered by his silence. *"Since when?"*

"Since now," Brody replied, very quietly.

Joleen blinked. He hoped she wouldn't cry, but if she did, he reckoned he could endure it, since he'd be driving away here in a minute or so. "It wouldn't be a payoff," she finally said, her voice gone small and a little shaky now. "The five grand, I mean. It would be one friend making a loan to another. And be honest, Brody. Maybe building that big, fancy house and barn at River's Bend is the first showy thing you've ever done, but that's pocket change to you, and you know it."

"Sorry, Joleen," Brody said. "Writing you a check for any amount of money is a message I just don't want to send."

Her shoulders sagged and she scuffed at the gravel with the toe of her white waitress shoe. It wouldn't be white for long, Brody supposed, but, then, Joleen wouldn't be a waitress for long, either.

She had the worst case of wanderlust Brody had ever seen.

"Well, *damn,*" she said finally, and the sorrows gave way to that showgirl smile of hers. "It was worth a try."

Brody laughed. "Good luck, Joleen," he said, "and be happy."

She was still smiling as he drove away, and waving one hand in farewell.

Women, Brody thought. There was just no figuring them out.

Carolyn rooted desperately through her wardrobe for something to wear besides her normal jeans, T-shirt and boots. Bottom line, she'd shot the fashion wad with the cotton sundress she'd worn to Bill's backyard barbecue, and recycling it for a date with Brody just didn't seem right.

"Why don't you wear the gypsy skirt?" Tricia asked. They'd closed the shop an hour early that day, and she'd stuck around to quiz an admission out of Carolyn—yes, she was going out with Brody that night.

It was no big deal, she'd insisted to Tricia.

"Are you kidding me?" Carolyn retorted. "The bid is in four figures. Whoever is so determined to buy that skirt isn't looking for anything that's already been worn."

"They'd never know," Tricia said.

"*I'd* know," Carolyn countered.

"Then maybe they wouldn't care if they *did* know," Tricia said cheerfully.

"Fat chance," Carolyn retorted, unearthing a black sundress with white polka dots and holding it up for a critical examination. When had she made the thing? It had to have been a long time ago, because she didn't remember it at all.

Tricia chuckled. "And yet you would have me believe this date with Brody was no big deal," she teased. "Why don't you just jump in your car and come out to the ranch? We'll ransack every closet on the place if we have to—between Kim and I, we must have *something* you could wear tonight."

"There's no time for that," Carolyn practically wailed, casting a speculative glance at the gypsy skirt, draped neatly on a hanger and suspended from the hook on the back of her bedroom door.

She *couldn't* wear that skirt.

For one thing, it didn't really belong to her.

For another, she might spill something on it, ruin it forever. *Then* what?

And for still *another* thing, Brody hadn't asked her to a formal gala at the White House or a coronation at Buckingham Palace—he'd offered dinner and a movie. She'd look like a fool, getting that dressed up for a blue-plate special at some country café, followed by a flick and popcorn.

She couldn't resist catching one of the ribbons between her fingers, though, and imagining how it would feel to be a princess for just one night.

"Wear the skirt, Cinderella," Tricia said gently.

"I couldn't," Carolyn murmured, sorely tempted to do just that. To be rash and reckless, for once in her life, instead of careful.

To be beautiful.

To be Cinderella.

Oh, but Brody Creed was a cowboy, not a prince.

Lonesome Bend was planted squarely in the real world, not in a fairy-tale kingdom, where fairy godmothers waved wands and pumpkins turned to coaches, mice to prancing steeds.

She was Carolyn Simmons, an ordinary woman, and she'd better remember it.

Tricia wasn't one to give up. "Well, then, just *try it on,*" she said, waddling over to stand next to Carolyn. With a sigh, she stretched to ease the pressure on her lower back and sighed, "I swear this kid is getting ready to audition for *Riverdance.* The way he kicks, he'll be born wearing tap shoes."

Since Tricia and Conner had been closemouthed about the sex of their baby, this was the clue Carolyn had been waiting for.

"Ah-ha!" she cried, jubilant, forgetting the skirt and all its magic for a much greater miracle, the formation of a brand-new human being. "You're having a boy!"

"Don't tell," Tricia said, in a conspiratorial whisper, putting a finger to her lips. "Outside the doctor's office, nobody knows but Conner and me."

"Why the secrecy?" Carolyn asked.

Again, Tricia sighed, but softly, and with an air of contentment. "We're not trying to be mysterious," she said. "It's just that . . . well, we're both sort of old-fashioned when it comes to having a baby. Not that long ago, nobody knew if they were having a boy or a girl until after their delivery. Now, people have the nursery furnished in either pink or blue and the name picked out months ahead of time. I'd rather have been surprised, and Conner agrees."

Carolyn studied her friend. "You're not superstitious, are you? One of those people who think it's bad luck to buy things for a baby before it's born? In case—in case something goes wrong?"

Tricia smiled. "No," she said. "I'm not. There is nothing wrong with this baby, trust me. He kicks like a mule."

Carolyn smiled back, relieved. "I don't suppose you want to tell me what you're going to name young Mr. Creed, now that the figurative cat is out of the bag?"

"Davis Blue," Tricia answered readily. "We'll probably call him Blue."

"Blue?" Carolyn asked. The Davis part needed no explanation, but—*Blue?*

"For Conner and Brody's father," Tricia said. "Davis's older brother. The story goes that the sky was a knock-out shade of azure when Blue was born—hence the name."

"I like it," Carolyn mused and, for the briefest of moments, she allowed herself to wonder what name she and *Brody* might give a child of their own.

"Me, too," Tricia agreed. "And don't you dare tell anybody. Davis and Kim don't know, and neither does Brody. We want our baby's sex *and* his name to be a surprise."

Carolyn made a zipping motion across

her mouth. Then she laughed again, out of pure joy at her friends' good fortune, and gave Tricia a quick hug.

"Now," Tricia said, with a little sniffle, once they'd had their girl moment, "back to the gypsy skirt. *Try it on.* I want to see what it looks like on an actual person, and heaven knows, I'm in no condition to model haute couture."

"Tricia."

"It's the least you can do," Tricia insisted, "after I told you my big secret."

Carolyn sighed, took the skirt from the hook, still on its hanger and held it against her chest, careful not to crush the ribbons. "Oh, all right," she said, starting for the bathroom. "But I'm telling you right now, it's going to look downright weird with a T-shirt."

Tricia went to the bureau, tugged open a drawer and extracted a wispy black silk camisole with spaghetti straps, waving it at Carolyn like a flag. "Wear this," she said.

Carolyn took the garment hesitantly—she'd worn it with a transparent shirt she'd owned, and subsequently discarded as impractical, a long time ago—

and gave Tricia a rueful look. "I don't know," she said. "It's pretty skimpy—"

"It's just us girls," Tricia reminded her, almost singing the words and shooing Carolyn toward the bathroom. *"Go."*

Standing at Carolyn's kitchen door, with the first shadows of twilight falling around him, Brody tried to remember the last time he'd made a fuss like this over a simple date.

Not since his high-school prom, he decided, hooking a finger under the collar of his starched white shirt even though the top three buttons were already undone. Kim had made him wear a penguin suit that night, as she'd done to Conner, too, and Brody had stabbed the girl—Becky? Betsy? Babs?—with the little pearl-headed pin while fumbling around trying to pin on her corsage. He and Conner, along with two of their friends and all four dates, had crammed themselves into the back of a rented limo and thought they were big stuff.

He smiled at the memory.

Remembered that he hadn't knocked.

He rapped his knuckles lightly against

the door frame. Through the frosted glass in the door's oval window, he saw Carolyn approaching to admit him, and even before she opened the door, his heart had shinnied up into his throat and swelled to three times its normal size.

Her light hair gleamed around her shoulders, looking soft enough to run his fingers through, and her perfect cleavage formed an enticing V above the black silk of her top.

After her face, though—her shy and lovely and slightly flushed face—it was the skirt he would remember until the end of his days.

It was composed of what seemed to be hundreds of ribbons and beads, and it swayed and shifted around her like a puff of glittering smoke, or shards of glass in a kaleidoscope.

"Wow," he said. He hadn't brought flowers, since she still had the roses from the other night, but now he wished he had. He wished there were a coach-and-six waiting on the street, instead of the car he'd borrowed from Davis and Kim.

Carolyn's cheeks were pink. Without

looking down—a skill he'd perfected since puberty—he managed to note that her nipples showed faintly through the black top.

"Wow, yourself," she said, after giving him a flirty once-over. Then she lost whatever bravado she'd summoned up and blushed again. "Do—do you think I'm overdressed? It was Tricia's idea to wear this—she nagged me into it—"

Brody reached out and rested an index finger lightly against her mouth—a mouth he hoped to kiss, and thoroughly, later on in the evening. "It's perfect," he said. "*You're* perfect."

She already had her purse handy, a thin little envelope of a thing she tucked under one arm. Obviously, she hadn't brought her toothbrush and a change of clothes for morning.

He tried not to read that as an omen.

"Thank you," she said, so belatedly that Brody had to scramble for a moment to recall what she was thanking him for.

Oh, yeah. Saying she was perfect. Well, that hadn't been such a stretch now, had it?

She *was* perfect.

He took her arm as they descended the outside stairs, the skirt whispering like poetry made visible with every move she made.

This time, she noticed he was looking and stopped, when they reached the bottom of the steps, to peer into his face. "Are you *sure* I'm not overdressed?" she demanded.

He chuckled. "As far as I'm concerned, lady, anytime you're wearing more than skin, you're overdressed."

That made her laugh, albeit nervously. But her feet came loose from the ground, where she'd dug them in a moment before, and Carolyn and Brody moved on toward the waiting car.

He might have blown it with the flowers, Brody thought, but he'd gotten this part right. In that getup, Carolyn would have had a hard time getting into the cab of his truck.

He opened the passenger-side door for her, waited while she and that amazing skirt got themselves settled in the seat.

She'd already fastened her seat belt by the time he slid behind the wheel.

He was wearing his best shirt and jeans, and a pair of boots that had cost more than his first car, but now he wondered if he wasn't the one who ought to be fretting about how they were dressed—or *under*dressed, in his case.

Carolyn sat rigidly in the seat, the sliver-thin purse on her lap, her gaze fixed straight ahead. In a sidelong glance, Brody noticed the pulse at the base of her throat.

He wasn't the only one who was nervous, obviously.

The realization relaxed him a little.

As for chitter-chatter, well, if Carolyn didn't feel like talking, it was okay with him. He was satisfied just to be sharing a car seat with her.

They drove through town and he thought she gave a little sigh of relief when they passed the Birdcage Café without stopping—*as if* he'd take her there—and then the Golden Spur Saloon and Steakhouse, but maybe he imagined it.

When he steered the car onto the

bumpy track leading to the Bluebird Drive-in, though, she turned and looked at him with widened eyes. Maybe she thought he doubled as a serial killer in his spare time and he was taking her somewhere remote, so she could be his next victim.

Creed, he thought, *you are losing it.*

Thanks to the generator he'd borrowed from his contractor—it was a noisy piece of equipment, but effective—the building containing the snack bar was all lit up. The ancient movie screen glowed white in the gathering twilight, ready for action.

Carolyn looked around, still wide-eyed, with her mouth slightly open.

"You wanted dinner and a movie," Brody said, watching her.

What if this was the world's dumbest idea? he wondered, while he waited for a reaction.

"You're not serious," she said, but there was a gleam in her eyes now, and that pulse at the base of her throat was beating hard.

Brody said nothing. He just shut off

the car, got out and came around to her side to open the door for her.

She put out her hand, and he took it. Helped her out.

She stood there, like a goddess dressed in dancing dreams, looking up at him. Her expression was one of amused bafflement. "I don't understand," she said.

"You will," Brody replied, still holding her hand.

He led her toward the snack bar, which had been filled with the caterer's assistants until a few minutes ago. By now, there was a single waiter, hiding in the back most likely, and he'd be gone, too, as soon as Brody could reasonably get rid of him.

Inside the scrubbed and scoured snack bar, the glass enclosing the popcorn machine gleamed, as did the counter.

A round table sat in the middle of the room, draped with a snow-white tablecloth and set with china and silver. Candles glimmered and flickered in the center and, except for the faint hum of the generator, all was quiet.

Carolyn was speechless. She looked up at Brody's face as though she expected him to say there was some mistake, they'd wandered into the wrong place, whatever.

Brody smiled and cocked an elbow at her so she'd take his arm, which she did after a moment's confusion, and escorted her to the table. He pulled back her chair, waited until she was seated and sat down opposite her.

The candlelight danced across her face and shimmered in her hair.

Right on cue, the rent-a-waiter appeared, with a bottle of French wine and two sparkling crystal glasses.

Carolyn drew in her breath, gave Brody another look of curious surprise and finally smiled back at him.

"When you said dinner and a movie, you weren't kidding," she said, as the waiter poured their wine and scurried off to the back room again, to await his next scene.

Brody grinned, picked up his wineglass by the stem, and waited for Carolyn to do the same. "There are some things," he said, "that I never kid about."

She smiled, and their glass rims made a bell-like sound as they touched them together. "This is like something—well, out of a *movie,*" she said.

The waiter returned with salads, set them down with a flourish and immediately vanished again.

The guy certainly knew when to get lost, Brody thought with approval, and his tip was getting bigger with every passing moment.

"This is delicious," Carolyn said, after spearing some salad with her fork and taking a cautious nibble.

Brody laughed. "You sound surprised."

She blushed prettily. God, he loved it when she blushed. "It's . . . I've never been on a date like this."

"That was the idea," Brody said. "Don't look now, but I'm trying to impress you."

"Well," Carolyn said, "you're succeeding." She looked at him from under her eyelashes, and a corner of her highly kissable mouth twitched. "What comes next?"

Brody pretended to be puzzled. Took

another sip of his wine instead of answering. But he was thinking, *You do, if I have anything to say about it.*

Carolyn, so quiet before, in the car, seemed bent on conversation now. "The Bluebird has been closed for years," she said, looking around. Her expression was nostalgic. "Tricia has a lot of old pictures of it. But surely the projector doesn't actually work—"

"We'll see," Brody said.

CHAPTER SEVENTEEN

Carolyn was amazed, and not just by the romantic dinner, the delicate dessert to follow, or the way the popcorn machine seemed to come on all by itself, like magic.

That Brody had even thought of something like this, let alone gone to all the trouble and expense to make it happen, blew her away.

They lingered in the candlelight until it was fully dark outside, and then Brody pulled back her chair, waited for her to stand and escorted her grandly back to Kim and Davis's car.

They drove over a couple of humps in the ground and stopped beside one particular rusted post, with a speaker attached.

"Don't move," Brody told her, with a twinkle in his eyes, "I'll be right back."

She turned to watch as he returned to the snack bar.

Sound crackled through the dented speaker on the pole outside the driver's side window, and light spilled across the darkened lot. Once, the Bluebird Drive-in would have been packed with all sorts of vehicles on a Saturday night, every space filled, every speaker clipped onto a car window, but tonight, apparently, it was theirs alone.

True to his word, Brody returned in a couple of minutes, carrying a silver wine cooler overflowing with fresh popcorn in the curve of one arm.

He opened the car door, handed Carolyn the popcorn and got in.

Imagining what buttered popcorn might do to the gypsy skirt, she set the cooler between them, on the console. When she closed her eyes, she felt dizzy, but the instant she opened them again, she was fine.

"I didn't have time to hunt down any of those cardboard buckets they usually serve this stuff in," Brody explained, with a nod at the popcorn, turning and fiddling with the speaker.

Music swelled into the car, accompanied by a few stereophonic screeches, and Brody winced as he adjusted the volume.

Only then did Carolyn look toward the movie screen, now awash in motion and color and light and opening credits.

One name jumped out at her.

Gifford Welsh.

Gifford Welsh, the man who'd single-handedly ended her brief and happy career as his daughter's nanny.

Shock washed over her, like water charged with electricity, stunning the breath from her lungs and making every nerve in her entire body sting like molten wax.

This must be what it's like to be struck by lightning, she thought.

More nausea and another spate of dizziness followed the shock and for a moment, Carolyn was afraid she might distinguish herself by throwing up a *second* time, in front of the same man.

"Oh, my God—" she whispered, incapable of more.

Brody had deliberately chosen a movie starring *Gifford Welsh.*

And why would he do such a thing? Because he'd heard all that stupid gossip about her supposed affair with the actor, *that* was why. He'd set her up, suckered her in with that romantic dinner in the specially refurbished snack bar—maybe the lovemaking had been part of the joke, too—and for what? To play a cruel, sophomoric prank?

"Oops," she heard Brody say, somewhere in the pounding void of furious humiliation that surrounded her. "Carolyn, I—"

Carolyn shoved the car door open, trembling, blinded not by tears but by injured rage. She scrambled out and immediately caught the toe of her shoe in the hem of the gypsy skirt—the *beautiful* gypsy skirt—and heard the fabric give way with a terrible ripping sound.

Over it all, on the gigantic screen, Gifford's face loomed, big as a building.

He was laughing, of course.

Carolyn lifted the skirt in both hands and ran, tripping over the rough ground, finally kicking off both shoes and leaving them behind.

"Carolyn!" Brody shouted after her, his voice gruff. "Wait!"

She didn't, couldn't wait. She couldn't be rational.

This was what she got, she thought hysterically, for believing she could be Cinderella, even for one night.

Brody caught up to her, took a firm hold on her arm, held her up when she would have lost her footing and taken a tumble.

"Listen to me," he said.

Carolyn was breathing hard, coming back to herself, and feeling even more wretchedly embarrassed than before.

Brody used the side of one thumb to brush a tear from her cheek; until then, she hadn't known she was crying.

"Shh," he murmured, and pulled her close to him.

Carolyn struggled at first, but then

she clung. She buried her wet face in his once-white shirt, smeared foundation and mascara and lipstick all over the front and let the sniffles turn to sobs.

And still Brody held her. "I'm sorry," he said quietly, his breath brushing past her ear. "Carolyn, I'm so sorry—"

Carolyn, I'm so sorry. The words echoed through her memory, spoken by different voices.

Her mother: *Carolyn, I'm so sorry, but I just can't take care of you anymore. . . .*

Social worker after social worker: *Carolyn, I'm so sorry, but the Wilsons— the Jeffersons—the Crosbys—think you'd be better off in a different foster home. . . .*

And, finally, Gifford Welsh: *Carolyn, I'm so sorry. I thought you felt the same way about me as I do about you. . . .*

"I wasn't involved with Gifford Welsh," Carolyn said now, her voice and her breathing as uneven as the ground around them. "I was *the nanny.* I looked after his daughter, Storm, and I loved that child and *I had to leave her* because he came on to me, while his wife was away, and—and—"

"Carolyn," Brody repeated, gripping her shoulders and resting his chin on top of her head. "Take it easy. It's okay. Everything is okay."

But another wave of fury crashed over her then, and she pushed back from him. "I can't believe I trusted you again, after what you did before. What am I to you, Brody? Just another notch on the bedpost? Well, here's a flash for you, cowboy—I'm a *real person,* with feelings!"

Brody didn't say her name again. Didn't say anything at all. He just looked at her, his hands hanging loose at his sides, that damned movie looming huge behind him like some Hollywood version of the Second Coming, and odd squeaks of dialogue and music piping from the rusty speaker disintegrating behind them.

A part of Carolyn stood back from it all, detached, silently observing that by now Brody was probably expecting her head to start spinning around on her shoulders or something.

"I want to go home," she said, with

hard-won dignity, after a few moments of awkward silence.

"Okay," Brody said, his voice hoarse now. "Let's go."

He took her arm, squired her back to the car and got her settled in the front seat, all without a word.

Getting in on his side, he rolled down the window, unhooked the speaker and gave it a hard toss. Then he started the car and they drove off, leaving the movie playing to an audience of ghosts and the lights burning in the snack bar.

The popcorn spilled into the backseat when they went over a bump, and Carolyn looked down at the gypsy skirt.

It was ruined, of course.

A metaphor for the evening.

A metaphor *for her life.*

So much for Cinderella. Brody wouldn't be around to try a glass slipper on her dainty little foot anytime soon, that was for sure.

Carolyn waited for Brody to ask if she'd seen her shrink lately, or maybe forgotten to take her medications, but he didn't say anything at all.

"I might have overreacted a little," she

finally said, hollowed out by all that searing anger, when they pulled up in front
of Natty McCall's house.

"Ya think?" Brody asked mildly, and
without a trace of humor.

He got out of the car, walked around
to her side, opened her door.

Barefoot, except for her ruined panty
hose, she clasped her purse—by some
miracle, she'd managed not to lose it—
to her bosom and walked as regally as
she could across the sidewalk and the
grass to the stairs leading up to her
apartment.

Brody saw her to her door, but despite the lack of space on the tiny landing, he somehow maintained a little distance between them. A muscle bunched
in his jaw, but the expression in his eyes
was one of pain, not anger.

"You'll be all right now?" he asked,
like he wasn't sure it was safe to leave
her in her own company.

Carolyn bit her lower lip, nodded.
"Yes," she said.

He held out one hand, palm up, and
for just a second, Carolyn thought it was
an attempt to make peace. Fortunately,

she realized he wanted her house key before she made an utter idiot of herself all over again by giving him her hand instead.

Brody unlocked the door for her, pushed it open. Handed the key back once she was over the threshold, and facing him.

Winston, who'd most likely been watching from the windowsill, jumped down with a solid *thump* of cat meeting floor, but he didn't hiss at Brody the way he normally would have done, or bristle out his tail.

He actually purred, and looped himself around the man's boots a couple of times in greeting.

Brody didn't acknowledge Winston; he was gazing straight at Carolyn. His throat worked, and the pain in his eyes, visible even though she had yet to turn on the overhead light in the kitchen, matched the dull ache lodged in the center of Carolyn's chest.

"Good night, then," he finally said.

"Good night," Carolyn choked out, with great effort.

Then Brody turned to leave, and Carolyn shut and locked the door between them. Flipped on the lights.

Winston meowed, looked up at her.

She made herself take a good look at the gypsy skirt.

Yep, it was in tatters. A total loss.

Numbly, Carolyn went into her bedroom, exchanged Cinderella's ball gown for jeans and a T-shirt and boots and returned to the kitchen.

"I've done it now," she told Winston, rummaging in the cupboards for the box of ginger tea. Her stomach was doing flip-flops.

Winston leaped back up onto his windowsill. "Reow?" he asked.

She patted his head, smiled sadly. Her eyes felt swollen, though she hadn't cried that much, and she probably had makeup smeared all over her face, and heaven only knew what her hair looked like by now, but none of those things mattered, because it was the same old story. Déjà vu all over again.

She'd been a sucker for a fantasy, allowed herself to believe in fairy tales. For just one night, she'd wanted to be a princess.

Was that so wrong?

Carolyn forgot about the ginger tea, opened another cupboard door and began taking down souvenir mugs, one by one.

Disneyland. The Grand Canyon. Independence Hall. The Alamo.

She'd never been to any of those places, but she could have described a family vacation to each one of them, complete down to the weather what meals she'd eaten at which restaurants. There would have been lots of pictures to anchor the memories, and choosing which one to put on the front of the annual Christmas card would certainly be a challenge.

At least she hadn't sent herself postcards, she thought ruefully, her eyes burning with another crop of tears.

In all, there were over two dozen mugs in her pitiful collection.

She'd been—all by her lonesome—to exactly three of the places represented: Boise, Idaho, Virginia City, Nevada, and Reno. Not even Las Vegas, for Pete's sake, but *Reno.*

It was pathetic.

Well, she was through pretending. Through with fairy tales. Through trying to be anybody other than Carolyn Simmons, the foster kid all grown up, with no family and no history and certainly no happy vacations to look back on.

Not that she felt sorry for herself—if anything, she was angry.

Maybe Brody had set her up tonight, and maybe he hadn't.

Either way, she'd acted like a maniac, and he'd avoid her from now on.

Which was probably a good thing.

Carolyn picked up the cup from Disneyland, recalled buying it in a thrift shop somewhere in her totally unremarkable travels and dropped it into the trash can, where it made a satisfying *clunk* sound.

Winston looked at her curiously, but did not seem overly concerned by her strange behavior.

That made one of them.

She dropped in the mug from the Grand Canyon next, and, striking its counterpart from Disneyland, it shattered.

By the time she'd finished, she had three cups to her name.

They were nothing fancy, but at least they commemorated places she'd actually *been to* once upon a time.

She'd always heard that breaking dishes could be therapeutic, and it seemed there might be something to that theory, because she'd begun to feel just a touch better than she had before, even though her head still ached and her stomach was still twitchy.

It was a rite of passage, getting rid of those cups, Carolyn decided, briskly lifting the heavy trash bag out of the bin, tying it closed and carrying it down to the larger bin next to Natty's detached garage.

Step one to becoming the real Carolyn Simmons.

Whoever the heck *that* was.

Conner watched with a wry expression in his eyes as Brody took a beer from the ranch-house fridge, popped the top and poured some down his throat.

The kitchen was dimly lit—Tricia was in bed, probably asleep, and Conner had answered the knock at the back door muttering, hair all messed up and clad only in a pair of sweat pants.

"What happened to your shirt?" he asked, taking in the large, colorful smudge on Brody's chest. A pensive frown followed. "Or is that *my* shirt?"

"Carolyn's face rubbed off on it," Brody replied, raising the beer can in a grimly humorous salute.

Conner helped himself to a beer of his own and padded over to the table where generations of Creeds, men as well as women, had carried on late-night conversations like this one.

"Sit," he said to Brody.

Brody took time to grab a second beer, for backup, before he sank into a chair.

"How did Carolyn's face happen to rub off on your—my—shirt?" Conner asked mildly. Brody saw amusement in his brother's eyes, along with a generous amount of sympathy. That last part pissed him off.

"It isn't your shirt," Brody bit out. "I bought it two years ago, in San Antonio."

"Whatever," Conner said affably. Then he sighed and went on. "I've figured this much out on my own—the big movie date must have been a bust for some reason," he said, "but you're going to have to help me out with the rest, if you want me to understand."

Brody drained the first beer, reached for the spare, decided to wait until some of the carbonation in his stomach fizzled out and drew his hand back empty. Shoved it through his hair. He'd stopped by the lodge after the debacle with Carolyn to pick up Barney before heading for the home-place, and that poor dog probably thought he'd fallen in with a crazy man.

Not that he seemed particularly shaken up, old Barney, bunking in with Valentino over by the stove as he was. The two of them just fit on the dog-bed, and they were both sound asleep.

Must be nice, Brody thought, figuring he'd never sleep again.

Conner snapped his fingers a few inches in front of Brody's nose. "Talk to me," he said. "You got me out of a warm bed, with an even warmer woman, and you owe me a reason."

Brody chuckled. "You want me to tell you what happened," he said.

"Basically," Conner answered dryly, "*yeah.* That would be a start."

"I'll be damned if I know," Brody answered. "One minute, we were having a great time, Carolyn and me. Wine, fancy food, a waiter—we had everything but a string quartet playing smooch music. Then it came time to watch the movie, and all hell broke loose."

Conner's expression was skeptical to say the least. "Come on, Brody. You're not seriously trying to tell me you don't know what happened? You were *there,* damn it."

"Must have been the movie," Brody said, reconsidering that second beer. Might as well down it, he thought. He wouldn't be driving back to River's Bend tonight anyway. Nope, he and ole Barney, they were spending the night.

"What was wrong with the movie?"

"It starred Gifford Welsh," Brody said.

"Oh, my *God,*" said Tricia, from the doorway to the hall.

She was barefoot, dressed in one of Conner's shirts and pregnant out to here.

"I tried to tell her it was an accident," Brody explained, "but she just *lost it.* Started babbling on about gossip and how she never had an affair with the guy—"

Tricia threw both hands up in the air, for emphasis. "*Honestly,* Brody," she exclaimed. "Do Conner and I have to watch you *every minute?*"

He reddened a little, and stiffened his spine, avoiding Conner's gaze because he knew he'd see laughter there. "How was I supposed to know she'd go off like that? Decide I'd chosen that movie on purpose . . . ?"

Tricia was standing next to Conner's chair now, with her hands propped on her hips and her stomach sticking halfway into next week and her head cocked to one side. "Those lousy rumors have been knocking around Lonesome Bend for *years,* Brody. How can you be the only one who's never heard them?"

Brody swallowed, still careful not to look at his brother's face. "Joleen might have said something about it once, but I didn't take it seriously."

Tricia patted Conner's shoulder and he pushed back his chair a little ways, so she could sit on his lap without being pinned between him and the table's edge. "Carolyn almost left town because of it, several times," she confided. "Between that and the stunt you pulled, it was almost too much humiliation for one woman to put up with. It's a testament to how much she loves Lonesome Bend and wants to make a home here that she didn't bolt a long time ago."

Brody's ears felt hot. "This is *my* fault?"

"Partly, yes," Tricia said. "You were probably one of the first people Carolyn ever allowed herself to trust—you have no idea what things have been like for her—and you *let her down.*"

"Tricia," Conner interrupted quietly, his arm around her, "you know Brody had his reasons for what he did."

Conner was *defending* him? Brody could barely believe it.

"We'll be lucky if Carolyn doesn't pull up stakes and take off for good," Tricia said, though some of the wind had gone out of her sails by then, and she was resting against Conner's chest. "Did you explain that you made a mistake?"

Brody closed his eyes to count to ten, but only got as far as seven before he had to blurt out, "*I* made a mistake? I practically refurbished the Bluebird Drive-in for one date and *I* made a mistake? Hell, Tricia, I didn't even look at the titles of those movies—I just grabbed a DVD and shoved it into the machine, and two seconds after I got back to the car, Carolyn was *freaking out.*"

Conner chuckled. "Sounds like most of the drama never got as far as the screen," he observed.

"Hush," Tricia scolded, giving her husband a light jab with one elbow. "This is *serious,* Conner." She turned to Brody. "You've got to talk to her," she insisted, as serious as an old-time preacher describing the torments of hell. "Right now, tonight."

"He's not going anywhere," Conner stated. "He's been swilling beer like his insides were on fire."

"I have not," Brody answered.

"Nevertheless," Conner reiterated, "you're *still* not going anywhere tonight."

Normally, Brody would have argued, just on principle, because he didn't take kindly to anybody—Conner in particular—telling him what to do. Trouble was, Conner was right. He probably wasn't over the legal limit on a beer and a half, but he wasn't exactly in his right mind, either, so why take unnecessary chances?

"You made her cry," Tricia accused sadly, spotting the makeup stain on his shirt. At least, he *thought* it was his shirt. Might be that he had it mixed up with one belonging to Conner.

"She went ballistic," Brody recalled, before finishing the second beer. "Granted," he said, when he'd caught his breath, "I should have checked out the movies before shoving one in the hopper, but it was an *honest mistake,* Tricia. Even if Carolyn *had* had an affair with Gifford Welsh, it wouldn't be any of my damn business, now would it?"

"This is all a big mess," Tricia said despairingly.

Conner gave her a one-armed squeeze.

"But it's *Brody's* mess, sweetheart," he reminded her. "And he'll have to straighten it out. In the meantime, let's go back to bed."

That now-familiar sensation of benevolent envy ground in Brody's middle. *He,* of course, would be sleeping alone, in his boyhood bed, unless Barney decided to join him.

And that didn't seem too likely, the way that dog was snoring.

Brody decided he needed a third beer after all.

Tricia got to her feet, and so did Conner.

While his wife padded back toward the bedroom, Conner paused to lay a hand on Brody's shoulder. "Go easy on the brew," he said. "You're going to have problems enough in the morning without waking up to a hangover."

Brody sighed, too stubborn to agree. "Good night," he said, in a grudging tone.

Conner merely chuckled, shook his head once and followed Tricia into the corridor.

*   *   *

Carolyn managed to get *some* sleep that night, though it was certainly nothing to write home about.

Not that she had a home or anybody to write to.

"Oh, stop it," she told herself, standing straight and tall in front of the mirror over the bathroom sink. "I've had it with your whining, Carolyn Simmons."

For once, there was no snarky answer.

Carolyn lifted her chin, squared her shoulders and critically examined her face.

Her eyes, rimmed with splotches of mascara, put her in mind of a raccoon. And they were puffy, to boot.

What remained of her lipstick was a pink mark on her right cheek.

And was she getting a cold sore, there, by her nostril?

Resolutely, she started the water running in the sink, scrubbed away the remnants of the Cinderella makeup job, and splashed her face with repeated palmfuls of cold water for good measure.

When she'd finished, she still looked bad, but she was clean at least.

She dabbed ointment on the budding cold sore and marched back out into the kitchen, where the gypsy skirt was draped over the back of a chair.

It wasn't a hopeless case, as she'd thought the night before, but it would require fairly extensive repairs. Along with Winston and a week's supply of sardines, she'd pack up the skirt, various sewing notions and her trusty machine to take to Kim and Davis's place, where she'd agreed to house-sit for the next week. Stitch by stitch, she'd put the garment—and the person she really was—back together.

With this mental to-do list rolling around in her brain, Carolyn put on a pot of coffee—she needed *something* to get her going—and decided to reward Winston with his favorite meal for breakfast.

The moment she peeled back the lid on the sardine can, however, the nausea was upon her.

She raced to the bathroom, holding

her hair back with both hands as she got very, very sick.

And in the midst of all that, it came to her.

She'd had wine the night before—several glasses of it—and, dazzled by all Brody had done to make the evening special, she'd never given a single thought to her special sensitivity to alcohol.

She *wasn't crazy,* she thought, with a rush of jubilation, even as another spate of retching brought her to her knees in front of the commode.

It was the wine.

Brody drove Kim and Davis's car up to their place first thing the next morning, to swap it out for his truck. While there, he'd feed the horses and have another look at the Thoroughbred, too. With luck, he could cadge breakfast from Kim, or at least a decent cup of java.

Down at Conner and Tricia's place, a man needed an engineering degree to run the damn coffeepot. Marriage and impending fatherhood, it seemed to

Brody, had rendered his twin brother a little strange.

He'd been keeping his mind busy with pithy observations like that one for much of the night and all there was of the morning so far, and it wasn't helping. Thoughts of Carolyn were just beneath the surface the whole time, and they broke through in every unguarded moment.

Even now, he thought a dinner and a private showing of a first-run movie put him in the major leagues when it came to creative dating. He'd seen the look of wonder in Carolyn's eyes when she saw the snack bar decked out for a romantic dinner for two. She'd been charmed, maybe even a little enchanted, exactly as he'd intended.

Okay, so he could have made a more sensitive choice when he chose the actual movie. He'd apologized, hadn't he? Once he understood what the hell she was so upset about, anyway?

He sighed and resettled his hat.

Well, it was actually *Conner's* hat, like everything else he had on this morning.

The question was, how could something so right have gone straight to hell in a handbasket the way last night had?

"Mornin'," Davis called, from the back door, when Brody came out of the barn. "Coffee's on."

"I'll be right there," Brody responded, pausing to watch Firefly at the corral feeder.

Now *that,* Brody mused, was a *horse.*

"Don't even think about it," Davis warned, materializing beside him to set his arms on the top rail of the fence and nod toward Firefly. "He's off-limits, Brody, and that's the end of it."

Brody gave his uncle a sidelong glance. "I can handle any horse," he said evenly. "I've got the championship belt buckles and the prize money to prove it."

Davis narrowed his eyes, and his tone was as solemn as his expression. "Your dad said something a lot like that once," he said. "It was the day I warned him to stay off the stallion we'd roped wild, up in the foothills, until he'd been gelded and had some time to calm down a little. Blue told me he'd never met the horse he couldn't ride, but I thought he was just talking, that he'd seen the sense in what I'd said. Next thing I knew, my brother was lying in the middle of the corral with his neck broken, and that stallion circling him like a buzzard, closing in, fixing to finish him off then and there."

Davis paused, took a ragged breath and gazed off into the middle distance like he could see the scene playing out in front of him, clear as crystal, even after so many years.

"I had the hunting rifle in the truck," he went on presently, without looking at Brody, "and I brought that horse down with one shot, right where he stood." He made a sound that might have been a laugh, but wasn't. "I thought there was still a chance that Blue would pull through," he added. "If I'd seen him tossed by one horse, I'd seen him fly off a hundred, and a couple of those times, he'd even broke a few bones. But Blue didn't move, didn't open his eyes. Kim called the ambulance, and I stayed there with Blue, in the corral, with that dead horse a dozen feet away, telling my brother it would be all right. 'Just hang on, help is coming. I'm here, Blue, right here, and I'm not going anywhere—'"

Davis choked up then, had to stop for a second or two to get a grip.

Brody waited, hot behind the eyes, while his uncle, one of the toughest men he'd ever known, pulled himself back together.

"You know what happened," Davis said, looking right into Brody's face now. "Your dad never came out of the coma. Six miserable weeks later, he was gone." The older man swallowed hard, and his eyes glistened with rare moisture. "I brought Firefly to this ranch to save his life, Brody. Nobody else wanted him, said he was worthless, nothing but trouble. But you hear me, son, and hear me well . . . I'll put a bullet in his brain before I'll let anybody—and I mean *anybody*—ride him. Do we understand each other?"

"Breakfast is getting cold!" Kim sang out, from the side porch.

Neither Brody nor Davis moved, or looked away from each other's faces.

"Do we understand each other?" Davis asked, for the second time.

Brody thrust out a sigh. "We understand each other," he replied.

Davis slapped him on the shoulder, and he even smiled a little, but his eyes were as serious as Brody had ever seen them. "I need your word, son," he said.

"You have it," Brody replied. "I won't ride the horse."

CHAPTER EIGHTEEN

Carolyn had just released a very disgruntled Winston from his crate into the wide-open spaces of the Creeds' erstwhile empty kitchen when she heard a vehicle drive up and stop with a squeak of brakes.

She glanced at the clock—it was a little after noon—before peeking out the window, half-expecting to see Kim and Davis, ostensibly well on their way to Stone Creek in the RV, with Smidgeon and Little Bit, returning for something they'd forgotten.

Instead, Tricia, cumbersome, climbed

from her Pathfinder, waving one hand in front of her face to dispel some of the dust she'd stirred up arriving.

Heartened, but at the same time feeling like one big bruise, exposed to every jostle and bump, Carolyn opened the side door to greet her friend with a smile and a wave. "You'd better get those brakes checked. I could hear them from inside the house."

Tricia smiled. "Don't worry. Conner made me promise to trade my rig for Kim and Davis's car until the mechanic in town can have a look at it. That's the main reason I'm here."

The *main* reason, Carolyn thought wryly, but not the *only* reason.

By now, Tricia would have at least an inkling about the things that had happened last night, at the storied Bluebird Drive-in.

"You look like five miles of bad road," Tricia observed bluntly, confirming Carolyn's suspicion and duck-walking toward her. Carolyn wondered idly—and very briefly—if her friend wasn't further along in her pregnancy than everybody thought she was. Tricia looked as though she might deliver baby Blue at any moment.

"Gee, thanks," Carolyn chimed merrily, holding the screen door wide so Carolyn could squeeze past and enter the kitchen. Immediately, she hung the Pathfinder keys from the hook nearby and took the ones for Kim's car.

The car Brody had picked her up in the night before, predisaster.

"But," Tricia went on, dropping into a chair at the table with a relieved sigh and tossing Kim's keys into her purse, "I'm happy to relate that Brody looks even *worse* than you do."

"I guess that's something," Carolyn replied, with a grim little chuckle.

Tricia's gaze had fallen on the gypsy skirt, neatly spread out on the table, awaiting rehabilitation.

"Yikes, Carolyn," she marveled. "What *happened?*"

"You've seen Brody?" Carolyn said, letting Tricia's question ride for the moment. She bit her lower lip and sat down, propping her chin in one hand. "Since last night, I mean?"

"He stayed at our place," Tricia answered, squinting a little. "You really do look awful, Carolyn. You're pale, and there are shadows under your eyes. And the *skirt*—what on earth . . . ?"

Carolyn spread her fingers wide and shoved all eight of them into her hair, along with her thumbs, shaking her head as she recalled the latest calamity to befall her love life.

If it could be *called* a love life.

"I freaked," she moaned. "Lost it. Ruined everything." She made herself lift her eyes to meet Tricia's. "First, I drank wine," she admitted.

"Oh, no," Tricia said.

"Oh, yes," Carolyn responded glumly. "But I've thought about this a lot, and I've decided that's no excuse for the way I behaved. Part of the reason, maybe, but not an excuse." She sighed before going on. "Okay, the few times I've ever indulged in alcohol have all proven . . . imprudent. I should have anticipated that, and skipped the wine, but I was dazzled, Tricia. Honestly *dazzled*. What *really* went wrong was, I got scared, because nothing could ever be as good as that date was shaping up to be—I'm pretty sure that's how my reasoning went, anyway—and something awful was bound to happen if I let myself believe for another second that— that—"

"That Brody might actually love you?" Tricia supplied gently, with a brief, reassuring touch to Carolyn's hands.

"I made the mistake of thinking he did, once," Carolyn said slowly. "And when I came to my senses, it was like being run over by a freight train. I spent a long time gathering up the pieces, Tricia, and putting myself back together." She managed a thin smile. "Problem is, I think I might have put some of those pieces in the wrong places."

"What happens now?" Tricia asked, after a sigh and a long pause.

"I fix the gypsy skirt and hope whoever's driving the bid through the roof is happy with the results," she said, fairly certain that Tricia had expected her to say she was packing up and leaving Lonesome Bend without a backward glance.

But she'd meant it when she promised herself she was through running, literally *and* figuratively.

Tricia's blue eyes twinkled with a sort of sad mischief. "Oh, I wouldn't worry about the bidder," she said. "She's a very understanding woman. One of *two* very understanding women, actually."

Carolyn felt her own eyes widen. "You know who . . . ?"

Tricia smiled and struck a comical glamour pose without getting out of her chair.

"You?" Carolyn whispered. *"You're* the mystery bidder?"

"Kim and I are going halves," Tricia answered, undaunted.

Now Carolyn was *really* confused. Both Kim and Tricia were beautiful women, and both of them had great bodies—normally—but they were built differently, and Kim was at least three inches taller than Tricia, so there was no possible way they could wear the same garment without extensive alterations.

"Why?"

"Because we've both seen how much that skirt means to you," Tricia said. "We were planning to wait a while, and then surprise you with it—for your birthday, maybe. Or Christmas."

Carolyn knew better than to get her back up and accuse Tricia of joining forces with Kim to offer her charity. They'd done this amazing thing because they were *her friends,* because they had the means and because they cared about her.

Her eyes filled. "Oh, Tricia," she said.

"Don't cry," Tricia said, waving her hand again, the way she had outside, when she was fanning away the dust. "If you do, I will, too, and then my nose will get all red and my eyes will practically swell shut and it *will not be pretty.*"

Carolyn laughed, giving her cheeks a swipe with the backs of her hands. "Not pretty?" she joked. "We can't have that."

Tricia smiled and sniffled once and said, "Well."

Winston, having scouted out the new surroundings, returned to the kitchen to wind himself around and around Carolyn's ankles in a figure-eight, purring like an outboard motor.

Evidently, he liked it here, at Kim and Davis's ranch house.

"The auction doesn't end until tomorrow," Carolyn mused aloud, looking at the skirt now. Even bedraggled and in need of mending and some serious sprucing up, it was still breathtakingly beautiful. "Maybe someone has outbid you by now."

"Nope," Tricia replied, with a smug little smile. "Ain't gonna happen. Our ceiling bid is so high, nobody will match it."

With a tentative hand, Carolyn reached out and touched the garment almost as gently as if it were a living thing, and suffering from various painful injuries. "None of it matters, now," she said. "The skirt needs too much fixing to sell to anyone, and I couldn't have let you and Kim go through with your crazy, wonderful and unbelievably generous plan anyway. Not once I found out what you were up to."

Carolyn's natural practicality reasserted itself. She'd call off the auction as soon as she got the chance, she decided, and keep the skirt for herself. Not that she had any more reason to wear it than before, because she didn't, but they shared something now, she and that once-glorious mass of beads and ribbon and fine cloth. They were both veterans of the Cinderella wars.

And they'd both been on the losing side.

A peaceful silence fell.

Tricia broke it with a soft "Come to our place for supper tonight, Carolyn?"

Carolyn grinned wanly, thinking how lucky she was to have friends like Tricia and Conner and Kim and Davis, among others. Not that she could trust either of those women any farther than she could have thrown them, when it came to their matchmaking schemes.

"So you can corral Brody and me in the same room and hope we'll kiss and make up?" she countered, though not unkindly. "No way, girlfriend. I'm not ready to deal with Brody face-to-face quite yet, and I'll wager the reverse is true, as well."

Tricia looked sad, but she clearly understood Carolyn's position, too. "I just wish you weren't all alone, that's all," she lamented. "You'll call Conner and me if you need anything, won't you?"

"You can bet on it," Carolyn promised. "And it's not as if I've become a
hermit, hiding out at some robber's roost
tucked away in the distant hills, after all.
I promised Kim I'd spend the nights
here, and basically hold down the fort,
but I'll still be going to the shop in the
morning, like I do every Monday."

Tricia brightened. "Speaking of the
shop—what have you decided? Are you
taking me up on my offer or not?"

Carolyn smiled. "I'd be crazy if I
didn't," she said. "No matter what happens, Tricia, I'm staying right here in
Lonesome Bend. I've had enough of the
gypsy life, and I'm through trying to escape my problems. I'm digging in for the
duration."

"That's great!" Tricia cried, delighted.

"I thought I'd start by hiring Primrose
to work for us part-time," Carolyn said,
profoundly grateful for the change of
subject. "If it's all right with you, of
course. She has some very interesting
ideas and, besides, she's a natural sales-
woman."

Tricia laughed, getting slowly to her
feet. "That she is," she agreed. "Go

ahead and offer her a job whenever you're ready. In the meantime, I'll make a preliminary deposit to the business account, just to get things rolling."

Carolyn was teary again. "You're sure you want to do this, Tricia? Really, *really* sure? Because I'd understand if you didn't, and I'd be fine without the shop—"

Well, maybe not *fine,* exactly—she loved the shop—but she'd survive, like always, and eventually thrive.

Tricia gave her one of those impulsive, Tricia-hugs, quick and awkward and wholly sincere. "Well, the *shop* wouldn't be fine without *you,* and neither would I. I'm *having a baby,* Carolyn, not a lobotomy. Before I came to Lonesome Bend to settle Dad's estate, I ran a gallery, remember? I love Conner more than I ever knew it was possible to love a man, and we'll both be crazy about this baby and all his brothers and sisters, but I *need* to be around art on a regular basis—I need color and texture and all the rest."

Carolyn certainly understood; art fed her soul, it was a form of prayer for her, of praise and thanksgiving

She recalled Tricia's arrival in town, a

couple of years ago. Naturally, there had been a lot of talk about her when she moved in with her great-grandmother and put the River's Bend Campground and RV park up for sale, along with the ramshackle Bluebird Drive-in. People had claimed Tricia was too citified for a town like Lonesome Bend, even though she'd spent summers there since childhood, and they were sure she'd be on her way back to Seattle and her old life before the ink was dry on the sales agreements for her father's properties.

Instead, Tricia had fallen in love with Conner Creed, married him and fit into the community like the proverbial hand in glove.

After walking Tricia to the garage and watching her drive away in Kim's car, Carolyn went back inside, feeling somewhat at loose ends.

She supposed that house should have felt lonely, as big as it was, with just her and Winston rattling around in it like a pair of pebbles in the bottom of a barrel, but it didn't feel that way at all.

It was a real home, a sanctuary where a man and a woman loved each other, day to day, through thick and thin, working separately and side by side to keep a ranch and an extended family going. There were memories here, practically tangible, and pictures on the walls and mantelpieces full of smiling faces and birthday cakes and Christmas trees and first cars.

In the hallway between the living room and the guest room where she'd be sleeping, Carolyn paused to look more closely at some of those photographs. One showed Brody and Conner and Steven on what was probably a fishing trip, a blond, sun-burned trio, none of them in their teens yet, beaming and holding up the day's catch.

Next to it was a shot taken on a long-ago Christmas morning—Brody and Conner posing in front of an enormous tree decorated with a hodgepodge of ornaments, each of them gripping the shiny handlebars of a brand-new bicycle. Steven, who had lived in Boston with his mother most of the year, wasn't in the picture, but there was a bulging stocking hanging from the mantel with his name stitched across the top, so he must have been expected to arrive for a visit soon.

Carolyn smiled, touched their faces with a fingertip, lingering a little longer on Brody's image. To look at them, a person would have thought they'd always had it easy, but of course that wasn't true.

Everybody, no matter how fortunate some aspects of their lives might be, had things to overcome. Dragons to face, and rivers to cross.

In Brody and Conner's case, it was a double loss: their parents had both died, in separate accidents, when the twins were just babies. And as much love as Kim and Davis had given these boys over the years, as much guidance and security, they'd still had their battles to fight, not only in the outside world, but also with each other.

Conner and Brody had been on the outs for years and, of course, Brody's wife and child had been taken from him, in a very cruel way.

Carolyn sighed and went on to the guest room, Winston romping at her heels like a kitten, to unpack the few things she'd brought from the apartment in town. Since she'd be going to the shop every day, she didn't need more than fresh underwear, a nightshirt, the usual toiletries and something to wear to work in the morning.

She put things away, closely supervised by Winston, and then decided to take two aspirin and grab a nap, hoping to shake off the last lingering effects of last night's apocalyptic events.

A little over an hour later, she woke up, her headache and the few remaining tatters of nausea gone at last. Feeling quite like her old, best self again, Carolyn smoothed her hair and headed for the kitchen, planning to have a late lunch—something light, like chicken noodle soup—and settle down to work on the gypsy skirt.

And there was Brody, big as life, sitting at the kitchen table, drinking coffee and reading a newspaper.

Carolyn stopped short, just inside the doorway from the dining room.

"I knocked," he said nonchalantly, without looking up from the paper, "but nobody answered."

"So you just walked in?"

"Pretty much, yeah."

"Well, I'll just leave you to your coffee and your newspaper," Carolyn told him hurriedly, turning to march right back out again.

He stopped her with a single word—her name.

She stiffened, but didn't look back at him. "What could you possibly have to say to me, after last night?" she asked, her tone even, revealing nothing of what she was feeling. Not that she exactly *knew* what she was feeling, because she didn't.

She was all a-jumble inside—happy and sad, scared and excited, angry that Brody was there and, at the same time, deeply, deeply relieved.

"How about 'I'm sorry'?" he suggested, from directly behind her.

How did he *do* that? How did the man cross rooms in the space of a heartbeat, without making a sound? It was uncanny. It was *spooky.*

She swiveled, squaring her shoulders, lifting her chin. He was close enough to kiss her—but he didn't.

"It's *my* turn to apologize," Carolyn said, drawing on all her bravery, and on her new determination to live in the real world like a rational human being with a right to be there, damn it—but not quite meeting his eyes. "You went to a lot of trouble to make last night . . . special. I should have known it didn't mean anything that Gifford Welsh was starring in the movie, but . . . well . . . I didn't, not at first, anyway. I'm not very proud of how I acted, and I am definitely sorry."

"Carolyn," Brody said again, this time with a smile in his voice.

"What?"

"Why won't you look at me?"

Because looking at you makes my clothes fall off, Brody Creed.

Like she'd ever say *that* out loud.

Brody laughed. "Looking at me makes your clothes fall off? Hot damn, that's the best news I've had all day."

Carolyn blinked. Put a hand over her mouth, horrified. Murmured, "Did I actually say . . . ?"

Brody's grin was a mite on the cocky side, and totally hot. "Yeah," he said. "You did."

"Oh, my God," she said.

"That was my reaction, too," Brody said, his eyes dancing as his gaze tripped down the front of her T-shirt. He pretended to frown. "Doesn't look like it's happening, though. Your clothes falling off, I mean."

She felt a surge of heat in her face, knew she was blushing—*again*—and wished she could vanish into thin air, like a wisp of smoke.

She couldn't, of course.

That was one thing about being real. No disappearing allowed.

"My clothes are staying right where they are," she said, with a notable lack of conviction.

"That's probably a good idea," Brody agreed thoughtfully, rubbing his chin, where a golden stubble was already showing. "For the time being, anyhow."

Carolyn tugged hard at the hem of her T-shirt and marched past him, headed for the cupboard. She needed a good, stiff shot of herbal tea, and she needed it now.

Brody watched with amusement as she gathered the necessary stuff.

"It's a damn shame, though," he observed, stroking his chin again.

"What?" Carolyn asked briskly, filling a cup with hot water from a special dispenser affixed to the sink.

"That your clothes didn't fall off," Brody said. "It would have been something to see."

"Would you like some tea?" Carolyn inquired, as though nobody had said anything about anybody's clothes falling off.

Least of all, hers.

"Uh—tea? Thanks, but no. I'm not a big tea drinker."

Carolyn made a face at him.

"Would tequila do it?" he mused, as though talking to himself. "Like in the song?"

"Brody," Carolyn said. "Stop teasing me, will you please? It was a slip of the tongue, that's all."

"Very Freudian," Brody agreed, with mock solemnity. "Especially the tongue reference."

"I did *not* make a 'tongue reference,' as you so crudely put it," Carolyn said loftily, but she was struggling not to laugh.

"There," Brody said, pointing. "You said it again. *Tongue*. You keep bringing it up—definitely Freudian."

"Stop it," she said, choking back a giggle.

Brody's grin broadened and went from sizzle to stun. "Fine," he said. "Build your tea, sit down and talk to me."

Talk to me. Yikes.

"About what?" she asked.

"Yourself," he said. "I told you about Lisa and Justin. Now I want to know what makes you Carolyn, so to speak." She was silent, preparing her tea. Pensive. But she approached the table and sat down, and when she had, Brody sat, too.

Folded his hands loosely and rested them on top of the open newspaper.

"Where should I start?" she asked, thinking aloud.

"Tricia told me you grew up in foster homes," Brody said quietly. "I'm sure that was rough, at least at times, but right now, I'm more interested in knowing why a Gifford Welsh movie would send you over the edge."

Carolyn sighed, took a slow sip of her tea and savored it. Or pretended to, that is. The stuff didn't seem to have any taste at all.

"It was partly the wine," she said.

Brody nodded. "I figured that out later," he said. "Another reason to apologize, Carolyn. I should have remembered that you can't hold your hooch."

She laughed softly, relaxed a little—but not for long. Whenever she thought of Gifford Welsh, she thought of Storm, running behind her car, screaming for her to come back, and the pain was still enough to double her over.

Brody took her hand. "Whatever it is, Carolyn," he said, "it's *okay*. But if we're going to mend fences, you and I, we have to be straight with each other, starting now. No surprises down the road."

Carolyn nodded, swallowed hard, even though she hadn't taken another sip of tea. "I know a lot of people think I had an affair with Gifford," she said, meeting Brody's eyes. "It doesn't happen to be true, but last night—last night, I thought you were . . . well . . . throwing him up to me. Letting me know that *you* knew. That's what set me off."

Brody waited calmly for her to go on, his eyes gentle and very, very blue.

Carolyn's fingers trembled when she picked up her cup to drink from it, so she set it down again, without bringing it to her mouth.

Winston, that unpredictable feline, leaped up into Brody's lap, purring and rubbing against his chest.

Brody chuckled and stroked the cat's back, comfortable with the interaction, but made no comment on the animal's apparent new opinion of his character.

The ball was still in Carolyn's court, it would seem.

Slowly, she told Brody what had happened at the Gifford mansion that day, unreeling the memories in her mind's eye as she spoke, reliving them.

She'd been attracted to Gifford Welsh—who wouldn't have been?—but he was *married,* and that meant something to her, if not to him.

She'd fled in a panic—much as Brody

had done the night Lisa called and told him she was carrying his child. She'd left Storm behind, unable to explain why she was leaving in such a hurry, and she'd regretted that ever since.

Carolyn had regretted abandoning a little girl, in almost the same way *she'd* been abandoned, and she'd blamed herself for other reasons, too. Had she unwittingly sent Gifford some kind of come-hither message, prompting him to make advances?

Was the whole thing *her* fault?

Looking back, it seemed strange that she'd ever believed such a thing. Carolyn had been his daughter's nanny, his wife had been away and he'd made a move on her.

Gifford, like everyone else on the planet, was responsible for his own actions.

"I shouldn't have left Storm behind like that," she said numbly, when she reached the end of the account. "But I was young and I was shaken up, and I didn't know what else to do but get the heck out of there, fast."

"You did what you thought was the

right thing at the time," Brody said. At some point, he'd taken her hand into his.

"So did you," Carolyn said. "When Lisa called that night, I mean."

He raised a shoulder, lowered it again. "I've decided to let myself off the hook for it," he said. "I can't bring Lisa and Justin back, or make things right for them, and it's time I quit trying." He paused, started again. "I came back to Lonesome Bend to settle down, start a family and build a legacy, and that's what I mean to do."

Carolyn looked at him, thinking how much she loved Brody Creed, how she'd loved him all along, though that love had evolved as she had, as Brody himself had.

He'd been a boy when they met, and she'd been a girl.

Now, he was a man, and she was a woman.

Whole other ball game.

They were at a crossroads, Carolyn realized. They could go their separate ways, sadder but wiser, or they could get to know each other all over again, from an adult perspective.

Carolyn knew what she wanted, but she wasn't at all sure Brody was on the same page, so she kept the words she most needed to say to herself.

Gently, Brody lifted Winston off his lap and set him on the floor.

Carolyn took a big gulp of her tea, just for something to do, and nearly choked on the stuff.

Brody leaned toward her, brushed her hair back off her right shoulder.

"There's one more thing I need to know," he said. "Those foster homes you lived in. Were they good ones?"

Carolyn pondered the question. Finally she sighed. "There were different levels of commitment, but basically I think everybody did the best they knew how," she said, coming to yet another deeply personal conclusion. "Including my parents, I guess."

Brody drew her out of her chair and onto his lap.

It seemed natural to put her arms around his neck and rest her forehead against his.

"I never knew my dad," she confided softly, and then waited for the strength to go on, to say the rest of it.

"Me, either," Brody said. "But we had Davis, Conner and I, and he handled the job just fine."

Carolyn nodded. "You're lucky—that you had Davis and Kim, I mean."

"Yep," Brody agreed. His arms were around her, but loosely, strong but making no demands. "Lucky on all counts, when it comes to kinfolks." He hooked a finger under her chin, lifted, and pulled back just far enough to look directly into her eyes. "And when it comes to you, Carolyn."

She blinked.

"I love you," he said. Just like that.

Talk about things that were too good to be true. "You do?"

He chuckled, and then flashed that dangerous grin at her. The one that made her wish her clothes would fall right off. "I just said I did, didn't I?" he teased. There was heat gathering in his eyes now. "But I don't mind repeating myself. *I love you,* Carolyn."

"Really?"

"Carolyn." Brody tried to sound stern, but the tenderness in his eyes spoiled the effect.

She blushed, confused and joyful and ridiculously shy. "I love you, too," she blurted out.

"Good," Brody said, his mouth close to hers now. "That's good."

"What happens next?" she murmured, as things shifted inside her, finding their level. Her pelvic bones seemed to be melting, along with her knees.

Brody arched an eyebrow. "We go to bed?" He was already slipping a warm hand underneath her T-shirt.

Carolyn gasped. "That's . . . a given—" she managed to say. "I mean *after*— next week, next month, next year—" He'd unfastened the front catch on her bra, and one of her breasts spilled, warm and ready, into his palm. His thumb chafed her nipple. *"Oh, God—"* she whimpered. He pushed up her T-shirt and then his mouth closed over her. *"Brody—"*

He enjoyed her freely, for what seemed like a deliciously long time, before lifting his head to meet her eyes and offer a belated reply to a question she'd almost forgotten she'd asked.

"I say we let next week, next month and next year take care of themselves and concentrate on what's happening right now," he said. And then he pushed back his chair and stood, lifting Carolyn in his arms. "Which bedroom is yours?"

Brody had barely *begun* to make love to her and already she was limp, completely at his mercy.

She told him where her room was.

And he carried her there, and their clothes fell off, and Carolyn's first orgasm came quickly, fiercely, rocking her very core, wringing a shout of glorious surrender from her.

"Brody!"

He had horses to feed, Brody thought, lying there in the twilight, still partially entangled with a sumptuously naked—and soundly sleeping—Carolyn. Not just Davis and Kim's horses, either, but Moonshine, too, over at River's Bend.

And Barney was down at Conner and Tricia's, awaiting his return.

Brody touched the tip of Carolyn's nose, then her lips.

She stirred, opened her eyes. Blinked, as though surprised to see him.

He grinned. "Gotta go," he said.

Carolyn, still half-asleep, looked immediately alarmed.

"To feed the horses," Brody clarified, placing a nibbling kiss on her mouth, "and collect my dog."

She swallowed. "Then what?"

"Then I'll come back here, if that's all right with you."

Her smile was sudden, a bright flash in the semidarkness of the room. "I have a better idea," she announced. "I'll come with you."

Simple as it was, Carolyn's statement struck at something deep inside Brody. His voice came out husky when he said, "Sounds good."

They shared a shower—somehow managing not to wind up making love again, although the temptation was strong—then got themselves dressed and, after Carolyn had given the cat a fish dinner from a can, headed for the barn.

Together, they made short work of the chores. They rode to River's Bend in Brody's truck, fed Moonshine, fetched Barney's bag of kibble from the lodge and went on to the main ranch house.

Carolyn, evidently suffering a sudden bout of shyness, waited in the truck while Brody went inside, politely refused Tricia's invitation to have supper with her and Conner and reclaimed Barney.

It occurred to Brody as they bumped over the road leading back to Kim and Davis's place that Barney and Winston the cat might not make for the best combination, what with their fundamental differences.

"Winston adores Valentino," Carolyn assured Brody, once he'd expressed his concern. "He'll get along fine with Barney, too."

She was right, as it turned out.

Barney and Winston met up for the first time in the middle of Kim's kitchen, eyeing each other like a pair of gunfighters at high noon.

The cat fluffed out his tail, and Barney sniffed curiously at Winston's nose, and the two of them turned away from each other and casually went their separate ways.

"See?" Carolyn said, taking one of Kim's famous casseroles from the freezer side of the refrigerator. "It's a nonevent."

Brody grinned, looking at the casserole dish in her hands. "You cook?" he teased.

She laughed. "No," she said. "But I do *reheat.*"

With that, Carolyn turned her back to him, setting the casserole on the counter and removing the foil covering.

Brody stepped up behind her, slipped his arms around her, and kissed the nape of her neck, delighting in the little shiver of response she gave.

"Speaking of reheating things," he muttered.

"Later," she said. "Supper first. We need our strength."

Brody tasted her earlobe. "Umm," he said.

Laughing again, she wiggled free, switched on the oven and set the temperature. *"Later,"* she repeated.

Later took its sweet time arriving, but

eventually, when they'd eaten and loaded the dishwasher, then rigged up a couple of blanket-beds for Winston and Barney, they took a second shower.

This time around, there was no resisting temptation.

There was also no condom.

Hours later, both exhausted, Brody and Carolyn finally slept.

CHAPTER NINETEEN

Brody's cell phone was ringing.

Carolyn's heart scrambled into her throat, and as deeply as she'd been sleeping only moments before, she was wide-awake in an instant, if still a little disoriented. Straining for the switch on the bedside lamp while Brody, muttering, groped for his discarded clothes, rummaged audibly and finally got hold of the phone.

"Brody," he answered, his voice raspy with sleep and worry.

Carolyn found the switch, and light spilled into the room. Although she'd slept through that other phone call, on that other night years ago, the similarities were still eerie. She could almost believe she'd somehow blundered into a time warp, and here was Lisa calling to say she was pregnant, and the whole heartbreaking scenario was starting up all over again.

"Conner," Brody said, his gaze locked with Carolyn's. "Stay calm. You have got to stay calm—we'll be right there, and we'll do whatever needs doing, I promise you. In the meantime, *hang up and call 911—now.*"

Carolyn clambered into her clothes, her eyes hot but dry, her throat thick with fear. *Call 911—now.* It was 2:00 a.m.

Dear God.

"Tricia?" she whispered, as Brody clicked the phone shut and got back into the jeans and work shirt he'd been wearing earlier, when they did chores.

Brody nodded. "She's having pains—bad ones, evidently—and Conner's in a panic."

"What if he's too panicked to call 911?" Carolyn lamented, as she and

Brody headed for the bedroom doorway at the same time.

"Conner," Brody said, striding through the darkened house, almost running, "is Conner. He's solid, through and through."

By the time they crossed the kitchen, Brody had his truck keys out. Winston and Barney were both up on all four feet, rising off their improvised beds, watching them.

"You'll have to stay here this time," Brody said to the dog, for all the world as though he expected the creature to understand. "Look after Diablo-cat for me."

Barney lay back down again, with a sigh, and Winston followed suit.

Moments later, Carolyn and Brody were in the pickup, barreling down the moon-washed driveway, headlights slashing the darkness.

Several minutes before they pulled up in front of the main ranch house, they heard the ambulance siren and saw its red light swirling in the gloom as it raced around the far bend and along the county road.

Brody was the first one inside the house, shouting his brother's name.

Conner appeared from the hallway leading to the bedrooms, carrying Tricia, wrapped in a quilt, her face pale as death. The quilt was soaked in blood.

Please, Carolyn prayed silently. *Just . . . please.*

"They're coming, Conner," Brody told his brother. "The EMTs are coming— probably turning in down at the gate right now."

Carolyn had never been in such a situation before, would have had no idea what she'd do if confronted with an emergency. Now, she knew—she automatically went straight up to Conner and touched Tricia's wan face.

"Tricia?" she said, firmly, but with a quaver. "Tricia?"

Tricia's head lolled against Conner's shoulder, but she opened her eyes to look at Carolyn. "Don't worry," she said, incredibly, and with great effort. "I'm okay, and so is Blue— This is just— I don't know what this is, but . . . don't worry . . ."

Don't worry.

Carolyn lifted her gaze to Conner's face. She'd never seen such fear, such anguish—or such inborn strength. Conner Creed was terrified, but no force on earth could have brought him down as long as Tricia and his unborn baby needed him.

Valentino began to bark hysterically as the ambulance siren grew deafening, and red light flashed against the kitchen windows like fire.

"Shh," Carolyn said, feeling sorry for him. Valentino was Tricia's dog, and his devotion to her was complete. The animal, like Conner, was quite literally beside himself.

Things happened fast over the next few minutes—Tricia was loaded onto a gurney and whisked into the back of the ambulance, an EMT taking her vital signs and starting an IV while Conner crouched on the opposite side of the stretcher, clutching her hand, murmuring to her.

Brody, standing nearby, beside Carolyn, was a living reflection of his brother's pain. The emergency lights washed over him, in their garish rhythm. Carolyn knew he felt much of what Conner was going through, because of that weird twin-connection, but he was no more likely to buckle under than his brother was.

Around Lonesome Bend, it was an accepted fact that the Creeds were tough, but, slipping her arm around Brody's waist, Carolyn wondered if anybody had any idea just *how* tough.

As the ambulance raced off down the driveway and practically took the turn onto the county road on two wheels, siren screaming now, Carolyn and Brody dashed back to his truck and followed.

Brody's face was grim as he drove, and Carolyn knew he wasn't just sharing Conner's agony now, he was reliving his own. Taking the full weight of the deaths of his wife and child, as surely as if the tragedy had just happened.

It came home to Carolyn then, with cruel clarity, that the accident wasn't just a memory, it was literally a part of him, something he'd have to confront over and over during the course of his lifetime.

The thought was worse than sobering. Something shriveled and shrank inside Carolyn, some hope she'd dared to cherish—again—but she drew a deep breath and refused to give in. If Brody and Conner could hold it together, she would, too, for their sakes, for Tricia's and the baby's, and even for her own.

Courage, like so many other things, was not something one did or didn't have; it was a decision, a choice.

Brody handed her his cell phone. "Davis and Kim will want to know what's going on," he said. "They're on speed dial—zero-eight."

Trembling, Carolyn took the phone, opened it, studied the unfamiliar keyboard briefly and put the call through.

Davis answered after two rings, his voice gruff with sleep and the almost universal alarm of receiving a phone call at that hour. "Brody?" he said. "That you?"

Carolyn found her voice, identified herself and explained what little they knew of what was happening.

"We'll be there as soon as we can," Davis replied, and then she heard him say, "Kim, wake up, it's Tricia—something's wrong . . ."

Kim must have grabbed the phone from her husband's hand, because hers was the next voice Carolyn heard. "Carolyn? Which hospital are they taking Tricia to? Mercy General?"

Carolyn relayed the question to Brody, who nodded and said, "Probably. Tell them we'll be in touch again as soon as we know anything more." He paused, his profile backlit by the lights of a passing car as they careened along behind the ambulance. "And tell them to *be careful* driving back, because we can't afford to lose them."

Carolyn repeated Brody's words to Kim, and the call ended.

The drive to Mercy General, a small but up-to-date facility that served not only Lonesome Bend, but also four or five small towns around it, was a half an hour.

It was the longest thirty minutes of Carolyn's life so far.

When the ambulance pulled into the bay outside the emergency room, Carolyn called Davis again, and verified that

Tricia had indeed been taken to that particular hospital.

She and Brody ran inside, after parking the truck, but Tricia had been swept away immediately, and Conner, of course, had gone with her.

In a way, it had been easier when they'd had to hurry.

Now, they were just pacing, back and forth, back and forth, high on adrenaline with no way to work it off.

Except for the people at the reception desk, Carolyn and Brody had the lobby to themselves.

Up until Tricia's arrival, evidently, it had been a slow night.

Brody went to the desk every few minutes, asking for news, and each time, the nurses on duty just shook their heads and said they didn't know anything yet.

Brody would pace again, and then return, only to be told the same thing.

Carolyn's heart went out to him, but there was no settling him down. He waved away the cup of vending-machine coffee she got for him, and words didn't help, either. What could she say, any-way—*everything will be all right?*

But maybe it wouldn't.

Maybe *nothing* would be all right, ever again.

Whoa, cowgirl, Carolyn told herself silently. *No news is good news.*

A few minutes later, unable to bear his agitation on top of her own, Carolyn simply walked over to Brody and put her arms around him. He stiffened and then relaxed against her, his face buried in her hair.

"I'm here," was all she had to offer. "I'm right here."

But maybe—just maybe—it was enough, because Brody's breathing deepened and slowed, and she felt his heartbeat against her cheek, gradually losing speed.

He propped his chin on top of her head, and a great, tremulous sigh went through him.

He never cried, not on the outside, at least.

Carolyn, in the privacy of her own heart, cried enough for both of them.

It was nearly 5:00 a.m. when Conner

reappeared, looking ghastly pale, shadows etched deep under his eyes—and smiling fit to light up the whole place and the surrounding night, too.

He came straight to Brody, and the two men, virtual mirror images of each other, stood face-to-face. For Carolyn, it was like looking at a pair of exquisite coins, both inscribed with the head of the same noble emperor.

"We got her here in time," Conner said, his voice a broken croak, cracked through with a joy so deep it must have been rooted in his very soul. "Tricia will be fine, and so will our son."

"Your son?" Brody echoed, finally catching up.

"Davis Blue," Conner confirmed proudly. "Six pounds, seven ounces of squalling Creed."

The transformation in Brody's face was a sight Carolyn would never forget. He was positively *illuminated.* "Davis Blue Creed," he repeated, in a tone of wonder.

"You don't mind, do you?" Conner asked his brother. "That we used up Dad's name, I mean, right along with

Davis's? We mean to call him Blue, but if that bothers you, Brody, there's still time to make a change—"

"Davis Blue Creed," Brody said again, savoring the name. "It's perfect, Conner. *Perfect.*"

"Can we see the baby?" Carolyn asked, her voice small. "And Tricia?" All of the sudden, she was feeling like an intruder, a bystander who didn't actually belong, and she wished she hadn't spoken so impulsively.

She felt like a third wheel—until Brody put his arm around her and drew her against her side.

"Later on," Conner told her quietly, smiling as he registered the couple's body language. "Tricia's sleeping now, and Blue will be in an incubator for a day or two, according to the doctors. Why don't you two go back to the ranch and try to get some sleep?" A wry look moved in Conner's happy, exhausted face. "You could feed the horses in the morning, too, come to think of it."

Brody chuckled, a raw sound, wholly good to hear, and slapped his brother lightly on the back. "Don't worry about the horses," he said. "I'll take care of them, Conner, and Davis's, too."

"And I'll help," Carolyn said.

Conner gave her an awkward hug. "Thanks," he said.

The hug he gave Brody was even *more* awkward, but it was genuine, too.

During the drive back toward Lonesome Bend, Carolyn and Brody were both too emotionally wrung out to talk much, but words weren't really necessary anyway.

Tricia would recover.

Blue would thrive, eventually.

At the moment, nothing else seemed to matter.

A week later, Conner brought his glowing wife and his brand-new baby son home to the ranch, where they were greeted with a brief and very low-key family celebration.

There were balloons, a big cake and piles of baby presents, tied up with ribbons the color of Blue's name.

Tricia was practically effervescent with happiness, beaming as friends and family admired the newest member of the Creed clan, but Conner guarded the both of them like a sentinel, and everybody understood when he squired his wife into their room to rest for a while. The diagnosis of Tricia's initial crisis was separation of the placenta from the uterine wall and, while she was fine now, she naturally tired easily.

Blue, meanwhile, remained in the kitchen, holding court and enchanting his grandparents.

Davis and Kim were absolutely besotted with the infant, and Brody looked, to Carolyn, as proud as his brother was. Steven and Melissa and their children would be arriving from Stone Creek soon, for a visit; Melissa and Kim planned to take turns spending nights at the main ranch house, so they could help look after the new baby.

Carolyn, looking on from the sidelines, thought it was a beautiful thing, a family in action, rallying around when their loved ones needed them. *Being there,* at any hour of the day or night, willing to travel any distance, putting personal differences and agendas on a back burner, at least temporarily, to lavish care on one of their own.

It was no wonder, she reflected, sitting there in Tricia and Conner's kitchen, that the Creeds had flourished, not just in this generation, but in all previous ones as well. In times of trouble *and* times of joy, they stuck together.

Carolyn marveled at that and, silently, she celebrated that such a thing was true.

Every night since Kim and Davis had returned, the day after Blue's birth, she and Brody had shared the three-quarter bed in the rustic cabin he jokingly referred to as "the lodge." The place made her apartment at Natty McCall's look like a palace, with its funny refrigerator and tiny microwave, but she'd been completely happy there, because she and Brody and Winston and Barney were together.

Neither she nor Brody had spoken of love again, let alone marriage, but, for the time being, it didn't matter. The lovemaking was exquisite, and they laughed constantly, she and Brody, and it was all right to live in the moment, because the moment was just fine the way it was.

For the first time in her life, Carolyn didn't have a universal shopping list of things that *had* to happen for her life to work. Just showing up for whatever came next, being present to it, seemed to be enough.

The days had been wonderfully ordinary: she helped Brody with the ranch chores.

She quietly stitched the gypsy skirt back to its former glory.

She took care of Winston and sometimes Barney, and she watched as Brody's big house rose against the sky, more complete with every passing day.

Now, in Conner and Tricia's kitchen, surrounded by friends and family, Brody laid a hand on her shoulder and bent to whisper in her ear. "Let's go," he said. "I have something to show you."

Carolyn nodded, a little flushed, and the two of them said the necessary goodbyes and left, riding in Brody's pickup, with Barney proudly ensconced in the backseat. Winston preferred to remain at the lodge most of the time, not being big on wheeled conveyances of any sort.

Brody drove to the new house, parked out front.

The windows reflected an apricot-and-gold sunset, and the roof and walls looked sturdy enough to weather a century or two of Creeds, being born, growing up, falling in love and marrying and having children of their own, getting old gracefully and, in their own good time, going to their rest.

The thought made Carolyn's heart swell.

Brody opened the truck door for her, and lifted Barney down from the backseat before walking toward the front entrance.

The double doors at the entrance were hand-carved, with the name *Creed* inscribed above them, on a massive lintel.

Carolyn paused to look up, admiring the effect, feeling the impact of that name lodge somewhere deep inside her, become an actual part of her.

Brody used his key, and one of the

doors swung open when he gave it a slight push.

He turned to Carolyn, the last of the sunlight shining in his face and hair, and held out a hand to her. "One day soon," he said, very quietly, "I hope to carry you over the threshold of this house as my wife, Carolyn."

She stared at him. "Is that a proposal?" she dared, after a long moment of courage-gathering.

Brody cocked a grin at her, and she took the hand he offered her. "No," he said. "That's a separate thing."

He pulled her into the big living room, and her eyes went immediately to the place above the magnificent fireplace, where the Weaver hung in her fine frame, a monument to grace and wisdom.

Carolyn smiled. In all the excitement over Tricia and baby Blue, and Bill Venable's safe but unexpected return from the forest fire in New Mexico—he'd caught Carolyn during one of her brief stops at the shop and told her he'd had some kind of private epiphany and was now willing to do whatever it took to win Angela back—she'd forgotten about

Primrose Sullivan's wonderful batik, awaiting delivery over at the shop.

"Primrose brought the picture over a few days ago," Brody said. "The contractor let her in, and some of the guys on his crew hung it for her, under her close supervision."

Carolyn could just imagine Primrose directing this man hither and that man yon, making them move the Weaver a few inches to the right, then the left, until she was satisfied that its position was absolutely perfect.

"Beautiful," Carolyn said, on a breath.

Brody took her into his arms, right there in the middle of the soon-to-be living room. "Marry me?" he asked, his voice husky.

Carolyn laughed for joy. Reality, as it turned out, was better than any fairy tale ever told. "Yes," she said. "I'll marry you, Brody Creed."

"Soon? So I never have to spend even one night in this house without you?"

Her eyes burned. "Soon," she confirmed. But there was still an element of their relationship that hadn't been settled. "What about Joleen?"

Brody grinned, his hands moving slowly up and down Carolyn's ribs, his head tilted slightly to one side. "Didn't you hear the rumors? Joleen ran off with one of her customers from the café. According to the scuttlebutt, it's love, a match made in heaven."

"You don't say," Carolyn said.

Brody nibbled at her mouth. "I *do* say," he murmured. "What about Mr. Coffee? The hot-shot firefighting pilot guy?"

"I knew who you meant," Carolyn answered.

Brody simply raised both eyebrows and waited, but his hands were still subtly busy at her ribs and the outer rounding of her breasts.

"His name is Bill," Carolyn said, in a coquettish tone, "and he's not a 'hotshot firefighting pilot guy' anymore. He agreed to take a year off from his job and work out of Denver as an airline executive while he and his new bride, Angela, and his very precocious daughter, Ellie, build themselves a family life."

Brody took a deep breath, let it out as a long sigh. "It seems to be a trend," he said, in a drawl that meant he'd be trying to make her clothes fall off for the next little while. And that he was bound to succeed. "People taking a chance on love, I mean."

"Seems to be," Carolyn agreed, watching his lips.

It was something, what Brody Creed could do with those lips.

He left her, walked over to the fireplace, took something from the high mantel and came back to her.

While Carolyn watched, amazed even after he'd used the words *marry me,* he dropped gracefully to one knee in front of her, held up a little velvet box and popped the lid.

An eye-popping diamond engagement ring glittered inside.

Carolyn gasped and put a hand to her throat.

Brody grinned a lopsided grin. "Here comes the formal proposal," he said. "Will you, Carolyn? Will you be my wife? For better or for worse, for richer or for poorer, in sickness and in health, 'til death do us part?"

Carolyn sank to her knees, so they

were approximately at eye level. "Yes, Brody," she replied, "I will be your wife, for better or for worse, for richer or for poorer, in sickness and in health, until death do us part. I will love you and I will honor you, but you can just forget that part about obeying, because that ain't gonna happen."

He laughed. "Fair enough," he said. "Will you cook my supper every night, and have my babies?"

"I will have your babies," she replied, smiling as he slid the ring onto her finger. "But I'm not much of a cook, so we'll have to work something out regarding supper. Breakfast and lunch, too, for that matter."

Eyes sparkling with amusement, and with love, Brody kissed her, lightly, briefly and with a hunger that aroused a corresponding need in her. "What if *I* make supper?" he countered. "I happen to be a pretty good hand with a skillet."

"I thought you might be," Carolyn said, slipping her arms around his neck and inclining her head toward the kitchen, "when I saw that fancy stove with all the burners."

"I wish this place had a bed," Brody grumbled, kissing her neck.

Carolyn drew him down, onto the floor, urging him on top of her just to feel the weight of him, the promise of his hardness and his heat. "Who needs a bed?" she asked, as his mouth descended to hers.

EPILOGUE

Carolyn and Brody were married in early August at sunset, on the former swimming beach at River's Bend, with the whole town and a good portion of Denver in attendance. Conner was the best man, Tricia the matron of honor and Melissa and Steven's oldest, Matt, proudly served as ring-bearer.

Davis, handsome and comically uncomfortable in his Sunday suit, gave the bride away, while Kim looked on with tears of pure happiness glittering in her eyes.

Carolyn wore the now mended gypsy

skirt, with a white camisole and a short silk jacket she'd made to go with the outfit, and Brody looked better than handsome in his jeans, crisply white Western shirt and sport jacket, his concession to formality.

Since it was summer, the sunset lasted well past the actual ceremony, gradually fading as a band struck up a romantic country tune inside the large, rented tent that stood where the lodge used to be.

There was dancing, and there was cake, but the evening was mostly a glad blur to Carolyn—whenever she looked at Brody, which was often, he was all she saw, and she knew by the expression in his eyes that he was under the same spell.

They were surrounded by friends and family, by music and light and love and laughter, but they might as well have been alone on the planet, just the two of them, they were so absorbed in each other. They'd eaten cake, and toasted each other with frothing flutes filled with ginger ale, and posed for endless pictures, images Carolyn knew she'd treasure for the rest of her life.

Davis, with a slight smile, walked up to them, shook Brody's hand and politely asked if he might dance with the bride, since he'd been the one to give her away and all.

Carolyn smiled up at the man she thought of as her father-in-law now, as well as her good friend, and she remembered something he'd said to her, a few days before the wedding, when they'd all gathered at the main ranch house for a family dinner.

"When you marry a Creed," Davis had announced, smiling at her, "you get all of us."

Now, as they danced, as Kim and Brody joined them on the plank floor put down for the purpose, Chinese lanterns casting a multicolored glow, Davis squeezed her hand lightly. "Welcome to the family, Carolyn Creed," he said, in that singular rumble of his. "And I don't mind telling you, you took your sweet time about it."

Carolyn—*Carolyn Creed*—laughed softly. "You sound like Tricia," she replied. "And Kim. Were Brody and I the only people in Lonesome Bend who didn't see this wedding coming?"

Davis grinned, and Carolyn smiled up at him as they danced. "Sure seemed like it," he said. "There were times when I would have liked to thump your heads together. It was Tricia and Conner, all over again. They couldn't see the forest for the trees in the beginning, either."

"You know, don't you, that you and Kim mean the world to Brody and Conner? And to Tricia and me, as well?"

"They're my brother's boys," he said quietly, "and the spittin' image of him, too. There's never a day that I don't miss Blue, and wish he was here with the rest of us, where he belongs, but if he had to go ahead and get himself killed, well, he left a fine legacy behind." He glanced over, saw Conner cutting in to dance with Kim and Brody pretending to protest, and Davis's eyes brightened until they shone. "I love them like my own." He turned his head again, to face her. "And you and Tricia are the daughters we've always wanted."

Carolyn let her forehead rest against

Davis's strong shoulder for a moment, overcome with emotion. "Thank you," she whispered.

Davis chuckled and gave her a reassuring squeeze, and then Brody cut in, and she was dancing with her man, her cowboy, her *husband.*

"I love you, Mrs. Creed," he said, smiling into her eyes. "And I'm fixing to kiss you, right here and now, so get ready."

She giggled.

He stopped the giggle with the promised kiss, complete with a pretty flashy dip and some serious tongue-action, and the whole gathering cheered.

"And I love *you,*" Carolyn replied, breathless, when it was over.

Brody curved a finger under her chin and lifted. "What do you say we get out of here, Mrs. Creed," he said, "and leave these good people to party on to their hearts' content?"

"I think that's a fine idea, Mr. Creed," she replied.

He led her outside.

They stood hand in hand in the weighted heat of an August night, watching the light of the moon and a bajillion stars dance on the surface of the river, singing as it passed.

In the morning, they'd be leaving on their honeymoon, location undisclosed, but Brody and Carolyn wanted to spend their wedding night in the new house. It seemed just right, for their life together to begin there.

Brody held on to her hand, and they walked toward home, following a glowing path of silvery moonlight.

It was magical. Something right out of a fairy tale but *better,* because it was real.

To Carolyn's surprise, they passed by the house and headed toward the barn instead.

Inside the entrance, Brody flipped the light switch and Moonshine blinked at them from his stall, sleepily munching on a mouthful of grass hay.

Carolyn smiled and moved to pat the horse's velvety nose, but Brody pulled her on past, stopping in front of the stall next to Moonshine's.

A beautiful, snow-white gelding stood in the center of his space, splendid enough to pull Cinderella's carriage.

Carolyn drew in her breath, laid a hand to her heart.

"He's yours, if you'll have him," Brody said gently. "A wedding present from your lovin' husband. His name's Sugarman, but you can change it if you want to. He's gentle, but he's spirited, too."

Carolyn, in her shimmery skirt and special jacket, stepped up and clasped the rim of the stall door in both hands, already shaking her head. "I wouldn't change a thing, Brody," she said, turning to look into the face of the man beside her. "Not about him, and not about you."

Brody kissed her gently. "When we get back from the honeymoon, well, I thought you might like to go riding with me. Maybe up to Hidden Lake?"

She smiled. "Brody Creed," she said, "You're the best thing that ever happened to me."

He grinned that megawatt grin of his. "Back at you, pretty woman," he said, bending his head to taste her mouth.

A warm shiver went through her.

"Isn't it about time you carried me over the threshold, like you promised?"

she asked, slipping her arms around his neck.

"I do believe it is," he replied, after pretending to consider the matter for a few moments.

With that, they left the barn, walking on that same path of light, and when they reached the house, Brody Creed swept his bride up into his arms, kissed her again and said, "Hold on tight, lady. I think we're in for quite a ride."

Carolyn smiled. She knew he wasn't just talking about their wedding night. He was talking about the rest of their lives.

* * * * *